DEAD MAN'S GOLD

He ran as hard as he could, giving it all he had, plowing through the snow like a bull, until he was near the rifleman, separated from him by a line of boulders. He bounded atop one of the boulders, saw the reloading man look up in shock—and Sam leaped, flying though the air with the pick in his hand, swinging down as he descended.

The man had dropped his rifle and gone for a pistol stuck into his belt, but the pistol caught and never came clear. Sam descended and brought the pick down hard, intending to strike with the flat of it and knock the man cold. But the pick had turned in his hand. The sharp, rusted prong of it hit Emmett Fish in the center of the top of his head, dug through bone, and sank into his brain. . . .

D1495256

**Other two-in-one Westerns from
Cameron Judd**

Devil Wire
Brazos

The Quest of Brady Kenton
Kenton's Challenge

Timber Creek
Renegade Lawmen

Snow Sky
Corrigan

Available from St. Martin's Paperbacks

DEAD MAN'S GOLD

CAMERON JUDD

St. Martin's Paperbacks

This is a work of fiction. All of the characters, organizations and events portrayed in this novel are either products of the author's imagination or are used fictitiously.

CONFEDERATE GOLD / DEAD MAN'S GOLD

Confederate Gold copyright © 1993 by Cameron Judd.
Dead Man's Gold copyright © 1999 by Cameron Judd.

All rights reserved.

For information address St. Martin's Press, 175 Fifth Avenue, New York, NY 10010.

ISBN: 0-312-94334-2
EAN: 978-0-312-94334-9

Printed in the United States of America

Confederate Gold Bantam Domain edition / December 1993
St. Martin's Paperbacks edition / June 2000

Dead Man's Gold St. Martin's Paperbacks edition / August 1999

St. Martin's Paperbacks are published by St. Martin's Press, 175 Fifth Avenue, New York, NY 10010.

10 9 8 7 6 5 4 3 2 1

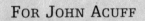

FOR JOHN ACUFF

CHAPTER ONE

By dusk the falling snow was thick, accumulating on the ground, the high stone ridges, the windswept conifers—everywhere except on the dead man who lay just below the narrow pass that led into Texas Gulch. Just enough warmth remained in his body to slowly melt the flakes that struck him.

A boy of twelve, Daniel Chase, stood rooted in the snow, staring down at this most unexpected find. He'd been headed home to the mining camp, humming to himself, his idle mind wandering. He'd almost fallen over the corpse.

The dead man was gray-haired, lightly bearded, maybe fifty years old. He looked very peaceful lying there on his back in the snow, as if he'd died swiftly and easily. But to the boy that serene appearance seemed ghastly.

Over in Texas Gulch, a dog barked. A shifting wind brought the scent of woodsmoke to Daniel's nose. A sudden desire to be indoors and away from snow, cold wind, and dead men overwhelmed the boy. Besides, somebody grown-up needed to be told about this. Daniel shivered and pulled his coat tightly around him. Then he cut a wide circle around the body and hurried along the trail and through the pass.

He trotted down the long slope toward the brown, smoke-belching, California mining camp that was home to him and a small but unusually diverse population of mining camp dwellers. The diversity was lost on the boy, who had no other experience of mining camps by which to make comparison. He did know, however, that Texas Gulch was thought to be the highest-elevated, most remote mining camp in all of California, because Crain Brown, one of the miners and residents, had told him so.

The dog Daniel had heard barking appeared. It was Arianna Winkle's dog, not a popular creature in the camp because it barked at night. Daniel liked the dog, though. Its pretty, thirteen-year-old owner he liked a lot more.

"How are you, Enoch?" he said to the canine, pausing to scratch around its ears. "There's a dead man up at the pass, you know it? You ought to run up and smell him!"

As if to obey, the dog bounded toward the pass, a natural gate that was the only known entrance into the three-mile-wide, generally circular, basinlike valley in which Texas Gulch stood. That is, if a shapeless splatter of low, rugged log buildings, which from a distance looked like scabs on the flesh of the land, could accurately be said to stand.

Daniel headed for a cabin at the northern side of the camp. Smoke was belching out its chimney into the gray sky. A fairly big cabin as mining camp cabins go, it was dwarfed, however, by another that stood in the middle of the camp, a virtual dormitory of a cabin built as a common dwelling for the original miners of this place. That had been a group from Pennsylvania who had wandered into the valley while trying to find a new route over the Sierras to the "diggings" on the other side. By accident, one of them struck color, and the group had wandered no farther. They had constructed this mining community, tried to name it Pittsburg Hill, but for reasons no one remembered, the name that actually stuck to the place was Dutch Camp.

The color hadn't lasted long and the original miners moved on. The place once called Dutch Camp was now called Texas Gulch by its newer and much smaller population of eighteen people, a population that was expected to grow swiftly come spring, when the snows were gone and word got out—as it was already beginning to do—that new gold had been found. There was still wealth to be made in the former Dutch Camp, and it was to assure that they held claim on the best of it when the gold season began again that the current Texas Gulch residents had opted to lay in food and provisions, cut massive supplies of firewood, and brave out the high Sierra winter rather than escape for the season to the warmer foothills below.

Daniel shoved the door open and walked in, bringing snow and wind with him, evoking howls of protest from four miners who were gathered around a table, playing cards. A pleasant fire roared in a big stone fireplace at one end of the cabin, though more than half the heat was going up the chimney with the smoke.

"There's a dead man up in the pass," Daniel announced from the open doorway.

"Close that door!" Sam Underhill bellowed.

Daniel obeyed. "There's a dead man up in the pass," he repeated.

"Fool boy!" one of the others, a surly man named Herbert Colfax, older than the other three miners, mumbled beneath his breath as he closed the lid on an ivory snuffbox he'd been using just as Daniel opened the door. "That wind almost blew away my snuff."

"I said that there's a dead man up in the pass," Daniel repeated yet again, a little louder.

"Oh, I'm sure there is," Colfax replied. "And what was it you said you saw back in the valley last week? A tiger, I think? And let's see . . . what work did you tell me your late father was in, before he took to mining? Vice president of the United States, you said. Yep, that was it. So I have every reason to believe you when you say there's a dead man in the pass." He winked across the table at Hiram Linfoot, another of the card players. "I'll bet it was that tiger what got the poor devil, you reckon, Hiram?"

Hiram and Ben Dillow, the fourth card player, laughed. Sam Underhill didn't.

"Daniel, this is just one of your tales, ain't it?" asked Underhill, a sandy-haired man who looked younger than his thirty-five years and was considered quite handsome by the ladies. He'd been quite proud of his looks in more youthful days, but he didn't dwell much on such things now that he was a little older.

"No," Daniel said. "There's really a dead man."

"Let's play cards," Colfax grumbled.

"Just hold on, Herbert," Sam said. "Daniel, you really do mean what you say?"

"Yes! I swear. How many times I got to say it?"

"The boy lies every time he talks, Sam," Colfax said. "He'll make a congressman before you know it. Maybe president."

"I think maybe he's telling the truth," Sam said.

"He'll get you up there, then laugh at you for having believed him," said Dillow, Sam's mining partner and fellow resident of this cabin.

"I'm not lying," Daniel said. "There's a man lying dead in the snow. It melts when it hits him."

Sam thought about that. "Then maybe that man's not dead yet." He laid down the cards and stood. "Will you show me the man, Daniel?"

"Yes."

"Underhill, are you really going out there?" Colfax asked.

"Yep. Why don't you come with me?"

"Think I'll stay."

"Come on, Herbert. In fact, all of you come. If there's really a man hurt or dead up there, I'll need help getting him down here. We can't just assume Daniel's telling a story."

"There's no dead man. The boy's a liar."

Daniel was almost in tears. "I'm not! I'm *not*! This time it's the truth!"

"It better be, Daniel," Sam said. "Come on, men. Just in case there's really somebody needing help."

Sam took his heavy bearskin coat from a wall peg, put it on, and slipped his slouch hat into place atop the thick and sandy hair of his head. He pulled a scarf-sized scrap of cloth out of his coat pocket and tied the hat in place, pulling the sides of the brim down like flaps over his ears. The other card players didn't budge.

Perturbed, Sam said, "Lead on, Daniel. You and me will go look even if nobody else will. Ben, I'm surprised that you, at least, won't come with me."

Dillow sighed and stood. "What the devil," he said, and went for his own coat and hat.

Hiram Linfoot got up and readied himself as well.

Colfax, outnumbered and facing the prospect of nothing to play but solitaire, stood with a sigh. "Hang and bury you, Sam Underhill. Hang and bury all of you. I'll come too, if for no more reason than to laugh when the little liar shows you for the fools you are."

Less than an hour later, Colfax was gazing at the corpse he'd just helped haul in, scratching his beard, and trying hard to catch his breath. Being several years older than most of the other prospectors, he tired easily. Despite his gasping, he continued to pace back and forth swiftly, unusually wrought up.

Laid out on the puncheon floor of the Underhill-Dillow cabin, the dead man looked even more placid than he had out in the weather. And more gray. His body had grown colder since Daniel had first seen him.

Dillow, whose experience raising, tending, and doctoring cattle and horses back in Kentucky as a very young man made him the closest thing the mining camp had to a physician, was examining the dead man closely, opening the shirt and studying the chest, lifting the eyelids and staring at the marbled eyes, peering inside the mouth and feeling around the back of the neck. Sam Underhill didn't know just what Dillow was looking for and wasn't sure that Dillow did, either.

"What do you reckon, Ben?" Sam asked.

Dillow reared back on his haunches and shook his head. "Don't know. I see no signs of violence. He ain't been shot or stabbed, and there's no unusual bruises to make me think he was beat."

"Natural death, then?"

"Believe so. Probably his heart gave out on him. I knew a man back when I was a boy who died climbing up a steep hill in the snow. It strains the heart something fierce."

"Why do you reckon he was coming here at this time of year, with the snows setting in?" asked Linfoot.

"Maybe he wasn't coming here," Dillow said. "Maybe he was just passing by."

Colfax, pacing back and forth very fast, snorted. "This ain't the kind of place a man passes by. We ain't located in the heart of Boston, you know."

Dillow eyed Colfax. "Why are you so nervous? Why are you pacing that way? You need to go out and drain your bladder or something?"

Sam Underhill said, "Ben, we've got a lady present." This was true; the bringing in of a dead stranger had drawn several other Texas Gulch residents to the Underhill-Dillow cabin, among them the lovely Marica Bolton, whom Ben Dillow liked quite well but was always managing to offend. It was a rarity for a mining camp to have any females—any of of the unsullied variety, anyway—but Texas Gulch had five, all of them of good repute. Sam continued, "All we'll be able to do for this man is give him a decent burial, and if we can, determine who he is and where he's from so we can notify his people."

"You search him, Sam," Dillow said, standing. "You're the man of the law here."

"That was back in Texas," Sam said. Indeed, back in the town of Underhill, founded by and named for Sam's famous father, Bushrod Underhill, the unwilling inheritor of the late Davy Crockett's mantle of peerless American frontiersman, Sam had been town marshal before he joined the rush to

California. "I don't suppose we have any *real* law in Texas Gulch."

"We don't have any real doctor, either, but I still have to do the job. Now do yours."

Given Marica Bolton's presence, Sam didn't fully undress the corpse. He did conduct a search of the dead man's clothes, but found no identification upon him. In the pockets he found a comb, a folding knife, a tinderbox, a matchblock, a snuff box, and a few scraps of paper with meaningless personal notes on them . . . but no name, nothing to indicate from whence this man had come, or why.

"Well, that's that," Sam said. "Unless somebody comes along asking after him and can identify him before he rots, we're not going to know a thing about him."

"Just a prospector looking for a new strike and a new dream, probably," said Kish Fleenor, a Texas Gulch prospector with a melancholy air, rather high voice, and philosophical bent. He wrote poetry, which he thought was a secret, though in fact everyone knew it. Colfax in particular despised him, but then, Colfax tended to despise everyone in varying measure.

Sam examined the dead man's hands. "No calluses on the hands. Soft. If he was a prospector, he hadn't gotten started yet."

"Look at the ring he's wearing," Marica said. She was the daughter of Art Bolton, a widower and Texas Gulch prospector who stood at her side. About twenty years old and quite pretty, Marica was the most idolized woman in Texas Gulch. The other females, none of whom were present at the moment, were Herbert Colfax's wife, America, and their plump and plain daughter, Letitia, whom everyone felt sorry for because she'd inherited her mother's unfortunate looks and her father's sour disposition, and the young widow Leora Winkle—whose husband had suffered a fit, fallen into a stream he was panning, and drowned the prior summer. Last and youngest of all was Arianna, Leora's thirteen-year-old daughter and the object of young Daniel Chase's undying affection.

Sam lifted the dead man's left hand and examined the ring. It was a plain, inexpensive band, widened at one point with a meaningless decorative scribble on it. Sam slipped it off and looked inside it, hoping to see a name inscribed, but there was none.

He held out the ring to Marica. "I suppose there's nothing wrong with you taking it, if you want."

She shook her head. "I'd as soon not wear a dead man's ring."

"I'd like it," Daniel Chase quickly said.

Sam handed Daniel the ring. "Here. Keep it in memory of our dead and unknown friend."

The boy slipped it on his ring finger, found it too loose, and twisted it onto his middle finger instead.

"It's sad that a man dies and is forgotten so thoroughly," said Kish Fleenor.

"It is," Sam agreed.

"Like a flower cut down in mid-blossom," Fleenor went on. "A gourd plucked too early from the vine."

"Bosh! There's men who die in the camps every day and are forgotten," said Colfax, speaking fast and restless. He was still pacing and nervous. "No reason to gush over this one. The way I figure it, he'd probably have come in and found the strike that should have gone to me. Good riddance to unwanted competition, I say. 'A gourd plucked too early from the vine.' Have mercy!"

"Colfax," Dillow said, "is talking out your backside a trick you had to teach yourself, or does it just run in your family as a gift of nature?"

"Ben, dang it," Sam scolded, "remember the lady!"

"Blast!" Colfax boomed abruptly and rather dramatically, stopping his pacing and patting about on his torso. "I've lost my pocket watch! I dropped it up there where the dead man was, I'll wager. Of all the bad luck!"

"If you dropped it up there, you may not find it until springtime," Sam said.

"Oh, I'll find it. I'll go right now and get it."

"I'll go with you," Bolton said. "It's dark now, and we'll need torches."

"Don't need any help, thank you," Colfax said sharply. He made his exit with a grand flurry and stomped off through the snow.

"What's the matter with that old goat?" Dillow asked. "He's acting even more peculiar than usual."

"I know," Sam said. "He was acting odd even when we found this body. He stayed off by himself, in the dark."

"Yeah. I noticed that."

"When will we bury this fellow, Sam?" Art Bolton asked.

"In the morning," Sam replied. "In the meantime, we'll lay him in my woodshed. It'll be good and cold there, so he'll keep."

CHAPTER TWO

THE NEXT DAY

Art Bolton, who had once preached as a lay-pastor in a Baptist church in Texas, said a few Bible verses and a prayer over the dead man, whom they buried deep in one of the empty holes left by some miner from the first days of Texas Gulch.

Such scars on the land abounded in a mining camp in its second generation. The Pennsylvanians of Dutch Camp days had damaged the land immediately around the camp very thoroughly before vacating the place.

Late the previous summer, Sam Underhill and a delegation of new prospectors from in and around the Brazos town of Underhill, had come in and taken another look at Dutch Camp, though they hadn't expected to remain. They had expected a quick and probably fruitless investigation of a site that everyone said was played out. But soon Herbert Colfax, of all people, had made a good strike right behind the abandoned log hut that now was his residence. A day later, Julius Setser had made a strike almost as good on a ridge outside town, and Joe Skinner, who traveled with his aging father in tow, had done the same yet again, at a different spot, within a week.

Dutch Camp wasn't played out after all. The first round of Forty-niners had simply been too eager, too sure they would find a better yield elsewhere, and had let impatience and the threat of severe winter weather move them out too quickly.

The new influx wouldn't be so foolish. Sam, who had helped organize the prospector group back in Texas, had counseled a cautious, patient approach.

"We'll not scratch here one day and run there the next," he'd said. "We'll work hard, and dig deep, and find gold that others have missed. We'll make our success by keeping our heads level and our noses to the grindstone. We'll keep news of our strikes to ourselves, as long as we can. We'll wait out the winter and guard our claims. We'll be wealthy before you know it."

So they'd settled into grubby little Dutch Camp and re-named the place Texas Gulch in honor of the state from which most of them had come.

When the man was buried and covered over, Colfax slapped the dirt from his hands and said, "Now you just watch. Somebody will come asking after him tomorrow and we'll have to dig him out again."

"I doubt that," Sam said. He looked up at the gray sky, which spat snow down onto his face. "There's going to be a hard winter. Before long it'll be hard for anybody to get to us, or for us to get out again."

"I hope we've laid in enough supplies to see us through the winter," Colfax grumbled. He was more his old self again, a mere grouchy old scoundrel, not pacing and nervous like the night before.

Sam said, "We've got more than enough."

Walking back down into the camp, Daniel Chase fell in beside Sam and held up his right hand. The dead man's distinctive ring was on his middle finger. "See it, Sam? Looks good, huh?"

Colfax frowned over at the ring from the other side of Daniel. "You'd best not wear a dead man's ring, Daniel," he said. "You know what happens when you do that, don't you?"

"What?"

"He comes back, that's what! Comes back looking for what was took from him."

Sam said, "Herbert, don't frighten him with nonsense."

But Colfax was having fun. He often toyed with Daniel, who had come to California from Tennessee with his older brother, Grady. The parents of the Chase brothers were dead. Grady and Daniel Chase had met and joined the Texas Gulch delegation along the way, but Grady had died of a fever shortly after, leaving Daniel alone in the world. The boy was now parented by the Texas Gulch community as a whole. He lived sometimes with Joe Skinner and his aged father, whom everyone called simply Old Man Skinner. Often he resided in the Underhill-Dillow cabin, or in the lodge house, as the big dormitorylike cabin was informally called.

"Don't believe him," Sam said. "Dead men don't come back."

"I know," Daniel said. "I'm not stupid. It's not ghosts that can hurt you. It's folks that's still alive you got to worry about."

"The boy's too smart for you, Herbert," Sam said. "Hey, did you find your watch last night?"

"I did indeed," Colfax said, and produced the watch to prove it.

"How did you manage to find it in the snow and dark?"

"Persistence," Colfax said. "With persistence, it's downright remarkable, the things a man can find." Colfax smiled, turned, and trudged away, whistling.

"He's in a remarkably good humor all at once," Sam said. "I can't imagine how he found that watch in the dark." He yanked playfully at Daniel's hat, a big flop he'd inherited from his deceased older brother. "You going to keep that ring for yourself, or give it to some pretty gal?"

"I'm thinking I might do the latter," Daniel said.

"Bet I know who she is."

"Maybe you do, maybe you don't."

"One word of advice, son: don't say where you got it. Most girls wouldn't be thrilled to know the ring a boy's given them has come off the finger of a dead man.''

"Arianna wouldn't care.''

"Bet she would. Women are like that.''

"I won't tell her, then.''

"You think you might just up and marry Arianna one of these days?''

The boy nodded firmly. "I will. You wait and see.''

Sam grinned. "Is she agreeable to the idea?''

"Not yet.'' Daniel paused, then looked up earnestly at Sam. "But she does want you to marry her mother.''

Sam felt his face changing color. "That's just little-girl talk, that's all.''

"She means it. She wants you to marry Leora. That'd make you Arianna's new father. Then, when I marry Arianna, I'll be your son-in-law. It'd be almost like being your son. That would be fine.''

Sam self-consciously yanked at the brim of Daniel's hat, wondering how red his face was.

"Why haven't you ever married, Sam?''

"Never found the right woman.''

"Arianna says you're handsome, and that she heard you've always had all kinds of women liking you.''

"Arianna thinks she knows my life history, does she?''

"Well, is she right?''

"I was a different fellow as a younger man. A little too carefree and high-spirited. I suppose I had my share of attention.''

"I wish I was handsome.''

"You are.''

"I'm too young to be handsome. I'll probably grow up ugly, like Grady was.''

Sam laughed. "You're a character, boy. You know that?''

As they trudged along, side by side, Sam thought about what it would really be like to marry Leora Winkle. It was hard to find anything wrong in the notion.

Daniel spoke. "Sam . . . there ain't no chance of what Mr. Colfax said being true, is there?''

"What, about the dead man coming back? No, son. That man's dead and gone, and whatever he's left behind, he's left behind for good. There's nobody, living or dead, likely to be coming to Texas Gulch with this snow setting in."

The next day, Sam Underhill huddled in his big bearskin coat and wandered through the mining camp, smoking a cigar and hoping he had enough of them to see him through until spring. He trudged over to where they'd buried the dead man the day before. The snow had covered the spot and made it hard to make out. He wondered how deep the snow would become before the winter was out. He knew that at some places in the Sierras, snow would pile up ten feet or more.

Puffing and thinking, Sam stared at the grave. Who was this man? Why had he been at the pass into Texas Gulch at such an odd time, and what had made him die? He'd been gray-haired, but not particularly old. Not the age one would expect a man to be if he was going to simply fall over dead.

On the other hand, Sam realized, his perceptions about age and vitality might be a little skewed, thanks to his own unusual father. Bushrod Underhill . . . frontiersman, Indian compatriot and also Indian fighter, hunter, settler, horse dealer, and American icon. Now somewhere above seventy years old—not even Bushrod himself knew exactly how old—the man was still as strong and energetic as one twenty-five years younger. Bushrod, though definitely mature in appearance, didn't even look his full age. His skin was weathered but not particularly aged, his hair with plenty of color still amid the white. And Bush Underhill could still wear out a far younger trail partner, Sam included.

"Sam!"

Sam turned. Daniel was coming up to him, kicking through the snow.

"What you doing, Sam?"

"Just smoking and thinking."

"Can I have a cigar?"

"Wait until you're grown. I doubt they're good for a man."

"Why do you smoke them, then?"

"I like the taste. And it's something to do. Hey, your finger looks a little swole up. That ring too tight?"

Daniel held his hand up and showed it to Sam. The finger was quite puffy, but not discolored.

"It is a little tight, but I don't think enough to hurt you," Sam said. "You want me to try to file it off?"

"Would it hurt my finger?"

"I'd try not to hurt you, but I can't promise."

"Then I don't want you to do it."

"Fine, but you need to quit pulling on it so the swelling will go down."

"I will. It'll fit Arianna's finger a lot better than mine."

"When you going to give it to her?"

"First chance I get. What you thinking about out here?"

"About my father."

Daniel grinned. He was deeply impressed that a man he knew had a father as famous as Bushrod Underhill. The boy, semiliterate, had struggled through several of the *Underhill Almanac*s which printers across the country were forever putting out, to the real Bushrod's chagrin. Daniel was quite eager to be persuaded that Sam's father really had once turned an alligator inside out, and killed a grizzly by sticking his head down its throat until it choked, like the almanacs claimed. He was equally enamored of the tall tales from the exaggerated biography of Bushrod that had sparked the nonsense to begin with.

"I hope I can meet your father someday," Daniel said.

"I hope you can, too. You'd like him."

"It must be wonderful to be famous."

"Pap hates it. He wishes nobody knew who he was, and that none of those lies about him had been told, and that he could live out his old age without folks bothering him . . . not that he's really old."

"But he has to be old by now."

"He is, in years. But still he's not old. I know that don't make a lot of sense . . . but if you knew him, you'd understand. I think he'll live forever, I swear."

"Are the stories true, about the box of dirt?"

Sam smiled. "The Eden Box, you mean."

"Yes." Daniel's eyes were unblinking, fixed intently on Sam as he awaited an answer. The boy had asked plenty of questions about the legendry surrounding Bushrod Underhill, but never had he addressed Sam about the Eden Box story before.

Sam puffed his cigar and stared across the valley. "It's true in part. There is an old box of soil, very rich, pure soil, that was given to my father by a dying woman, many years ago. A very old black woman, who'd outlived all her masters, and was full of plant cures and legends and healings and superstitions. And that woman did tell him that the dirt in it was the last of the soil of Eden. And she did say that if my father would imbibe a little of that soil each year, that the passing of time would have little effect on him, that just like her he'd live on, and on . . ."[1]

"Does he really eat that dirt?"

Sam grinned. "He does. My mother puts a few grains into his cornbread at the start of every year. She thinks he doesn't know it—Pap always scoffs at the Eden Box notion, at least before other people—but the truth is, he does know she does that, and never lets on to her that he's aware of it. I think that maybe he believes in it, but doesn't want to admit it. So it's easier to go ahead and let his wife give him the soil in 'secret,' so he never has to own up." Sam puffed again, and grew thoughtful. "The odd thing is, Daniel, that my father really doesn't seem to get old as fast as other men. He never grows sick. He's as strong today as he was when I was a little boy."

"So it really is dirt from the Garden of Eden?"

[1]*The Glory River*, Book 1 in The Underhill Series

Sam laughed. "Of course not. That was just a foolish old tale from a superstitious woman."

"Then why doesn't your father get old?"

"He does get old. He just does it better than most, for some reason. He's blessed, I suppose."

Sam tossed his cigar away and listened to it sizzle out in the snow.

"I'm hungry," Daniel said.

"So am I. Ben's cooking stew. Let's go inside and see how far along it is."

CHAPTER THREE

Ten horsemen rode in the mountains, horses struggling in the snow, breath and bodies steaming.

"It's no use, Jordan!" one of the riders called to the man in front, a weathered, lean fellow with a pitted, dark countenance and black eyes. "We got to turn back!"

"Not without Dehaven!" the pitted man replied firmly. He urged his weary horse on, through the next fresh drift of snow.

"We're going to get ourselves trapped in these damned mountains!"

"We're not giving up, Remine! Not until we find Dehaven!"

In a clearing on the other side of the drift, the riders stopped, letting their horses rest. The ten horses drew close together, seeking one another's heat.

"Ross is right," said a dark-haired young man who was in many ways the image of the pitted leader, but without the pox scars. This was Searl Mahaffery, younger brother of Jordan. "He's got away from us, Jordan. We may as well admit it and go back."

"Back to where, Searl? And to what? Dehaven has took it all! The gold . . . everything we've worked for! We planned it all perfectly. Performed it all perfectly. Got away perfectly. I'll not have it ruined by one man. He took everything we earned.''

"Everything we *stole*, you mean," muttered one of the other riders.

"What was that, Perry?" said Jordan Mahaffery, the pitted man. "You got something to say, you say it out to be heard!"

"All I said was, we didn't earn that gold, we stole it. And Dehaven stole it from us. Sure, it makes us mad. Sure, it leaves us back where we begun. But the man, and that gold, ain't worth dying for. There's a lot of gold in California. We can steal more of it. I say forget about Dehaven. Give the man his due for outwitting us, and let's get out of these mountains before we freeze to death."

Jordan Mahaffery replied, "It's the principle of the thing. I want my gold back."

An even-featured man who appeared to possess a mix of racial bloodlines cleared his throat and spoke in a smooth, almost soothing voice. "Jordan, listen to me. You've got to consider our situation. We've come out here without being ready for this kind of weather, particularly in these mountains. The horses are worn out, and there's no trail to follow. Perry is right. Dehaven has gotten away from us."

"Besides," threw in Emmett Fish, another of the band, "Dehaven has probably froze to death by now. No reason for us to do the same." Fish had a strong Georgia drawl and teeth the color of rust.

Jordan Mahaffery appeared to be thinking very hard. At last he spoke. "You got to ask yourself: why would Dehaven have run to such a place as this, especially in the winter? Why not take that gold and go to San Francisco or some other town, where he could spend it?"

"Because he'd know that we'd search every town until we found him," replied Searl Mahaffery.

Jordan Mahaffery nodded. "That's right. So he was coming up here to huddle with the gold through the winter. Figuring that the snow and such would keep us from following. Figuring that before the springtime come, we'd forget about him and move on. Then he could take that gold at his leisure and go off and enjoy it.''

''I can't believe Dehaven would try to winter over in such a place as this,'' said Conner Broadgrass, the dark-complexioned man with the smooth and diplomatic way of speaking. He was one of the few who could counter Jordan Mahaffery and get away with it. ''There's no place here for a man to live, no settlements or diggings, no shelter. And Dehaven is no mountain man. He'd never survive.''

''There *are* some diggings nearby,'' Mahaffery said. ''There's Dutch Camp.''

''Never heard of it,'' Emmett Fish said, spitting into the snow.

''I have, though I admit I'd forgotten about it,'' Broadgrass said. He'd been in California since well before the start of the Gold Rush, and had robbed, gambled, and womanized his way through almost every mining camp that had sprung into being since color turned up in Sutter's millrace. ''But even if there's still shelter to be had at Dutch Camp, Jordan, the camp is abandoned. There'd be no food, no company. Dehaven would never go to such a place.''

''I've heard Dutch Camp ain't empty,'' Mahaffery replied. ''There's a new group who come in and started prospecting there again. Word is just beginning to get out. More rumors than anything else . . . but the talk is, there was a group of folks who bought enough food and supplies to last a full season for twenty or so folks, and hauled it up into these mountains.''

''I don't believe it,'' said Bert Mongold, the burliest of the ten. The son of a St. Louis swindler who himself was the offspring of a Natchez Trace bandit, Mongold had been criminal since he'd been able to walk. ''Why would anybody prospect played-out diggings?''

''Because maybe the diggings didn't prove to be played out after all,'' Mahaffery replied. ''And maybe they figure to winter over to guard their find, and to get the fastest start on the mining season come warmer weather. And maybe Dehaven heard about it, and figured that kind of place was the safest for him to be. If I heard rumors about Dutch Camp, then he could have, too. Hell, the man talked to every stranger he met, anyway, so he'd be likely to hear the latest rumors. I despise the man for what he's done to us, but even I'll admit he's got a winning way about him with people.'' Mahaffery paused. ''Maybe that's why I was fool enough to trust him.''

Broadgrass spoke again. ''Even if Dehaven is at Dutch Camp, Jordan, we still face a problem if we go after him. Look at the sky. This snow isn't going to stop. If we stay in the mountains much longer, we're likely to be snowed in. Maybe until spring. And what if Dehaven isn't there? What if we go to Dutch Camp and find the people there have abandoned it like the first group did? We could be trapped in these mountains without food or supplies.''

''We'll take the risk. I ain't giving up that gold,'' Mahaffery said firmly. ''Dehaven *is* at Dutch Camp. I can feel it. And we're going after him.'' Mahaffery looked from face to face. ''Anybody wants out of this, let him leave. But whoever doesn't stick around gives up his cut of that gold once we get it back.''

''*If* we get it back,'' muttered Emmett Fish.

''We will get it back,'' Mahaffery said. ''But we've wasted enough time jaw-flapping. This snow is piling up by the minute. We're going to Dutch Camp, gents, and we're going to peel the very hide off Dehaven when we catch him.''

The other nine cast glances at one another. There was fear in the eyes of all but Broadgrass, whose immobile countenance always hid whatever he might be feeling. But no one countered Jordan Mahaffery. It wasn't wise to do such a thing.

''Let's go, big brother,'' Searl Mahaffery said. ''Lead the way to Dutch Camp. You reckon they got any pretty little ladies there?''

"At a mining camp? Ain't likely," Mahaffery replied. "Probably just a bunch of greasy miners with beards to their bellies."

"And Dehaven with them."

"That's right. And Dehaven with them. Now let's go."

The snow fell harder, but the riders pressed on.

Arianna Winkle shivered under her heavy coat and trudged through the piling snow, thinking how much better things were back home in Texas.

Just now she didn't remember the miseries she had suffered in the height of Texas summers, when she'd fantasized about dwelling in snowy, cold mountains just like those now surrounding her. Now that she was living out that midsummer's fantasy, she found little to like about it.

"Enoch!" she yelled, her breath gusting white. "Enoch! Here, boy!"

She waited and looked around. There was no sign of Enoch, no barking or scrambling in the snow.

A dreadful thought came: might somebody have done something to Enoch because of his habit of barking at night? She instantly suspected Herbert Colfax, whom she despised. Or Crain Brown, who put on such a nice front to cover the unpleasant, harsh person he really was. Arianna was good at sensing the personalities and characters of people, despite what veneer they put over their true selves. Either Colfax or Brown were the kinds who might have shot or poisoned Enoch on the sneak.

"Here, boy! Enoch!"

Still the dog did not appear. She looked all around in the vast whiteness. What if Enoch was hurt, and buried in the snow, unable to help himself?

"Enoch!"

She continued on toward the pass. Because of the lay of the land, the snow was drifted more heavily toward the wide, notchlike opening. She never much liked going beyond the pass into the mountains; it made her feel cut off from the protection of the little society of Texas Gulch. But for Enoch's sake she went on, whistling and calling the dog's name.

Unexpectedly, she heard her own name called, from behind her. "Arianna!"

Arianna winced. That was Daniel Chase's voice, an unwelcome one. She didn't really dislike Daniel—she felt very sorry for him as an orphan, in fact—but right now she didn't really want him bothering her. Besides, she could tell that he liked her, which made her uncomfortable. He was a year younger than she, after all. And he was not the kind of boy who could appeal to her, even if he were older.

She went on, pretending not to hear, hoping she could clear the pass before he caught up with her.

"Arianna!"

He was too close now for her to pretend she hadn't heard him. Oh, well. Maybe he could help her find Enoch. She turned and saw Daniel lumbering up through the snow, stepping high and wide and kicking up white dust all around. He had his usual big grin on his face.

He reached her, out of breath, red-nosed from the cold. "Where you going, Arianna?" he panted.

"Through the pass," she said.

"He's gone again?"

"Yes. I'm worried about him. There's snow now. He could get trapped out in it."

"I saw him yesterday. When I was coming in to tell about the dead man. He was heading up toward the pass, right up through this very place, matter of fact. He goes out of the pass a lot. I've seen him chase varmints and such a long way beyond it. He'll be back."

"Not if he can't make it through the snow."

"He can do it. You know how a dog his size travels through snow, don't you? He jumps!" Daniel performed a little demonstrative hop, advancing himself another couple of feet. "Then he does it again." Another jump, and suddenly he was uncomfortably close to her, grinning more broadly. She backed away a little.

"Want me to help you look for him?" he asked.

"Well . . . yes."

"Come on, then."

They walked together through the ever-deeper snow. "Hey, Arianna, I got you something," Daniel said. He stuck out his hand.

She looked at the ring that lay on his palm.

"Where'd you get it?"

Daniel remembered Sam Underhill's advice about not telling her it was a dead man's ring. "Sam Underhill told me I could have it. I put it on and it got stuck on my finger, but a few minutes ago, I was able to get it off. I don't want it no more. So you can have it. It won't stick on your finger, your hands being smaller and all."

Given the romantic symbolism associated with the acceptance of rings, Arianna wasn't sure she should take it. But she did like baubles, and didn't own a ring just now.

"Thank you," she said, reaching out and taking the ring off his palm. She slipped it on her biggest finger and found it too large, her hands being very slender. So she tried it on her thumb, and it fit perfectly.

"Wearing a ring on your thumb!" Daniel declared, and laughed. "I never seen nobody do that before!"

She shrugged and continued walking, battling the snow, hoping he understood that there was no significance in her acceptance of his ring. "Enoch!" she called. "Here, boy!"

Daniel fell in beside her. The snow grew more obstructive as they entered the pass, but both of them managed to keep going.

CHAPTER FOUR

An hour later, well out into the craggy Sierra wilderness, a somber Daniel turned to Arianna and said, "We have to go back."

"But we haven't found Enoch."

"But the snow, Arianna. Look how deep it's getting. If we don't get back, we may not be able to."

Arianna looked around, and knew Daniel was talking sense. They'd wandered far, calling for Enoch and getting no response. The snow was deep enough now that it was hard to hold out much hope for the dog, if in fact he'd been caught out here. It broke her heart to think about it.

A noise made Arianna pause.

"Daniel, did you hear that?"

"I didn't hear nothing."

"I did. It might have been Enoch."

Daniel listened hard, but shook his head.

"It came from over that way," Arianna insisted. "I'm going to go look. Then we can start back."

"Arianna, I don't think we're going to find Enoch."

Arianna was paying no attention, already pushing through the snow in the direction from which she'd heard the noise that had drawn her ear. "Enoch!" she called. "Enoch! Can you hear me?"

Daniel started after her. "Arianna, come back."

She kept going, calling for her dog.

"Arianna!"

She clambered over a fallen tree that was piled and slick with snow. She slipped, coming down hard on the log. The snow, however, softened the impact and she got up quickly.

"Are you hurt?" Daniel reached her and put out a hand toward her.

"Leave me alone!" she declared, irritable. "Go away! If you're worried about getting home, then go home now. I'll come later, with Enoch."

"Arianna, you got to go back. It's too cold. There's too much snow."

"I'll not! Not without Enoch!"

"Enoch may be waiting for you at home right now. I think we should—" He cut off suddenly, turning his head slightly.

"Do you hear him, too?" she asked.

"I hear something. But I don't think it's . . ." His voice trailed off.

"What is it?"

"Be quiet!" he said in a sharp whisper.

"Daniel . . ."

"Look!" he said, bending slightly at the knees and pointing down a slope to their west.

Arianna saw them. Men on horses, making their way along through the snow, and having a hard time of it. They were traveling along the foot of the ridge.

Daniel and Arianna slowly knelt, letting the deep snow hide them.

"Who are they, Daniel?" Arianna whispered.

"Don't know. Odd, men traveling like that in this snow. Who in the world . . ."

"Daniel, let's go home."

Daniel nodded. When the riders had passed below, boy and girl stood and began walking as fast as they could, which was not fast at all, toward the pass. It seemed terribly far away, and Arianna felt foolish for having come this far, even for Enoch.

"Those men scare me," she said to Daniel between harsh gasps for air.

"Nothing to be afraid of," Daniel said, trying to sound manly. Arianna could tell, though, that he was scared of them, too. There was something out-of-place and disturbing about such a group, in these mountains, during a season such as this. Only some desperate reason could make men willing to plunge into this wilderness at this time of year.

Arianna and Daniel were halfway back to the pass when another sound brought them to a stop. They glanced at one another, then veered to the left, scrambling over some fallen timber that was deeply encrusted with fresh snow, forming a distorted natural sculpture. Both Arianna and Daniel fell more than once as they clambered over the timber, but in the end they made it, and were rewarded by the sight of Enoch, the straying dog, yapping at them from a recess among the logs. The dog had apparently climbed on the timber, probably chasing some woodland creature, and had slipped into the deep recess, from which he had not been able to get out again. Though the crevice had imprisoned Enoch, it had also protected him from the snow and wind.

"I'll get him," Daniel said. He flopped onto his belly, reached down, and extricated the twenty-pound mongrel.

"Here you go," Daniel said blandly, handing Enoch to Arianna, knowing he was very much the hero of the moment, but trying to be nonchalant about it. Arianna hugged the dog and planted a big kiss on the side of his snout. Daniel was instantly and obviously jealous of the dog.

He made a face. "You know, I've thought a time or two that I might like to get a kiss from you sometime. But now that I know you kiss dogs, I ain't so sure."

She was too happy at the moment to worry about insult. "Thank you, Daniel," she said sincerely. "He'd have died in there if you hadn't found him."

"It was nothing. Now we'd better keep moving. Look

yonder—it's so white you can't make out the far peaks. That means the snow's coming in even heavier.''

"Do you think those riders are near?"

"I think they've moved on. Come on."

They continued, Arianna insisting on carrying her dog, even though it slowed her.

"Let him down, Arianna," Daniel said. "He'll follow us."

"No. He'll run away again."

"You're making us have to drag along, way too slow."

"Just keep going. I'll keep up."

They rounded the side of a hill, taking heed to their footing. Daniel was cheered to catch sight of the familiar pass into Texas Gulch, but the vision was quickly erased by a new sweep of falling snow, driven hard on the wind. For a frightening moment Daniel realized just how easy it would be to become hopelessly lost in such weather. He recalled campfire stories about mountain people who had frozen to death mere yards from their own homes, as lost as if they'd been a hundred miles out in the wilderness. He tried to lock in mind the exact spot where he'd seen the pass, so he wouldn't lose course.

The wind shifted again, and he saw the riders. They were riding single file, laboriously, on a diagonal path up the face of the final slope leading to the pass. Daniel stopped at once, and Arianna, having also seen them, stopped just behind him.

"Daniel, they'll get to the pass before we do," she said.

The wind swirled, and the falling snow thinned out for a few moments.

Enoch snarled in Arianna's arms, barked, and leaped free of her grasp.

"Enoch!" she said, sharply, but hardly louder than a whisper.

Her caution was pointless now. Enoch bounded through the snow, down the slope, barking loudly at the riders. The two youngsters saw the riders turn their heads, see the dog

. . . and then one pointed. Up the slope. At them.

Daniel and Arianna glanced nervously at one another, both knowing it would be futile to run.

"It's probably all right," Daniel said, watching as three of the riders turned their horses off-course and began riding up the ridge toward them. Enoch was barking and bounding, making a defiant show, but keeping well away from the advancing horses and men. "They're probably just travelers wanting shelter. Nobody to worry about."

"Yes," Arianna said. "Just men lost in the snow. They'll probably help us get in safe to Texas Gulch."

They stood there together, waiting for the advancing men to reach them.

"I'm worried, Sam," Leora Winkle said. "Arianna disappeared earlier, looking for her dog, and she hasn't come back."

Sam looked into Leora's face, pretty despite the lines of concern that tracked along it just now like thin trail marks traced on a map. "Do you think she'd have gone beyond the pass in this weather?" he asked.

"I don't know . . . I didn't think she would. That's why I let her go. Maybe I didn't think at all. I was . . . distracted today."

Distracted. Sam knew what that meant. She'd been grieving again for her lost husband. Sam felt sorry for Leora, but at the same time wished she'd find a way to put that loss behind her and take notice that there were other good and available men in the world, the most prime example he could think of being the one standing before her now.

"Might she be visiting at someone's cabin? Have you asked around for her?"

"I've been almost everywhere, every place she'd go," Leora said. "She's nowhere. And Daniel is missing, too. Mr. Colfax said he saw Daniel earlier, looking for her. I suppose they're together somewhere."

"I doubt they're far away, Leora. I'll go look for her. There's still a lot of daylight left."

"There's a place she likes to go, farther back in the valley. Where those white rocks are that the sun shines on in the evening."

"That's where we'll find her, I'll bet. Or more likely, I'll meet them already coming back. I'll find her for you. I promise."

"Thank you, Sam."

"My pleasure."

Leora left the cabin and hurried back through the snow toward the lodge house. Sam watched her go, and frowned. He'd just promised to find Arianna, a foolish pledge. His father had taught him never to make a vow he couldn't be sure of keeping. There was always the terrible chance that Arianna and Daniel had wandered too far, and had gotten lost or cut off from getting back. If so, they might not be found until the spring thaw, and maybe not even then. But Sam decided not to dwell on that possibility. He'd assume for now that he'd find both youngsters quickly.

Sam filled his water bottle from the drinking bucket, and dropped some sun-dried meat into a pocket. He considered loading himself up with his rifle and other gear, but it was hard enough to move through thick snow even without burdens. He'd forgo the weaponry in favor of unencumbrance.

If Ben Dillow was handy, he'd ask him to come too. But Ben was off somewhere else, and Sam wasn't inclined to go looking for him. He'd just make a quick hike out into the valley, round up the children, get them home, and enjoy Leora's praise.

He paused once before he set out, wondering if he was taking this all a little too lightly. Maybe he should organize a full search, take gear and weapons . . . but no. Leora was a worrier, always exaggerating things. It was possible that the youngsters were right here in the camp, just hidden away. Maybe Daniel had finally persuaded Arianna to give him a kiss, and they were off holding hands somewhere.

Probably the boy had given her that ring by now.

Tightening his hat onto his head, Sam left his cabin, paused to strap snowshoes onto his feet, and trudged out into the white.

CHAPTER FIVE

Arianna tried to hide her fear, but couldn't. She stared into the leering face of Searl Mahaffery, felt the pain of his big, rough hand around her wrist, smelled the stench of his breath in her face, and desperately wished she could run away. She was at the base of the slope, encircled by the riders. Daniel struggled in the grip of Bert Mongold, off to the side.

Enoch was up on the slope, growling, snarling, and occasionally barking at the group below, but staying far away.

"Tell me, dear thing, are all the little gals as pretty as you where you come from?" Searl asked her.

"Let me go!"

"Where do you come from? Dutch Camp?"

"Texas Gulch," she said. "Please, I want to go home!"

"Texas Gulch? Where the hell is Texas Gulch?"

Arianna tried to pull her wrist free. He tightened his grip, shoving his ugly face closer. "I asked you, where is Texas Gulch?"

"It's Dutch Camp," she said, fighting tears. "My mother is there. I want to go to her."

Searl grinned. "Your mother? Texas Gulch sounds like my kind of place. Is she as pretty as you? You don't find many mining camps with pretty gals about them, you know." He turned and winked at his companions. "Tell you what, dear thing, you give me a little kiss and maybe I'll let you go to your mama. What do you say?''

She turned her head away, sickened at the thought of kissing this man or having him kiss her. She looked at Daniel, pleading helplessly with her eyes. But Daniel was as entrapped as she was. And just as scared.

''You didn't answer my question about your mama, girl,'' Searl said, yanking her wrist. ''I asked you if she was as pretty as you.''

''Yes.''

''My, my. Lord have mercy! That's a thing to picture . . . two pretty things there together. Hey . . . in the night, do you ever see your mama and your daddy getting friendly . . . You know what I'm talking about?''

She was beginning to feel ill. ''My father's dead,'' she said. ''I want to go home.'' She looked at the faces of the men around her. No sympathy. Several very scary grins. One or two looked hungry in a way that terrified her. ''Don't hurt me.''

''Let her go!'' Daniel yelled, writhing and tugging in the grip of his own captor. ''Let us both go!''

''Shut up, boy,'' Mongold muttered at Daniel in a bored tone. Daniel might as well have been a mouse struggling in Mongold's big hands, for all the good his escape attempts were doing.

The dog up on the hill barked more intensely. One of the riders muttered a wish to shoot the cussed thing.

Daniel managed to turn and kick Mongold hard in the knee. Mongold roared, cursed, and struck Daniel in the face with a fist almost as big as the boy's head. Daniel's body jolted and he made a guttural noise. A second blow made him go limp. Mongold let him fall into the snow.

''Believe I may have hurt him,'' Mongold said. ''Ain't it a shame!'' He grinned at his partners, but grimaced as he reached down to rub the kicked knee.

Searl Mahaffery shoved his face against Arianna's, rubbing abrasive whiskers against her skin. ''Mighty pretty gal, you are," he muttered. "Pretty as a picture."

"Searl, she's hardly out of the cradle!" an outlaw named Reed Van Huss said. "Naught but a baby, that one! You're old enough to be her daddy."

"Maybe he is," said another of the band, Perry Winters.

Arianna began to cry and tried to pull away, but couldn't.

A hand gripped Searl Mahaffery's shoulder. Searl looked up at the stern face of his elder brother, the only man there, perhaps with the exception of the inscrutable Conner Broadgrass, who didn't seem to be finding this performance amusing.

"Searl," he said, and gave a little turn of his head to indicate Searl should step aside.

"You wait your own turn, Jordan," Searl said.

"There'll be no touching this girl," Mahaffery replied. "I'll not see her hurt. Let her go."

Mumbling a few obscenities, Searl freed Arianna, rose, and stomped back to his waiting horse.

Mahaffery knelt before the weeping girl. "Honey, are you afraid?"

She looked at the man. He looked at lot like the one who had just tormented her, though older, a little uglier, and with skin that bore the pitted scars of a long-past pox. But his kindly tone gave her hope. "Yes, I'm afraid."

"You don't need to be. I won't let him hurt you."

Emmett Fish said, "Hell, Jordan, you're ruining the fun." The others chuckled, except Searl Mahaffery, who was far too furious.

"You say you live where?" Mahaffery asked her.

"Texas Gulch."

Mahaffery smiled, as gentle and kindly as the friendliest schoolmaster. "Well! I didn't know until you said so that they'd changed the name from Dutch Camp. Why Texas Gulch?"

"Because most of the people there came in from Texas." She was sniffling now, not fully crying. Glancing over at

Daniel, she saw him still lying, unmoving, in the snow, and she worried about him.

"Texas, eh? What part?"

"Mostly from around Underhill."

"Underhill, Texas! Heard of it! That's where the famous Bushrod lives, ain't it? Somewhere in the Brazos country?"

"Yes."

"You from there?"

"Yes."

"Well! You know Bushrod Underhill?"

"Yes."

"He ain't in Texas Gulch, is he?"

"No. He's still in Texas." She started to mention Sam Underhill, but some cautious instinct told her to volunteer little information to these men, even to the one who seemed kind.

"I'll bet you've got lots of food, good shelter, and supplies laid in for the winter."

"Yes."

"Because, you know, I think me and my friends here might have made a mistake. We might have come into these mountains too late in the year to get out again. We might have to come live at Texas Gulch for a while."

Arianna blanched at the idea of these men infiltrating her own community. The prospect was purely dreadful.

"Tell me something, sweetheart," Mahaffery said through the most disarming of smiles. "Have there been other newcomers to Texas Gulch lately?"

"No."

"Are you sure about that?"

"Yes. It's just all the regular people."

"Then where did you get this?" He reached out and took her hand, lifting it, and pointing to the ring on her thumb.

A murmur of surprise ran through the circle of riders. "That's Dehaven's ring!" Ross Remine said.

"It was a gift to me," Arianna said, pulling her hand away.

"From a man? Gray-haired, friendly sort?"

"No. From him. From Daniel." She pointed at Daniel's still form. Tears formed in her eyes and she feared Daniel was dead.

"Really? Is he your little beau?"

"No. He's just Daniel the orphan boy."

"Mighty odd mining camp, I must say," Mahaffery commented. "Widows, pretty little girls, and orphan boys. Tell me: where did Daniel get this ring?"

"I don't know."

"Well, you know where I think he got it? I think it must have been given to him by a man named Frank Dehaven. Because Frank used to have this ring. He's an old friend of mine. I think he must be in Texas Gulch, and he must have made friends with Daniel. Now, maybe Frank ain't calling himself by his real name. He does that sometimes, uses different names. But he's a little older than I am, and with grayish hair. Fairly fine-looking figure of a man. That sound like anybody you know in Texas Gulch?"

"No. Is Daniel dead?" She was beginning to draw in her breath spasmodically, on the verge of breaking into sudden, out-of-control sobs.

"No, no. Just knocked a little silly, that's all. But you know what? I bet we do need to get him into Texas Gulch, where we can put him in a warm bed and make sure he's well. Would you like to go back to your mother?"

"Yes. But don't let him bother her." She flicked her eyes toward the sullen Searl.

"He won't bother you or her. I won't let him. He's my little brother, and I can keep him under control. Now, let's go, sweetheart. My name's Mr. Mahaffery. What's yours?"

"Arianna Winkle."

"Arianna. Pretty name to go with a pretty girl." He grinned at her in a downright heartwarming manner. "You and me can be friends, I believe."

"You promise to keep him away from my mother and

me?'' She cast another glance at Searl Mahaffery, who muttered a curse beneath his breath.

"You bet I will. He's the bad boy of the family. But I'll keep him in line." He patted her shoulder. "That your dog up there?"

"Yes."

"Barks a lot, don't he?"

"Sometimes."

"Would you like your dog back?"

"Yes."

Mahaffery stood and turned to Emmett Fish. "Emmett, go and fetch that dog for Arianna here, would you?"

"Fetch the dog? How am I supposed to fetch it?"

"Just take care of it, Emmett. You can follow our tracks in. Arianna's going to show us the way to Texas Gulch. Right, sweetheart?"

Arianna didn't want these men coming to Texas Gulch, but knew she had no choice. "Yes," she murmured.

"Bert, scoop up the boy there before he gets the chilblains. You fetch that dog, Emmett, then follow us on in. We'll lead your horse in for you."

Arianna, though intimidated, made herself ask a question: "What are you going to do when you get to Texas Gulch?"

"Well, honey, I think we're going to try to find out more about how that ring you wear came to be in Texas Gulch. When did Daniel give that ring to you, sweetheart?"

"Today." She didn't like him calling her "sweetheart," but wasn't bold enough to tell him so.

"I see. Interesting. You want to ride on my horse? You can sit in front of me and I'll pull this big coat around you. Keep you warm."

She nodded, knowing again there was no other choice.

Bert Mongold managed to get the limp Daniel Chase onto his own saddle, and swung up behind. Somehow he got a grip on the boy and managed to hold his horse's reins as well. Daniel sagged and swayed, and made groaning sounds that Arianna was relieved to hear.

The riders, all but Emmett Fish, pushed on through the almost inpenetrable snow. Fish watched them with a sour expression, and began trudging up the slope toward the dog, which barked madly at him. He muttered a few curses, and called for the dog to stay put.

Of course it didn't. When he drew nearer, Enoch turned and bounded off through the snow in big, arcing leaps. Emmett Fish swore some more and trudged on after it, taking mental note of every landmark so he wouldn't get lost.

Fish wasn't fully sure what he was supposed to do. As best he could figure it, he was putting on an act for the girl's benefit, to keep her trusting and compliant until they reached Texas Gulch. After that, it wouldn't matter. Take care of it, Jordan Mahaffery had said.

He knew how he intended to take care of it. He wasn't about to carry some barking dog across the wilderness just to please some teary-eyed little girl.

He looked after the retreating riders, who were making slow progress across the white mountain landscape. Emmett Fish despised rugged country. Give him a good, level, well-liquored town anytime. The notion of spending an entire winter in these mountains was disgusting. He hoped they had a lot of good whiskey in Texas Gulch.

He watched the horsemen for a few moments more, then checked his rifle and turned to look for the dog.

CHAPTER SIX

Sam Underhill was glad his father wasn't here to see his son make such a mockery of all the common sense and trailsmanship he'd tried to ingrain in him through the years.

Sam felt quite a fool. He'd made the twin errors of over-confidence and easy assumption. He'd assumed it would be simple to find Arianna and that he could handle the task alone. But he'd meandered over a big part of the valley and so far hadn't found a sign of her or Daniel. Not a track, not a peep of sound.

So maybe they weren't here at all. Perhaps they had gone the opposite direction, out through the pass into the mountains beyond. If so, and if they hadn't returned in Sam's absence, they were probably in severe trouble right now. Maybe dead. Dear Lord, what had he done, taking such a cavalier attitude?

Sam would have kicked himself if it would have done any good. He should have alerted all the men of Texas Gulch, had them spread out and search systematically until Arianna and Daniel were found. He should not have come out here alone and unarmed in this land of bears, mountain lions, and coyotes.

The sun was westering. Before long he'd have to end his search. He imagined facing Leora Winkle and telling her he'd failed to find her daughter, and now it was too late to do anything further because night had come.

He struggled against mounting panic. Arianna and Daniel *had* to be here. He *had* to find them.

Sam cupped his hands around his mouth. "Arianna! Daniel!"

No replies came except the echo of his own calls off the high, encircling ridges.

He drew in a deep breath and decided there was but one thing to do. He had to rush back to Texas Gulch as quickly as possible and hope that he'd find the children already there. If not, he and the men of the mining camp would have to make torches and form search teams. They'd have to position themselves at high places on both sides of the pass, and build huge bonfires both to keep them warm through the night, and to serve as guidelights for the missing youngsters. And they'd have to pray hard.

"Arianna! Daniel! Can you hear me?"

Empty echoes mocked him.

He shifted his coat, rehoisted his trousers, and put his snowshoe-clad foot out to begin the journey back to Texas Gulch. Curse the snow! It was piling faster and deeper than he'd anticipated. He'd not make it back quickly enough. Had to try, though.

A few steps later, however, he stopped. Something had caught his eye up on a bluff to his right. He stopped, put his hand across his brows, salute fashion, to shield his eyes, and studied the faint spot of color. It was too high and far away for him to be sure, but he thought it might be a small human being. Arianna or Daniel, or both huddled together. Might they have climbed the bluff, looking for shelter in a cave, and gotten stranded on the ledge?

"Daniel! Arianna! Is that you I see?"

Whoever or whatever it was, there was no answer. He prayed he wouldn't find them up there frozen to death from exposure to the cold wind.

He squinted harder, unsure whether he was seeing human

forms at all. It might be no more than a colored, eroded boulder that the wind was keeping free of snow accumulation.

But the more he looked, the more he believed that what he saw was human . . . but unmoving.

No, dear Lord, no . . . don't let me be too late. Please.

Sam began looking around for a route up the slope. He wondered how Arianna and Daniel had managed to reach such a place. Well, if they could, he could too.

He studied the area above the ledge with concern. Though the snow was still new enough not to have accumulated to dangerous levels, the slope above the ledge was of just the right angle and conditions to be favorable to snow slides. A little more accumulation, and this could become the site of small, continuing avalanches all winter long. Just one more reason to get those children away from this place . . . if that was really who he saw.

Sam rubbed his face, trying to ward off chill, blinked his eyes several times, and spotted a possible climbing route. Removing his snowshoes, he laid them aside for retrieval after he came down again. Putting hand to stone, he made the first heave. So far, so good. He found another handhold, and a crevice to accommodate his foot, and rose another half a yard.

The stone face of the bluff was cold, and the wind and stinging snow made it difficult to concentrate on where he was going. As he climbed, he glanced up repeatedly, making sure he wasn't losing his bearings and drifting away from the ledge where they were . . . *if* they were.

Keep climbing, old fellow, he urged himself. *You've got to find them and bring them home. Just keep climbing.*

Emmett Fish had thought it would be easy to shoot the dog and be through with it. But the blasted creature was running him all over creation, ever deeper into the wilderness and snow, and he was afraid that he'd lose his way back to that pass if he went any farther. Every time he tried to line up his shot, the dog would dart away.

He would have been willing to let the dog go free and freeze to death out here, but the beast had made the mistake of annoying him. Shooting the thing had become an issue of personal satisfaction.

Ah, there it was! Just ahead, up on the crest of a small rise, looking back at him as if beckoning him to follow yet another distance. Anger surged. A dog, a mere *dog*, was playing a game with him!

Fish wanted to scream at the animal, but that would be counterproductive. ''Come here, fellow!'' he called warmly, and whistled. ''Come here just a bit closer! Old Emmett's got a little something for you!''

The dog wagged its tail, bounded toward him a couple of leaps, and eyed him with interest.

''That's right! Come on now, boy! Good doggy!''

He raised his rifle slowly, cocked it, and sighted in on the dog's midsection when he saw the beast turn its head, peer through the driving snow to its right, and begin to bark madly.

Fish lowered the rifle. The dog had smelled something, seen something.

He looked hard in the same direction as the barking dog. Images of himself being devoured by some hungry bear filled his mind. Or were bears all in their dens right now?

Fish decided to take no chances. He'd not expend a rifle ball killing a dog when there might be something dangerous nearby. He stared a little longer through the swirling snow, thinking maybe he *could* see something there, after all . . .

The dog barked in a new frenzy, and bolted off over the rise and out of sight.

Emmett Fish gazed through the snow, squinting, brows lowered.

A *man*? Was that really a man he saw out there?

''Dehaven! Is that you?''

He received no answer. The figure, barely visible, just stood there, seemingly looking back at him.

"Dehaven! It's Emmett Fish!" He paused. "Dehaven? I came to warn you that Mahaffery's come looking for you! He's mad as hell because of you taking the gold . . . but don't you worry. He's gone down into that mining camp! He thinks maybe that you're there with the gold! But if you're here, and you still got the gold, you and me could take it . . . we could get clean away. I'd never do a thing to betray you, Dehaven!"

The figure did not move or reply. Emmett took a few steps closer, trying to see better, but the snow was still thickly falling.

"Dehaven? Is that you? I swear, I wouldn't betray you! It'll take Jordan a while to find out you ain't at that mining camp. We could be long gone by then . . . but we got to move quick, before the snow gets deeper."

No answer. Was that Dehaven he was seeing?

Maybe, maybe not. Maybe it wasn't even a man. Just a tall stump or a wind-twisted young tree.

But it surely did look like a man, just standing there. He raised his rifle again. He stepped closer yet, then cussed loudly.

It *was* a tree. Nothing but a blasted, dead tree that nature had chanced to sculpt into something roughly the shape and size of a man!

Disgusted, he lowered the rifle, and turned back to head for the pass. The devil with that dog, and everything else. He was hungry and cold and in need of shelter, ready to follow his companions into Texas Gulch.

Sam Underhill was praying hard now.

The rock he climbed was nearly sheer and cold as a block of ice. The wind was growing stronger. And he was more certain than ever that no greater fool had ever followed the gold trail to California than Sam Underhill.

"Lord," he said aloud, "if you get me out of this, I swear

I'll become a preacher. I'll give everything I got to the widows and orphans. I'll turn missionary to the heathen Chinese. I'll do anything at all, if you'll just let me get home alive. And those children. Especially those children.''

But he feared they were already dead. Up on the ledge above him, frozen to death.

Sam paused to let himself regather a little strength. At least the exertion was keeping his muscles warm. He breathed hard for half a minute, then put forth a new burst of effort. He climbed the final distance. Cutting his eyes upward, he saw the edge of the ledge within reach. He'd done it! But he dreaded what he was sure he would find when he made the final pull.

Putting a hand up, Sam gripped the rim of the ledge and pulled. No good footholds here, just smooth rock. He strained hard.

Sam's head cleared the rim of the ledge. He would have laughed at the irony of it all, if he could. There were no dead children on that ledge. No children at all.

Just colored stone. The very possibility he had considered and rejected. A mound of oddly colored stone, cropping out onto the ledge.

The discovery brought him some relief—at least the children weren't dead up here—but it was relief with a dark edge. As far as he knew, they still remained lost. And he'd just expended most of his strength, and almost the entire remaining light of day, climbing up a bluff for nothing. He'd never make it back down again, and to Texas Gulch, in time to get search teams going before dark.

He hoped that maybe Ben Dillow or somebody else with some sense about them had become aware of what was going on, and had already started looking for the children on their own steam.

He realized that by now they might be looking for him, too.

He pulled himself up onto the ledge and crawled into a space behind the very wedge of colored stone that had deceived his eye. Here he was cut off from the wind, and when he huddled just right, could actually avoid even the driven snow.

The thought of simply staying here to wait out the night came to mind, but was dismissed. Too dangerous. A shift of wind could bring the cold and snow in right at him. If he went to sleep he might freeze to death.

He decided to stay here long enough to rest his muscles and regain his breath, then climb back down again before all the light was gone. Then he'd hurry back to Texas Gulch.

He closed his eyes, listening to the howling wind and the endless, barely audible rattle of snowflakes pelting stone. The natural world seemed a vast, dangerous, but coldly splendid place just now.

Opening his eyes when he noticed a sudden diminishing of the snowfall, he realized what a spectacular view he had from this place of the great basin that held Texas Gulch. The sun was closing on the western horizon, nearly invisible behind the clouds, but revealing its presence as a smear of gray light. Quite a piece of creation, this was! But wild and indifferent to the men who tried to exploit it for the gleaming bits of gold it had to offer. Sam remembered words his father had told him: *a man who knows his proper place in the scheme of life is a wiser man than most, but also a much more sober one*. Sam was beginning to understand what that meant.

Time to climb down again.

Leaving his place of refuge, he turned and positioned himself to edge down over the lip of the ledge. His fingers were almost numb, so he wriggled them a few moments, then got a firm grip on the stone and began to descend.

He wasn't at precisely the same spot he'd come up, and was halfway down before he realized that this was a potentially serious problem. He'd veered into an area with fewer handholds and footholds. But he went on, occasionally slipping, but not falling.

At last he reached an impasse. Nothing but smooth stone

below, and several yards yet to descend. Too far to jump.
Further, it was getting darker, and he couldn't see well in
any direction. Should he drift left or right? Or would he
have to climb back up and try to find some new route from
there?

Left, he decided. That's how it would be. The stone was
rougher in that direction. More to hold on to.

Sam began edging, inch by inch, in that direction. The
light was fading far too fast, and he rushed a little. It was
a mistake. His foot, barely caught in a small crevice, slipped
free and made his body slip to one side and turn slightly.
His right hand lost its precarious grip, and with his heart
leaping to his throat, he plunged, pounding down the slope
into a dark, hidden area below.

CHAPTER
SEVEN

In the white world beyond the pass, the tree that Emmett Fish had seen was no longer there. As soon as Fish had turned and vanished, the "tree" had moved, and become a human being.

The man had waited only long enough for Fish to gain enough of a lead that he could be followed without becoming aware of it. The man had learned a lot from that little burst of information Fish had yelled up to him when he thought he was Dehaven, whomever that might be. The implications were troubling.

He followed Fish's tracks through the falling snow, utterly silent.

While Sam Underhill had been climbing carefully up a bluff far down the valley toward what he had thought would be the two missing children, the people of Texas Gulch were slowly emerging from their cabins to encounter an unexpected and chilling sight.

Jordan Mahaffery had ended all pretenses of gentleness toward Arianna Winkle by the time the exhausted horses came through the pass and in sight of Texas Gulch. Once there, Mahaffery had remounted his horse, with Arianna directly in front of him. By the time the riders reached the edge of the mining camp, Mahaffery had his pistol out and

pressed to the temple of the girl. She was too scared even
to cry.

To Mahaffery's right, Bert Mongold had the now-semi-
conscious Daniel Chase hefted upright in the saddle before
him, with Mongold's pistol stuck up under the boy's chin,
keeping his head propped up. Mongold wore a big smile.
He loved this kind of thing.

Mahaffery, for his part, was calm and businesslike. When
a sufficient number of startled, gaping people had gathered,
he nodded in friendly style and said, "Howdy to you all.
Texas Gulch, I believe you call this place now? Well, folks,
I just want you to know that your population has just increased. Your cooperation with us, your new guests, is advised, or else the population could as easily make a sudden
decline."

Ben Dillow stepped toward Mahaffery. "Lower that pistol!" he demanded. "What kind of man are you to threaten
a little girl?"

Mahaffery clicked back the lock of his pistol. "I advise
you to stop where you are, unless you'd like to see me blow
this pretty young lady's brains out through her skull. Am I
speaking with sufficient clarity?"

Dillow halted and stood glaring at Mahaffery. Mongold
chuckled. Back in the crowd, Leora Winkle, who had just
then emerged to see her daughter in such straits, let out a
scream and ran toward Mahaffery.

"Uh-uh," Mahaffery said, shaking his head. "No,
ma'am. I don't advise it."

Dillow put out his arm and caught Leora as she began to
pass him. "Hold up, Leora. He'll kill her if you don't."

"That's right," Mahaffery said. "You're an intelligent
man, sir. A veritable scholar of common sense. I will indeed
kill this young lady, and Mr. Mongold there would gladly
kill that sorry scrap of a boy, if any one of you attempt even
the slightest interference with anything we do here. Is that
understood?"

No replies were heard beyond a few subtle mutters and

growls and the pitiful sound of Leora Winkle sobbing into her hands.

"By the way, my friend," Mahaffery said to miner Julius Setser, who was creeping about the edge of the little crowd, "I do see that pistol you're trying to conceal. And that's not at all what I meant by 'cooperation.' " Mahaffery raised his pistol, sighted down it, and shot Julius Setser through the heart. Arianna jerked like a puppet with its string yanked. Setser fell, twitched, and died in the snow as screams rose from the onlookers and people reflexively backed away from the new-fallen corpse.

Mahaffery began to reload his pistol, arms still wrapped around Arianna.

"Someone take the pistol from that dead man and hand it to my brother here," Mahaffery said, indicating Searl just to his left. "That, my friends, is what I meant when I talk about quick population decline. Need I give any further demonstrations?"

"Who are you, and what do you want from us?" Dillow said.

"Who I am is Jordan Mahaffery. This man to my left is Searl Mahaffery, my younger brother. Not at all a refined young man, I have to tell you. I advise you to keep your wives and daughters away from him, if you can." Mahaffery finished his reloading, meanwhile, but kept the pistol in his hand. "To my right is Mr. Bert Mongold, a vicious sort of devil who enjoys inflicting death in slow and colorful ways. Be very, very polite to him at all times."

Mongold, beaming, nodded at the people of Texas Gulch, acknowledging his due acclaim.

"These others with me are Mr. Lennis Yeager, Mr. Ross Remine, and Mr. Conner Broadgrass, three men you don't want angry at you." He turned and looked behind him. "Ah, yes! And yonder, walking through that pass behind me to join us, is Mr. Emmett Fish. Not the smartest man, Mr. Fish, but quite good at following directions. Completely lacking in scruples. I once saw him hack an old man to death for stepping on his sore toe.

"And over there are Joe Legarde, Reed Van Huss, and Perry Winters. Not much wickedness in this world those three haven't done, and not a bit of it they wouldn't do again.

"That's who we are. As for what we are, we're thieves. Scoundrels. Murderers. The lowest breed of mankind, and quite content with our station. Only one thing disturbs our peace, and that's when what's ours is taken from us. Which, sorry to say, is what's happened. And that's why we've come here to you."

"No one here has taken anything from you," Dillow said.

Mahaffery grabbed Arianna's arm and jerked it straight up so suddenly and so hard that the girl gasped and her mother screamed.

"Look at this girl's hand," Mahaffery said. The light was fading and so was his deliberately ironic facade of friendliness. "There's a ring on her thumb. I know that ring. There's only one ring like that. I know the man who wore it. And I want to know, right now, no delay, where that man is." He let go of Arianna's hand and turned his pistol toward Dillow. "And if I don't find out, I'll kill you, sir."

"I don't know where that ring came from," Dillow said.

"I do." The speaker was Marica Bolton. She stepped around from the rear of the clump of scared people.

"Well, ma'am!" Mahaffery said, actually smiling at the sight of this previously unnoticed pretty lady. Beside him his younger brother whistled low and muttered something. He was grinning, too. "Pleasure to meet such loveliness in a dung pit of a mining camp like this. Do tell me what you know."

"That ring came from the finger of a dead man."

"Yes . . . I remember now," Dillow said. "She's right."

Emmett Fish, cold and glum and silent, reached the clump of outlaws and swung into his saddle, from where he peered across the gathered people of the mining camp.

Behind Fish, unseen by any, a shadowy figure had also entered the pass, drawing only close enough to hear what was said, but remaining out of sight.

"Mister, I'm talking to the lady just now, so you can keep your damned mouth shut," Mahaffery said to Dillow. "Dead man, did you say, ma'am?"

"Yes. He was found dead at the pass."

"And where is he now?"

"Buried."

"And how, ma'am, did this dead man become dead?"

"He was found dead. Mr. Dillow believes the man's heart failed him."

"Mr. Dillow?"

"That's me," Ben Dillow said.

"Fine. Then you tell me, Mr. Dillow, what became of whatever baggage the dead man had with him?"

"There was no baggage."

Mahaffery raised his pistol, aimed, and sent a ball hurtling just past Dillow's head. It almost struck America Colfax behind him. She screamed and ran to her husband. Arianna, close to the pistol when it fired, squeezed her eyes tightly closed. She bit her lip so hard her teeth almost broke the skin.

Mahaffery again began reloading the pistol.

"Mr. Dillow, the next time you lie to me, I'll shoot you through the face. Do you understand?"

Marica Bolton strode to Dillow, glanced at him, then stepped boldly between him and Mahaffery. "Would you shoot a woman, sir?"

"Ma'am, I'd shoot John the Baptist, Paul the Apostle, and in the right circumstances, my own mother."

"Mr. Dillow didn't lie to you. There was no baggage with the dead man. There was only his body."

"And who found it?"

"The boy there. Daniel."

Dillow whispered to her, "I wish you hadn't told him that."

"Ah!" Mahaffery said, looking over at Daniel, who was now looking around bleary-eyed, softly groaning every now and then. "So the boy found the body, alone . . . then came into town and informed the rest of you. And Dehaven—that's the name of the dead man, by the way—was collected and buried, all but his ring. Is that it?"

"That's it."

"So we have only the boy's word that nothing else was found with the body."

Marica Bolton blanched, realizing the trouble she might have just brought upon young Daniel. "Daniel never said that nothing was found with the body. He never said anything about that at all, either way."

Dillow stepped up beside Marica. He tried a new tack, no belligerence or defiance. "Mister, we'd like to answer your questions, but maybe we could understand things better if you explained what this baggage you talk about is supposed to be."

"Gold, sir. Gold, and gold aplenty. Stolen from a bank vault many miles away from here, by myself and my partners here, at the cost of a few lives, none of them ours. Then Dehaven, one of our number, managed to take that gold for himself and flee with it. We pursued him, tracked him to these mountains . . . and now we're being told he's dead and that the gold hasn't been seen at all." Another pause. "I, for one, am skeptical about that."

"Maybe this Dehaven hid the gold himself, before he got here."

"Hid the gold, then conveniently died. I find that hard to believe."

"You can search this camp. You'll find no gold beyond what we've grubbed ourselves."

"We *will* search this camp, sir. And we'll even dig up Dehaven's grave, come morning. Capable man that you seem to be, we'll give you the honor of the task. Then we'll take a look at that corpse and see if there are any signs of violence against him." As the wind howled and the snow suddenly became a little heavier and colder, Mahaffery looked the group over and gave a final pronouncement. "It's my belief that some of you, maybe all of you, have sinned the sin of greed. I believe that Dehaven did come to this camp. And I believe that some of you, maybe all, killed him for the sake of the gold he carried. And I believe that gold is here, hidden. And I want it."

Herbert Colfax, scowling, spoke up for the first time. "It ain't true, my friend. There was no gold seen by any one of us. I helped carry the dead man down from the pass. I can tell you there was no gold on him. So if anybody found gold, it was the boy, before any of the rest of us even knew there was a dead man."

Dillow wheeled and barked at Colfax, "What the devil are you trying to do, Colfax? Get a little boy tortured or killed?"

"I'm speaking the truth, that's what I'm doing, and I'll make no apology for it! I'll not be misused, nor see my family misused, for the sake of some lying orphan child!"

"Enough of that!" Mahaffery said. "All possibilities will be examined and explored. The truth will come out quickly enough. And when my partners and I leave this place, we *will* have our gold. And it makes no difference to any of us whether we leave this camp with a living population, or a dead one." He let the dark implication sink in. "Now . . . it's dark, it's cold, and the snow is heavy. I see a long, big log building back yonder. What is that? Some kind of common dwelling you folks share?"

"Some here share it. It was built back when this place was still called Dutch Camp," Colfax volunteered. "It's been divided up with partitions and such, so a lot of folks can live in it at the same time."

"We'll go inside there, then. All of us. And if there are any others living in this camp who aren't out here, I want them brought to me—man, woman, bed-baby . . . all of them. Don't try to hide anyone or anything, for we'll be exploring every inch and every cranny of this hellhole, and there'll be no secrets kept. Any who try to hide anything from me and my companions, anything at all, will not live to see another springtime. Any questions?''

"You're very clear, sir," Colfax said.

Dillow muttered, "Why don't you just ask him to rear up a little higher in the saddle so you can kiss his rump without so much strain, Colfax?''

"Don't mock the gentleman," Mahaffery said to Dillow. "He's got the right idea. He understands how things stand. The quicker all of you do the same, the better off you'll be.''

Mahaffery spoke to his men. "Emmett, you and Lennis get a couple of these folks to help you see to the horses. I presume there's some sort of stable. Lennis, it'll be your task as long as we're here to make sure the horses stay tended and fed. For now, the rest of us will get these folks herded together in that big cabin, and we'll search this camp for guns and such. And find some food! I'm nigh starved.''

"I'd advise guarding the pass as long as we're here, Jordan," Broadgrass said. "If there's anyone hidden out here that we don't yet see, they might get out in the darkness, before we're even aware of them.''

"You're a wise man, Conner. Reed! Perry! Joe! You three get a couple of big fires blazing up in that pass. And stand guard to make sure nobody gets out. You—Dillow! Is there any other way out of this valley?''

"None," Dillow said glumly.

"Very good, then. We'll all stay here together. Reed, Joe, Perry, we'll have some food up to you soon. And we'll work out some shifts so nobody has to stay up there all night. Make those fires big, you hear? Light up that whole pass, and get yourself plenty of heat.''

Mahaffery turned back to the people. "Folks, pleased to be with you all. You behave, you cooperate, you'll be fine. You don't, and you'll wind up like that fellow there.'' He pointed at the body of Julius Setser. "Now let's get out of this weather, what do you say?''

CHAPTER EIGHT

The three outlaws designated by Mahaffery trudged up to the pass, taking with them wood from one of the several massive woodpiles around Texas Gulch, the fuel set aside to get an isolated mining camp through a long and cold winter. As they entered the pass, the shadowy figure that had followed Emmett Fish moved, hesitated, then moved again, slipping back toward the mountains.

Minutes later, as the flames of two bonfires rose, illuminating the gap, the unseen man watched from outside the circle of light. For a long time he waited, then at length turned and quietly moved farther into the darkness and away from the light.

Sam Underhill rolled over and did his best to groan, but the impact of his fall had temporarily paralyzed his lungs, and he couldn't draw a breath.

Sitting up, he felt the reflexive panic that comes from the inability to breathe, and struggled to suck in air. A few moments later his body cooperated and he breathed in ragged gasps. The panic subsided, but in its place came pain. He felt as if two giant fists had grabbed him like a wet rag and given him a wringing in opposing directions.

"Dear Lord," he muttered. "That was indeed a tumble."

He turned his body a little. His ribs were sore, but not

sore enough to make him think he'd broken any. That much was good. He wriggled his toes, turned his feet, drew up his knees and straightened them again. Everything worked. Nothing broken there. He checked his hands, his arms, rolled his shoulders. Everything was in operating order, though he ached all over and figured that before long he'd have enough bruises to make him look like a map.

Once he'd decided that providence had spared him any major injuries, he turned his attention to the place where he'd landed. He was in nearly total darkness, though the last lingering traces of daylight were still visible through some sort of opening above him. He saw he was inside some enclosed place, apparently a vertical cavern, or pit, at the base of the bluff.

He looked around, but the darkness spread to all sides. He stood, very slowly, still testing his body. He bumped his head, though, and stepped forward to seek more room.

Snow drifted down around him, through the opening above, but only a little. He scuffed his boot on the stony soil beneath his feet and found it relatively free of accumulation.

He dug around in the folds and pockets of his bearskin coat. The coat was a gift given him by his father and mother prior to his departure to California. Bushrod Underhill had shot the bear himself on a hunting venture into Arkansas five years earlier, and had considered it the prize bear of a long hunting career. He'd saved the skin to make a coat for himself, but when Sam had announced his intention to become a Forty-niner, he had bade his wife to make the coat to fit Sam instead. So this garment had a lot of meaning to Sam Underhill, and as he thought about it, he realized its heavy protection probably accounted in large part for how he'd managed to take such a fall without serious injury.

At last he found the matchblock he sought. Breaking a match off, he knelt, shielded it with his body, and struck fire. By the flaring light he looked around him, as far as the light would allow. Yes, he was in some sort of pit, probably

another entrance to one of the many caverns running
through the mountains around the Texas Gulch basin. There
were plenty such caves, new entrances constantly being
found by the prospectors as they poked around the landscape
looking for gold.

The match burned to Sam's fingers and he shook it out.
Standing partially, but keeping his head low, he crept a little
farther to the center of the pit, then knelt and lit another
match. By its light he studied the floor. Ah, yes. Just as he'd
hoped. There were dried evergreen needles, twigs, even a
few old and dried branches that had fallen or blown into
this hole over the years. He shook out the match, and in
blind-man fashion felt around his feet and gathered twigs
and tinder. Heaping these, he struck another match and lit
a fire. The dry materials caught easily, and by their flames
he gathered a few of the bigger sticks and added them to
the blaze. He piled on yet more fuel and soon had a small
but wonderfully warm and light-generating fire, sheltered
from the wind by the walls of the pit.

Remembering his notice of the angle of the slope high
above him, he considered his good fortune that no snowslide
had yet occurred here. If this pit had filled with snow there
would be no fire to build here, nothing to do but try to
struggle out some way before he froze in a crystalline pool
of deep, icy white.

He tried not to think too much about the fact that the
snow, if it kept falling, might pile up on that slope enough
to bring on that first avalanche at almost any time. A man
could die a hard death under the sudden crush of such a
snow mass.

Sam sat down beside the fire, feeling like a great, weary
bear in his heavy coat. He simply stared and breathed for a
time, forcing himself not to worry about snowslides and
other dangers he could do nothing about, and merely to take
pleasure for a few moments in being alive and relatively
unhurt. He must have fallen right through the opening above
him, which was not much bigger than the base of a prairie

schooner at its widest point. He was fortunate indeed to have avoided striking the sides of it as he went through. He said a prayer of thanks, then another for the welfare of Arianna and Daniel.

Sam added a little more fuel to the fire and stood slowly. "Well," he said aloud, "I guess I need to figure out how to get out of this hole."

He looked around, on all sides. Beneath a small, flat rock outcrop he found a crevice that led deeper into the mountainside, a small cavern opening that might go back mere yards, or might lead into some vast cave. It was large enough to accommodate a crawling man, but there was nothing to gain by plunging into the heart of a dark mountain. Other than that small cave mouth, however, there was no other evident exit from the pit except for the hole above.

He looked up at that hole, and examined the pit walls beneath it. These were not of pure stone; they also contained quite a bit of soil and imbedded, broken gravel. If he had a sharp knife, he might be able to dig himself handholds and footholds, and gradually work his way up and out again. But he'd not brought his knife. He marveled at his own foolishness. He'd never neglected carrying his knife before.

Sam studied the slope of the walls and saw exactly what he feared he would. He was effectively inside a giant bottle, the walls sloping in, narrowing toward the opening. This place seemed naturally engineered to let a man fall in easily enough, but not to get out again.

The fire, burning hot and fast and fueled by very dry materials, began to die. Sam scrounged about and found more wood. It wouldn't last long, though. Not much burnable material had chanced to find its way through that opening and into this pit.

When the blaze was going nicely again, Sam evaluated his predicament. Clearly he couldn't scale walls that sloped inward . . . but as he examined them again, he realized that one side of the "bottle" was more vertical than the others.

A man with a climbing implement might make his way out up that wall—with luck.

But he had no climbing implement. All the sticks he'd found were dried and dead, nothing worthy of crafting into a makeshift pike, nothing big enough to use as a climbing pole. Nor were there sufficient rocks about to enable him to heap up a mound high enough to take him within reach of the opening.

He began to think about how he might be in this hole for a very long time.

It was worth worrying about. He had a fire for now, but soon the fuel would be gone. Though sheltered from the direct impact of the weather, the pit still was cold. A man could freeze to death in here. Or starve. Or . . .

"Whoa, Mr. Underhill," he said to the flickering light on the cavern walls. "Hold up there right now. That kind of thinking kills a man faster than the elements. There'll be a way out. You just got to find it. This hole is no match for a determined man. Just got to look about and—"

He cut off abruptly, and held his silence for a long time. He had moved, and his own shadow had moved with him, allowing firelight to reveal something he hadn't seen earlier.

Sam drew closer and knelt before what he'd found and slowly shook his head.

"My friend, I have to tell you that it's no encouragement to find you here."

The face that stared back at him did not move nor speak. In fact it was hardly a face at all, just what was left of one after a couple of years of decay. Empty eye sockets examined him. What little flesh remained stretched across the skull of the dead man wasn't much more than yellowed, dry leather, badly eaten by rot and insects. The mouth hung open, and the clothing, what remained of it, was mere tattered rags hanging on bone.

"Two dead men found within the same week," Sam said. "One fresh dead, the other long dead. Strange times, these."

The fire was dying again, so Sam once more replenished

it, then began a closer examination of the corpse. From the clothing and situation of the fellow, he suspected he'd found an ill-fated Forty-niner, probably from back in the Dutch Camp days. Probably he, like Sam, had come into this natural trap by some accident.

But if so, why hadn't his companions noticed he was missing, and come for him?

That question bothered Sam more than he wanted to admit. From the moment he'd realized that climbing out of here wasn't going to be easy, a faint hope had held that, if nothing else, he could count on Ben Dillow or somebody else coming to look for him. He could yell, try to send up smoke, do something to get attention . . .

But wouldn't this man have done the same? Yet no one had come for him. He'd died here. And from the upright posture, Sam was sure he hadn't died immediately upon his fall into the hole. Folks don't usually tumble into a seated posture and stay there.

"You are not an encourager, my friend," he said. "Not a bit of it."

Ah, but he might be a benefactor, Sam thought. *He might have something on him I can use to get out of here.*

Sam was a little more squeamish than he liked others to know, so it wasn't easy for him to touch the dead man. But he did so, pushing the body gently to the side and examining what he found around it. There was a pistol near one of the hands. It was old and rusted, the lock snapped down, the flint still in place, the wooden grip half decayed away . . .

Dear Lord . . . A dreadful possibility came to Sam only then. He looked at the side of the skull. Sure enough, there was a rounded hole, and on the other side, a shredded exit wound.

This poor man had put a pistol ball through his own brain.

Sam pulled his hands away. Touching a dead man was bad in itself; touching one who was dead because he chose to be was worse, somehow. But a moment later, Sam resumed his examination of the man's body, feeling through the trousers and wrapping his hand around what was left of the man's legs. Hardly thicker were they now, than Sam's own forearms, and little more than bone with hide on top.

He paused when he detected a clean break in the right thighbone.

Now he understood. This poor fellow had fallen in, broken his leg, and rather than die a slow death alone, had opted to use his pistol to end things more quickly.

"Poor old soul," Sam whispered. "I'm mighty sorry for how things ended for you."

It came to mind that if this man was a Forty-niner, he might have some kind of tools. But he found none. No pan, no shovel . . . but wait! On the corpse's belt, left side, was a sheath with a knife still in it. Sam slid it free. The sheath had protected the knife from moisture and rust. He turned it, examining it in the firelight, then glanced at the vertical section of wall leading to the upper opening.

Maybe. Just maybe.

He slid the knife into one of the many pockets and pouches he'd sewn into the inside of his coat, and continued to search the corpse. He found a couple of gold nuggets, which he kept, and a picture locket, open. Whatever image had been inside had decayed away. A wife or fiancée, probably. He felt another burst of pity for this unknown man.

The knife and the rusted pistol. That was pretty much it. This man hadn't brought much with him into his final resting place. Sam still wondered why no one had ever come looking for him.

Possibly, he thought, *the reason nobody came is that nobody knew he existed. Maybe he wasn't one of the miners who founded Dutch Camp. Maybe he came across the mountains into the valley, and was prospecting in secret, fearing the people in the camp might drive him out.*

A decent theory, though he couldn't know if it was true. But it did make him wonder if there might be another route in and out of the Texas Gulch basin besides the pass.

Sam went to the far side of the pit and sat down. He dug

around in his coat until he found some of the meat he'd brought. Ben Dillow had joked before that a man could live for a month off the stray food he could find tucked away in that big coat of Sam's. He slowly ate some of it while he looked at the wall he was going to attempt to climb. Always plan your actions, his father had often advised him. A man who acts without a plan is a man soon mourned by those he left behind.

At length Sam stood. The fire was low again. One more round of searching and gathering wood, dried evergreen needles, and such. One more restoring of the blaze. As an afterthought Sam even added some of the ragged clothing of the dead man.

The light rose in the pit, and smoke billowed toward the hole through which Sam would attempt his exit. Taking several deep breaths, he went to the vertical section of wall, wriggled his arms and legs to warm the muscles, and with the knife gouged out a hole big enough to accommodate the toe of his right boot. He wedged his foot into the foothold, and hoisted himself up. Once there, Sam gouged a second hole, higher up, for his left foot. On he went, foot by precarious foot, slowly making his ascent.

CHAPTER NINE

He was almost halfway up before he slipped and fell. It happened fast, the result of one of the gouged footholds giving way under his weight, and he barely managed to land on his feet. Standing, he brushed himself off, found the knife where he'd dropped it during the fall, and checked himself over for possible new injuries.

Nothing. Relieved, he looked over at the dead man and said, "Lucky that time. I might have busted my leg like you did." He paused, thinking how it must have been for the poor fellow. Probably the man had sat there looking at that same vertical wall Sam was now trying to climb. Probably he'd realized that he could use his knife just as Sam was using it now and gotten out of here . . . if only his leg wasn't broken.

No wonder the man had been driven to put a pistol ball through his own skull.

Sam didn't linger. He went back to the wall, began his climb anew, and this time made it even higher before falling. Once again he escaped injury, though he did abrade his left thigh badly and come down painfully hard on one heel.

The fire was almost gone now. Sam felt a mounting sense of desperation. He needed light to climb, and he'd expended almost all the meager fuel in the pit. He tried again to climb, and this time didn't fall, but still he was forced to descend again because he simply ran out of light. The fire dwindled to almost nothing.

Discouraged, Sam plopped down in the darkness and leaned back against the wall of the pit. He'd been so close to escape! But now, with the fire gone, there was nothing to do but wait for morning.

He found a comfortable space between two boulders, huddled back in his big, protective coat, and closed his eyes. His final thought before sleep came was of his friends and neighbors back in Texas Gulch. He wondered if they were safe and warm in their beds, the children having been found in his absence. He hoped so. Another part of him hoped the men of the town were out with torches, scouring the valley, searching for him.

Even if they were, they'd not find him tonight. He made himself relax and accept the situation as it stood. It wasn't long before his breathing slowed and his head sagged.

In the pit, with no company but the leathery corpse of an unknown man, Sam Underhill slept.

In Texas Gulch, no one was sleeping.

In the lodge house, home normally to several residents who had afforded themselves a touch of privacy by dividing it into chambers, with the erection of canvas screens, the entire population of Texas Gulch—minus Sam Underhill— was crowded. The canvas screens were gone, torn down with enthusiasm by Bert Mongold at the orders of Mahaffery. Mongold had ripped down the barriers with such violent destructiveness that he had seemed more animal than human to those who watched.

Now Mongold seemed eager for more meaningful violence. He paced about, mumbling and making guttural sounds, watching an interrogation now under way, with Mahaffery as questioner, young Daniel Chase as subject. Daniel was still slightly groggy and disoriented from the blow he had suffered at Mongold's hands up beyond the pass.

"I'm going to ask you again, son," Mahaffery said gently. "I want you to think hard, and tell me what you might have found at the same time you found Mr. Dehaven's body."

"I didn't find . . . nothing."

"Maybe you did. Maybe you're just a little addled right now and can't recall it. Maybe there was something lying beside Mr. Dehaven in the snow. Maybe you picked it up, and put it somewhere else."

"There was . . . there was . . ."

Mahaffery leaned forward, intent.

". . . There was nothing."

Mahaffery leaned back again. Mongold swore loudly, then said, "Let me have a try with him, Jordan. I'll make him talk."

"Stay out of this, Bert. We'll do it my way."

"He's lying to you!"

Mahaffery said, "I don't think he is."

Mongold snorted disdainfully.

Leora Winkle let out a screech on the other side of the room. Mahaffery looked just in time to see his younger brother take a hard slap across the face from the woman.

Leora was drawing back for another slap, when Searl Mahaffery grabbed her arm and stopped the blow. He doubled up a big fist and pulled it back . . .

"Searl!"

Searl stopped his fist in mid-swing. His elder brother had risen and was striding toward him.

"She slapped me, Jordan! The shrew slapped me!"

"He insulted my daughter," Leora said, her face even redder than the handprint clearly visible across Searl Mahaffery's stinging face. "What he said to her no mother should have to hear spoken to her child!"

"All I said was that the little gal's pretty enough to—"

"Searl, shut up. Now," Mahaffery said. He hadn't raised his voice, yet the command bore the authority of a shout. "There'll be no more of this kind of behavior."

Searl gaped. "Jordan, you shot a man to death before

these people! And you're telling *me* I should act the high-stocking gentleman?''

''I shot a man to make a point that had to be made. You'll stay away from this lady, and her daughter, or you'll deal with me. You understand me, Searl?''

Searl glowered. Turning away, he swaggered off to a corner and plopped down on a stool.

Mahaffery turned to Leora. ''I beg your pardon for my brother's behavior, ma'am. He's not a couth man.''

''You, sir, and your brother, may both go to hell,'' Leora said, eyes unblinkingly staring into his.

Mahaffery arched his brows, flaring his nostrils in anger, then paused and chuckled. ''You are a high-spirited woman as well as a lovely one,'' he said. ''Two fine qualities, those.'' He turned and headed back over to resume his interrogation of Daniel Chase.

''High-spirited, he says,'' Texas Gulch prospector Copp Nolen muttered to Ben Dillow, who sat beside him. They were across the so-called lodge house from the place where the little drama had just played out. ''So she does seem to be. That ain't the humble, meek little Leora Winkle I've known before.''

''She's protecting her child. That brings out a new aspect in a woman,'' Dillow replied.

''She surely did slap the fire out of Little Brother over there.''

''Refreshing sight, I thought.''

''Tell me something, Ben. What do you think's going to happen come morning?''

''Mahaffery's already said he'll have the dead man dug up. He'll look over the corpse and see that the man wasn't shot or stabbed. Then he'll know we weren't lying to him, that we haven't killed the man and taken his gold for ourselves.''

''There ain't wounds on the body . . . right?''

"None. I looked him over close. Whatever killed him, killed him from the inside."

"What if they *did* come to believe, for some reason, that any of us killed the man?"

"I don't want to think about that."

"There'd be threatening and torturing, trying to make somebody talk . . . you reckon?" Copp suggested.

"I'd say so."

"You *sure* there was no mark of violence on that corpse?"

"I'm sure. But I don't know that it will matter in the end. These devils are going to end up killing us all, anyway."

A pause. "You don't mean that, do you, Ben?"

"I do. These are desperate and wicked men. They've already murdered one man in cold blood, right before our eyes. Once we become useless, they'll not leave us alive to cause them trouble later. This protect-the-ladies, play-the-gentleman act that Mahaffery's putting on will vanish fast once he has nothing more to gain from us, I'll bet."

"How do you know so much about it?"

"Because I know Mahaffery's type." Dillow paused. "I was a constable once, back in Kentucky. I had to deal with a lot of such folk. The frontier always draws that kind."

"You were a constable? Then why did you let them make Sam Underhill the marshal here, instead of you?"

"I've been a man of the law once. That's enough. Besides, in truth there is no real law here, not even Sam. He was just willing to take the title. I doubt he ever anticipated anything like this coming up."

"Speaking of Sam . . . Ben, he ain't here."

"I know."

"So where is he?"

"I don't know . . . but the fact he ain't here is the one thing that gives me some hope. If Sam is out there, and they don't know it, then that's an edge we've got on Mahaffery. Our one and only edge."

"Not much of one. One man, alone. And all the rest of us under the gun."

"Don't underestimate Sam Underhill. He's got more gravel in his craw than a dozen average men. There's a lot of his daddy in that old boy. I just hope he knows what's going on. Otherwise he might just stumble into the midst of it and be caught along with the rest of us."

The door opened, and Emmett Fish and Ross Remine entered, bearing armloads of weapons. Dillow shook his head.

"There's my rifle. And my pistols, too. And every other durn weapon in this mining camp, judging from the size of the load they're carrying."

"We're helpless, then. No weapons at all, and all of us hostages."

A few moments of silence followed this somber evaluation.

Nolen broke the silence. "So we'll dig up the body, and they'll see that the dead man wasn't killed by us. What then?"

"I think they'll turn to the idea that the man either dropped or hid the gold out in the mountains on his way here. Most likely they'll go to where his body was found, and dig about in the snow. Or have us do it for them."

"Maybe there really is gold up there."

"There could be. But I hope we don't find it."

"Why? They'd go away then."

"They'll go away, and leave us moldering as corpses."

"You believe they'll kill us even if they get their gold?"

"Like I said: they'll never leave folks alive who've witnessed them commit murder."

On the other side of Dillow, Herbert Colfax grunted. He'd been sitting there, listening, silent until now. "That's nonsense, Ben Dillow. You don't know what they'll do."

Nolen looked around Dillow at Colfax. "Ben may be right, Colfax. We did witness them murdering Julius. That makes any one of us a potential witness against them."

"Julius was sneaking about with a gun. He brought it on himself."

"Just whose side are you on, anyhow?" Nolen asked.

"My side. Me and my family's side. And I'm not giving up and declaring myself doomed just yet, no matter what Dillow here believes."

"I hope you're right and I'm wrong," Dillow said. "But I see little grounds to be optimistic about these scoundrels."

Copp Nolen abruptly asked Colfax, "Herbert, what time is it?"

Colfax pulled his pocket watch from under his vest. "Three in the morning."

"Found that pocket watch, I see. Remarkable that you could find it out in that snow, in the dark."

"What are you trying to say, Copp?"

"Nothing. Just commenting that it was remarkable that you could go out in the snow, in the dark, and find that pocket watch."

"I was lucky."

"Yeah. Tell me. Did you find anything else while you were poking about in the snow up there last night, all by yourself?"

Colfax rose and faced Nolen. "I don't like what you're implying, Copp."

Dillow said, "Herbert, sit down. And Copp, keep your mouth shut. You're attracting some unwanted attention our way."

Colfax turned to see Searl Mahaffery striding toward him. The red mark left by Leora Winkle's hand was still clearly visible on Searl's face.

"Set your fat backside down again, old man," Searl commanded.

"Show some respect for your elders, boy," Colfax replied.

Searl Mahaffery's fist rocked Colfax's jaw. The older man staggered and made a deep, guttural noise, but did not fall. America Colfax cried out on the other side of the room, where she had been seated, weeping and scared, beside Marica Bolton, receiving comfort and reassurances from the kindhearted younger woman.

"Sit down, Searl!" This came from Jordan Mahaffery. "You too, old-timer."

Colfax, hand gingerly on jaw, glanced down at Nolen, and softly said, "You'd best be careful, throwing around allegations at a time like this."

"In your seat, old man!" Jordan Mahaffery commanded again, more harshly.

Colfax strode across the room and sat down beside his wife. She wept and laid her head on his shoulder, her broad shoulders heaving.

"Herbert's right," Dillow said. "You ought not have said what you did, Copp. You were hinting pretty strong that he might have found that gold last night."

"If a man can find a missing pocket watch in the dark, he might find something else, too. Or more likely, he never had lost that pocket watch at all. Maybe he stubbed his toe on that cache of gold while we were fetching the body, and went back up to claim it later. Remember how he was staying back in the dark while we were up there? Remember how nervous he was after we brought back the body? Remember how he refused to let anyone go back with him to look for his watch?"

Dillow whispered, "If speculation like that got to the ears of our new friends, you could get Colfax killed really fast."

"I don't trust Colfax. Never have."

"You've also never liked him, and he's never liked you. But don't let that get us off track. If there's any hope of making it through this, we have to work together. And trust each other."

"I'll never trust Colfax. I don't have it in me. And as far as dangerous speculations go, you heard how Colfax was trying so hard before to persuade Mahaffery that poor little Daniel yonder had probably found the gold. Did you see anybody else trying to throw off blame that way? Old Colfax was mighty quick with his *own* accusations, it seems to me.''

Dillow sighed and leaned back. Maybe Nolen had a point, though he hoped not. He'd hate to think that even sour old Herbert Colfax would be willing to betray and endanger his friends and fellow miners for the sake of a cache of stolen gold.

A desperate desire to find some way out of this predicament overwhelmed Dillow, but all he could do was sit there, helpless. With all the weapons in the hands of the outlaws, and every resident of Texas Gulch held hostage, he could do nothing.

No, he reminded himself, there was one resident yet who wasn't hostage.

''Sam,'' he murmured toward the underside of the roof, ''I hope you're out there, and that you've figured out what's going on, and that you've got some way in mind to get us out of this. Because for the life of me, I surely don't.''

''What'd you say, Ben?'' Copp Nolen asked.

''Nothing, Copp,'' Dillow replied. ''Just talking to myself.''

CHAPTER TEN

Slowly and warily, Sam Underhill picked himself up one more time from the rocky floor of the pit. Sore now . . . no, beyond sore. Since the first welcome morning light had spilled into the hole, he'd tried three times to climb his way out. Three times he'd fallen. And three times, he was thankful to discover, he'd managed to break no bones.

The bruises, though, were going to be a sight worth seeing.

He stood and looked sadly up at the sky beyond the hole. Would he never find a way out of here?

"The devil with this!" Sam muttered. "I'm not going to die down here in this hole!"

He'd dropped his knife again, so he looked for it. There it was, on the floor, the blade cleanly snapped off at the hilt.

He gazed at it, fighting despair. *Now* what would he do?

His eye turned to the dead man. Walking over, he eyed the fellow. "Friend, is there a chance at all you've got anything for me that I haven't found yet?" He nudged the corpse to one side with his toe.

What was revealed had been previously covered by the dead man's corpse. Sam stared down at it thankfully, and picked it up.

It was a small rock pick, typical of the sort prospectors carried. The handle was made of hardwood and had a thick varnish finish, and was not at all rotted, even for having been nestled up against a dead man for Lord knew how long. The head of the pick, though badly rusted, was still sharp and strong.

"Thank you, my friend," Sam said with honest emotion. "Thank you. What you've given me here very well may save my life. I'm only sorry it wasn't able to save yours."

The ground had begun to freeze, so the dirt, gravel, and rubble that filled the makeshift grave of the dead outlaw was much more difficult to dig out than it had been to put in. Further, none of the laborers had slept the night before, which made exhaustion loom all the closer. Still they worked hard, under the constant threat of the guns of Mahaffery's men.

Dillow slowly stood up in the hole, letting his straining back relax as he leaned on his shovel. Mahaffery paced back and forth in the snow with a cigar in his hand. Dillow said, "We just got down to the body."

"Haul him out, then."

Dillow was thinking about how satisfying it would be to ram his shovel suddenly into Mahaffery's belly and give it a hard twist. Just a pleasant fantasy, that was all. To really try it would get him killed. "We've got a little more dirt and rock to clear before we can get him out."

"Then why are you standing there working your jaws instead of your shovel?"

In the hole with Dillow was Fleenor, the would-be poet and philosopher. The pair of them went back to their labors, and within three minutes had the body exposed. Thanks to the cold weather, decay and stench were minimal.

With effort, and help from Crain Brown and Joe Skinner, they managed to haul the stiffened dead man out of the hole, where he was dumped without ceremony in the snow, landing facedown. Fleenor and Dillow climbed out. Emmett Fish came over and knelt by the body. He'd always found the dead fascinating. Searl came near, too, and stood beside Fish.

"Roll him over," Mahaffery ordered. Emmett Fish obeyed, revealing the face to the outlaws.

Searl Mahaffery leaned over and spat tobacco juice into the dead man's face. "Howdy, Dehaven," he said, and cackled with laughter. "You're looking kind of sickly."

"Searl, don't dirty him up more than he is. I want to be able to examine that body for wounds. Get down there and strip the clothes off him."

"I ain't stripping the clothes off no dead man!"

"Then get out of the way. If you won't be useful, at least don't be underfoot for those who are."

Emmett Fish did the job instead. When the gray, mottled, and late Frank Dehaven lay naked in the snow, Mahaffery knelt and began examining him thoroughly, even looking through the hair for hidden entrance wounds from a bullet or blade. Eventually he stood.

"What'd you find?" Searl asked his older brother.

Mahaffery's answer was to shove the corpse back into the hole with a single hard push of his booted foot.

"No bullet holes or nothing, huh?"

"Not a one. It appears we've been told the truth. Dehaven wasn't killed. The old thief up and died on his own."

"Maybe they strangled him, or beat him to death."

"It would show."

"Maybe they smothered him."

"Why would they smother him instead of just shooting him and being done with it?" Mahaffery was beginning to sound irritable. "It isn't like they knew we were going to be showing up to look him over."

Searl spat into the hole on the dead man again.

"Cover him up," Mahaffery ordered Fleenor and Dillow.

"So where do you reckon the gold is, if these folks didn't take it from him?" Remine asked.

"Either he hid it or dropped it. If he hid it, we may never

find it. If he dropped it, that probably happened somewhere near where he died."

"Up in the snow?"

"That's right." Mahaffery turned and called to Conner Broadgrass. "Broadgrass! Gather up the menfolk and herd them up to the pass." Mahaffery looked over the glum assembly of his hostages. "It's going to be a day of pleasure for you folks. You're going to dig in the snow, just like children."

Arianna Winkle, standing beside her mother, did not hear a word Mahaffery said. She was too distracted by a sight that only she had noticed: Hiram Linfoot was sneaking away from the group of hostages, unnoticed by Mahaffery or his distracted guards. Arianna dared not breathe. She inwardly cheered for him. *Run, Mr. Linfoot! Get away from them! And find help for us.*

She didn't know how he could find help by running back into the enclosed, unpopulated valley instead of toward the pass, but she didn't dwell on that. It was satisfying merely to see someone getting away.

"What are you looking at, girly?"

Arianna snapped her head around to look at the bulky Bert Mongold. "Nothing."

Mongold turned in the direction she had been staring, but Linfoot dropped to the ground just as Mongold looked his way. Arianna thought he'd dropped too late, but Mongold didn't seem to have seen him. She noticed that Mongold was squinting badly. Bad eyes. *Good thing for Mr. Linfoot,* she thought.

Mongold turned back to Arianna. "Did I see something move out yonder?"

"I don't know what you saw."

"You speak up, girly! Tell me if there was somebody out there! My eyes ain't the best."

"I saw my dog running across," Arianna lied.

"That was all? Your dog?"

"Yes."

"I don't want you talking to my daughter," Leora said, putting her arm around Arianna's shoulder. "Speak to me, if you have anything to say to either of us."

"I'll talk to the girly if I want," Mongold said. He stepped forward and looked down at Arianna. "You sure it was just a dog?"

"Yes, sir."

Mongold stared at her a few moments. "My, my, but ain't you a pretty little thing. There's a few lessons I could teach you, little gal, if you was just a year or two older."

Leora stepped between Arianna and Mongold, which placed her uncomfortably close to the stinking, ugly man. But she did not flinch back from him. "I told you: I don't want you talking to my daughter. Especially not that kind of talk."

Mongold grinned at her; his teeth were brown as dirt. "That kind of talk, eh? What kind of talk do you mean? This kind, maybe?" He leaned forward and whispered in Leora's ear.

Leora's knee came up fast and hard, and caught the big man in the groin with a force scarcely less than that of a sledgehammer. Mongold sucked in two lungfuls of breath in record time, made a strange, high sound, and backed away, doubling over and growing brilliant red in the face, gripping himself in a most indiscreet fashion.

"Was that the kind of attention you were talking about, sir?" Leora asked him.

The other outlaws howled with laughter. Even Mahaffery seemed amused, and an uncharacteristic smile crossed the usually inscrutable face of brooding, deep-thinking Conner Broadgrass.

Mongold slowly raised his crimson, bleary-eyed face to look up at the hard-as-iron, coldly beautiful visage of Leora Winkle. "I'll kill you for that," he said in a very tight and pain-wracked voice.

Daniel Chase had been in a daze through most of the

night, even while being questioned by Mahaffery, but the coming of morning had restored him. He ran over to Mongold, stopped just outside the bent-over man's reach, and said, "You wouldn't dare threaten her if Mr. Underhill was here!"

Over by the hole, Dillow closed his eyes and thought, *Oh, no.* He'd hoped that word of the existence of Sam Underhill wouldn't reach the ears of the outlaws.

Mongold tried to kick at Daniel with the side of his foot, but the effort was rather pitiful and drew more laughter from the other outlaws. The residents of Texas Gulch were enjoying it, too, though they dared not show it.

"Mr. Underhill wouldn't be afraid of you! He'd tie you up into a ball and roll you down the mountain!"

Shut up, boy! Dillow was thinking. *Just keep your mouth shut!*

"Get away from me, boy," Mongold said, slowly trying to straighten. His face was still very red and he was breathing strangely.

Arianna shifted her eyes leftward. Hiram Linfoot was on the move again, darting through the snow and back into the valley. Just a little farther and he'd be over a rise and out of sight. She prayed for him, silently.

Mahaffery said, "Who's this Underhill the boy speaks of?"

Dillow had a sudden inspiration. "He's talking about Bushrod Underhill," he said quickly, hoping no one would counter him.

"Bushrod Underhill?"

"That's right," Dillow said. "Bushrod Underhill, who ropes the moon and rides tornadoes like they were horses and drinks the Great Lakes dry when he's thirsty. I tell the boy tales to entertain him, and he takes them a bit too seriously at times."

Dillow glanced around at the faces of the other people of Texas Gulch, and saw a lot of confusion, but also some dawning understanding of what he was doing. For the first time some of those people seemed to be realizing that Sam wasn't with them, and that with one of their number, especially one so capable and intelligent as Sam, free and able to act in the background, there might be hope.

"Is that right, boy?" Mahaffery asked Daniel.

Daniel glanced at Dillow, confused, but read the message in Dillow's eyes and obediently said, "Yes."

"Bushrod Underhill, eh?" Mahaffery said. "I've read some of them almanacs. Old Bushrod's quite a character, eh, son? A bigger wildman than even old Davy Crockett was in his day."

"That's right," Daniel said, beginning to rise to the occasion. "And if he was here, he'd whup you all!"

"So he might, but he ain't here."

"Mahaffery." The speaker was Conner Broadgrass, and he was pointing back into the valley.

Arianna felt her heart sink as she saw that Broadgrass had spotted Hiram Linfoot just as he topped the rise. Now Mahaffery saw him too, and snapped his fingers twice.

"Emmett Fish! And you, Mongold! Go after him!"

Mongold twisted his head, watched Linfoot scramble away, then looked back at his chief, perplexed. "Jordan, I can't hardly walk, much less chase a man through the snow!"

"You got enough energy to be talking filth to decent women and little girls, you got enough to make yourself useful. Get your rifle and go after him, now! And when you catch him, don't feel inclined to mercy. Let's make a good lesson out of that man, hmmm?"

Fish and Mongold set out through the snow, pursuing Hiram Linfoot toward the heart of the valley, Fish moving much more quickly than Mongold and soon leaving him behind.

CHAPTER
ELEVEN

Sam Underhill sat at the edge of the hole at the top of the pit, legs dangling into the space below. He was sore, out of breath, and cold, but very happy. Out at last! If not for finding that pick, he might never have gotten free.

He bowed his head and said a prayer. Then, with head still bowed, he looked into the hole again, and spoke his silent gratitude to the silent dead man now unseen down there. Before commencing his climb out of the pit, he'd taken time to move the corpse into the small cavern beneath the stone outcrop, and laid him there on his back, arms folded across his chest. It was a final gesture of respect for an unknown man long passed on, and his thanks for the life-saving gift of the little rock pick.

Sam rose, looking around the bright landscape. Time to head home. He marveled to think that what had started as a simple hike to bring in two straying children had turned into an all-night ordeal. He wondered if his peers were out searching for him.

Most of all he wondered what had happened to Daniel and Arianna.

He paused to eat a few bites of jerked meat from one of the pockets of his bulky coat, then rose and began looking for the snowshoes he'd left at the base of the slope the day before. He couldn't find them; snow had covered them thoroughly.

He sighed and made the best of it. The snow wasn't so deep yet that he couldn't make it even without snowshoes.

Sam began hiking through the white valley back in the direction of Texas Gulch.

Progress was slow, and an hour passed before Sam topped a small rise and saw that he was nearing the final stretch to the mining camp. He also saw something else, which confused and dismayed him.

A man was running, scrambling wildly, through the snow, coming roughly in Sam's direction at first, then veering to the south. The way he moved, the wild manner in which he looked over his shoulder and then ran harder, made Sam wonder what kind of demon was on the fellow's trail.

Sam looked harder, squinting, and recognized the man as Hiram Linfoot.

He started to shout at Hiram but didn't. Something unusual obviously was happening here. He realized he needed to understand it before he threw himself into the middle of it.

A second figure came over the hill, racing after Hiram. A man with a rifle. And behind him, a long way back, a second man, much bigger and quite a bit slower, but also armed. The second man had an odd gait, as if he was injured.

Both the pursuers were strangers, as best Sam could see from this distance. Strangers in Texas Gulch? With the snow piled high in the pass and the mountains virtually impassable?

How did they get here? And when? And why were they chasing Hiram Linfoot?

The first pursuer stopped and dropped to one knee in the snow, raising his rifle. Linfoot kept running, hard. Sam opened his mouth to shout a warning, but Linfoot went out of range and the man with the rifle didn't fire. Sam watched

him rise and continue chasing Linfoot, who was making for
the rugged country at the northern side of the basin. *Good
move, Hiram. You can lose them if you make it into the
rocks.*

The second pursuer was still coming on, but even slower
than before. A big man, he looked like he might drop exhausted at any moment. At his speed it would take him five
minutes at best just to catch up with his companion.

So Sam decided not to worry about that second pursuer
yet. The smaller one at the lead of the chase was the most
dangerous one to Linfoot. Hefting up the pick, wishing he
had his rifle, Sam began running across the uneven country,
trying to close in on the man from the side, and if possible,
to do so without revealing his presence too quickly.

The most worrisome possibility was that the second pursuer would draw close enough to see him and yell a warning
to the first, but a glance revealed the second pursuer was
not to be seen. Sam figured the man had dropped, probably
exhausted. Good.

There was Hiram, running up a slope and not doing too
well at it. He fell twice, mired in drifting snow. The man
after him dropped to his knee again, raised the rifle, aimed
carefully, and this time did fire.

The rifle's crack was thin and empty in the vast open
space of the valley. Sam glanced at Hiram, and grimaced
when he saw his friend throw his arms out and up, and fall
in the snow.

The rifleman hurriedly engaged himself in reloading, giving Sam, who was now driven by fury, the best opportunity
he was going to find. He ran as hard as he could, giving it
all he had, plowing through the snow like a bull, until he
was near the rifleman, separated from him by only a small
line of boulders. He bounded atop one of the boulders, saw
the reloading man look up in shock—and Sam leaped, flying
through the air with the pick in his hand, swinging down as
he descended.

The man had dropped his rifle and gone for a pistol stuck

into his belt, but the pistol caught and never came clear. Sam descended and brought the pick down hard, intending to strike with the flat of it and knock the man cold. But the pick had turned in his hand. The sharp, rusted prong of it hit Emmett Fish in the center of the top of his head, dug through bone, and sank into his brain.

Fish shuddered and died before he hit the snow, his weight pulling the pick out of Sam's hand and taking it down with him.

Sam landed atop the corpse, rolled off, and came to his feet. He stared at the dead man with the pick buried in his head, and felt a numb horror. He'd just killed a man!

All at once he was back in Texas, about a decade and a half back, with his father and brothers, fighting a band of ruffians who believed the Underhills bore ransom. That night Sam Underhill, then a much different, less settled kind of fellow, had killed another human being for the first time. He'd tried to hide the horror of it behind bravado back then—that was his way in those days—but the feeling was one he'd never forgotten.[2]

He felt it again now.

Remembering that the slower, second pursuer might reappear at any moment, Sam went for the dead man's weapons. He took the rifle, finished the reloading job, and commandeered the dead man's shot and powder as well. He stuck the pistol into his own belt.

It felt good to be armed again . . . though even now he didn't know what in the devil was going on, why Hiram Linfoot had been chased down and shot, or who this fellow was he'd just pickaxed to death.

Sam ran toward the hillside where Hiram lay in snow that was swiftly turning red around him. Hiram was alive, but his wound was bad. Blood was flowing frighteningly fast.

"Hiram . . . it's me, Sam!" He dropped to Hiram's side. The man had managed to roll himself over onto his back.

[2]*Texas Freedom*, Book 2 in The Underhill Series

He blinked up numbly, almost stupidly, at Sam's face.

"Sam . . . Sam, they've shot me."

"I know, Hiram. But the man who did it is dead. I killed him. Just now. Who was he?"

"Bad men . . . they're in the camp. Several of them . . . come looking for gold . . . that the dead man had stole from them."

"The dead man Daniel found in the pass?"

"Yes . . . Dehaven, they called him. Dehaven."

Sam glanced back. Still no sign of the slower-running pursuer. Perhaps the man had given up.

He looked at Hiram's pallid face and saw that death was coming. "Tell me what's happened, Hiram."

"They came in . . . they already had Arianna, Daniel . . . guns to their heads. They took everyone in the camp hostage . . . searched the houses, took all the weapons. The dead man . . . he'd been one of them . . . he'd taken gold from them that they'd all stolen somewhere . . . they chased him into the mountains, all the way to Texas Gulch . . . he died, trying to reach the mining camp . . . now no one knows where the gold is . . . they'll kill us in the end, Sam. They'll kill everyone."

"Hiram, are you sure of all this?"

"Yes . . . they've already killed Julius . . . now they've killed me, too."

Sam wanted to assure Linfoot that he'd be fine, but it would be a lie, and he and Linfoot would both know it.

"You say they had the children. So Daniel and Arianna are alive."

"Yes . . . they'd found them out beyond the pass. Took them prisoner."

Sam was glad to know the children hadn't frozen to death, though it appeared their predicament at the moment was not much better. "You're sure all the weapons in the camp are taken?"

"All of them. And all the people . . . kept under guard every minute. I was the first to . . . try to escape . . ." He actually laughed a little, bitterly, and blood came to his lips. "Didn't do . . . too well, I guess. I don't even know . . . where I was running to. I just had to try."

"I know, Hiram. And I'm sorry it went bad for you."

"They don't know . . . about you, Sam. The bad ones don't know that you even exist . . . it's up to you, Sam, if our people . . . are going to be saved."

Something changed in Hiram's face, very suddenly. A moment before, his body had been animated. Now it was empty. He was gone.

Sam stood slowly and stared down at the corpse of his friend. All this was too much to take in. Texas Gulch taken by outlaws. People murdered. A dead man's lost gold endangering the entire camp. It seemed very unreal.

Sam felt the twin weights of responsibility and terror descend upon him. He had to help his people . . . but what could one man do, alone, minimally armed with weapons that weren't his own, against an entire band of armed desperadoes?

The only edge he had was that they didn't know he existed. He needed to keep it that way.

He had to make the outlaws believe that it was Linfoot who had killed the rifleman. And that Linfoot was still alive. That might draw some of them out, hunting for Linfoot. Maybe, a few at a time, Sam could deal with them.

Sam slung his newfound weapons and gear across his shoulder, reached down, and picked up the body of Hiram Linfoot. Carrying Hiram in his arms like an oversized baby, he staggered back down the slope, trying his best to stay in the tracks already made. He reached the ridge of boulders near the place where Emmett Fish lay with a pick through his brain, and worked his way behind them. No way to avoid leaving tracks, but his father had always told him not to worry about that which couldn't be helped. With any luck, that second pursuer wouldn't be a clever man, and wouldn't realize there had been a third man here besides Linfoot and the first pursuer.

*   *   *

With Hiram Linfoot's body lying nearby, Sam peered over the snow-covered rim of the boulders before him and watched the slower pursuer finally appear. The man must have taken a long rest. He walked slowly even now, and kept rubbing his groin as if it pained him.

Sam listened to the man curse in astonishment as he found the body of the man with the pick in his head. The bigger fellow knelt and looked at the appalling sight, making a face of disgust. He looked at the tracks that went on up the hill, but did not study or follow them.

The man muttered something, picked up the body of the pickaxed man, turned, and made his way back in the direction he'd come, heading for Texas Gulch. Burdened, he was especially slow now. Sam watched him a long time; the fellow had to dump the corpse and rest several times even before he was out of sight.

When the man was finally gone, Sam rose, wondering if he should have simply shot the fellow while he had the chance. It would have given him one less enemy to face later.

He picked up Hiram's corpse again, took a deep breath, and began making his way slowly back into the valley again, where he'd hide Hiram's body somewhere. He'd find a hole, or a hollow log, or a crevice in some bluff. He'd like to do better by Hiram, but for now any resting place would have to do. He was sure Hiram would have understood, and under the circumstances, agreed.

As Sam traveled, he watched new, gray clouds coagulating in the sky. Good. More snow would cover tracks and blood and any other sign back at the death scene.

And maybe give him a little more time to figure out what the devil he was going to do.

CHAPTER
TWELVE

Mongold's voice still had a tight, pained sound, and he continually shifted from one foot to another while he stood, talking intently to Mahaffery. It would be a good while before he'd be back to his old self again, thanks to Leora Winkle's sledgehammer knee. He'd never made it all the way in with Fish's corpse, but had dropped it out in the valley.

"The man had to have had that pick on him, hid somewhere," Mongold said. "Either that, or he found it while he was running, somehow. Because he gouged it clean through Emmett's head. An ugly sight. You'll see, when you see his corpse. I got it within a quarter mile of here before I had to leave it. We'll need to fetch Emmett in soon, or we'll not be able to find him. It's snowing hard again."

"And Emmett's guns . . ."

"Gone. I reckon the running man took them."

Mahaffery swore softly. "So one's gotten away from us . . . and now he's armed. There's no chance that Emmett wounded him before the fellow pickaxed him?"

"I don't know. There were some bad tore-up tracks, heading up a hillside . . ."

"And you didn't follow them?"

"No."

"Why the hell not?"

"Because . . . because Emmett was lying there, dead, with his head split open. I figured you'd want to know. And because the guns was gone, so I knowed this other man was armed now. I was afraid he might be lying in wait for me. And besides . . . I was hurting from what that woman did to me. She hurt me bad, Jordan. It still hurts."

"You're useless, you know it, Mongold? I should never have sent you with Emmett. I should have sent Broadgrass, or Remine, or somebody else with sense and a little courage. That running man should have been tracked down while we had the chance. Now, with the new snow coming in, there'll be no way to track him."

Mongold looked at his chief for a long time before speaking. "I don't take well to being treated as a coward, Jordan."

"Then don't act like one. Thanks to you letting up your chase we now have an armed man roaming around the valley. A source of trouble for us . . . one you allowed to come about, Mongold."

"What does it matter, Jordan? We'll find that gold wherever Dehaven dropped it. We can leave here, then, and that fellow can roam the valley forever, if he wants."

Mahaffery drew close and spoke quietly. "Nobody's going to be roaming any part of this valley when we leave here. They know our faces, our names, and what we've done. Do you understand me?"

Mongold thought it over, then nodded when the implication set in. "I should have gone after him, Jordan. I'm sorry."

Mahaffery lost some of his anger. "What's done is done. We'll catch him again. He's got no food, and the people here say there's no way out of this valley except the front pass." Mahaffery paused. "Just don't make any more mistakes, Mongold. We can't afford them."

"I won't."

"Good. Good." Abruptly, Mahaffery passed into a better frame of mind. "You know, Bert, I'm hungry. Let's get

some of the women here to fix us up some food. We'll eat
. . . then we'll leave Emmett's corpse where you dropped it.
I don't want our hostages knowing about him being dead.
Might give them notions that we can be overcome.

"Meanwhile, once we've eaten, we'll get some digging
started up in that pass and see if we can't put our hands on
that gold, and get all this over with as soon as possible."

Mahaffery paced back and forth in a gully beaten through
the snow at the pass, nibbling on bread and meat and glowering as the captive men of Texas Gulch dug in the snow.
A vain search, so far. Though they had begun digging right
at the place the body had been found, widening the circle
as they went, no gold had turned up.

Mahaffery chewed his beef and hated the late Dehaven.
He hated him for having taken the gold for himself, for
having lost or hidden it, and most of all, for dying and
taking with him the secret of where the gold now was.

One of the digging men tripped on something in the snow,
and fell. Mahaffery instantly became interested. "What did
you find?"

Kish Fleenor climbed back up on his feet, brushed himself
off, and looked at what he'd stumbled on. "I tripped over
a rock."

Mahaffery swore at him. "Next time you fall over something, it'd best be that gold."

"I'm so starved I can hardly work," Fleenor said, em-
boldened by anger, hunger, and lack of sleep. "When are
you going to let us eat?"

"When you find that gold, there'll be food," Mahaffery
said, and took a big bite of his bread, chewing slowly while
Fleenor watched.

Joe Skinner moved closer to Dillow as work began again.
"Ben," he said, softly and without looking at him, "I want
to ask you something."

"What's that?"

"I been thinking . . . if we find that gold, what's to keep them from just killing us?"

"Nothing that I can see."

"Do you think they would? Kill us, I mean?"

"I don't really know what would happen. My strong suspicion is that they'd kill us all. But I think that's going to happen, eventually, even if we don't find the gold."

"You really think that?"

"The moment we cease to be useful to them, either by finding the gold, or by failing to find it for so long that they cease to believe the gold *can* be found, then I think they're going to be ready to rid themselves of us. We're one of two things to them: tools or threats. So the key for now is to remain useful for as long as we can, and pray for the chance to make something happen." He paused, thinking of Sam Underhill. "Or for a miracle to come."

"So the best thing we can do right now . . ."

Dillow finished for him. "Is to keep on digging, and to find nothing. But we have to keep them believing that we're just a hair away from finding the gold . . . yet never actually find it."

"Because we want all the time we can get."

"That's right."

"For us to make something happen . . . or for a miracle."

"That's right. So, Joe, spread the word among the others, quietly, without being heard. Look for the gold, but don't find it . . . even if you *do* find it. Do you understand what I mean?"

Mahaffery yelled, "You two hush the talking. Get to work!"

"I'd like to ram this shovel through his neck," Dillow muttered.

Skinner moved off to the right a few paces and began to dig in a fresh patch of snow. The sky, grayed over and heavy, was spitting flakes again, already beginning to refill the snowy chasm the searchers had created. Dillow was glad. More snow meant a slower and less certain search.

More time to remain useful to the outlaws . . . more time to remain alive.

He wondered again what had become of Sam Underhill, and whether Sam had any notion of what was going on in Texas Gulch.

Back in the sprawling, so-called lodge house, Daniel Chase was restless in body and mind. And he was already very tired of being imprisoned, tired of these harsh, stinking outlaws pacing around with their guns, eating in front of hungry people, insulting the ladies, threatening the men, displaying their weaponry like strutting cocks showing off plumage . . .

Daniel had endured all he could stand. Time to change the scenario a little.

There were advantages to being a boy, being small, being sneaky. A boy could do things a man could not. And boys always knew secrets. Sitting there among the women, listening to the snoring of Old Man Skinner, father of Joe Skinner and the only truly old person in the camp, Daniel had remembered a secret of his own. Something that maybe could make a difference.

Lennis Yeager of the outlaw band paced back and forth in the lodge house, bearing his rifle and wearing two pistols. He seemed irritable and bored. His hostages were bored, too, all of them ignoring him and brooding in private worlds. Every now and then Yeager would pause to kick at the boot of Old Man Skinner, stopping his snoring for a few seconds. And occasionally Yeager would go to the door, open it, and look out almost wistfully toward the pass, where most of his companions were standing guard over the men of the mining camp as they prospected the snow for that lost gold. At least there was something going on up at the pass.

There was a second guard in the lodge house, too, the evil-tempered Searl. But he was sleeping in his chair in the corner, hat tilted over his eyes and rifle lying crossways on his big chest. He seemed to be sleeping, anyway; Daniel had been eyeing him and wasn't really sure. Maybe Searl

was faking, just waiting for someone to make a wrong move
so he could have reason to shoot them and break the bore-
dom. If he was faking, though, he was doing it well. His
chest moved up and down, slowly and consistently, with the
breathing rhythm of a true sleeper. Daniel decided that Searl
really was asleep.

Yeager went back to the door again and opened it. Cold
air and snow blew in as he stared up at the pass, his profile
visible to Daniel. But suddenly he stepped forward half a
pace, putting the door between Daniel and himself, and at
that moment Daniel moved.

He'd always been a fast and silent boy. His motion was
so sudden and unexpected that only a couple of people in
the place noticed he had moved at all, and they did not react.
The people here were quickly learning not to react to anything, because that tended to draw the attention of their cap-
tors.

A big, homemade wardrobe stood beside one of the shut-
tered windows. Daniel darted behind it, got the shutter open
without a sound, and was out the window in exactly five
seconds. From the outside, he pushed the shutter closed
again just as Yeager eased the door shut and began pacing
once more. Yeager passed the empty place Daniel had been
moments before, and did not even notice the boy's absence.

Arianna, one of the two who had noticed what Daniel had
done, for the next five minutes held her breath every time
Yeager passed the place Daniel had been. At last she realized the man was hardly aware of those around him, and
ceased to worry so much. Whatever Daniel was up to, he'd
gotten away with it so far.

Her dog, Enoch, had returned to the mining camp the day
before, and now slept at her feet. She scratched at his ears
with her shoe.

Outside, Daniel was bounding through the snow like a rabbit, keeping cover between himself and the pass up above,
where men who looked like black, moving spots in the snow
labored under armed guard. Daniel slipped down to the rear,

lower section of the camp, near the place they had buried De-haven, and reached a nearby crumbled old cabin, one of the first ever built here, a relic of the first days of the Gold Rush. Too shabby and broken-down for use as a residence, the cabin was simply left alone by most of the people of Texas Gulch, or occasionally scavenged for a log or shingle to make a repair on one of the better dwellings. But for Daniel it had been a place of play, refuge . . . and treasure-stashing.

He entered the cabin through its broken door. There was no floor but the earth itself, hard-packed, cold, and dusted with snow that managed to infiltrate the very inefficient roof. Daniel paused a moment just to enjoy being here, in a hidden place, for now out of reach of outlaws and danger. He thought about and hated the men who terrorized this camp. Texas Gulch and its people were all Daniel Chase had in the world. He loved them. The murder of Julius Setser had shocked and infuriated him. He'd decided even then, while he'd been lost in a fog of stupor and horror, that he would do something, somehow, to stop these men.

He still didn't know exactly what that would be, but sitting there in the lodge house, watching that cursed guard pace back and forth, he'd remembered a certain item that would make a very handy tool just now.

Daniel moved a log that seemed to have simply fallen out of the crumbling wall to its current spot by chance, but which in fact was strategically placed to cover a well-wrapped item behind it. Daniel pulled that item out, a bundle of oiled cloth tied up with string.

Squatting on his haunches, Daniel untied the string and unrolled the cloth. Examining his little treasure, he found everything in good condition. Nodding with satisfaction, he put what he'd recovered in the pocket of his coat.

Daniel went back to the door of the cabin, looked right and left, and headed out into the snow. Climbing back up the slope and ready to turn left back toward the lodge house along the same path he'd come, he glanced up at the pass again, expecting to see the distant laborers just as before.

Instead, they were much closer, and heading in his direction, coming back down from the pass toward the lodge house.

Daniel dropped into the snow, sucking in his breath.

He was almost sure that the big one, Mongold, had looked right at him.

CHAPTER THIRTEEN

Food had never tasted so good.

Ben Dillow ate his meal of fatty meat, bread, and water as if he were a king at his banquet rather than an endangered, trapped miner reluctantly allowed a few bites by his captor. The others ate with similar relish.

Mahaffery, meanwhile, paced back and forth in the crowded lodge house, looking quite unhappy. No gold had been found, and this delay bothered him. But even the doomed must eat if they are expected to have the strength to work.

When Dillow had gotten down the last of his food and literally licked the juices and crumbs off his fingers, he stood and approached Mahaffery, who turned a glaring eye on the upstart.

"What do you want?"

"We need sleep. You've got us all working out there, and none of us slept last night."

"You could have slept. No one stopped you."

"It's difficult to sleep when you've just been overrun by men with guns."

"Not my problem, friend. You'll sleep once the gold is found."

Dillow could believe that. A long sleep indeed would follow the finding of that gold. An endless sleep. He'd reached the point of hoping that Colfax indeed did have the gold, and would keep its location secret as long as possible. Buying time, that was the key to survival.

"Sir, these men are exhausted. Even your own men are tired."

"Go sit down, Mr. . . . ."

"Dillow. Ben Dillow."

"Whoever. Sit down, shut up, and give an ear to me." Mahaffery raised his voice and spoke to the group in general. "In fact, all of you give me an ear. I got a few things to say."

Silence fell. Mahaffery walked back and forth a few times, gathering his thoughts. He cleared his throat and spoke.

"You think me a hard man, I'm sure. You think right. I am a hard man, but fair. You're tired and afraid, I know, but you'll have your rest. Tonight you'll get your sleep. Or if you find that gold before then, you'll have your chance to rest even earlier."

Copp Nolen and Ben Dillow, the latter having now returned to his seat, exchanged a glance. Mahaffery was following a simple but sensible strategy: throw the enticement of coming rest to weary men to make them work harder. Then, when their labor bears its fruit, line them up and shoot them down.

Mahaffery went on, his voice booming loud in the wide, low cabin. "The thing for you to do, all of you, is to co-operate completely. Don't complain, don't try to run. One of your number did that earlier. I sent two men after him, and your friend paid the price. He's lying dead out there in the valley."

Arianna lowered her head, sadly remembering how she'd inwardly cheered for Hiram Linfoot when she saw him slipping away.

"Let this man's death be a warning to you," Mahaffery said. "Don't think you can outwit, outrun, or out-think us. You can't. Just cooperate, and you'll stay alive. Cross us,

and you'll pay the same price as your man out there somewhere in the snow . . . what was his name?'' Mahaffery
turned to Ben Dillow as he asked this, and Dillow knew that
the outlaw chief had come to perceive him, at least in some
measure, as a leader and spokesman for the people of Texas
Gulch.

"I believe that would be Mr. Hiram Linfoot," Dillow
said quietly.

"Hiram Linfoot," Mahaffery repeated. "Well, Hiram
Linfoot is now a dead man because he was foolish enough
to think he could run away. Don't anybody else be foolish,
all right?" He looked from face to face, like a schoolmaster
making sure his lesson had sunk in.

"I'd like to ask the right to go fetch Hiram's body so he
can be given a decent burial," Dillow said.

"Mr. Hiram Linfoot can lie where he fell, and feed the
scavengers," Mahaffery said.

Dillow looked around the group. "You're missing a man.
The one you call Emmett."

"Emmett Fish is in another cabin, sleeping," Mahaffery
said. "His reward for work well done in taking care of the
runaway Linfoot."

Mahaffery paced about a little more, ranting about the
need for cooperation. He was tired, too, and it showed.

Mahaffery suddenly cut off in midsentence. "Somebody's missing," he said. "Where's the boy?"

Dillow looked around. Sure enough, Daniel Chase wasn't
to be seen.

Mongold said, "Jordan, I thought I seen him outside
while we were coming in from the pass."

"Why didn't you speak up?"

"Because I looked closer and decided it was just a
shadow on the snow. The sun was in my eyes."

"You and your bad eyes . . . you can't see fifty feet past
the end of your nose on your best day. Hell, I want that boy
found! Even a little runt like him, running around free, could
be dangerous."

Dillow had a sudden realization: *Maybe Mahaffery's not as sure of himself as he likes to put on, if he worries that much about no more than a child getting loose.*

"Broadgrass, Remine, I want you two to go out and find that boy. Find him fast, before he gets away. Bring him directly to me when you do, and—"

"I'm right here," Daniel stepped out from behind the wardrobe. "I ain't been nowhere. I'd just fell asleep back there, that's all."

Mahaffery stared at him, silent, then suddenly seemed to lose all interest. He turned his back on Daniel, and said, "Back up to the pass, gentlemen. We've got much more digging to do."

Trudging wearily back up toward the pass for what promised to be more hours of digging in snow, Dillow managed to get close to Copp Nolen.

"Tell me, Copp," he whispered, "did something strike you odd about the way Mahaffery talked about Hiram being killed, and this Emmett fellow being somewhere taking a nap, and all that?"

"Indeed it did. That man's covering up something. Telling us what he wants us to hear."

"My feeling is precisely the same. I'm even wondering if it's this Emmett fellow who got himself killed instead of Hiram. Or maybe they killed each other."

"Hard to imagine Hiram having the brass about him to kill anyone. And how would he do it, with no weapons?"

Dillow thought about that one for a while. "Maybe it wasn't Hiram who did it. Maybe Sam did it."

"I hadn't considered that. It is the kind of thing Sam would do."

"Yep. I can tell you one thing: if Sam Underhill's alive, and if he knows what's happened in Texas Gulch, he's already trying to do something about it. Let's just hope Sam has some kind of plan."

* * *

Sam Underhill had no plan at all.

He sat in a deep niche on a rocky ridge, staring out across the valley and at the gray sky overarching it, watching yet another round of snowfall come down. There was little wind at the moment, though, and the snow fell slowly and peacefully. All in all it was a beautiful, placid scene, quite different in mood from the way Sam felt just now.

He looked down at the weapons he'd taken from the man he'd hit with the pick, and wondered what a lone man could do against an armed gang so desperate it would gun down a fine fellow like Hiram Linfoot, just for running away. He figured that the more stalwart men of the community, such as Ben Dillow, probably were doing what they could, or at least trying to . . . but if Hiram's story was right and the outlaws had all the weapons, what could Dillow or anyone else on the inside do?

Sam had built a small fire, situated perfectly in the rock niche to hide the smoke until it had time to disperse and become invisible in the falling snow. Heat reflected off the rocks and back onto him. He'd nibbled a little more of his food and pondered that before long he'd have to do a bit of hunting or snaring.

Sam sighed, stood, and walked toward the outer part of the niche. There he examined the high, encircling mountains, and tried to think logically, instead of emotionally, about his situation and that of his friends. The honest fact was, he wasn't likely to be able to do much for them alone. A gang of outlaws against a group of unarmed men, women, and children didn't add up to odds likely to be improved much by the addition of one mere camp marshal armed with commandeered weapons. No, Sam decided, he'd have to find help.

The only way to do that, though, would be to make it out of this valley, through the nearly impassable snows of the Sierras, then down to the lower diggings and towns. Once there, he'd have the hard task of persuading others that his wild tale of an outlaw gang, holding a group of people hostage in a mining camp that most still believed was deserted, was not a delusion. Even if he could do that, he wasn't sure he could convince anyone to go back into the dangerous mountains with him, all the way back—if possible—to Texas Gulch, and into likely battle with armed outlaws. And by that time, how might the scenario have changed? The outlaws might have killed off the entire population by then.

Not much of a plan, to be sure, but all he had. Sam, discouraged and deeply worried, again eyed the mountains. The first step in trying to find help was to get out of the valley. He couldn't do this by way of the pass, considering that he'd have to travel right through Texas Gulch to reach it. Besides, the outlaws probably had the pass guarded.

The only way out would be to find another way over the mountains. Another pass. The general consensus at Texas Gulch was that no such alternative pass existed. And if this proved accurate, Sam faced some serious mountain climbing, burdened with weapons, lacking ropes or equipment, and without sufficient food to see him through.

He lifted his eyes to the sky and prayed again. *Lord, I need help. I don't know what to do, and I need help.*

But when he looked at the mountains again, no new pass had miraculously appeared, and no fresh ideas had sprung into his mind.

More discouraged than ever, he returned to his fire, sat down again, and lowered his head for a few minutes of sleep and, he hoped, mental refreshment that might give rise to a plan.

CHAPTER FOURTEEN

The few minutes became an hour. Sam slept deeply, but awakened fast—his usual pattern at times of tension. He moved stiff, cold muscles, rose, and added more fuel to the fire. He noticed that the snow had, for now, stopped. Hoping he had literally dreamed up some inspired plan, he searched his brain and found . . . nothing.

Discouraged and depressed despite his hour of sleep, Sam wandered again to the opening of the niche and gazed over the valley. Such beauty! But he couldn't appreciate the splendor while his own people were in danger of losing their lives. And Julius Setser and Hiram Linfoot were already dead.

Sam traced the outlines of the peaks against the sky and despaired of finding another route out of this huge, ragged-edged basin. He slowly followed the lines of the mountains as they circled around, until his vision caught something on the side of one of the nearer slopes. Not really close, but close enough that he was almost sure what he saw was a man.

He stared as hard as he could, wishing he had a spyglass. It *was* a man, alone, moving across the snow. But who? And why?

Most of all, how?

Judging from the man's direction of travel, Sam was

nearly sure the fellow had come into the valley from the side opposite the pass at Texas Gulch.

Another way in . . . another way out.

Sam settled down to watch the distant figure creep across the snowy landscape, very steadily, making good progress considering the snow. An experienced wilderness traveler, obviously.

Before long, Sam realized that the man was about to move out of his sight. Couldn't have that. He needed to meet this man and find out from him how he'd entered the valley. Maybe this newcomer would even be a source of help.

Sam kicked snow over his fire, gathered his weaponry, and began to descend to the lower part of the valley. He tried to anticipate where the man would go, hoping he could keep him in sight or at least stand a reasonable chance of relocating him if he did lose him. He wondered if the man was aware of him, maybe watching him even as he watched.

Sam did lose sight of the man. It was inevitable, given the rugged land, and when Sam came out an hour later onto a broad, sloping meadow where he had anticipated the man might emerge from the foothills, he saw no sign of him. This bothered Sam to a degree that surprised him; he actually struggled against tears.

The newcomer, coming when he had, had given Sam hope. The thought that there might be something approaching the supernatural in this unexpected appearance had whispered across Sam's mind, barely acknowledged, but definitely there. An answer to his prayer for help, maybe. Now he wondered if he was just foolish.

Had he not watched the man for so long, it would be easy to believe that he'd simply imagined him.

Sam looked at the area from which the man had been traveling. Somewhere beyond those ridges, there was surely a route out of the valley. In theory, he might find it. In reality, he was more likely to starve or freeze to death trying.

He found another place to make a camp, and built himself a lean-to shelter of the sort his father had taught him to make years ago. He made a fire and settled down to pass the night. Come morning he would make a decision. Either he would go on and try to get out of this valley, and down the mountains for help, or he would walk back to Texas Gulch, reveal himself to the outlaws there, and try to persuade them to spare the lives of his people.

Odd, he thought, managing to smile. He'd never taken seriously the idea that he was the law in Texas Gulch. It had seemed a pointless, silly idea before. Now it didn't feel that way. He felt a real sense of responsibility.

Sam slept soundly again. The night was deep and cold and long, but Sam was comfortable throughout. Strangely, when he awakened at the first glimmer of dawn, the fire still burned high. It had been replenished by a man who sat nearby, huddled in a big bearskin coat, similar to Sam's, and topped by a heavy woolen blanket. An identical blanket had been laid across Sam while he slept.

The man stood and grinned. He had a ragged beard now, mostly white, but other than that, looked the same as he had when Sam had last seen him in Texas.

Sam stared, disbelieving, then rubbed at his eyes. Rising, he went to the man and wrapped his arms around him, embracing him with the deepest affection.

"Hello, Pap," he said. "You don't know how fine it is to see you again."

"Fine to see you, too, son," Bushrod Underhill replied. "Though I'm sorry for the trouble that's come on your mining camp."

"How do you know of that?"

"I came along at the right time to witness it . . . enough of it, anyway. And I'm glad I've found you safe, Sam. Because you and me together have some work ahead of us."

"I can't believe you're here, Pap."

"Well, I am here. I had it in mind for a long time to make this journey and see you."

"But in the winter? The mountains and the snow . . ."

Bushrod's lips parted, but for some reason he hesitated a

moment before he spoke. "You know me, son. That kind of thing makes little difference to me."

Sam was struggling with emotion. "What work are you talking about?"

"We've got to save your mining camp, son. You and me, against a small army of armed outlaws. How do those odds strike you?"

"Mighty uneven," Sam said.

Bushrod's own eyes were glistening. "That's right. With you and me both here, they don't stand a chance."

Weary and scared, facing a new morning under the gun, the people of Texas Gulch ate glumly of the meager food prepared for them by the women. Over it all the intimidating Jordan Mahaffery stood watch, far more somber and intense today than the day before. He walked back and forth, speaking to no one, every glance full of threat and fury.

"Look at him!" Copp Nolen said to Dillow as he bit off a hunk of hard biscuit. "All pompous and huffy, like he's making a great sacrifice just allowing us to eat!"

"Pompous and huffy isn't how I'd term his manner today."

"What, then?"

"Dangerous. There's more anger in him. He's beginning to face the possibility that he may not ever find his gold."

Mahaffery pulled out his pocket watch, glanced at it. Less than a minute later he did it again.

"Eager to get us digging in the snow again," Nolen said.

"Yep."

"Know what I believe? I believe Colfax already has the gold."

"So do I."

"How long before Mahaffery gives up and decides there'll be no gold found?"

"Don't know. Not too soon, I hope."

A sudden burst of activity on the far end of the lodge house startled everyone in the place. Art Bolton had come to his feet, dumping his plate on the floor, and was lunging at Searl Mahaffery, who'd been standing close and closer yet to Art's daughter Marica as she served sausages from a griddle. He'd been speaking to her softly, grinning, hiding his words from the others. She'd gradually reddened and looked more upset . . . and just now, Searl had touched her. On the shoulder at first, but then his hand had trailed down . . .

"Get your hands off my daughter!" Art Bolton yelled as he threw himself at Searl Mahaffery. Marica screamed and jumped back. Art's body bumped the griddle and sent it falling, sausages dumping out across the puncheon floor. Searl went down, Bolton atop him, the latter's fists flying, pounding the younger man's face and head.

Some of the outlaws hooted and whooped, enjoying the moment at Searl's expense. But Searl was at a disadvantage only a few moments. Younger, stronger, and meaner than Art Bolton, he quickly threw the man off him, came up, and went for his pistol. Marica screamed again, and for a moment all believed that the younger Mahaffery was about to shoot the man. Instead he pistol-whipped him, laying open a small but ugly cut across the side of Bolton's face.

Cursing through clenched teeth, Searl was about to pound Bolton a second time, but Jordan Mahaffery got to him and pulled him away.

"Don't kill him, Searl," Jordan said. "We need every digger we got."

"He attacked me, Jordan. Came right at me! Knocked me down!"

"I saw what happened. A father will do that kind of thing when somebody goes to bothering his daughter."

"I'll kill the bastard, Jordan! You ain't stopping me!"

"I *will* stop you. We need the labor, Searl. Unless you want to dig out that whole mountainside yourself."

Nolen and Dillow shared a glance. What Mahaffery had just said was, oddly, a relief to hear. Dig out that whole mountainside . . . though they didn't take that literally, it did give hope that Mahaffery wasn't going to give up the search quickly.

"Let me make an example of him for the others!" Searl pleaded. "There's enough here to dig without him. Let me put a hole through his head!"

"No!" Marica yelled, and threw herself down, wrapping her arms around her father's shoulders and covering him protectively.

"You'll kill no one," Jordan said.

Searl and his older brother stared at one another from a distance of six inches. Jordan's stare held the longest.

"I'll bide my time," Searl said. "But not forever."

"If you hurt my father," Marica said, "I'll kill you myself."

Jordan Mahaffery suddenly seemed to lose interest in all this. "That's enough," he said, turning away from Searl and back to the hostages. "Finish that food, and head out to the pass, every damned one of you men! You women, you stay here and clean this mess up. And somebody bandage this fool on the floor." He shoved at Art Bolton with his foot. "Ross, you stay here and guard these folks. You too, Mongold. And when this one gets over being addled, bring him up so he can dig, too."

"I'm staying down here . . . with her," Searl said, pointing at Marica.

"Afraid not, Searl. I want you to help keep watch up at the pass."

"Hell! I was up there three hours last night!" Indeed, Mahaffery's men had been guarding the pass in pairs all night, keeping two huge bonfires blazing, making sure no resident of Texas Gulch managed to escape . . . or tried to come up and do any grubbing for lost gold in the snow on their own behalf rather than Mahaffery's. Given the huge amount of firewood that the Texas Gulch people had laid in to see them through the winter, there was no lack of fuel for the bonfires, and the guards used the wood freely to fight off the cold.

"You'll be up there for more hours than that today. This afternoon, maybe we'll let you come down here and sleep a bit . . . if you'll keep your hands off the women."

Searl muttered a curse and wheeled, stomping away from his brother in very little-boy style. Jordan Mahaffery looked disgusted and shook his head.

"Come on," he said. "We've got a lot of snow to sift."

Four hours later, the forced laborers had cleared much more snow, but still no gold had been found. Art Bolton had showed up after an hour, still dizzy and disoriented. He did his best to work, but it was difficult for him.

For his part, Dillow worked hard, not talking to anyone. He kept his eye on Jordan Mahaffery and didn't like what he saw. Mahaffery was glowering, impatient, edgy. Worse, he'd produced a flask from his coat and had been taking pulls on it all morning.

Mahaffery, though heartless and cruel, was at least somewhat sensible in how he dealt with his hostages. He sought to keep them alive and functioning as long as he needed their slave labors. But drunken men were often different men than when they were sober.

Dillow hoped that Mahaffery would put the flask away for good. But it kept coming out, again and again.

CHAPTER FIFTEEN

Dillow was clearing a snowdrift, working near Kish Fleenor, when the latter stumbled over something in the snow and fell backward. Fleenor tried to use his shovel to catch himself, jamming it not into the ground, but into the ankle of Dillow.

Dillow howled in pain and collapsed, gripping his injured extremity.

"What'd you stumble over?" Mahaffery said, running to the spot. The obviously injured Dillow was of no concern to him at all.

"Don't know," Fleenor said. "Ben, I'm sorry. I didn't mean to—"

"Hell with him!" Mahaffery said. "Find whatever you tripped over!"

Fleenor felt about in the snow, put his hand on something, and rolled it out.

Just an old piece of dropped firewood.

Mahaffery let out a long string of vile words and produced his flask again. "Keep digging!" he yelled to the laborers, who had stopped work to watch the commotion. "Move that snow and find that gold. Hell, find it in the next hour, or I'll kill you all!"

Work resumed at a nearly frantic pace.

"My ankle's hurt," Dillow said. "Let me go back to the lodge house and wrap it up in something."

Mahaffery cursed him thoroughly and drank from his flask again, then waved Dillow dismissively in the direction of the lodge house.

"I'll guard him on down," Searl said quickly.

"I don't care what you do," Mahaffery muttered.

Searl seemed surprised, but delighted, to hear this. He grinned slyly, behind his brother's back, and to Dillow said, "Come on, you. Let's go."

Dillow didn't want to go, now that Mahaffery had ceased to concern himself with keeping Searl away from Marica. But when he expressed his change of mind to Searl, the latter began to kick and curse him. Dillow managed to get himself upright, even to put a little weight on the injured ankle. He began hobbling toward the lodge house, Searl prodding him on.

Daniel had been put to helping the women with the food and dishes, and so was present when Dillow and Searl Mahaffery reappeared at the cabin.

"You hurt, Mr. Ben?" Daniel asked when he saw how Dillow was limping.

"Took a knock on the ankle. I don't believe it's bad, but I need to wrap it up."

Searl was already beelining for Marica Bolton, whose face blanched as soon as she saw him.

"Hello, sweetheart," Searl said, drawing near. She was washing dishes in a big kettle, and backed away from it, hands dripping.

"Get away from me."

"No! No! You're taking everything all wrong, honey. I don't want nothing but your help. In fact, I'm mighty sorry I offended you earlier. I swear on my mother's grave, we came back only because we got a hurt man here. Dillow there needs some cloth wrapped around his hurt foot. You can do that for him, can't you?"

Marica looked distrustful, but eyed Dillow a moment, saw he was really hurt, and nodded quickly.

"I can do that."

"Yeah, I knew you could. I'll bet there's all kinds of things she could do to benefit a man. Eh, Mongold?" Searl winked at the big outlaw guard.

"That's right, Searl." Mongold's grin was big. With Jordan not present to keep things under control, there was no telling what might happen here, and that suited Mongold.

Remine, more loyal to the cause than either Searl or Mongold, did his duty and said, "You'd best watch out, Searl. I don't believe Jordan would like you bothering that woman."

"Bothering? Who's bothering?" Searl's ugly grin beamed toward Marica, who had just sat down to tear a rag into binding strips for Dillow's ankle. "I could show you 'bothering.' And maybe I will." He winked at Marica and sat down beside her. She scooted away. He laughed and scooted after her, until she was on the end of the puncheon bench.

"Leave me alone," she said, and rose with the torn strips to go to Dillow.

The ankle looked a bit swollen, and the shovel had made a significant abrasion on the skin, but Marica quickly made it look better by washing it clean and applying the cloth strips. As she knelt, working, Searl came and knelt beside her, putting his arm over her shoulder and winking at Mongold.

"Mighty pretty lady, you are. Got you a husband?"

"No."

"Want one?"

"Get away from me."

"I'd make a good husband. I could do all the things a husband does. One thing most of all. Let me show you. Bet you'd like that, huh?"

She violently pulled out of his clutches. "Get away from me!"

Old Man Skinner rose from his seat and tottered over toward Searl. Too old to labor at the pass, he wasn't too old to understand what kind of men these were or what was going on before his eyes.

"You leave that woman be!" he demanded, lifting his walking stick as if to use it for a club.

Searl came to his feet and spun, grabbing the stick and clouting the man on the side of the head. Old Man Skinner fell. Daniel yelled in alarm and ran to the elderly man's side.

"Don't hit him!" Daniel begged, placing himself protectively over the old fellow just as Marica had protected her fallen father earlier.

"Well, the little hero! I'll hit him if he don't keep out of my way! Never had no use for meddlesome old fools . . . or young ones." Searl glanced at Marica. "Of course, maybe I'd be nicer to him, and to everybody, if somebody in particular would be a little nicer to *me*."

Marica rose. "You make me sick. I hate the look of you, the way of you, the smell of you." She paused, lip trembling, and there was in her manner a visible change, a line crossed only with the greatest effort of self-sacrificing will. In a weakened voice, she went on, "But if you'll leave these others alone, if you'll stop your threats and your cruel ways . . . then—"

"No, Marica!" Dillow said. "Don't say it. Don't . . . don't."

But Searl already knew what she'd been about to say, and was grinning again. He tossed the walking stick to the floor, went to Marica, and gave her a long kiss on the mouth before the entire population of the lodge house. He was obviously enjoying shocking his watchers as much as he enjoyed the kiss itself. Remine, meanwhile, grinned and looked nervous. Mongold chuckled loudly.

The kiss went on endlessly, Marica stiff and struggling against it, Searl lewd in his manner, his hands moving freely upon her. Across the cabin, America Colfax wept quietly, and someone murmured, "God help us."

Marica pulled away enough to speak. "Please, not here . . . not before these people."

"Why not?" Searl said, closing his mouth upon hers again. "We'll give that little boy there some lessons in manhood. And remind that old man of things he's forgot."

Old Man Skinner began to sing a mournful hymn about the end of the world. America Colfax wept more loudly. And Ben Dillow began to rise, determined to get his hands on Searl Mahaffery's neck and break it if at all possible, no matter what they did to him in turn.

Daniel was faster than the limping Dillow. He grabbed the walking stick and began to pound Searl with it. Searl roared, let go of Marica, and grabbed the stick away. He swung it at Daniel, but Daniel dodged it and ran back to the corner. Searl flung the stick to Mongold's feet.

"Keep that thing away from these people, and I'll let you have a turn with her."

Mongold nodded eagerly and put his heavy foot atop the stick.

In Old Man Skinner's song, Judgment Day had come and the unsaved wicked were being banished to the lake of fire.

Searl advanced, got his hands on Marica again. He kissed her harder and began tugging at her dress. Dillow started to rise, but his hurt ankle turned on him and forced him back down.

At that point, Marica vomited, a violent, forceful heaving. Searl cursed and backed away, foul matter on his chin, down his front. He spat and swiped at his tongue and swore.

She knew she was in trouble. "I'm . . . sorry . . . I tried not to . . ."

Searl drew back his arm to backhand her, but suddenly Daniel was there, at Searl's side, arms extended up and hands gripping a small pistol. This was the treasure he had taken from the ramshackle cabin: an old flintlock with a damaged grip, but still functional. A small, secret inheritance from his late brother. He'd had only three pistol balls for it, and only three charges of powder, but he'd loaded it carefully and knew it would fire, if he could find the courage to pull the trigger.

It had been his plan to slip this pistol to some reliable adult, such as Ben Dillow, but the opportunity for that hadn't come.

"I'll kill you!" Daniel yelled.

"Why you little cuss, where'd you get that pistol? Huh? Speak up, boy!"

Remine was frozen, too stunned by this odd development to move. Mongold began to advance, but the walking stick under his foot rolled beneath him and made him stumble. He went down on one knee, out of balance.

Searl tried to grab the pistol, but Daniel darted back, evading him. He cocked the pistol.

"I'll kill you!" Daniel repeated.

"You ain't got the courage, boy." Searl groped for the pistol again.

Daniel shot him between the eyes.

For maybe three seconds, utter silence held in the lodge house. Mongold rose, staring at the dead body of Searl Mahaffery, and the paralyzed Remine looked like a man about to wet his trousers.

Without a word, Daniel darted toward the same window through which he'd escaped earlier, grabbing his coat and hat from off a peg on the wall as he went. He was out of the lodge house before either Remine or Mongold could react, and running through the snow back toward the big valley.

More silence. Then Old Man Skinner started his song again.

Up in the pass, Jordan Mahaffery turned his head toward the lodge house.

"Did you hear that?" he asked Conner Broadgrass. "Sounded like a shot."

"I did hear."

"What the hell's going on down there?"

"I'll go find out for you, if you want, Jordan."

"I'll come, too. Most likely Searl's involved if there's some kind of trouble. He always is."

CHAPTER
SIXTEEN

Dillow watched closely as Jordan Mahaffery stood staring at the dead body of his younger brother. Little emotion beyond surprise showed in the outlaw's face, and soon even that faded . . . but Dillow was sure that an emotional and possibly violent explosion was imminent. The killing of Searl Mahaffery might prove to be the spark of judgment day for the people of Texas Gulch.

"Who did this?" Mahaffery asked at last. His voice was soft, ominous-sounding.

Dillow was about to step forward and manfully shoulder the blame, but the realization came that he had no pistol and therefore could hardly claim to be the shooter. In that moment of hesitation on his part, America Colfax made all valiant intentions moot by chiming in, "It was the boy! Daniel Chase! He had a little pistol in his coat pocket!"

Dillow thought drolly what a wonderful family the Colfaxes were. Always ready to make sure their own hides were safe, and the devil take the rest.

"The *boy*, you say?"

"That's right, sir. No one else had anything to do with it. Oh, please, sir, don't hurt any of the rest of us for a thing we never done!" America Colfax whined like a cur. Just then Dillow despised her as much as he often despised her husband.

"My brother . . . shot to death by a boy." Mahaffery stood absorbing that. Dillow braced for that emotional explosion. "Twenty-three years of life . . . and he's shot between the eyes by some cussed little boy."

Mahaffery chuckled. Dillow couldn't believe it. The chuckle grew into a deep, spastic laugh.

"Wouldn't you know it'd be something like that!" Mahaffery turned to Conner Broadgrass. "Don't it just seem to fit, somehow, Searl having his sorry life brought to an end by a snot-nose boy?"

Broadgrass replied, "It does indeed, Jordan. Tragic. Just tragic."

"A *boy*!" Mahaffery laughed until his eyes watered. Pulling out a handkerchief, he dabbed the tears as mirth gradually subsided. "Oh, well. So it goes. No loss to the world, eh, Conner? In fact, the world's probably a better place with Searl gone."

Broadgrass again agreed.

Mahaffery took a swig from his flask and wiped his mouth with the handkerchief, which he then unfolded. Stooping, he laid it over his brother's face.

"Still, I have to respond to this. Can't let this go unpunished." He stood and looked around. "Where's the boy?"

America Colfax was again more than glad to provide information. "He went out the window, sir. He's probably running back into the valley to hide."

"Still got his pistol?"

"Yes, sir."

"We'll have to assume he's also got powder and shot, then," Mahaffery said. "I wonder how that boy managed to hide that pistol from us? Anyway, Conner, you take Remine there and head out after him. He should be easy enough to track in the snow. Bring him back alive, unless he forces you to kill him. I'll decide what to do with him then."

Dillow had to speak up. "He's just a boy, Mahaffery. And he only shot your brother because he was trying to protect the honor of a woman your brother would have raped right here before the eyes of all these people.''

''My brother was a sorry piece of dung, and that I won't deny,'' Mahaffery said. ''I'll not miss him, and won't pretend otherwise. Don't worry, friend. I probably won't kill the boy. But I do have to bring him in.''

Mahaffery took a final look at his brother's covered face, then turned to Mongold. ''Get him outside, Bert. We'll bury him right away.''

Mongold nodded and quickly got to the task.

Mahaffery drained another swallow of whiskey, left the lodge house, and trudged back up the beaten, snowy path to the pass, returning his attention to more important matters.

As Dillow anticipated, the actual burying job wasn't given to the outlaws. Dillow and Nolen were assigned the task. As they had with Dehaven, they opted to bury the dead man in a pre-existing hole left from the old Dutch Camp days. This was fine by Mahaffery, who seemed to desire no particular ceremony or special treatment for one more dead man, even if that dead man happened to be his own brother.

The hole, however, was filled with rocks and trash, and there was cleaning out to be done before it could accommodate its unmourned new occupant. Mahaffery seemed impatient to have it all done as quickly as possible.

As they worked, Dillow and Nolen talked quietly to one another, momentarily out of earshot of Mahaffery and his men.

''Think they'll catch Daniel?'' Nolen asked.

''Maybe. But Daniel's slippery. He just might get away.''

''He'll freeze to death if he does. Better to be caught than to freeze.''

''Don't take Daniel lightly. The boy is a survivor. He's explored this valley more than anyone else in the camp, and Sam Underhill has told me more than once that Daniel knows more caves and nooks and crannies and hiding places than you could count on five hands. He could give them the slip easier than you or me. And if he can find shelter—a cave, maybe—he might make it.''

''I hope so. Hey, maybe he'll find what's become of Sam.''

''You never know. I'm beginning to grow concerned about that, by the way. You'd think Sam would have shown himself by now . . . done *something*.''

''Maybe something bad happened to him.''

''I hate to consider it.''

''Or maybe there's just nothing he can do, one man against a small army of outlaws.''

''Sam's unarmed out there, I think.''

''What? How would you know that?''

''When they brought in the weapons they'd rounded up the first night, I saw Sam's rifle and pistol both among it all. I only thought about that earlier today, though.''

''Why was he out there to start with?''

''I had a chance this morning to talk quietly to Leora. It seems she'd asked him to go out and find Arianna and Daniel, who'd gone missing at the time. We know now they'd gone out of the pass, but Sam went back into the valley to search. Took his snowshoes, but apparently no weapons.''

''So even if he does know what's happening here, there's probably nothing he can do.''

''With no weapons, there's not a thing I can think of he could do for us. For that matter, against so many, and them as mean as they are, I don't know what he could do if he had a dozen rifles.''

Mahaffery walked up to the hole, suddenly out of patience. ''Hell, Searl's not worth this much trouble!'' he said, looking at the amount of rubble still awaiting removal. ''You two get out of there. Forget about it. Searl doesn't have to have a grave.''

''You don't want to bury your own brother?'' Dillow asked.

''Nope. Not when we can haul him out in the valley

somewhere and dump him. Let the varmints and the buzzards eat him, if they can stand him.''

"Not a close and sentimental family, you Mahafferys,'' Dillow muttered.

Mahaffery heard, but took no offense. "My brother wasn't even a human being, friend. He had not a trace of goodness in him, nor loyalty. He'd have betrayed me in half a breath if it would have benefited him. I'm not sure why I even let him stay around . . . I suppose I'm made of more loyal stuff than he was. But loyal or not, I'll not waste my time burying trash when I need to be digging for treasure. Come on up out of there. And get back up to that pass and find me that gold.''

"He's a clever little devil, I'll say that for him,'' Broadgrass said, referring to Daniel Chase. "And a lucky one, too . . . unless this isn't luck. Maybe the boy knows this valley well.''

"He came to the right place, no doubt of that,'' said Remine.

The trail through the snow had been quite clear, all the way from the lodge house and far back into the valley. Remine and Broadgrass had followed it with ease, anticipating an equally easy capture, unless the young fellow laid some kind of ambush with that pistol he had.

They'd found no ambush—not yet, anyway—but it did appear that Daniel Chase had found a way to present them with an interesting puzzle.

He'd run more than a mile, straight to a stream that splashed through a short and rocky course at the base of a jagged knoll in the midst of the valley. The stream ran out of one hillside cavern, went on for no more than a hundred feet, then vanished again into the earth, swallowed by another cavern after having made only the briefest of appearances in the sunlit world.

Either cavern opening was big enough to accommodate a man. Daniel had obviously stepped into the stream, following it into one of the openings . . . but which? He might have entered either place; a stream revealed no tracks.

"We'll have to split up," Broadgrass said to Remine. "You go in that cave, I'll go in that one."

"But the boy has a pistol, Conner. He could be lying in wait for either one of us."

"It's a chance we'll have to take. We have our orders."

"Forget our orders. We can tell Mahaffery the boy tried to hide in a cave and fell in a hole too deep to get him out. He'll never know the difference. And the boy'll just freeze or starve out here, so he won't be a problem either way. He's just a boy."

"A boy who just killed a grown man by shooting him between the eyes," Broadgrass reminded Remine. "Don't take him lightly. As for him surviving: these mountains, I'd wager, are full of caves. In a cave, if it's deep enough, the temperature will stay mostly the same all year round. And a boy as clever as that one could set rabbit snares, snag trout from streams . . . he'll not die."

"I don't want to go in these caves. He could shoot either one of us."

"Maybe you want us to go back to Mahaffery and tell him you decided to disobey him."

Remine glared at the other. "Very well, then, we'll look in these caves. But I don't think it's worth the risk, just for a damned kid. I'll take that entrance there."

"No. That'll be mine. It's smaller, and I'm smaller than you. You go in that bigger one there, where the water flows out. Look at it this way: he's most likely in the cave I'm going into. He'd have chosen it because he'd figure a grown man would be less likely to follow him into the smaller cave."

Remine thought about it, nodded, and stepped into the creek. "That's hellacious cold water," he said.

"You won't be in it long," Broadgrass said.

"Ain't you going in the other cave? Because I'm not

going to bear all the risk here, Broadgrass. We go in, we go in at the same time. Equal risk.''

''I agree. It's the only fair way. I'll see you in a few minutes. One of us should have the boy by then.''

Remine advanced against the cold, rushing water, stooped, and entered the cave from which water emerged. Broadgrass made a show of going into the other entrance at the same time, but quickly ducked to the side, just inside the cave mouth, and hid in the shadows. There he waited.

A minute later he heard a muffled shot echo out of the cavern Remine had entered. It sounded like a pistol shot. Broadgrass stepped out of his cave and onto the bank. He'd had a feeling, for some reason, that the other cave was the one Daniel Chase had selected.

A few moments passed before a pink tinge began to appear in the water running out of the other cave. Broadgrass shook his head. Poor, gullible Remine. Well, at least Broadgrass had managed to verify which cave the boy had entered without taking a bullet himself.

A half-minute later, Remine's body came washing down the creek, out of the cave, floating on its back. He'd been shot in the chest, and his eyes were dead marbles, staring up at the sky without blinking. He floated down the icy creek, and hung up at the mouth of the opposite cave entrance. The water passed around him, making him move and bob. Slowly he rolled over, turned by the water. More color spread in the creek, then was swallowed by the receptacle cavern.

Broadgrass surmised that Daniel must have positioned himself just deep enough in the cavern, and in just the right position, to let him see the limned outline of any other person who entered the cave after him. A simple shot to the mid-chest area was enough to do the job. A more perfect trap could hardly have been made. Remine, like Broadgrass, had anticipated it, but he'd been foolish and subservient enough to let Broadgrass talk him into making himself the first potential target.

Broadgrass had to admire the boy. A devilishly clever lad, this one. He'd managed to do in two grown men in one day, and Broadgrass was hanged if he was going to see the boy punished after showing that kind of ingenuity.

"I take my hat off to you, son," Broadgrass called into the cave that had belched forth Remine. "Just such a scheme is the very kind I would have come up with. I admire you, my friend, and now I'm going back to report that you've killed Mr. Remine, but not, unfortunately, before he killed you, too. They'll not look for you if they believe you're dead." Broadgrass paused, then reached beneath his coat and pulled out a packet of pemmican.

"I'm laying some food here by the cave mouth. You can get it later, when you've satisfied yourself that I'm really gone, and that this is no trap. You take that food, make it last as long as you can. Find yourself a shelter somewhere. Trap yourself some rabbits, catch some fish. If you're as clever as I think you are, you can survive until the spring. And by then, all this will long be over, one way or the other." He paused. "You'll probably be the only one of your people left by then. But you deserve to survive. You proved yourself worthy here today."

Broadgrass waited for an answer, but none came. He hadn't really thought one would. But he knew Daniel was in there, listening.

"I salute you, young man. Take care of yourself. I'm going back now, and if you'll keep yourself hidden, you should have no more trouble from any of us."

He looked over to where Remine floated and bobbed at the mouth of the other cave. He muttered, "Good-bye, my friend. One less with which to divide that gold . . . if ever it's found. Ten of us before . . . now only seven. Life truly is but a shadow. Well, good-bye."

Broadgrass trudged away, through the snow, back toward Texas Gulch.

CHAPTER
SEVENTEEN

Sam Underhill ate slowly of the rabbit meat his father provided perfectly roasted on a spit, and listened to Bushrod recount his long journey from Texas to California, a journey made, the aging frontiersman said, just to see a son he missed, and to walk through some country he hadn't yet explored.

Sam listened, but it was a bill of goods he wasn't buying.

"Pap," he said at last, laying aside a bone gnawed clean. "Tell me the *real* reason you came."

"What are you talking about?"

"Pap, it's winter. You've come all the way from Texas, trudged up mountains in heavy snow, and so far all I hear from you is that you just hankered to see me. But there's more to it than that. There has to be."

Bushrod Underhill looked quite offended. "You had a mystic vision, did you, that tells you I lie to my own son?"

"It doesn't require a mystic vision to see that it would take more than a desire for a family visit to draw you this far, this time of year. Besides, I can tell there's something on your mind."

"Of course there's something on my mind. You've got a mining camp full of innocent people, overrun by a horde of outlaws and murderers. You're probably facing a mass execution of men, women, and children before this finishes.

And to counter all that, there's just me and you.''

"But you didn't know any of that when you left Texas. It's not why you came."

"I don't know why you find it so hard to believe that I'd come see you just because you're my son."

"In the dead of winter? In the mountains?"

"Like I said, Sam: you know me. Inconvenience never stopped me from doing anything I wanted to do. Besides, it took me a mite longer to track you down than I thought it would. There's not many below who know there's anybody at Dutch Camp."

"It ain't Dutch Camp now. We call it Texas Gulch."

"Hallelujah. I'm all for honoring the great state where thrive the Underhills."

"Something's wrong back home, Pap, and you're not telling me."

"Boy, the something that's wrong lies across this valley in that mining camp. I suggest we concentrate our minds and efforts on that."

Sam studied his father's face. Bushrod was hard to read when he wanted to be, but some pains even he couldn't hide. Despite Bush's protestations, Sam saw veiled things buried deep in the frontiersman's familiar eyes, things that hurt.

"Pap, just tell me one thing, and I'll leave it be for now: is it Ma?"

There might have been the quick glint of a tear in the old frontiersman's eye, but Sam couldn't be sure. "No, son. It ain't your mother."

"But there is something."

"I told you, Sam. I just wanted to see you. We'll leave it there, all right?"

A hundred dreadful possibilities were playing through Sam's mind, but he knew it would be futile to pursue them right now. "Whatever you want, Pap."

Bushrod nodded. "What I want is for us to rid your little community of the vermin that's infested it."

"I want the same. But I ain't been able to figure out how."

Bushrod was somber. They'd joked before about how the odds had swung in their favor, now that two Underhills were together, but the grim truth of what faced them hung heavy as a stormcloud about them. Two lone men, minimally armed, bore the duty of rescuing an entire community of endangered innocents.

"Tell me what you know, Pap, and how you came to know it."

"What I've learned I've learned by chance, Sam, or by some design bigger than our own. It happened that as I neared the final stretch up to this valley, heading for the entrance pass, I saw the riders, struggling up through the snow. I watched them—they didn't see me—and witnessed them taking two children hostage. One of them was Arianna Winkle, from back home, though she's growed considerable since I last saw her, and I didn't know her at once. The other was a boy, a stranger to me."

"Daniel Chase," Sam cut in. "He's an orphan, sort of a child of the whole mining camp. He came to us with his older brother, and then the brother died and left him alone."

Bushrod paused after hearing that, a look of concern on his face. Sam understood. Bushrod's own childhood had placed in him a deep sense of affection for and protectiveness toward orphans.

Bush went on. "I was too far away to do aught about the taking of the children, and I'd counted ten of them scoundrels. Wasn't much I could do.

"But I was able to hear enough to begin to get a notion of what was going on, and when I determined they were going to ride in to your camp, I followed. But one of them broke off from the rest—for some reason, he was chasing a dog, Arianna's dog, I think—probably just trying to keep the poor girl trusting them until they could reach the camp. But of course this fellow ends up ready to shoot the dog instead. He saw me, though, through the snowfall. I stood still as a stone, hoping that my clothing, the blurring of the snow, all that, would camouflage me. But he spoke to me. Called me 'Dehaven.' The name mean anything to you?''

"Dehaven . . ." Sam recalled what Hiram Linfoot had told him before he died. "That was the name of a man we found dead in the snow just outside the pass, the evening before the outlaws came in.''

"This fellow, apart from the rest of his group, was making me an offer—or making this Dehaven an offer, from his point of view—to divide and take some gold, and to run off and leave the rest of the group without. I made no answer, just stood there. Eventually he wandered off, figuring that his eyes were playing tricks on him in the snow, I suppose.

"When he'd gone on a distance, I followed, wanting to see what this gang was up to. I came up into the pass after dark, and hid there, and listened. And I heard it all.

"Your camp is hostage, Sam, all of them. This Dehaven fellow had taken stolen gold from the others and tried to keep it all for himself.'' Bushrod told the story as he'd been able to piece it together from what he'd heard. "The leader of the gang, a man named Mahaffery, killed one of your people that first night, Sam. Shot him dead, before the others, because the man was sneaking a gun on his person. And I knew right then just how serious a danger all the people there are in.''

Sam said, "All you're telling me confirms what I was told by a man who managed to get away from the camp . . . though he was mortally wounded at the time he told me.''

"So there's *two* Texas Gulch people dead?''

"Yes. You remember Hiram Linfoot? Came to Texas about six months before we headed for California?''

"I do remember him.''

"He's the second who was killed. He'd gotten away, and told me, without all the details, the same things you just did. But, Pap, if you were in the pass that first night, why didn't you just sneak on in the rest of the way, instead of coming all the way around and over the mountains?''

"Because this Mahaffery put watchmen at the pass," Bushrod said. "I was driven out by their approach before I could get all the way in. But I knew I had to get in somehow. I'd looked for you among the people, and hadn't been able to spot you. I thought maybe I'd just overlooked you. I had to find out. I circled and explored all through the mountains the next day, until finally I found a new way into the valley."

"I've always heard there is no other way in besides the pass," Sam said.

"The general wisdom is wrong. There is one. High and narrow, hard to reach, but it's there. And I found it."

"How?"

"I've got a nose for these things. Like Dan Boone used to say, 'The land can tell you a lot when you know how to read it.' "

"So you came all the way around, and into the valley, just to look for me?"

"Mostly. And to help the others, too. They're my people, too, after all." Bush smiled at his son. "I'm mighty relieved I've found you alive, Sam. I was afraid, when I didn't see you amongst the people, that something bad had befallen you since last I'd heard from you."

"I'm still among the living . . . for now."

"Yes, thank God. Well, I've told you my tale. Now let me hear yours."

Sam took a deep breath and started at the beginning. He told Bush, briefly, the history of Texas Gulch, and of those who prospected its environs. Most of the people Bush already knew. He was particularly saddened to hear of the death of Leora Winkle's husband, a man he'd always thought of very highly.

Sam described, with some shame, his own ill-advised, inadequately prepared-for jaunt into the snowy wilderness for what he'd thought would be a quick find of two missing children. But if his father judged him harshly for having ventured out without weapons and adequate planning, he said nothing of it. Sam figured that lecture would probably come later.

Sam also told how his search for the children had been providentially timed. It had gotten him away from Texas Gulch just in time to avoid being taken as one of the hostages of the Mahaffery gang.

Sam described his fall into the pit and the finding of the rock pick, which he'd used not only to get himself out of a quite literal hole, but to kill the rifleman who'd mortally wounded Hiram Linfoot.

"I hid Hiram's body, and the second man who'd been chasing him never saw me, nor did he see Hiram dead. I can only suppose the outlaws must believe that Hiram's still alive out here, alone, and that it must have been Hiram who pickaxed that fellow to death. Hiram himself told me, before he died, that the Mahaffery gang doesn't even know I exist . . . unless, of course, someone has told them since."

"Either way," Bush said, thinking, "it's a good thing you played that hand as you did. Whether or not they know about you, they do believe that Linfoot is still alive and roaming around . . . and likely they'll try to search him down at some point. Maybe we'll get a chance at them, a few at a time, that way."

Sam felt daunted. "It frightens me to consider that there's only two of us, and so many of them."

Bushrod's eyes twinkled. "But we're Underhills, remember? And an Underhill can shoot a hole in the moon and spit through it. An Underhill can light his pipe from the flames of the sun. And an Underhill can belch and knock down a grove of California redwoods. Says so right in the almanacs."

"As I hear it, there's only one Underhill who could do such wonders, and I'm looking at him. But don't tell me you've taken to believing all those tales you profess to despise so," Sam said.

"Son, in the situation we're in, we'd both best start believing them. For what we're going to have to pull off is nothing less than a miracle."

CHAPTER
EIGHTEEN

Conner Broadgrass reported the death of Ross Remine in his usual impassive style. And he told his lie about the supposed death of young Daniel Chase in such a bland and convincing manner that tears came to almost all the Texas Gulch residents who heard it and had no cause to disbelieve it.

Ben Dillow didn't weep. The news about Daniel filled him with sorrow, but even more with fury, and he decided on the spot that he would, somehow, get this camp and these people out of this horrific situation, or sacrifice his life trying.

America Colfax did shed tears—despite the fact she'd been more than ready to feed Daniel Chase to Mahaffery for the sake of her own sagging and sallow hide. Herbert Colfax did not cry. He seemed lost in his own deep brooding, his thick brows descending low across the bridge of a hawklike nose, deepening the crease that ran along its top and the furrows in his forehead.

Broadgrass had returned at a time when the work at the pass was at a temporary stop so the exhausted men could rest. So hard had they been pushed, and in such a mentally and physically draining manner, that even Mahaffery had been forced to see that efforts had to slow down a little, or they'd stop of their own accord.

Mahaffery didn't seem concerned about Daniel's fate, but Dillow noticed that the outlaw blanched a little to hear that one more of his men, Ross Remine, was dead.

That makes three gone, Dillow thought, for he'd decided already that Mahaffery's claim that the one named Fish was off somewhere, resting, was a lie. The man was dead. Hiram Linfoot, or an accident—or maybe even Sam Underhill— must have gotten Fish. *Ten outlaws to begin with, now down to only seven. They've got the weapons, and therefore the odds are still theirs . . . but not quite as heavily as before.*

That two of the outlaws had died at the hand of a mere boy inspired and humbled Dillow. If Daniel Chase had the wherewithal to take one of his enemies with him to the grave, shouldn't a group of grown men be able to do as well?

Dillow had accepted the fact that any or all of them might die before this was done, but he pledged to himself not to die without taking a member or two of the Mahaffery gang along for the same ride. He'd not let young Daniel outdo him. He'd honor the orphan boy's memory with the blood of the same outlaws who had killed him.

Mahaffery was obviously troubled and trying to think, but his drinking wasn't helping him. He paced back and forth in the lodge house, staggering slightly this way and that, so that the hostages seated around him were careful to keep their feet out of his way so as to avoid tripping him and maybe getting shot for it.

Mahaffery was red-faced, red-eyed, and swearing with every breath. Ben Dillow could hardly blame him. Mahaffery had come here to recover lost gold, only to find it elusive. And three of his men, including his own brother, were dead.

Dillow took some satisfaction in Mahaffery's unhappiness, but it also worried him. Mahaffery might decide to give up his gold quest early. If so, the people of Texas Gulch would probably not live to see another setting of the sun.

But Mahaffery wasn't through quite yet. He barked an

order, and under guard, the weary men of Texas Gulch
trudged up the slope to the pass, to spend more long hours
prospecting the snow for stolen gold.

Through the white valley, Sam and Bushrod Underhill
walked together, father and son, heading toward Texas
Gulch.

It was a terrible burden to carry the fate of an entire group
of people in one's hands, Sam thought. But an easier burden,
now that his father was here. Maybe Bushrod Underhill really couldn't shoot holes through the moon or drink the
Great Lakes dry, like the almanacs claimed, but he still was
Bushrod Underhill, frontiersman, survivor, companion.
Most of all, father. Sam needed that right now.

"There it is," Sam said, when the mining camp at last
came into view. It was, from their vantage point, nothing
more than a few squares and rectangles of dull brown
against a backdrop of white. He watched the plume of
smoke rise from the twin chimneys of the big lodge house.
"Looks remarkably peaceful, considering."

The pair of them stood there, watching the camp. Sam
lifted his eyes to the pass and could barely make out the
forms of men up there, digging in the snow, widening the
search area ever more. Men under the gun. Good men,
working like slaves because their lives, and the lives of their
neighbors, and in a few cases, their families, depended on
it.

Suddenly it was all overwhelming, impossible . . . and
Sam turned his head away.

"I don't know what we'll do, Pap," he said. "We've
talked, figured . . . and we still have no answer."

"Maybe we've got part of one," Bush said. He touched
Sam's shoulder. "Take a look, son. Then back up, slow,
and let's you and me drift into these rocks over here."

Sam looked. Coming toward them, out of Texas Gulch,
were two men bearing a burden. They struggled slowly
through the snow, heavily laden.

Bushrod reached beneath his coat and brought out a familiar spyglass, one Sam had seen him use all his life. Pressing it to his eye, adjusting it, Bushrod looked for a few moments and said, "Sam, they're carrying a corpse."

Sam winced.

"Take a look."

Reluctantly, Sam took the spyglass, found the image, and brought it into focus. He didn't recognize the men who carried the body. Two of the outlaws. The body was wrapped, the face hidden. Judging from the size of the dead man, Sam figured it could be Ben Dillow, maybe Jack Gray, Leora's brother.

He lowered the glass slowly. He and his father drifted to the side, hiding themselves behind a conglomeration of boulders as the corpse-bearers slowly advanced in their direction.

"Let's get them, Pap," Sam said. "Let's eliminate two pieces of the problem right now."

"Let's do."

Reed Van Huss and Lennis Yeager were not happy men, and expressed their displeasure to one another as they stumbled and staggered through the snow, bearing the wrapped corpse of Searl Mahaffery. Who did Jordan Mahaffery think they were, anyway? Why did two of the best thieves on the continent—in their own estimation, anyway—have to serve as mere guards and corpse-carriers for Jordan Mahaffery? Though both had always admired Mahaffery's skill as a criminal organizer, schemer, and technician—it was he who had conceived and carried out the brilliant robbery that had netted them the gold Dehaven had taken—just now they saw nothing to like in the man. Just a sorry drunk, throwing his weight around, making everyone around him labor while he stood swigging from his flask like some minor king.

"I've got half a mind to dump old Searl right here on the ground and forget about it," Van Huss said. "Why should we go trekking any farther through this snow? This is far enough.''

Yeager, though agreeing with the emotion of Van Huss's statement, was a more practical man. ''We dump him here, and we'll just be sent back to redo the job. Let's put up with the headache and carry him back a little farther. We'll find someplace among the rocks to lay him. Or we'll hide him beneath a snow drift if we have to.''

''Hell, it isn't going to matter,'' Van Huss said. ''We'll be out of here before long anyway.''

''You think we're getting out of here before spring? You think we could get down that mountain in this kind of snow?''

''I could. Just find that gold; give me my share, and I'll be gone.''

''You'd never make it. Hey, see those rocks yonder? Let's go dump him there.''

The other was agreeable. They struggled with the body toward the place they'd chosen, and were almost there when two unfamiliar men rose before them, rifles leveled. One was young, the other white-haired.

''Hold just as still as your dead friend there,'' the old one said. ''Or you'll find yourself in the same unhappy condition he's in.''

Van Huss and Yeager glanced at one another. They'd always been able to read each other well, and did so now.

''Let us lay down this body,'' Yeager said.

''Let him drop,'' the white-haired man replied.

But they didn't drop Searl; they squatted slowly and laid him gently on the snow, as if he had been the dearest friend they'd ever had. They moved as one, abruptly, pulling pistols from beneath their coats and throwing themselves in opposite directions, finding the nearest cover as they cocked their weapons.

The two outlaws didn't know who these strangers were, but they'd be hanged before they'd let themselves be taken without a fight.

*   *   *

In the lodge house, Jordan Mahaffery snapped up his head.

"You hear that?"

"Gunshots," Mongold said.

"What the hell . . . ?" Mahaffery grabbed his rifle from the corner and headed out the door and around the lodge house. Another shot sounded from out in the valley, a high, cracking sound at this distance.

Mongold came to Mahaffery's side. "Reed and Lennis must have run across trouble. But who? The one who me and Emmett chased?"

"Has to be. Who else could it be?"

"But there were more shots than I'd expect from them finding one unarmed man."

"Maybe that runaway got his hands on a weapon, somehow. He managed to find a pick to kill Emmett with, didn't he?"

Another shot, then another, closer this time.

"Hey!" Mahaffery exclaimed. "There they come!"

Mongold didn't see Van Huss and Yeager nearly as quickly as Mahaffery had. But soon even his piggish, myopic eyes spotted them. Both were running as hard as the snow would allow, back toward Texas Gulch. They leaped snow drifts and bounded over the rugged terrain with the kind of grace and athletic prowess often inspired by mortally dangerous encounters.

They were breathless by the time they reached Mahaffery and Mongold, and leaned over with legs bent, hands on knees, gasping out white clouds of steam.

"Two men . . . tried to take us," Yeager managed to get out.

"*Two* men?" Mahaffery said.

"Yes . . . Never seen them before."

Van Huss found his voice and added, "One of them was young . . . the other an old fellow."

"Almost had us, too," Yeager said. "But we moved . . .

quicker than they'd anticipated. Did you hear ... the shots?''

''I did. Did you hit them?''

''No. And they didn't hit us. We were lucky. They had rifles, us just our pistols.''

''Two men ... how in the devil? And where did they come from?''

''No idea, Jordan. No idea.''

''The younger one ... might he have been our running man, the one Mongold and poor old Emmett chased?''

''We'd have known him. It wasn't him. I swear, these two were strangers.''

Mahaffery let out a slow breath. ''Get back inside. Let's go have a word with the good people of this sorry camp. I have a feeling some of them might know who this pair is. If there's somebody living elsewhere in this valley, some-body here's bound to know about it.''

CHAPTER NINETEEN

The gunshots had been heard up in the pass, too. The men laboring there were brought down, at Mahaffery's orders, and stood up in the trampled snow outside the lodge house. The other hostages were lined up alongside them. The sky had cleared momentarily, though new clouds were thickening on the horizon, and the sun was bright on the snow, making them all squint and wince.

Mahaffery paced before his hostages like a commander before troops with whom he is not pleased.

"I want to know one thing: who are they, and which of you knew of them?"

No one replied.

Mahaffery stopped pacing and stared into individual faces. "Why am I getting no answer? Two of my men were nigh killed today in that valley, attacked by a pair of men they'd never seen before. Now, if there's others living in this valley, some one of you is going to know it."

When no one answered again, Ben Dillow cleared his throat and tried to find something to say, just to keep Mahaffery's steam from rising any further.

"What did they look like?" he asked.

"What kind of question is that?" Mahaffery shot back. "Is there a whole damned population of folks living back in that valley so that you have to get a description to know which ones we're talking about?''

Dillow wasn't going to spar with this man. He said no more.

Mahaffery said to Van Huss, "Tell them what they looked like.''

Van Huss gave a remarkably thorough description, considering the tense situation in which he and Yeager had encountered the pair.

Letitia Colfax sniffled and whimpered, "Oh, it sounds like Mr. Sam and Mr. Bush!''

Dillow sighed. There'd be no more keeping secret the existence of Sam Underhill.

Dillow himself had to wonder who the older man could be. The description sounded like Bushrod Underhill, of all people, but that was impossible. Bushrod was still in Texas.

Mahaffery's nose was three inches from Letitia's broad face almost as soon as she spoke. "What'd you say, girl?''

"I said, it sounds like Mr. Sam and Mr. Bush.''

"And who might they be?''

"Sam and Bushrod Underhill. But it isn't possible that it's really—''

Mahaffery slapped her, evoking a screech. "What are you talking about, heifer? Are you trying to mock me? Bushrod Underhill? Hell, I thought maybe it was Father Christmas!'' He slapped her again.

Herbert Colfax, going crimson, stepped out of the line and pointed into Mahaffery's face. "Don't you hit her again!''

Mahaffery did hit her again, harder, staring at Colfax while he did so. "What do you aim to do about that, old man? Get your fat rump back where it was, or I'll turn your two cows here over to Mongold and let him do what he wants with them.''

Colfax's breath was coming hard. He tried to speak but couldn't. For a moment he hesitated, overwhelmed by fury, then, with effort, he made himself step back into place. Letitia stood with her face buried in her hands, crying. America Colfax looked like she could faint where she stood, her face as white as snow.

It was the first time in Dillow's memory that he'd actually felt sorry for Herbert Colfax. Just now he'd have killed to protect the man and his family.

The time had come to speak up. Dillow cleared his throat and said, "Mahaffery."

The outlaw turned. "Speak up."

"The young lady wasn't mocking you. There is a Sam Underhill who lives among us. You might consider him the closest thing we've had to a community leader, if you want."

Mahaffery strode over and faced Dillow. "Go on."

"The people of this mining camp came from Texas, for the most part. The town of Underhill stands on land that was given by Sam Houston to Bushrod Underhill for his part in putting down the Tripplerite Conspiracy that would have given the Mexicans a foothold in Texas."[3]

"Pass over the history lesson and get to the point," Mahaffery said.

"Sam Underhill is the son of Bushrod. The real Bushrod, not the make-believe almanac version of the man. Sam led this band of Forty-niners here, and has been a leader among us ever since."

"So why wasn't he among you when we took over this sorry place?"

"He was out searching for two lost children, that's why. The same pair you came riding in with, pistols to their heads, being the brave and fearless man you are." The sarcasm had been irresistible.

Mahaffery ignored it. "You're telling me that the younger of the pair who attacked my men is Sam Underhill. Son of the great Bushrod himself. So who was the older man?"

"I can't tell you, Mahaffery. But Letitia was right. From

[3]*Texas Freedom,* Book 2 in The Underhill Series

the description, I'd have to say it sounds like Bushrod Underhill.''

''So Bushrod Underhill came to Texas Gulch, too?''

''He did not. Which is why it can't really be him. Yet the description of him matches, right down to the last detail.''

Mahaffery pondered matters a few moments. ''So Sam Underhill has found himself a mysterious partner who looks like his pap in Texas. Interesting situation. But it won't matter. We'll kill them both all the same, no matter what their names are or how famous their pappies might be.''

Just then, farther down the line, Herbert Colfax said, ''Mr. Mahaffery . . . sir . . . there's something I need to say.''

Dillow frowned. There was something odd and strained in Colfax's speech. It sounded like it had taken an excruciating effort to get the words out.

''Speak up, then.''

Colfax frowned and tilted his head, putting one hand on the side of his head. ''I want to tell . . . you . . . that . . . uh, that there's . . . the gold, you see . . . I'm sorry, I'm sorry . . . I don't feel very well right now.''

He made an odd, gurgling moan, twisted his face strangely, and collapsed slowly to the ground.

High in the rocks of one of the many ridges that made up the great stone circle enclosing the valley holding Texas Gulch, Sam Underhill sat listlessly, staring at the ground before him as his father silently paced back and forth.

Sam spoke first. ''We didn't handle that particular battle too well, eh, Pap?''

Bushrod mumbled something Sam couldn't make out. Sam didn't ask him to repeat it because it really didn't matter. Nothing said now could alter the fact that they'd underestimated the two they'd tried to capture. Though they themselves had escaped unharmed, they'd also failed to so much as nick either of the outlaws.

And the only edge they had, the element of surprise, now was lost. By now Mahaffery had heard those two outlaws' entire tale, no doubt, and probably was making plans to defend against, or maybe even hunt down, the troublesome pair out in the valley.

"We're fools, Sam," Bushrod said at length. "A pair of fools not up to the task that's been given us. But you're a young man. You've got an excuse. I'm old and experienced. I should have handled it better."

"I was just getting ready to say that *I'm* the one who has no excuse."

"The truth is, neither one of us do," Bushrod said. "But there's no point in chasing water that's already flowed away, as old Tuckaseh used to tell me back in Coldwater Town. We've got to move on from here. Maybe, if we look long enough, we can find some advantage we gained from what happened, even if we don't see it yet."

It was a positive suggestion, and a good one to hear, but as Sam reviewed the fiasco of the failed attack, he could find nothing, and admitted this to his father.

Bush looked stoic. "I reckon I just proved that old Bushrod can't shoot a hole through the moon after all."

"Neither one of us is anything more than a man," Sam said. "We're facing a situation that there truly may be no way to get out of."

"Don't say that," Bush said sharply. "The moment you decide there's no way out, you've lost. And we mustn't lose."

"No." Sam paused. "We mustn't. Because there are good people down there. And children. For the sake of the children alone, we have to find a way."

Something odd occurred right then. Bushrod's look changed, and his eyes reddened. He turned his back on his son very quickly, but his shoulders heaved and he could not hide it.

Sam watched in amazement as his father wept. Bushrod

Underhill was shaken, deeply so, and Sam was sure it was not merely because of one failed gun battle.

"Pap, you're going to have to tell me sometime."

Bush drew in a deep breath, and straightened his shoulders. The quaking subsided. With his back still turned, he said, "Tell you what?"

"Whatever it is you haven't told me yet. Whatever it is that really brought you all the way here from Texas."

There was a long silence, then Bushrod said, "We'll be talking a lot, you and me, once we're through all this. Once we have your people free."

"You can tell me now, if you want."

But Bushrod had nothing to say.

They laid Herbert Colfax on a pallet inside the lodge house, but he would not lie still. He kept rocking, moving, as if trying to roll himself over, but he couldn't make it. The left side of his face drooped stiffly, as if the corner of his mouth was being pulled down by an unseen finger. His left arm lay motionless at his side, hand twisted oddly, fingers curling up.

"Oh, Herbert, please, please lie still!" America Colfax pleaded through tears. Her daughter, already shaken and never strong even in good times, huddled in a corner, knees drawn up, face hidden—to all appearances a young woman making a strong attempt to become a fetus again.

Dillow was at America's side, watching Colfax's odd motions. Any hostility he'd felt toward this fellow couldn't survive now. The man was pitiful and wretched, and Dillow felt sorry for him.

"It's apoplexy, America," he said to the crying woman. "I've seen it before. He can't really help what he's doing . . . it's just that his body won't obey him anymore."

She cried, refusing to look at her husband. Mahaffery stood behind America and Dillow, a few feet back, looking on silently. To Dillow's surprise, the outlaw was actually being relatively humane in this situation. He'd allowed Colfax to be brought inside, his family with him, and when he learned that Dillow served as a doctor substitute in Texas Gulch, allowed him to enter, too.

"I think he's trying to say something," Mahaffery said.

Dillow looked into Colfax's eyes, watched his struggling attempts to move his face. He saw at once that Mahaffery was right.

"Herbert . . . are you trying to talk?"

More strain, more twisting of the one side of the face that would still move. And this time, a bit of noise, but no words.

"Herbert, don't try. I'll get you something to write with."

Colfax relaxed then, lying back, but his body still seemed strained and awkward. The stroke had hurt him badly, and Dillow felt no optimism about Colfax's survival.

Dillow rose and looked back at Mahaffery, who nodded his permission for Dillow to search out writing materials. All Dillow could find was a slate and bit of chalk that Arianna Winkle used when her mother gave her schooling. Dillow held up the slate and let Colfax take the chalk in his right hand. Colfax, however, was left-handed by nature, and it was difficult for him to write on the slate, which Dillow held up for him. Letters kept showing a tendency to come out turned backward, but still the apoplectic man managed to produce scratchings that could be read.

He wrote slowly and laboriously, his breath catching and face reddening. Then he lay back, still gripping the chalk.

Dillow turned the slate and looked at it. America ceased hiding her face and read, too, and Mahaffery stepped over and looked down as well.

"What the devil . . . ?" the outlaw muttered.

Colfax had written: HID THE GOLD.

CHAPTER TWENTY

"What's he mean by that?" Mahaffery said, intense all at once. "What gold? *My* gold?"

Whether it was good or bad that Colfax was revealing this now, Dillow could not say. But the dam was broken and whatever flowed over now would simply have to come.

Dillow leaned over and spoke into Colfax's face. "Herbert, I'll take the chalk from your hand and put my finger in its place. When I ask you a question, you squeeze once for yes, twice for no."

It seemed that Colfax tried to nod.

Dillow did as he had said. "Herbert, is the gold you wrote about gold you've mined?"

Two squeezes.

"Is it the gold that Mahaffery and his men have been searching for?"

A pause, then a single squeeze. Mahaffery saw it and cursed.

"Are you saying, Herbert, that you have Mahaffery's missing gold?"

Again, a single squeeze.

Mahaffery dropped to his knees, shoving Dillow aside. He put his own finger into Colfax's hand. "You saying you got my gold, old man?"

Colfax, looking as scared as his facial paralysis would

allow, gazed into the outlaw's face and squeezed his yes.

"Why, you sorry old thief! All this time, you've had my gold, and you said nothing?"

Another single squeeze.

"Well, you devil, before you die and go to hell, you're going to tell me where it is . . . ain't you!"

Another squeeze. A yes.

"Give him the chalk and the slate," Mahaffery directed Dillow.

Dillow went to Colfax's opposite side and picked up the slate as before, first dusting off the prior words with the heel of his hand. He put the chalk into Colfax's hand, then helped him lift his arm, propping it to let him write.

Colfax wrote: NO.

Mahaffery cursed thoroughly. "Old man, you don't co-operate, and I'll let you watch me cut your wife's throat, then your fat daughter's."

"Wait a minute," Dillow said, forcefully. "He wants to write more."

Dillow cleaned the slate; Colfax wrote again.

PEOPLE FREE.

"He wants you to let the people here go," Dillow said. "Then he'll tell you where the gold is." *Good for you, Colfax,* Dillow thought. *Maybe you're a better man than I ever thought. What you're trying to do might not work, but at least you're trying.*

"Does this old fool think he can lie there and tell me what to do?" Mahaffery glared down at Colfax. "You're dying, old man. But your wife and daughter ain't. Keep in mind that the situation could change."

A tear streamed down Colfax's face. Dillow fought emotion himself: a pure, righteous anger that made him want to take Mahaffery's throat in his own hands and squeeze the life from the man. For a few moments he seriously thought of doing so, but gave it up. Mahaffery was armed, and he wasn't. He'd never succeed.

But if Mahaffery threatened the lives of the Colfax

women, he decided, he'd attack him right there, and die with Mahaffery's throat in his teeth.

Mahaffery put his face inches from Colfax's. "Old man, you're going to write out where that gold is. No games from you, no promises from me . . . except one. If you'll tell me where that gold is, I'll see your family treated well. I'll see that, no matter what, they survive this."

Colfax was listening. Dillow couldn't blame him. What man wouldn't care about the safety of his family more than about any other matter? But he hoped Colfax had the sense not to believe Mahaffery. The outlaw would have no reason to keep his pledge once he had what he wanted.

"You going to help me out, old man? You going to make sure your women are safe and sound after you're gone?"

Colfax blinked his wet eyes rapidly. The meaning was obvious.

Mahaffery grinned and put the chalk into Colfax's hand. Colfax began to scratch the chalk over the slate.

Dillow closed his eyes. It was almost over now. Mahaffery was about to be handed his gold, and what would happen after that he could not say, but he wasn't optimistic.

Dillow heard something clack against the puncheon floor. He opened his eyes.

America Colfax was sobbing all at once. Dillow looked at Colfax's face and saw why.

Herbert Colfax was dead. A second stroke, probably, silent and quick. The chalk, falling from his fingers, was what had made the clacking noise on the floor.

Mahaffery, a little slow to comprehend what had just happened, finally did a moment or so later. He turned the slate he'd been holding and cursed loudly.

Colfax, though he had tried hard, had managed to produce nothing more than a few indecipherable, childish scribbles.

Mahaffery rose and smashed the slate against the wall. America Colfax sobbed louder and went to her dead husband, while Letitia made whimpering animal sounds that were quite pitiful.

Dillow perceived this moment as the most precarious he and his fellows had faced from the moment all this began. The one man who knew where the gold was hidden was dead. It would take Mahaffery only a few moments to come around to the possibility that Colfax might have told his wife or daughter where the gold was, which would lead to interrogation, maybe torture. Dillow knew Colfax well enough to believe that he'd probably kept the matter of the gold secret even from his own family. All the ugliness would lead nowhere but to more frustration and anger on Mahaffery's part . . . and probably to a mad search of the camp, and a mass killing at the end of it all.

In such moments inspiration often comes, and it came to Dillow right then.

He turned to the rampaging Mahaffery and said, ''That's it, Mahaffery. I reckon there's no point in me holding out any more.''

Mahaffery turned his frown on him. ''What are you talking about?''

''It's just that I know what'll come next. You'll want to hurt these women on the chance that he told them where he hid that gold. But please don't do that, for I know he didn't tell them. He told me instead. Colfax and I were in this thing together . . . and we hid the gold together. He didn't let on just now, trying to protect me, I guess. But I'll not hide the truth anymore.''

Mahaffery drew his pistol. ''Tell me where the gold is, right now.''

''I can't describe the location to you. Too complicated to explain . . . you'd never find it that way. I'll have to lead you to it.''

Mahaffery studied him silently, then said, ''You're damned right you will. And if you're lying to me, I'll make you die a hundred deaths.''

"You're mighty rude to those who offer to help you, you know it, Mahaffery?"

"Watch your mouth, my friend. I'm not a man who abides insult."

"You'll abide mine. Because right now I'm the only hope you have of ever putting your hands on that gold."

Mahaffery stared coldly at him, but it was obvious that Dillow's disrespectfulness was, paradoxically, gaining Dillow some respect from the outlaw. That daredevil defiance was the very kind of attitude Mahaffery himself would have had if the roles in this scenerio were reversed. Dillow had anticipated just this reaction, and it gave him a certain sense of power to see that he'd correctly gauged his foe's mental processes. These outlaws might be bold and cruel, but there was a shallowness about them, too, that a clever man might be able to manipulate to his advantage.

"Very well, Dillow," Mahaffery said. "I have no desire for your respect. All I want is my gold. And I want it now. Take me to it. But tell me first how I can be sure you really know where it is."

"You can't. All I can tell you is that Herbert Colfax and me found that gold alongside the corpse of Dehaven, even before young Daniel found the body. We hauled that gold out and hid it well, planning to get it in the spring, divide it, and go our way." Dillow glanced at America Colfax and her daughter. Both were still silently crying, but listening intently. He wondered if they believed what he'd told Mahaffery, or saw the design behind his lie.

Mahaffery said, "So all this time you've known where that gold is, and you've said nothing."

"It's a lot of gold. Colfax and I were banking on the hope that you'd give up eventually, vacate this place, and leave the gold to us."

"So you let your own people work under our guns, and let men die, and still you kept your mouths closed."

"Like I said, it's a lot of gold. And if we'd told you

where it is, you'd have killed us all as soon as you got your hands on it.''

Mahaffery's lip twitched, and he smiled, just a little, just for a moment. ''And once I get it now . . . what do you think I'll do?''

''I'm going to ask that you spare us. There's not a thing I can do to make you do that, but I can tell you that I'm a man with influence among these people. I'll keep them quiet. No one will ever tell about what you and your men have done here. You have my promise.''

''So that's what I'm to rely on: your promise.''

''It's all I can give you. But I'm in the same situation. I have nothing but your word to go on. So let's exchange our pledges, so to speak. I promise to put that gold into your hands, and to keep all these people quiet, if you'll promise to spare our lives in the end.''

Mahaffery gave Dillow a smile worthy of Old Scratch himself striking a bargain for a human soul. ''You have yourself an agreement, Dillow. I'm a reasonable man, after all. The way you said it is the way it will be. I get my gold . . . and you get your lives.''

CHAPTER
TWENTY-ONE

Dillow limped out of the lodge house, trying to remember if there was ever before a time he'd felt this tired, body and soul. This ongoing ordeal had drained from him something vital that he wasn't sure could be restored with any amount of future rest. But he had to hold on a little longer. He had a plan, a desperate one, but one that might work.

The guarded people of the mining camp stood in a cold cluster, watching him approach. He addressed Perry Winters. "Mahaffery wants you to bring everyone back inside. And he wants to talk to you, Van Huss, and Legarde."

"It wouldn't hurt you none to use the word 'Mister' every now and again," Winters said.

"Please accept my apology, Mr. Winters." Dillow struggled not to let too much sarcasm come through, knowing it wouldn't pay.

The people were eager to get inside. It was cold and the clouds had moved from the horizon to cover the entire sky. Dillow turned to the group. "Herbert Colfax is dead," he said. "A natural death. Apoplexy."

There were no strong responses to the news. A few lifted brows and a few shaking heads with sorrowful faces. That was all. These people were simply too weary, and had already seen too much dying, to react much to news of one more passing. They walked toward the lodge house, from which Mahaffery himself now emerged. He pulled out his flask and took a sip as he watched the people file past him to go inside and find places to sit, or more or less collapse. Dillow came in last, glancing at Mahaffery as he went inside. He limped across the room and sat down on an empty spot at the end of a bench, near Art and Marica Bolton.

Bert Mongold closed the door and leaned against the wall with rifle in hand, picking at his teeth with a splinter and eyeing Marica Bolton and Leora Winkle alternately. Lennis Yeager held his post at the opposite end of the room, and Conner Broadgrass, leaning in a corner, looked typically mysterious, brooding, and confident.

Outside, Legarde, Van Huss, and Winters gathered around Mahaffery, who gave them an uncharacteristically warm grin and, even more uncharacteristically, offered them his flask. "Take yourselves a good swallow," he said jovially. "It's mighty cold out here."

"Thank you, Jordan," Van Huss said, taking the flask, draining away a mouthful, then passing it on to Winters. Strange, Mahaffery being generous with his liquor. The man seemed to be in a revived and optimistic mood.

"I guess you heard the old man died," Mahaffery announced as the flask finished its round and came back to him. He pocketed it. "Apoplexy. But forget about him for now. I have something for you to do. I want you to go hunting for me. Manhunting."

Van Huss, who had already had one encounter with the men he was sure Mahaffery wanted hunted, looked quite unhappy, but Winters and Legarde, both of whom loved a chase dearly, perked up considerably. Better to be doing something, anything, than this endless standing guard over a bunch of snow-digging gold searchers who seemed unlikely to turn up anything more valuable than rocks and frozen dog dung.

Mahaffery went on, "I want you to put an end to these men in the valley, this Sam Underhill fellow, and the old man with him. The old man must be some stray hermit prospector, maybe some holdover from the old Dutch Camp days. And then there's the possibility of a third man, that being the runaway who Emmett and Bert chased, the one named Linfoot. And if Linfoot is alive, he's probably got Emmett's weapons.''

''You want these men brought back or killed?'' Winters asked.

''I want no more people to guard, no more mouths to feed. Rid us of them for good.''

Van Huss, making no effort to hide his unhappiness with the assignment, said, ''Jordan, if all three of us go, that leaves only you, Lennis, Bert, and Conner to guard all these people.''

''We've got the guns; they don't. Besides, they're all too weary to cause any problems.''

''So am I,'' Van Huss muttered. ''And I've almost been killed once today already.''

''Cheer up there, Reed. Things are about to take a better turn.''

''You have a new lead on that gold?''

''I do. The old man who died on us claimed at the end that he found the gold before we ever arrived here, and hid it. The one named Dillow claims to have been in on it with him. Me and him are going to make a journey out to fetch it.''

The three others exchanged glances. ''You believe this ain't a bluff?'' Van Huss asked.

''The dying one had nothing to gain by bluffing. I believe it's the best possibility we've been handed so far.''

''What if Dillow tries to make a break from you out there?''

''I can handle him. Besides, I don't plan to still have him with me when I come back, if you follow me.''

They nodded. Good. It was time to reduce the numbers here a little. Even an unarmed and exhausted group of people posed a threat when they outnumbered their guards.

''Don't you think somebody should go with you? Just

you and that man alone . . . he might find a way to get a drop on you.''

"Don't worry about me. You three just go get rid of this Sam Underhill character, and anyone else straying around in this valley.''

"What if we can't find them?''

"Keep looking until you do.''

Mahaffery stood in the center of the lodge house and looked around at the sullen people.

"You'll be happy to hear that, for the moment, work up in the pass will cease,'' he announced. "You people will remain here, inside this building. You'll be closely guarded, and I do hope you've learned by now the sheer foolishness of trying to get away.''

"What are you going to do with us?'' asked Jack Gray, brother of Leora Winkle.

"What we do with you is entirely in your own hands,'' Mahaffery replied. "You cooperate and you'll be just fine.''

Young Arianna surprised them all with quite a bold question: "Did you kill Mr. Colfax?''

"No, young lady,'' Mahaffery answered. "Mr. Colfax up and died all on his own. I'm very sorry it happened. Now, if you'll excuse me, Mr. Dillow and I have some business to deal with. The rest of you, just be patient, stay where you are, and maybe this will be over soon.''

At the mention of business with Dillow, Conner Broadgrass, who had been half-napping where he leaned against the wall, the brim of his hat pulled low, looked up quickly and shifted his hat back.

"Where's the other three of your men?'' Art Bolton asked.

"Resting in another cabin. Close by and ready to give aid if any of you prove foolish enough to attempt anything rash in my absence.'' Mahaffery turned to Yeager. "Lennis, put some of these women to cooking. And be sure to save some of the food. Mr. Dillow and I are likely to be hungry when we get back.''

Without further discussion, Mahaffery ushered Dillow out of the lodge house. Broadgrass moved to a window and watched the pair trudge toward the pass, Dillow limping badly, yet staying slightly ahead of Mahaffery, who was armed with his rifle and two pistols, along with a knife and hatchet.

Some of the clouds had turned the color of indigo. A light snow, which looked fated to become heavier, was peppering down. Broadgrass looked at the sky speculatively, then back down at the departing pair again. After a few moments he went back to where he had been, leaned into the corner, and pulled the brim of his hat low once more.

''Mama,'' Arianna Winkle said to Leora, ''that Mr. Mahaffery lied about the other guards resting.''

''What do you mean?''

''I just looked out the back window, and saw them. They're walking back into the valley, with guns. Like they're going hunting.''

Leora thought about that, and about Sam being out there. She pursed her lips tightly.

''Mama, what's wrong?''

''Nothing, dear. I'm just tired.''

''Do you think they're going hunting, Mama?''

''Yes. I do.''

''Then why would Mr. Mahaffery lie and say they were asleep in another cabin?''

''Because it's in his nature to be wicked, and tell lies, and do other bad things. And I suppose he'd rather all of us believe that there are more guards right here in the camp, than to know they're really gone off into the valley.''

''Where do you think Mr. Dillow is going with Mr. Mahaffery?''

''I don't know, dear.''

''Do you think he will be all right?''

Leora paused, then admitted, "I don't know."

"I hope he is." Arianna sat down beside her mother and nestled close. Although she was at an age when she had begun the process of pulling away from her mother, trying to be independent, she now was childish again, clinging. "Mama, I miss Daniel. I cry when I think about him."

"So do I."

"I wish he hadn't been killed. I wish this was over." The girl hesitated, then said something her mother had never allowed her to say about other human beings. "I hate these men, Mama."

"I hate them, too, Arianna. And I hope they all die, every one of them, very soon."

Arianna rested her head on her mother's shoulder for a few moments, then said, "Is it wrong to feel that way?"

"Maybe," Leora said. "But I find I can't help it."

"I wish Papa was still alive."

"Yes, sweetheart. Right now I miss him very much."

CHAPTER TWENTY-TWO

"Is that the fastest you can move?" Mahaffery said. "This snow will worsen. I don't want to be trapped out in the mountains in the midst of a storm."

Ah, Dillow thought defiantly, *but that's the very idea, my friend.* "I can't move any faster. My ankle pains me. And I've never been able to move fast on snowshoes."

"How far to the gold?"

"Not far." But it would be far. He'd keep hiking, trudging, turning, moving from ridge to ridge, ever farther away, until by the time greedy, murderous Mr. Jordan Mahaffery realized that he'd been lied to and there was no gold to be had, he would have no idea where he was, or how to get back. This, at least, was Dillow's intention. He didn't plan for Jordan Mahaffery to ever set foot again in Texas Gulch.

Dillow knew it wasn't much of a scheme, and had the distinct disadvantage of likely costing him his own life right along with Mahaffery's, but maybe, God willing, it would work. What was the point of trying to save himself, anyway, when there was no hope of anything in the end but death at the hands of the outlaws? If Dillow was going to die, he intended to take at least one of these devils with him. Maybe, somehow, the others would then have a chance.

The pair trudged on, deeper into the mountains. The snow heightened some, but was still far short of the near-blizzard that had been under way the night the outlaws first came to Texas Gulch.

Travel was laborious, which began to worry Dillow. The point was to go as far as possible, as fast as possible. Otherwise Mahaffery would easily find his way back. Gritting his teeth because of the pain in his ankle, Dillow sped up. His breath was coming in great heaves.

"Stop," Mahaffery said at last. "Stop right here. I don't trust you."

Dillow, truth be told, was glad to stop, for he was exhausted. He turned and panted, his white breath mixing with Mahaffery's.

"Don't . . . trust me?"

"That's right." Mahaffery gasped a few times before going on. "I don't believe you and that old man carried that gold out this far."

"We did."

"No. No. Not that old fellow. I don't believe you."

"Believe what you want. We'll go back and you can keep us digging in that snow until the next century, and you'll find no gold, for it ain't there to be found."

"Then where is it?"

"I told you, I can't describe it. I just have to take you to it."

"Where, though? A hole in the ground? Up in a tree? Under a rock?"

Dillow glanced ahead and picked his spot nearly at random. "Up in those bluffs," he said, pointing at a high rock ridge ahead of them, its distance hard to determine because of the spitting snow.

Mahaffery looked at the bluffs unhappily. "How high?"

"Maybe halfway up."

Mahaffery frowned longer at the high ridge. "I don't believe you. You'd not have had reason to hide it so well. You didn't know we were coming to search for it."

Dillow's mind raced. He wasn't a habitual liar, so he

didn't contrive stories easily. But he managed to speak quickly enough to sound believable.

"We *did* know you might be coming," he said. "Dehaven was still alive when me and Colfax found him. He talked."

"The hell!"

"He told us he'd taken gold, and that some men were after him for it. He said you were bad men who would search all creation, if you had to, for that gold. He said we'd get half the gold if we'd help him, but he died right after that. So we decided all the gold was for us, and hid it well, as far away as we could from Texas Gulch in the time we had."

"If you knew we were coming, why weren't you prepared?"

"We didn't really believe anybody would come this far, with the weather going bad. We hid the gold and figured that was precaution enough. Then we left the body to be found by someone else, and from then on played ignorant of it all . . . until Colfax spilled the truth with his chalk and slate."

Mahaffery looked at the sky. Snowing even harder now, but not intolerably. "We don't have much time. We need to get that gold quickly."

Thank God, Dillow thought. *He believes me.*

They headed for the bluffs, Dillow praying for the strength to make it that far, much less to climb.

Van Huss grew more angry the farther he advanced into the valley with the other two manhunters.

"I can't believe I'm here, doing this," he said. "Damn it, I should've taken my leave of Mahaffery long ago. And I sure shouldn't have let him set out alone just now with that Dillow."

"What are you thinking, Reed?" Winters asked.

"I'm thinking he has it in mind to get that gold and try

to make it out of the mountains with it, all alone. Keep every bit of it for himself.''

''You really think so?''

''I do. I do. I don't trust Mahaffery anymore. You wait and see. He has it in mind to cheat us out of that gold.''

Sam and Bushrod Underhill were perched high on a Sierra ridge, well hidden, watching the three armed men move through the valley below them.

''They've come hunting, I believe,'' Bushrod said. ''Hunting us. Look . . . I believe one of them was one of the pair we fought with earlier.''

''Well, if hunting's their intent, let's give them a bit of sport, Pap.''

''Sport? No, no, son. Sport is for pleasure . . . and it's for the sportsman to bring it about, not the game. Besides, this ain't a sporting hunt those men are engaged in. This is war.''

''Meaning what?'' Sam asked.

''Meaning that we won't worry about sporting chances. In war, a man does what he has to do to kill his enemy.''

''I believe you may be thinking of doing some sniping at our friends down there,'' Sam said.

''So I am.'' He pointed at the three gunmen, now much closer. ''See yonder tall fellow? Black coat, brown hat? He's my target.''

''I may as well pick one, too,'' Sam said.

''No. Save your shot to cover me while I reload afterward.''

This suited Sam, who wasn't the long-range rifleman his father was, anyway. Through the back of his mind flicked a thought he'd had many times over the years: *my father is indeed a remarkable man*. The old fellow had just traveled all the way from Texas and climbed the snowy Sierras, but to look at him and see him right now, even in such a tense and dangerous situation, he might be on a pleasure outing with one of his grandchildren no more than a mile or two from home.

Bushrod sat upright, taking a classic rifleman's stance. He

sighted down the long barrel, which did not waver at all, but held as rigidly as if it had been clamped in place. A steady hand, had Bushrod Underhill.

Sam watched the advancing men below, wondering if they had any clue they were about to be fired upon. He focused on the tall man—Perry Winters, though Sam could not know his name—and waited for his father to fire.

He saw Winters pause, look around . . . then up, right at them. Sam knew the moment had come.

"Good-bye, friend," he whispered, and half a second later, Bushrod Underhill's long rifle cracked and spit fire.

In the lodge house, Conner Broadgrass snapped up his head, listening.

"Did you hear it, too?" Mongold asked.

"I did," Broadgrass replied. "Gunfire in the valley."

Another shot followed, then a third.

"They've surely got a battle going," Yeager said. He shuddered, remembering his own fight with those two valley-roamers. It had scared him more than he wanted to admit.

"I'm going out there," Broadgrass announced.

"What?" Yeager said. "In direct violation to what Mahaffery told you to do?"

"He'd want one of us to go help them out. Sounds like they've found some real trouble." Another distant crack punctuated the statement. "See there? I'll be back soon." He headed for the door.

"You better not do it, Conner," Mongold said.

Broadgrass didn't reply. He reached the door and opened it.

"Conner, you're leaving only two of us here to guard all these people!"

The door closed behind Broadgrass and he was gone. He circled the lodge house, through the snow, and headed for the valley. Mongold went to the window and watched him a few moments.

''There he goes,'' Mongold said. ''Mahaffery will nail his rump right to the wall for breaking his orders, just you wait.''

''No, not Broadgrass, he won't,'' Yeager said with some evident bitterness. ''Broadgrass never has been under Mahaffery's thumb. Broadgrass believes he's smarter and better than any one of us.'' He hesitated, then added, ''He may be right. Maybe we ought to be following him instead of Mahaffery.''

''You'd trust Broadgrass above Mahaffery?''

''Yes. I believe I would.''

Outside, Broadgrass continued toward the valley as fast as the snow would allow, to all appearances an eager warrior intent on reaching the fight as soon as possible. But as soon as he was over a rise that blocked any possible view of him from the lodge house, he darted to the left and circled around, keeping behind cover, and headed for the pass.

It was impossible to make it all the way to the pass without coming into a potential line of view of the lodge house, so there was no choice but to take the risk. The battle in the valley was of no interest to him. What intrigued him was what was going on beyond the pass . . . Mahaffery and the man named Dillow. Going for that gold. Alone.

They'd not be as alone as they expected to be.

Whatever Mahaffery was up to, Broadgrass intended to know. And he wasn't about to accept on blind trust that Mahaffery, with that gold in hand, would ever come back to Texas Gulch at all.

Once he came into potential view of someone in the lodge house, he moved quickly. Sometimes a man could make up in speed what couldn't be had in stealth. But there was no good speed in this falling snow. He tried to run but could manage little more than a fast trudge. Still, he made the pass unchallenged from below, and when at last the lodge house passed behind him and out of sight, he was sure he'd succeeded. They hadn't seen him.

CHAPTER
TWENTY-THREE

Sam Underhill sighted down his rifle, squeezed the trigger, and felt the slam of the rifle butt against his shoulder. Being quite bruised and sore from his ordeal at the pit, the recoil hurt a lot. He pulled back behind the boulder that was his cover, waited for the gunsmoke to clear, then peered over. He ducked again, quickly, grimacing as a rifle ball struck the stone and threw chips and dust in all directions, stinging him badly.

Beginning to reload, he glanced over at Bushrod, who was taking new aim himself. He fired just as Sam was slipping the ramrod back into its thimbles.

"You hit him?" Sam asked.

"No," Bushrod snapped.

Sam shook his head, held his breath, and dared to peer over the stone again, hoping to find another, better target. Bushrod, meanwhile, was reloading with the kind of remarkable speed born of long experience.

"Pap, once again we ain't doing too well," Sam said.

"You think I don't know that?" Bush replied sharply. He finished loading, then mumbled, "At least I hit mine."

"You just wounded him, that's all."

This was true. Perry Winters, the tall fellow Bush had chosen to take the first rifle ball, had taken the wound in the side and fallen back with a yell. But he'd quickly scrambled away, leaving a trail of blood as he went, and found cover in a snow-filled gully. Since then he'd managed to fire off several shots. Every time Sam suspected the man had passed out from shock or maybe bled to death, he'd pop up again and shoot. It was he, in fact, who had almost taken off the top of Sam's head with that last rifle ball.

Sam raised his rifle and fired again. He drew back behind cover.

"Get one?" Bush asked.

"No," Sam said.

"Dang 'em. Harder to kill than a nest of ticks." Bushrod positioned himself, ready to take his turn at firing. "Maybe we took the wrong approach to this, Sam."

"Maybe so." Sam was half reloaded by now. But he was getting worried. Emmett Fish had not possessed a wealth of either powder or shot, and before long, Bushrod would be left to fight this battle alone, for Sam would have expended all his ammunition.

Bushrod raised up, took careful aim, then fired. He dropped again with a dour look on his face. Sam didn't even have to bother to ask how that shot had gone.

"Sam, there was three of them to begin with. Now, whenever I rise to fire, I only see two. What happened to the third man?" Bush wrapped a ball in patching and positioned it for a ram down the long, rifled barrel.

"I don't know. Maybe we killed him."

"No. We haven't killed anybody yet. He's out of view somewhere. And I don't feel very comfortable about it. What if he finds a way to sneak around on us? See them rocks there? If he came up there, he'd have us shot before we knew he was upon us." Bushrod finished reloading.

"Then maybe we should move. Try to get up there ourselves. Take the high ground," Sam said.

"Then lead the way, son."

They eyed one another, did a quick, silent three-count, and rose as one. For a few moments they were exposed, and in that moment the men below fired, one at a time. One ball struck a stone near Sam and spanged off to the left, singing into the snowing sky. Sam twisted away, a reflex action, and fell.

"Sam? You hit?" Bushrod said, ducking and turning.

"No, I just—"

There was no time to complete the answer. A second rifle below barked, and Bushrod jerked and pitched to the side, falling hard into the snow.

Sam stared at him, horrified. Bush lay on his side, eyes wide and suddenly quite glassy. The old frontiersman was staring at his son, unspeaking, mouth slightly open. He did not blink, did not breathe.

"Pap?"

Bushrod remained silent and unmoving.

"Pap . . . *Pap*!" Sam touched his father, shook him gently. "Oh, Pap, no . . . no . . ."

Sam opened his mouth and let out a scream that rebounded off the stones behind and above him, and out into the broad valley, the terrible echo of it coming back moments later, like mockery.

He heard one of the outlaws below give a hoot of triumph, and laugh aloud.

In the mountains beyond the pass, the wind began to whip up and the snow fell faster. Squinting against flakes that peppered his face, Mahaffery turned to Dillow and asked, "How much higher?"

They were halfway up a rugged slope, one they'd climbed with much strain. Here the wind was bitterly cold and the terrain so rugged that Mahaffery was growing even more skeptical about the claims of his companion. This seemed an unlikely place in which to have hurriedly stashed a cache of gold.

"Just a few more yards," Dillow said. He pointed. "See that bluff there, and the flat space above it? There's a little cave up there, just a small hole in the rocks. That's where the gold is."

Mahaffery looked hard. "Where? I don't see anything."

"You can't see the opening from down here," Dillow said. "Come on . . . you'll see it when we get up atop that bluff."

Mahaffery glowered. "You're a liar! What are you trying to do? Get me up here and get me lost? Maybe get me on that bluff and push me off?"

"You're way too suspicious, Mahaffery," Dillow replied. "You want your gold or not? We can turn back now and go back to Texas Gulch if you want to."

Mahaffery hesitated. "Hell, go on," he said. "We'll go as far as that ledge, but no farther. And if I find there's no cave and no gold there, I'm going to put a rifle ball through your brain on the spot. I swear I am."

Mahaffery shoved Dillow roughly. They continued to climb.

Bushrod Underhill's breath came back to him suddenly. He gasped and groaned, and Sam Underhill laughed aloud in pure, wonderful relief to hear it.

"Pap, I thought they'd killed you!" He knelt beside his father, rubbing snow on his face, trying to rouse him.

Bush breathed hard, blinking, making faces in protest of the cold snow being rubbed against his skin. Groaning again, he sat up. "Killed? No. Not me. I'm tenacious as a bad habit, son."

"Where are you hit?"

Bush made a face of pain and moved his right shoulder. "Here, I think."

But when Sam examined the shoulder, he found nothing but a crease cut through Bush's clothing, and to his surprise, the rifle ball itself lodged right against Bush's shoulder. He probed into the tear in Bush's clothing and popped the ball out. "Take a look at that, Pap! You'll probably never see that happen again! That ball hit at just the right angle to knock you over like a club, but not to penetrate."

"It sure knocked the wind out of my bellows when I

fell,'' Bush said, eyeing the ball that by all rights should be inside him now. ''Couldn't breathe for a few seconds.''

''You were staring like a dead man. I thought you *were* a dead man.''

Sam was looking into Bush's face, examining his eyes for evidence of concussion, when those eyes suddenly cut upward and widened. ''Sam, look out—''

The butt of a rifle pounded Sam's head from behind, very hard. Sam yelled and sprawled. Bushrod crabbed back for space, reaching for his pistol.

Reed Van Huss, who had so loathed entering this fray, had certainly risen bravely to the occasion now that he was in it. While Legarde and Winters had kept the Underhills occupied with gun battle from below, he had found a way up the slope toward their hiding place, creeping up and staying out of their view, managing to surprise them.

Van Huss stepped across Sam and swung his rifle up again, ready to club Bushrod. Sam, though, got a hand out and wrapped it around Van Huss's ankle, pulling hard and tripping the man before he could swing.

Ironically, the action saved Van Huss's life. Bush's pistol blasted just as Van Huss fell. The ball that would have passed through the center of Van Huss's forehead sailed off into the snowy sky instead.

Van Huss fell atop his rifle. Sam got up, intending to throw himself atop Van Huss and pin him, but the clout to the back of his head had staggered him pretty badly. He stumbled to the left and fell beside Van Huss rather than on him.

Bushrod, meanwhile, came to his feet, backing off and trying to bring his rifle into position to shoot.

Another shot fired from below, singing past the old frontiersman. Bushrod moved back, getting out of the line of fire from below, and raised his rifle.

Van Huss, however, had taken advantage of that extra moment of movement to get up again. He charged at Bushrod and was able to deflect the rifle muzzle before Bush had a chance to aim and fire. He wrenched at the rifle, trying to pull it free of Bushrod's hands, and was surprised at the iron grip of the old man. Swearing, he reached for Bushrod's throat with his left hand while still holding the rifle with his right.

Bush, who had been gripping the rifle in standard shooting position, let go of it with his right hand and drove a swift punch into Van Huss's face. The outlaw went down on his knees with a grunt, but didn't lose his grip on the rifle. Bushrod kicked him, then kicked again, but by sheer luck, Van Huss managed to grope out and wrap his hand around Bushrod's foot as it kicked at him the second time. With a heave he threw Bush off-balance, and back to the edge of the steep slope down which the Underhills had been firing.

Sam was on his feet again, and went for Van Huss, but not before Van Huss at last was able to wrench the rifle out of Bushrod's hands. At the same time, he shoved, and Bushrod teetered a terrible second, then toppled, rolling and sliding down the rocky slope, toward the very rocks behind which Winters and Legarde had taken cover.

Sam struck Van Huss from behind, but the blow mostly glanced off the outlaw's shoulders. Sam's head was spinning; he felt weak, and his skull ached where Van Huss's rifle butt had struck him. Van Huss wheeled, cursing. He'd tossed aside Bushrod's rifle, but there was a knife in his hands. He lunged at Sam with it, the blade aimed directly at Sam's heart.

Sam remembered the pistol he'd taken from the body of the man he'd killed with the pick. Reaching for it, he found only air. The pistol had come out of his belt and lay on the rocks behind him. There was no way to go for it, though, while he was occupied with dodging his enemy's blade.

Below, Bushrod came to a stop, battered and grimed and aching, at the base of the slope. He'd rolled as free as a stone, unable to stop himself, but he'd done the only thing a man could do in such a circumstance, and that was to relax his body as much as possible as he rolled, and to try to roll sideways, log-style, rather than head over heels. Thus, when he reached the bottom, he had to lie there only a couple of moments, moving fingers and toes and so on, to surmise that he was still in one piece.

Bushrod got up as quickly as he dared, and began looking around for a refuge.

He'd realized even as he fell that he was descending right into the snake pit, so to speak, and sure enough, the unwounded gunman, Legarde, appeared almost as soon as Bush was upright, raising his rifle and shooting hurriedly at the prize that had all but rolled into his lap. Fortunately for Bushrod, the shot was too rushed, and missed him by at least two feet. Bush debated with himself only a moment—Run for cover? Attack while his foe's rifle was empty?—and opted for the former when he saw the fellow pulling out a pistol. Bush scrambled behind a big stone just as the pistol fired. The ball struck the stone and rebounded with a high, singing whine into the sky.

Bushrod saw his moment and seized it. Unless the man had a second pistol, something Bush was willing to bet against, he was at this moment unarmed. Bush reached to his belt and pulled out a bone-handled hunting knife that had been given to him many years before, back when Bushrod had lived in Missouri, by another old Missouri frontiersman then in his waning years: Daniel Boone. Locking the knife firmly in his hand, he came from behind the boulder and headed straight at the momentarily unnerved outlaw, who was fumbling about, trying hard to get his pistol reloaded in record time.

Meanwhile, atop the rise, Sam was engaged in a struggle for his life. Van Huss was a madman, slashing with his knife, cursing and shouting at Sam, trying to keep him off-balance. And Sam *was* off-balance, but not because of the noise. He was dizzy, too dizzy to see straight, and it took great effort to keep Van Huss in focus. For the moment Sam was engaged mostly in a dodging contest, trying to avoid the wild slashes of Van Huss's blade.

As he had earlier while trapped in that pit, Sam regretted deeply having failed to bring his own knife. He also regretted not having bothered to remove that pick from the skull of the fellow who had shot Hiram Linfoot. Right now any weapon would be welcome. He flicked his eyes away from Van Huss for a moment, looking for that pistol he'd lost. There it was, well out of reach, and blocked from him by the man who was doing his best to kill him.

Below, Legarde screamed. Bushrod had just stabbed him, not a deep wound, but right in his middle. A few inches up, and he could have been pierced through the heart. He danced back, bleeding. Bush came at him like a fighting dog, switching the blade in his hands so that now he could stab with a hammering motion. He knocked Legarde down with his body, making him lose his weapons, then rolled off and bounded up again. Legarde was deeply unsettled to see such agility in an obviously aging fellow. What kind of man was this?

He had little time to think it over further. Bushrod was upon him again, swinging the blade down, stabbing Legarde in the shoulder. The man screamed and twisted, turning his back unwittingly.

Bushrod buried the blade in Legarde's back.

Legarde hardly felt this one. Shock was beginning to set in. But he lurched away before Bush could pull his knife free, and staggered off toward the place he'd been hidden before with Winters. The knife was still lodged between his shoulder blades.

Again Bushrod was fortunate. Legarde had happened to position himself in a way that blocked Winters from getting a shot at Bush. Realizing the precariousness of the situation, Bushrod scrambled away, seeking cover.

On the top of the slope, Sam Underhill had just closed his hand around a stone. Not much of a weapon, but all he had. Summoning his strength, he heaved it at Van Huss, striking him on the nose. Van Huss yelled and staggered backward. Sam ran and leaped over him, hoping his dizziness wouldn't make him fall, and landed near the pistol he'd dropped. He grabbed it, cocked it, turned . . . and snapped the pistol without effect in the direction of Van Huss.

The percussion cap had come loose, at the worst possible moment. The pistol couldn't fire at all.

With nose bleeding, Van Huss came at Sam again, a wild, killing glitter in his eyes. Sam threw the useless pistol at him and hit him on the nose again. Van Huss howled, blood flying. Sam ducked low and dove at his knees, bringing Van Huss down.

They struggled there, rolling about, pounding one another, biting, head-pounding . . . men in primal, mortal battle, doing their best to kill one another. Van Huss, with his knife, held the distinct advantage.

But somehow Sam managed to strike Van Huss's head very hard against a stone on the ground, stunning him. He grabbed Van Huss's knife hand and tried to get the weapon free, but Van Huss managed to hang on. When it became evident that Sam was ultimately going to get the weapon, Van Huss brought up his other hand, hit Sam hard on the ear, then tried to shift the knife from one hand to the other. All he managed to do was drop the blade. It landed on its side on his chest. Sam groped for it, but Van Huss got his hand on the weapon first. Sam grabbed the wrist, and again there was a struggle for possession.

The men somehow came to their feet, fighting for the knife, hardly aware of where they were, dancing a lethal ballet together. Then, before either realized it, they were at the edge of the slope. Van Huss's foot slipped and he fell, dragging Sam with him. Together they rolled, still gripping one another, pounding down the very course that Bush had plunged along a little earlier.

When they hit the bottom, Sam found that Van Huss was struggling no more. His grip went weak, and Sam quickly pulled away from him.

The knife was sticking deep into Van Huss's chest, moving a little with each breath, blood gurgling around the place it entered the flesh.

Sam wondered if he had stabbed the man without really being aware of it. No, he hadn't, he realized, because he'd never really controlled the knife. Van Huss had simply rolled on the blade and stabbed himself.

"You . . . Underhill . . ." Van Huss muttered weakly, looking at him.

Sam knew right then that what Hiram Linfoot had told him in his last moments was no longer true: the outlaws holding Texas Gulch now *did* know that Sam Underhill existed and was alive in this valley. These manhunters had known exactly who they were searching for, at least in his case. Word had gotten out.

Bushrod appeared at Sam's side, looking down at Van Huss.

Van Huss's eyes shifted toward Bushrod. "You . . . old man . . . who are you?"

"I ain't *that* old, friend. Well, actually, I suppose I am."

"But who . . . ?"

"My name's Bushrod Underhill."

Reed Van Huss arched his brows, looked quite surprised, and died without ever speaking another word.

CHAPTER
TWENTY-FOUR

"There's another one gone," Sam said. Only then did he remember the other two, whom Bush had been dealing with below. "Pap, where—"

"Don't worry," Bushrod interrupted. "They're gone. One dragging along with a bullet wound in his side, the other with my old Boone knife still sticking out of his back. Heading back for Texas Gulch, and no doubt hoping they make it before they die. They just up and gave up the fight on me." He paused and shook his head. "I surely do hate to lose that knife."

"Let's go after them, Pap. We can stop them before they get very far."

"Maybe we should just let them go. Let them tell stories about the two wild madmen who did that to them, and killed their partner besides. Maybe the whole gang will get scared and leave."

"You believe that?"

"No."

"Then let's go after them. If we succeed, there's three of them gone. Three! The odds would improve a lot."

"Son, you've got a mind about you. Maybe you're even smarter than your old Pap these days. Come on. Let's go catch them."

*   *   *

Broadgrass paused for breath and stared through the falling snow, looking for Mahaffery and Dillow. Their trail was clear in the white, though their tracks were filling remarkably fast. He wondered why they had come so far.

Something was wrong about all this, and he was beginning to suspect what it was. This Dillow fellow wasn't leading Mahaffery out here to retrieve hidden gold. Dillow—a clever man, Broadgrass had perceived from the moment he first saw him—was leading Mahaffery out here to try to kill him, or at least get him lost.

Broadgrass stood there, thinking. Much farther, and even he himself might become lost. And what was the point of going on, anyway, if there was no gold at the end of the trail?

Time to turn back to Texas Gulch.

As he turned, he wondered if Mahaffery really would become lost, or get himself killed. That would be an interesting scenario, to be sure. And not necessarily a bad one. Broadgrass had known for a long time, by instinct, that he was a better and more clever man than Mahaffery. He'd allowed Mahaffery to lord over him only because it had seemed prudent, and because Mahaffery's scheme to steal that gold had been so obviously a wise and workable one, the kind of plan Broadgrass would have come up with himself. But Broadgrass was sure he never would have lost the gold again, like Mahaffery had. No mindless fool like Dehaven would ever have gotten the best of Conner Broadgrass.

The snow began to obliterate the landscape in a vast bleakness. Broadgrass looked back and saw his own tracks rapidly filling. No more time to waste. He began trekking back toward Texas Gulch.

"Conner!"

Broadgrass wheeled, looking all around.

"Conner . . . is that you?"

Mahaffery's voice! Broadgrass peered through the snow and tried to find him. He sounded far away and muffled.

"Mahaffery! Where are you?"

"I can see you, Conner! Stay where you are! I'm coming to you!"

Broadgrass obeyed, though he didn't like being approached by someone he couldn't see. Years of living in a world governed by untrustworthiness and suspicion had left him edgy about such things. But this was Mahaffery, not a stranger, and from the tremor of Mahaffery's voice, it sounded like the man was in trouble.

He saw him then, a dark, faint figure struggling his way across the white mountain snowfield.

"I see you, Jordan. I'm coming to you now," Broadgrass said.

When he reached Mahaffery, he found the man panting, weak, and seemingly in pain. He was gripping his left wrist, his fingers hanging limply, looking bluish from cold.

"You're hurt, Jordan."

"My wrist. It's hurting bad. I don't know if it's broken. But it hurts."

"Your fingers are freezing. We need to get you to some warmth before they get frostbit. Here . . ." He pulled a rag handkerchief from his pocket and wrapped it around the hand, making Mahaffery grimace every time the hand moved.

"Where's Dillow?"

"Gone. The bastard tried to kill me, and almost did. Got me up on a bluff where he said the money was hidden, then tried to shove me off. It almost worked, but in the end, it was him who went over the edge, not me."

"And there was no gold."

"No. No gold. It was nothing but a ruse. He wanted to play the hero for his people. Get me out here on the pretext of finding that gold, and get me lost or dead. I should never have let him come so close to getting the best of me."

Broadgrass was thinking the same thing. "How'd you hurt the wrist?"

"Catching myself on the ground when he first knocked me over. Damn, it hurts!"

"Anything else injured?"

"Left ankle's a little painful, but nothing so bad I can't walk on it. Truthfully, I'm relieved to be able to feel it. If it was numb I'd be worried about keeping my toes. It's bitter cold out here."

"This ain't fit weather for a man to venture out in, Conner. The winter's here to stay, and I think we are, too. And I'll tell you something else: I'm beginning to think we'll not find that gold. That old Colfax fellow could have hidden it anywhere."

"There's one hope yet," Mahaffery said as they trudged along, following the ever-dimming backtrack through the snow toward the pass. "He might have told his wife or daughter."

"Something you should know, Jordan. There was gunfire out in the valley," Broadgrass said. "Our men must have run into this Sam Underhill and the old man, whoever he is."

"I hope it went well for them. I can't afford to have those two alive, either. No way to know how close they've been to us, and how much they may have seen or heard."

"Jordan, none of this is going to matter if we don't find that gold."

"I know. That's why I want to get right to work on those Colfax women." Mahaffery stumbled right then, almost fell, and swore.

"You all right?"

"I'll make it. But let's hurry. The snow's coming down even faster now. But there's something I want to know from you first: why are you here? I told you to stay with Mongold and Yeager and guard our prisoners."

It was a delicate situation. How did one explain direct disobedience? Broadgrass usually relied on his quick mind to see him through such situations, but just now inspiration was lacking, and the answer he gave sounded feeble and false even to himself. "I can't explain it, Jordan. It was just a feeling I had that you were in trouble. I knew I had to come after you.''

Mahaffery looked at him without expression for a few moments. ''So you've turned mystic on me, have you?''

''I told you I couldn't explain it. But it's a good thing I followed my instinct, don't you think?''

''I believe I could have made it in without you.''

Broadgrass had no more to say, and the silence was not comfortable for him.

''You said there was gunfire in the valley. If anything, it seems to me you would have gone there, to lend a hand,'' Mahaffery said.

''I set out to do just that, Jordan. It was after I was outside and heading their way that the feeling struck me that you needed help.''

Mahaffery's stare was almost as cold as the wind. ''You shouldn't have left that lodge house to help either me or the others. You should have done what I told you and stayed where you were.''

''I suppose you're right.''

''You wouldn't have had it in mind to try to desert us, would you? Were you trying to see if there was still a chance you could make it out of the mountains?'' Mahaffery paused, then added, ''Or might you have had it in mind to take the gold for yourself, like Dehaven did, if I'd managed to put my hand on it?''

''That's a serious accusation, Jordan.''

''So it is.''

Broadgrass, lacking any good reply, let a haughty look, and silence, do his talking for him.

Mahaffery studied him for several moments. ''I suppose we should get back,'' he said.

For a couple of seconds a distinct possibility materialized in Broadgrass's mind. They were alone here, and Mahaffery was already injured. He could kill the man with a deft blow, a slash of a blade, a clubbing from a rifle butt. Kill him and leave him to be buried in the snow until spring. He could return to the lodge house and assert his own authority in Mahaffery's stead. The weaker minds and wills of the others of the outlaw band would in the end acquiesce to his own. He could determine for himself whether the Colfax women knew where the old man had hidden the gold.

But this he would not do. As hard a man as he was, and as many wickednesses as he had done, he found he couldn't actually kill Jordan Mahaffery.

"You're right," Broadgrass said. "We do need to get back, before we lose the way."

They trudged on together, side by side, neither willing to let the other fall behind and out of view. *Interesting situation,* Broadgrass thought. *We've now entered a level of mistrust we've never had between us until now. The first dose of poison . . . and just how strong it will grow, it's too early to tell.*

Maybe he should have killed Mahaffery after all. A mistrustful Mahaffery was an enemy more potentially ruthless than any man would want to deal with.

CHAPTER
TWENTY-FIVE

There was blood in the snow, so much of it that the Underhills could have tracked Legarde and Winters even without the big tracks that the two hurt and stumbling men left behind them. It was their guess that the gun-shot one was leaving most of the blood. Legarde's knife wound was not as likely to bleed so profusely, especially if he still had the blade stuck in him. Bushrod had already commented to Sam on the man's wisdom in not instantly pulling the blade out of himself. A blade in a man's flesh is bad, but not nearly as bad as one stuck in and pulled out again. The man who pulls the blade out again is the one who bleeds to death inside himself.

Neither man was surprised when they soon encountered a dark, unmoving form lying facedown in the snow. One set of tracks continued on past the point where Legarde had abandoned his wounded and weakening companion. ''One more of them dead, Pap,'' Sam said. ''We're making some progress, anyway.''

But when they reached the body, Bushrod rolled the man over, studied his face, put his head to his chest, and said, ''This man's still alive.''

Perry Winters's eyes fluttered open and he looked at the two Underhills. ''You've killed me,'' he said.

"Not yet," Bushrod replied. "You're still among the breathing of this world."

"I'm shot . . . bad. The bleeding's going to kill me. Tell me your names . . . I want to know who's ended my life."

"My name's Bushrod Underhill. Don't believe half of what you've heard about me. The other half, do believe it. This here's Sam, one of my boys. And what's your name, young man?"

"Winters . . . Perry Winters."

"Son, listen: you are bleeding bad, and indeed you may die. I suggest you spend some time talking to Jesus before it comes time for him to talk to you. But let me take a look at your wound. Sometimes not every wound is as bad as it seems."

Winters closed his eyes, maybe on purpose, maybe because he'd just passed out. Bush opened the man's coat, studied the blood clotting in his clothing, then lifted the shirt.

The bullet had entered Winters from behind, passing deeply through flesh and lodging just below the skin on his lower left torso. Bushrod reached for his knife, and remembered that it was no longer with him, but still riding in the shoulder of an outlaw who was probably now almost back to Texas Gulch. He took Perry Winters's knife instead.

A small incision was sufficient to expose the ball, which literally rolled out of the wound into Bushrod's hand. He held it up for Sam to see, then pocketed it. He'd never been one to waste lead that could be remelted into new ammunition.

"That one was enough of a clean-through wound that this young man may prove lucky," Bushrod said. "Sam, you got a clean rag on you?"

"Mostly clean."

"Is it snotty?"

"No."

"Then we'll consider it clean enough."

Sam produced the linen handkerchief, which Bushrod

poked into the wound. With his finger he probed it in as deep as it would go, then with the knife blade he pushed it even deeper. Winters didn't budge; indeed he was passed out, and a good thing for him, for what Bushrod was doing would have been excruciatingly painful if he'd been conscious. Bush rolled Winters slightly to the side, and found the bloodied tip of the handkerchief poking out of the other end of the tunneling wound. He grasped it and slowly pulled the entire rag through. It came out richly red with blood, but also carrying some grit and fragments of Winters's coat and shirt that had entered the wound with the ball.

"If he's lucky, that ought to clean him out good enough to let him heal without much festering," Bush said. "Want your rag back, Sam?"

Sam eyed the gory cloth. "Don't believe so."

Bush tossed it aside. "Come on, Sam. Help me hoist him."

"What are we going to do?"

"The only decent thing a man can do. We're going to build this fellow a shelter and a fire and give him a chance to live."

"Why should we care what becomes of him?"

Bushrod looked sharply at his son. "Vengeance is the Lord's, boy, not ours. The moment we come to treat the hurt and captive like they were nothing but dogs, then we've turned into nothing better than that rabble that's holding your people hostage in the mining camp. So give me a hand with him. And consider this, Sam: if we can bring this fellow around enough, we might be able to persuade him to tell us a little about what's going on in the camp. We can get to know our enemy a little better, and like old Tuckaseh used to tell me, 'An enemy known is an enemy half defeated.'"

"What about the other half?"

"With the other half, you just have to do the best you can."

*   *   *

Arianna Winkle sat with the pieces of her broken slate in her lap, trying to piece them back together like the segments of a puzzle. She'd been heartbroken to find the slate shattered, for she'd always loved the schoolwork she did under her mother's tutelage, and prized the slate dearly. She wondered who had broken it, and why, and also what the chalk lines and markings visible on some of the pieces would say when the slate was put together again.

Sorry as she was about the shattering of the slate, she was grateful that trying to put it together again at least gave her something to do. Right now she longed to lose herself, to leave this terrible place mentally, even if she could not physically. But it was hard to keep her mind on her task while poor old widowed America Colfax continued to wail beside the corpse of her dead husband.

"Arianna?"

She looked up and was surprised to see Letitia Colfax before her, smiling sadly. Arianna didn't know what to think; Letitia had never paid her any heed before.

"Hello," Arianna mumbled.

"Can I sit down and talk to you, Arianna?"

Arianna, feeling shy under the attention of someone who had always seemed in a different world than she, mumbled an invitation for Letitia to join her.

Letitia sat down and looked sorrowfully at the broken slate.

"I just want you to know it wasn't Papa who broke your slate," Letitia said earnestly. "It was the bad man, Mahaffery. Poor Papa was trying so hard to write down where the gold is, so that the bad men would go get it and then leave us alone, but he couldn't write. That man Mahaffery threw the slate against the wall. I'm sorry."

Arianna looked at the pieces in her lap. She hadn't even known Herbert Colfax had used her slate. That must mean it was he who put those strange and intriguing scribblings on it. "That's all right," she said. "It wasn't your fault. And it's just a slate."

"I hope you don't hate Papa for having hidden that gold," Letitia went on in her soft, rather high voice, which she kept barely above a whisper. "I'm sure he didn't mean to do anything wrong. He never told Mama and me about it."

Not knowing what she should say, Arianna just nodded.

Letitia was in the mood to talk about the father she'd lost. "Papa was a good man. He could be harsh and mean sometimes, the way he talked to people, but he was a good man."

Arianna put another piece of the slate back into place and studied the chalk marks on it. "Letitia, did you say your father was trying to write something when the Mahaffery man broke the slate?"

"Yes. He was trying to write out how to find the gold, so that all our lives could be saved. He was an unselfish and good man, Papa was."

Arianna studied another fragment, then pieced it into its proper position. "I don't think he was trying to write words, Letitia. It looks to me like—"

The door burst open and Mahaffery stormed in, gripping his wrist. Broadgrass was right behind him. Their entrance was so swift, unexpected, and loud that every soul in the place started, and some came to their feet. Arianna lost a few pieces of the slate off her lap onto the floor, and quickly bent to retrieve them. Her mother, who had been standing on the other side of the room, fighting a sense of imminent emotional and mental breakdown, came over and joined her, putting an arm protectively around Arianna's shoulder. Arianna huddled against her, eyeing Mahaffery with hatred, then decided she didn't want to sully her vision with the sight of the wicked man and turned to peer around the edge of the shutter and across the snowy valley.

Yeager seemed revitalized by the reappearance of his leader. "Did you find the gold, Jordan?"

"Hell, no," Mahaffery said. Then loudly, to all: "Somebody give me a strip of cloth. I got a hurt wrist needs binding."

Marica Bolton, ever bold and levelheaded, moved to fulfill the command. Everyone else sat stock-still, staring fearfully at Mahaffery.

"You didn't get the gold?" Mongold asked.

"That liar never knew where the gold was. Or if he did, didn't lead me to it. His intent was to get me out there and try to kill me, or maybe get me lost in the mountains." Mahaffery raised his voice to make sure everyone in the place heard him. "None of it matters anymore. Mr. Dillow is now a very dead man."

Marica Bolton went white and looked like she was struggling not to faint. Letitia Colfax buried her face in her hands and sobbed loudly. Jack Spillane muttered something bitterly. The spirit of gloom well known to every captive of Texas Gulch deepened greatly. Old Man Skinner began to sing his Judgment Day hymn again, but Joe, his son, gently quieted him. Arianna, meanwhile, suddenly had trouble drawing her breath. Mr. Dillow . . . dead?

"Dillow died because he forced me to kill him. He died because he was fool enough to believe that he could outwit me," Mahaffery said. "Don't any of you make that same mistake." He looked around. "Where the hell is that cloth for my wrist?"

Marica stepped up with a strip of cloth torn from the same sheet that covered Colfax's corpse. "Here . . ."

Mahaffery yanked the cloth from her hands, and threw it on the floor. "I'll have no dead man's shroud cloth around my wrist. Get me a clean cloth, woman!"

Marica turned away, searching. Finding nothing handy, she sat down and began to tear away a long strip at the hem of her own dress. Mongold stared at her exposed ankles as she performed the task.

Mahaffery took a pull from his flask and glared hatefully around the room. "Maybe the time has come to show you people just how serious I am about finding my gold. *My* gold! It was taken from *me*! And this is no game we're playing here! I want my damned *gold*!"

Art Bolton found his courage and stood. "Mr. Mahaffery, if it was in the power of any of us to give you your gold, then we'd do so. And we'd do all we could to help you leave this place so that we could try to live our lives again ... if our lives will ever be the same after witnessing such cruelty and wickedness as you've done. But we don't have your gold, sir. And if it's true that Herbert Colfax hid it, then none of us know where he did so."

"Maybe some of you do," Mahaffery said. "Maybe that fat, weeping daughter of his over there knows. Maybe his mindless widow over there, caressing his corpse, knows. Maybe we could find a way to jar her memory."

Bolton stepped forward impulsively, face reddening. "Mr. Mahaffery, there's not a man here who will stand by and see you do harm to two bereaved and innocent women! We'll die, to the last man, before we let that happen."

"Indeed you will." Mahaffery turned to Mongold. "Bert, lift your rifle and shoot Mr. Bolton through the head, if you please."

"What?" Mongold asked, not sure he'd heard rightly.

Just then Arianna jumped to her feet, spilling fragments of the slate from her lap onto the floor. She was staring out the window through the shutter crack. "It's Mr. Dillow!" she declared. "He's not dead!"

The timing of her shout was providential for Art Bolton, for it drew the attention of all and took the steam out of Mahaffery's execution order. Art Bolton sank back into his seat. His daughter, dress trailing the cloth strip still not quite fully torn from it, rushed to him, wrapped her arms around his shoulders, and wept.

"What'd you say, girl?" Mahaffery asked Arianna.

"It's Mr. Dillow! He's walking in from the valley! I can see him!"

"From the valley? Even if he was alive, he wouldn't come from that way."

Arianna, still peering out the window, seemed to deflate. She lowered her head. "It's not him," she said. "It's *not* him.'' She turned and sat down again, the broken slate pieces about her feet. She clung to her mother and cried.

The order to shoot Art Bolton forgotten in the distraction of this new development, Mongold had moved to the window and thrown the shutter open. His piggish eyes squinted hard. ''It's Legarde,'' he said. ''And he's staggering bad. I think he's hurt.''

''What about Reed and Perry?''

''They ain't with him. He's alone.''

CHAPTER TWENTY-SIX

Two minutes later, after Lennis Yeager had gone outside and helped the weak and stumbling Legarde make it into the lodge house, the people inside, outlaw and hostage alike, stared in shock and fascination at the bone-handled knife that still was lodged deeply in Legarde's back. The half-frozen man lay facedown on the puncheon floor, pallid and very weak, staring glassily across the floor at nothing. His back rose up and down, making the knife move.

Mahaffery, still gripping his injured wrist, squatted and examined the knife, but did not touch it.

"Who did this to you?" he asked Legarde.

"The older one . . . older, but strong. He's killed me."

"You ain't dead yet. The younger one was there, too?"

"Yes."

"Describe them both to me."

Legarde, as best he could, fumbled out a description, and many glances were exchanged in the lodge house, hostage to hostage.

Mahaffery rose slowly and looked around at the people, settling on Copp Nolen. "The younger one he described: Sam Underhill?"

"It sounds like Sam, yes."

"And the older man? Bushrod, I suppose."

"Well, sir . . . impossible though it is, the description sounds exactly like him."

"Bushrod Underhill," Mahaffery repeated. "Bushrod Underhill, who you all say you left in Texas, has now magically reappeared in a mountain valley in California in the dead of winter. Am I really expected to believe that?"

"Sir, I ain't saying it is him. I'm saying it sounds like him."

"There's something else," Joe Skinner said. Mahaffery turned to face him. "That knife sticking into your man, there . . . that's Bush Underhill's knife. The Boone knife."

Every eye focused on the knife again. "My word!" Copp Nolen said. "It *is* at that!"

"What's this 'Boone knife' talk?" Mahaffery asked.

Nolen replied, "That knife there belongs to Bushrod Underhill. It was a gift to him from Daniel Boone, when the pair of them both lived in Missouri, in the Femme Osage country, during Boone's last years."

"So now we've not only got Bushrod Underhill roaming the valley, having appeared from nowhere to kill my men, but we're invoking the ghost of Daniel Boone," Mahaffery said coldly. "Do you people take me for a fool?"

Skinner said, "I'm just telling you the facts: that knife is familiar to us all, and it most definitely is the knife that Daniel Boone gave to Bushrod Underhill. Bushrod has carried and used it proudly ever since."

Mahaffery cursed, drank from his flask again, and in doing so generated a spasm in his hurt wrist. He turned to Marica. "Where's that binding cloth? How slow can you be, woman?"

"Please . . . tell your man not to kill my father!"

"Hell, I'd done forgotten that. Mongold, let him be."

Mongold grunted and looked a little disappointed.

Marica reluctantly let go of her father and rose. When she'd eyed the outlaws long enough to persuade herself they really weren't going to shoot her father, she stooped and finished tearing the cloth strip from her skirt hem. Rising, she held it up for Mahaffery. The outlaw held out his injured wrist, and she bound it silently.

"Very good," he said, wriggling his fingers. "Much better. You see, Miss Bolton, how much more smoothly things go when you people are cooperative?"

"Help me, Jordan!" Legarde begged pitifully from the floor. "I need a doctor."

Mahaffery knelt beside his subordinate. "I'm mighty sorry, but there is no doctor. The closest thing to one, as I understand it, was the late Mr. Dillow."

"Then get me a preacher . . . I don't want to die, Jordan. I ain't ready. I ain't ready!"

"I'm mighty sorry for you, my friend."

Suddenly Legarde was bitter. "It's your fault, Jordan! I should never have joined you! I never should have come into these mountains! All you've done in bringing us up here is get us killed . . . Searl, Emmett, Ross, Perry, Reed . . . now me."

"Yes," Mahaffery said softly, the gentle tone failing to disguise a quick-rising anger. "Now you." He reached over, grasped the knife, and jerked it out of Legarde's back. Joe Legarde screamed, then fainted.

"You shouldn't have done that," Fleenor said. "He'll bleed inside the wound now."

"I know," Mahaffery said. "But it doesn't matter. There's nothing I could do for him, anyway."

For almost a minute, silence lingered in the lodge house. Bert Mongold and Lennis Yeager stared at their dying companion on the floor, and at their leader, who paced around, drinking again.

It was Yeager who spoke up first.

"Jordan . . . I want a word with you." He glanced about. "Private."

Mahaffery swept his eyes over the people. "Private. Not much chance of that." But he came closer to Yeager and ducked his head toward him, waiting. Mahaffery's eyes were very bloodshot.

"Say what you got to say."

"Now that I think about it, maybe Bert and Conner should hear this, too."

On the floor, Legarde made a strange, wheezing sound. His breathing became more ragged.

Mahaffery sighed. "All right." He called the others over, and waited for Yeager to begin.

"Jordan, we have a problem situation here."

"Indeed we do. It's called missing gold."

"No. Beyond that. Look at us, Jordan. Four of us left. Ten to begin with, and now just four! Dear God, who could have imagined such a thing would happen?"

"All for the best, if we find our gold," Mahaffery replied. "Fewer ways to split it means a greater amount for us all."

"I don't believe we're going to find that gold. I don't believe anybody knows where it is, and even if they did, finding it in this snowfall would be all but impossible."

"So maybe you should just leave, Lennis."

"You're drunk, Jordan. You've stayed half drunk, or more, ever since you started pulling on that flask of yours. You've always been a smart man, a good leader . . . but all at once you don't seem to think things through. Look at us . . . four men left alive, once poor Joe dies on the floor there."

As if in reply, Legarde made a guttural sound, another wheeze, and his color went from pallid to gray. His head flopped to one side, and a trace of blood appeared at the corner of his mouth and trickled to the floor.

"Four of us to guard these people! We've got the weapons, sure, but they've got the numbers. And we can't stay awake twenty-four hours a day. It's only a matter of time before they find an advantage and turn on us."

"You'll notice there's not as many of them left, either," Mahaffery replied. "Seven men left to our four, and one of their seven is older than Adam. And none are armed."

"There's also four women and a girl."

"You're worried about women?"

"I'm worried about all of them, worried about everything. A woman can stab or shoot as easy as a man can. Hell, we've already seen your own brother killed by a little boy!"

"If a man takes care of himself, he needn't be shot either by man, woman, or boy."

"That's a weak answer, Jordan, and you know it. Face the facts! How long do you think we can go on this way? We're snowed in up here. The odds of making it out of these mountains now are slender. What are we going to do? Spend the entire blasted winter standing guard over these people?"

"That's not what I had in mind," Mahaffery said.

"All right, so we shoot them all. We've still got the two out in the valley to contend with, this Sam Underhill and whoever the hell the other one is. And maybe a third one out there, too, if the one who killed Emmett is still alive. And those men *are* armed! We're in a true predicament here, Jordan."

"I want my gold," Mahaffery replied flatly. "I'm willing to take some risk for it."

"It's my gold, too. It's all of ours. And all of us have *already* taken risks for it. But I, for one, am not willing to die for it. It was a goodly amount of gold, but not worth this."

The discussion, rising toward an argument, went on, but the outlaws kept their voices too low for anyone nearby to hear the conversation.

Arianna Winkle, meanwhile, had pieced the slate fragments together on her lap again, and was studying Colfax's final scribblings very closely.

Jordan Mahaffery just then swore loudly, looked at Yeager with disgust, and pulled out his flask for another swallow, never breaking his gaze from Yeager's. He was clearly growing angry, but still remembered to keep his voice low. "All right, Lennis. You've let us know how un-happy and worried you are. So what do you suggest we do about it? You say we can't leave. You say we can't stand guard over these folks all winter. So what does that leave?"

"I don't know the answer. Maybe we ought to go ahead and shoot these folks and be done with it."

"I believe you may be right. But there's a way to go about that by which we can solve more than one of our problems at a time."

"What do you mean?"

"I mean I got an idea brewing as to how we can draw them two out of the valley and to us . . . and then we can rid ourselves of all our problems here at once. It might get a little bloody, a little ugly . . . but we have to do what we have to do."

Yeager swiped a dry tongue over his lower lip. "Say what you mean, Jordan."

"Later. For now, I want to know you trust me, and that I can count on you to do what has to be done when the time comes."

Yeager's eyes swept across the faces of Broadgrass and Mongold, trying to read their thoughts. "Well . . . I reckon we may as well go on as we are for now."

"Good man, Lennis. I knew you could be relied on. Meanwhile, we still have a chance at finding where the old man hid the gold. I ain't convinced he didn't tell his fat womenfolk there."

Mongold said, "Want me to work on them for you, Conner?"

"I think we'll make better progress with a kinder ap-proach to begin with," Mahaffery said.

"What should we do with Joe, and the other dead man?" Yeager asked.

"Pull Joe in the corner for now. As for old dead Colfax, leave him where he is. He's going to help us out a little later on, when it comes time to draw our unseen friends out of the valley."

CHAPTER
TWENTY-SEVEN

The shelter of poles and evergreen boughs had gone up quickly; both Bushrod and Sam had built hundreds much like it over the years, using whatever natural materials were at hand. With a fire blazing far enough away to ensure that the shelter didn't catch fire, but not so far away as to be useless for heat, they made Perry Winters as comfortable as possible.

"I'm dying," Winters said several times. "I can feel the dying going on inside me."

"You may yet live," Bushrod replied. "I truly believe you could go either way. But if you make up your mind you're going to die, you probably will."

"I don't understand why you're doing this for me," Winters said.

"Just because a man forces you to shoot him like a dog doesn't mean he *is* a dog," Bush said. "I'm sorry you chose to attack us, sorry I had to put a rifle ball through you. But what's done is done, and now we'll try to put you right again. And maybe, in return, you can tell us some things we need to know."

Winters, his voice wracked in pain, said, "About what's happening back in the mining camp, you mean."

"Precisely so," Bush said.

Winters thought it over only a moment or two. "Yes, I'll

tell you. Why the hell not? I owe Mahaffery nothing. I expect the bastard's already got the gold for himself and is
trying to run off with it. I hope he freezes to death. He
probably sent me out here to get killed. One less to share
his gold with.''

"This gold, tell us about it.''

Winters did so, describing to Bushrod and Sam his own
road into the gang of Jordan and Searl Mahaffery, two
worthless, criminal brothers who had only one advantage
between them, that being Jordan's keen criminal mind. Winters proved a good and succinct storyteller, describing how
the gang came together, how the elder Mahaffery concocted
a scheme that would get into their hands enough stolen bank
gold to keep them all in liquor and women for months, and
how they'd managed to pull it off with hardly a hitch.

But Frank Dehaven, perceived by all to be Mahaffery's
closest friend and ally in the gang—closer even than Mahaffery's own animalistic brother, Searl—had cheated them
all by taking the gold for himself. He'd fled, but they'd
found his trail and tracked him into the mountains, finally
determining that he was bound for the old Dutch Camp. He
described the encounter with the two children in the mountains, and from there on, the story became more familiar to
Bushrod and Sam.

But Winters knew many things they didn't yet know, and
told them freely, and with such an ease and fervor that both
Underhills could see that he was telling the truth. He presented every event and told of every death, including the
death of Colfax. That news shocked Sam. Colfax was older
than most of the miners, indeed, but Sam had never perceived him as a candidate for sudden death. As far as Sam
was concerned, Mahaffery was as responsible for Colfax's
passing as for the death of Julius Setser. It was probably the
mental distress of the ordeal that triggered Colfax's fatal
attack of apoplexy.

More intriguing than the news of Colfax's death, though,
was that of the deaths that had beset the Mahaffery gang

itself. Sam ticked them off on his fingers, calculating. Assuming that the one who made it back to camp with Bushrod's knife in his shoulders was dead or soon would be, there were only four outlaws left in Texas Gulch out of the original ten. So astonished by this was Sam that he insisted that Winters himself name off the dead, which he did, from Emmett Fish on through Joe Legarde, who had abandoned him bleeding in the snow.

"I hate him," Winters said of Legarde. "He left me to die, and dead I would be even now if you two hadn't helped me. But I hate Jordan Mahaffery all the more. I was a fool to come out here just because he told me to."

Winters was tired when he finished his talking. He'd spoken with intensity, expending energy that best would have been kept. The Underhills held silence and waited for him to go to sleep, which happened in seconds.

"Pap," Sam said, "only four of them left! Maybe not even that, if Mahaffery really has gone on after that gold."

"Do you really think Ben Dillow knows where the gold is? Would he have been the kind to scheme with Colfax to hide it?"

Sam recognized the question for what it was: rhetorical. Both he and Bushrod had known Ben Dillow for years, and knew the kind of man he was. He'd never have taken part in a scheme to hoard gold at the expense of his peers and neighbors. Sam shook his head. "No. He'd never have done it. Which means he lied to Mahaffery."

"And why would he do a thing like that?"

Sam could see only one answer. "He was probably trying to lead Mahaffery away from the camp, so he could kill him, or lose him in the wilderness."

"A thing possibly to be achieved only at great risk to his own life," Bushrod said. "And that *does* sound like the Ben Dillow I know."

Sam figured that his father was right. He wondered where Ben Dillow was at this moment. Had his scheme worked?

"Pap, Mahaffery might be dead, or gone for good, if Ben's succeeded."

"Yes. But we can't know, sitting out here."

"Then maybe it's time for us to quit sitting out here," Sam said.

Back at the lodge house, Mahaffery was seated on a stool, leaning forward with elbows on knees and an earnest expression on his face. On a bench before him were the Colfax women, both wide-eyed and very afraid despite Mahaffery's best efforts to look friendly and harmless.

"I want you to know my sincere sorrow over the death of your husband. Of all the men here, he was the finest and best, and I thought highly of him. I see the doubt in your face, but it's true. I'd have not seen harm come to him, I honestly assure you."

The women simply stared, their disbelief of this obvious liar almost humorously palpable.

Mahaffery, who had been working hard to make his fulsomeness believable, paused and went on. "It's out of respect for Mr. Colfax that I'm asking . . . not demanding, but *asking* . . . that you tell me where he hid the gold. Because I'm sure he told you something . . . he obviously cared deeply about both of you. He loved you so much—he wouldn't have left you in the dark."

The women blinked and struggled against tears and remained silent.

"Mrs. Colfax . . . please." Mahaffery reached out and touched her hand, and she drew it back like it was snake-bitten.

"He told me nothing."

Mahaffery swallowed again, harder. A vein made an appearance on his right temple.

"He must have told you."

"He didn't. I'm sorry. If he had, I'd tell you, so you'd take your cursed gold and go away!"

"I'm trying, ma'am, to be patient. To treat you as I know

Mr. Colfax would have wanted. I encourage you to co-operate with me. I promise, some of the gold will go to you—a very generous portion.'' He looked for a moment at the hostages. ''You might even save some lives through your cooperation.''

The Colfax women were none too keen mentally, but even they understood the subtle-yet-clear threat in Mahaffery's words.

''She's told you,'' Letitia spoke up, as loudly as her innate timidity would allow. ''He didn't tell us anything. If we knew, we'd tell you.''

Mahaffery's face lost its battle to remain tranquil-looking. He glared at Letitia. ''I don't have to continue to take such a kind approach, you know. I could have both of you telling me everything you've ever heard in your lives, in a matter of moments.'' He indicated Mongold with a toss of his head. ''I've got a man there who would be glad to help persuade you. He's already asked for the privilege.''

Letitia's eyes reddened, but she bravely held back tears. ''I really need to visit the outhouse,'' she murmured.

His hand shot out and closed around her wrist. ''You'll visit the outhouse when I tell you you can. You'll eat, you'll sleep, you'll sneeze and you'll cough when I tell you you can, and not before.''

''You're hurting me!''

''I haven't even *started* to hurt you, you ugly cow!'' He squeezed the wrist for a few seconds more, then relaxed, and when he did, his manner suddenly was gentle again. He patted Letitia's hand. Not as bold as her mother had been, she dared not pull it away.

''Now, let's begin again,'' he said. ''I want you both to tell me anything, anything at all that the late Mr. Colfax might have told you about where that gold might be.''

Over in the corner, while the interrogation of the Colfax women went on, Arianna stared at the slate, now fully pieced together on her lap. She studied the markings closely, frowning, her face an image of concentration.

Her mother, troubled by what was going on with the Colfax women and trying to block it out, sat down beside her. "What are you doing, darling?"

"Nothing," Arianna said. "I'm just looking at the slate."

"I heard that Mr. Colfax dropped that slate and broke it before he died," Leora said.

"No," Arianna replied, half distracted and now tracing the chalk markings on it with her finger. "No. It was the bad man who broke it. Letitia told me. He was mad because he couldn't read what Mr. Colfax had put on it."

Leora studied the seemingly random chalk marks. "Sad," she said. "He couldn't even make his letters. Apoplexy is a terrible thing."

"Yes," Arianna said. She brushed a finger across one of the slate shards, obliterating the mark on it. She repeated this action with the other pieces, until at last the slate fragments were erased, and the last attempted communication of Herbert Colfax to the world he was leaving disappeared for good.

Sam was sleeping deeply in the evergreen bough shelter, and what made him awaken he never knew. When he sat up, Bushrod was already awake, slumped over like a very weary man. Perry Winters lay on his back. Sam could barely make it all out by the tiny, faint beams of firelight that pierced through and danced in the gaps in the shelter walls.

"Pap?"

Bushrod lifted his head; his silhouetted form looked back at Sam. "Our friend here has died, son."

"What? But I thought the wound wasn't bad."

"I suppose it was worse than we thought."

"Pap . . . you sound like you're weeping."

Bush didn't answer at once. "I can't deny it, Sam."

"You're weeping for that dead outlaw?"

"No. Not for him. Though I suppose that every man has

something in him worth weeping for when it's forever gone.''

"If not him, then why?"

Again Bush paused. "I'll tell you soon enough. Not here. Not in the dark.''

"Why not?"

"Some things are easier said by daylight.''

Sam felt a cold terror inside him. He'd never seen his father this way, never heard him sound so irrational.

"Pap, I don't like you being this way.''

Bushrod sat up straighter, and when he spoke his voice was stronger. "You know, Sam, I've been thinking about what you said earlier. About how we can't just sit out here. The more this is allowed to drag on, the more dangerous it will become.''

"Pap, let's talk about what's bothering you.''

"Let's don't. Not now. Let's talk about what we need to do about our problem at Texas Gulch.''

"Pap, you listen to me. There's something that's been . . . *haunting* you. You're holding it back from me. You've been sitting up in the night, alone, weeping. Tell me what's wrong!''

"I'm going to lie down now, Sam. I'm weary. Tomorrow . . . we'll talk some more.''

"We'll talk now!''

"No. Not tonight. Tomorrow. I promise. We'll talk then.''

Sam swallowed his anger. Bushrod was not a man to be forced to do anything. "You'll tell me why you really came here?''

"I'll tell you whatever needs to be told. Now, pardon me while I drag our dead friend out of here.''

Sam watched as his father labored briefly, pulling the corpse of Perry Winters out into the snow. While he was outside, Bushrod replenished the fire, then reentered the shelter.

"Pap, I want to ask you something . . . do you think the

time's drawing near that they're going to commence killing hostages?''

"I do.''

"So what can we do?''

"I really wish I knew, Sam.''

CHAPTER TWENTY-EIGHT

Nothing is private for those living under the gun. In the thin, cloud-filtered winter sunlight of the morning, the hostages were lined up outside and allowed, one by one, to use the privy nearest the lodge house, while a grumpy-looking Mongold and a nervous Lennis Yeager stood guard over them.

Among them were the two Colfax women, scared and weary, but unharmed. Their interrogation by Mahaffery the evening before had ended without violence done to either. Mahaffery had simply lost steam somewhere along the way while the effects of exhaustion came on, accompanied by a growing comprehension that these simple women really didn't know where the gold was hidden.

The line of hostages stretched all the way back past the corner of the lodge house. Though usually Leora Winkle kept Arianna close beside her, today they were apart, Arianna holding back toward the rear of the line as it advanced.

When at last the necessities of life had been dealt with, the sullen people moved back inside the lodge house. A minute after they were back inside, Leora was engaged in a quiet, desperate search. Where was Arianna? Leora dared not draw attention to her daughter's absence out of fear it would bring harm to Arianna when she was found, but with her heart in her throat she desperately looked about the lodge house, peering into corners and even under benches.

At last she saw the note, tucked under the pieces of broken slate, which lay on the floor near the bench where Arianna usually sat. Leora sat down and spread her skirt to cover the slate, then casually reached down a few moments later and took the note, which was scribbled on a torn scrap of foolscap.

MAMA, IT WASN'T WORDS ON THE SLATE, IT WAS A PICTURE MAP. I'VE GONE TO GET THE GOLD SO THEY'LL LET US GO. I LOVE YOU. ARIANNA.

By this point, searching the pass seemed futile and foolish, but on impulse Mahaffery had put them at it again. The men of Texas Gulch had once more trudged to the crest of the gap, there to labor anew, moving old snow and fresh snow, looking for gold that no one believed would be found. Hadn't Colfax admitted he'd hidden it somewhere? Yet dig they did, because Mahaffery, seeing his hope of finding the gold through the Colfax women now withered away, clung to the faintest hope that maybe Colfax had never really hidden the gold at all, and it really *was* still waiting for them out there in the snow, behind a stone or under a drift that nobody had happened to touch yet.

The circle the diggers made was quite wide by now, and the few remaining outlaws were challenged to keep their eyes on all the men at once. Kish Fleenor, who had gradually worked his way to the farthest edge of the snow clearing, suddenly made a break and darted toward the trees.

Lennis Yeager raised his rifle and fired. Fleenor grunted, threw his hands out to the side and pitched facedown into the snow. He did not move.

Yeager was already half reloaded before the other men fully comprehended that Fleenor was dead.

It was more than Jack Gray, the kindhearted and gentle uncle of Arianna, could bear. A great and unfamiliar fury aroused him to unplanned action. He lunged with his shovel at Bert Mongold, knocking Mongold's rifle out of his hands. But Mongold, though big, was quick when he had to be. He whipped out his knife and had it between Gray's ribs even before Gray could draw back the shovel for a second swing. Once, twice, three times Mongold stabbed. The shovel fell from Gray's fingers and he collapsed into the snow.

Mongold recovered his rifle and gazed down at Gray, then at Fleenor. After a moment he shook his head at Yeager. "Another couple of them gone," he said. "Oh, well. At least we've evened our numbers a little more."

Yeager wasn't listening. His attention was raptly turned to the west, his eyes looking at something out in the wilds of the mountains.

"Bert, there's a man out there. Maybe two."

"What?"

"I saw it, just now. Very clear. A man, and beyond him, I'm almost sure, another one. But they're gone now."

"Maybe that Dillow fellow's alive after all."

"Then who's the second man?"

"Could be the pair from the valley, gone out into the mountains. We didn't guard the pass last night. They could have gone out of the valley without us knowing."

"I don't think it was them. I've seen those two, remember? This was somebody different."

The outlaws gazed into the wilderness several moments in silence.

"It's the law," Joe Skinner said. "The law has followed you murderers up here, and they'll hang you when they get their hands on you."

"Shut up," Yeager muttered.

New snowfall began, light at first, quickly increasing. Yeager looked into the gloom and shrugged. "Well, I *think* I saw somebody, anyway.

"Let's go back down, Bert," Yeager said. "We need to let Mahaffery know what's happened. He'll have heard the shooting. Besides, we're gaining nothing digging in this snow. The gold ain't here."

Skinner asked, "Will you at least let us carry down these two men you've murdered?"

"Bring them on, or leave them to lie. It's all the same to me," Yeager replied.

The shooting had indeed been heard down in the lodge house, so the people were already braced to learn of more losses by the time Yeager and Mongold returned, herding the corpse-bearing prisoners before them. The sight of the bodies of Jack Gray and Kish Fleenor, carried down and laid out side by side in the snow outside the lodge house, lowered a pall of despair over all the hostages. Tears and wails rose among the women, and Old Man Skinner.

Leora Winkle shed no tears. She was too numb, too afraid. She looked sadly at the body of her valiant brother and couldn't even find a word to quite fit the odd emotions that she felt. As worried as she was about Arianna, she was actually glad at that moment that her child was not here to see her uncle lying dead in the snow.

They all wondered how and why the two had been killed, but no one asked. Reasons were beginning not to matter. This place had begun as a refuge of hope for new life and wealth that was no further away than the spring. Now it was hell, and nothing made sense.

Jordan Mahaffery fell to talking to his men—Yeager and Mongold nervous-looking; Conner Broadgrass still calm and seemingly unworried—and Copp Nolen approached Leora during those moments of distraction.

"I'm so sorry, Leora," he said.

"Mr. Nolen, Arianna is gone."

"Gone?"

"Yes . . . this morning, when we went to privy, she was there, and then she wasn't. Back inside the lodge house, I found a note from her." She described briefly the matter of the broken slate and Colfax's final markings, misinterpreted, apparently, by all except Arianna. "She's gone to find the gold, Mr. Nolen, and plans to bring it back and give it to Mahaffery, and bring all this to an end.''

Copp Nolen turned a little pale. "I hope she doesn't do that.''

"Why?''

"Ben Dillow believes . . . *believed* . . . that as soon as Mahaffery gets his gold, he'll have all of us shot. We've witnessed murders done. We could harm him and his men with what we know.''

"Oh, no.''

"Leora, do you have any memory of Colfax's map? If I could figure it out, like Arianna apparently did, I could go where she must be going. I could stop her from bringing back that gold. And maybe I could hide her somewhere where she could survive, where she would be safe.''

"Does any such place exist here?''

"I don't know. I wish I did.''

Leora wracked her brain, trying to remember the map, but all she could conjure up in her mind were general, shapeless, fluctuating markings that had meant nothing to her because she was persuaded at the time that they were nothing but scribbles. "I can't recall any of it. But Arianna studied it closely . . . then erased it all.''

"She memorized it, I'm sure. She's always been a clever girl that way.''

Leora smiled and nodded, but there was pain in her eyes and it was obvious she was wondering if she would ever be privileged to see that clever girl again.

Nolen thought hard. "That gold, if truly hidden by Colfax, can't be far from the pass. He wouldn't have had the time, strength, or need to have carried it far. He must have stashed it somewhere right at hand. So that map must indicate someplace within easy reach.''

"But you've dug up the entire pass, more than once, and there's nothing.''

"There's plenty of rocks and trees and so on around there that haven't been explored. I suppose Mahaffery will put us onto that next, unless he decides to just say the devil with it all, kill us, and be done with it.''

Those words, too casually spoken, brought tears to Leora. ''I've got to find my daughter, Mr. Nolen.''

''Consider this, Leora: she may be better off having gotten away. If the worst happens, they won't be able to get her along with the rest of us.''

Leora thought this over. ''Yes. Yes. Mr. Nolen . . . Copp, do you mean it when you say you'd find her and take her to safety?''

''Of course I do . . . if I can.''

''I want you to try. Please.''

''Well . . . I will. But how can I get away? They watch us every moment.''

''Arianna did it. You can, too. You *must*.''

He remembered the sight of Kish Fleenor lying freshly killed in the snow. He'd tried to get away, too. But what could he say to this pleading mother?

''Very well, Leora . . . I'll do my best.''

''It's all I can ask, Mr. Nolen.''

CHAPTER
TWENTY-NINE
.

Afternoon came, and the men of Texas Gulch dug again. Absurd, forced labor, slavishly done in driving snow, under the eyes and guns of increasingly desperate men. When they'd descended to the lodge house the last time, bearing the corpses of Gray and Fleenor, and the news—which Mahaffery had discounted as a trick of the snow—of Yeager's sighting of two distant figures out in the mountains, all had been sure the digging at the pass was finished for good.

Mahaffery had surprised them all by sending them back again. But the more perceptive of the exhausted laborers realized that this might be good. As long as they were digging, Mahaffery still saw them as useful. As long as they were useful, they had a chance to live.

Copp Nolen worked with greater energy than he had since the ordeal began, because he was powered by purpose. He'd worked his way to the edge of the cleared expanse, and was shoveling snow into a great, long mound, all the while keeping his eye on the guards and the others, looking for his chance. He'd told none of the other men what he planned to do. Only Leora Winkle knew.

The mound was high enough for his purposes now, and situated just so as to allow him to use its cover to reach a long, deep ravine that ran down one of the many slopes just beyond this place. Nolen felt a nervous terror, but also a sense of anticipation and the cooperation of fate. The snow was a heavy screen, cutting visibility. The mound he had made, seemingly an unplanned by-product of digging snow, was plenty big enough to hide the maneuver he had planned, and the guards seemed lost in their own thoughts.

The snow grew even heavier after a few more minutes had passed. Gray sky hung low, laden with freezing moisture. It might snow for hours yet.

"Hell with this!" Nolen heard Mongold say. "There's no point in going on, Lennis. Let's get them back down to the lodge house."

Lennis Yeager drew closer to his fellow guard. "I agree. And Bert . . . I don't believe we should come up here and dig anymore. It's a waste of time, and I'm tired of freezing my backside off."

Unseen by either guard through the veil of snow, and equally out of view of his fellow hostages, Copp Nolen cast himself over the mound he'd made and sat flat in the snow. With his shovel he began sweeping snow over his legs and feet, hiding them. Then he lay down on his back and pulled more of it across his torso, covering everything but his face. Across his face he laid his shovel, resting it so that its contours gave him breathing space.

He couldn't lie here long without freezing, but he could make it long enough.

He heard the guards rounding up the men. *Please, God,* he silently prayed, *don't let them count the men. Make them careless right now.*

There was no count. He heard the men moving away from the clearing, back into the pass. Now, if only his own friends didn't unwittingly betray him by noticing and pointing out his absence, he should be in the clear.

He rose, breaking out of the hiding snow like a resurrected corpse. Brushing himself off, he entered the cleared area again, which was rapidly refilling, and trotted across it.

He'd made it. He was free of them, for now. Free to search for Arianna Winkle, and, God willing, to stop her from finding and taking that gold back to Texas Gulch and thereby, with the best of intentions, sealing the doom of every hostage there.

The returning outlaws found Mahaffery staring out the back window of the lodge house, the shutters wide open and wind and snow blowing through. Mahaffery didn't seem to care that it was, nor that the diggers had given up.

"Why you letting in the snow and wind, Jordan?" Yeager asked.

Mahaffery continued to stare out into the whiteness. "They're out there," he said. "Watching this place. Can you feel them watching? I'm even pretty sure I saw one of them, creeping out there along one of those ridges. They're there, no doubt about it. Watching us."

"You've been drinking again, Jordan," Yeager said. "Maybe you just imagined what you saw. Maybe it was a 'trick of the snow' on your eyes." There was no small amount of contempt in the way he threw back at Mahaffery the same bland attitude of discounting that Mahaffery had given his own claim of seeing men out in the mountains . . . though by now, Yeager himself was secretly beginning to wonder if Mahaffery might be right. The falling snow, combined with perpetual weariness, could present all kinds of false visions to a man.

Mahaffery shook his head, produced his flask, unstoppered it, and turned it upside down. Not a drop remained in it. "No, Lennis. I'm not drunk. It's been empty since last night." Mahaffery pulled the shutters closed and turned to Mongold. "I'm glad you men came back; I was about to send Conner up to fetch you. Bert, when the snow clears, I want you to haul out the late Mr. Colfax. With our friends out there within eyeshot, the time has come to put him to use."

"What are you going to do?" America Colfax asked.

"Something that should bring Sam Underhill and his old companion, whoever he is, trotting right down here to give themselves up. You should be proud of your husband, ma'am. He's about to become a hero.''

Arianna was sure she had waited too long. By now her absence was probably noted by the outlaws. Maybe they were tormenting her mother like that wicked man Mahaffery had tormented the poor Colfax women. Perhaps she'd made a mistake in escaping.

Hidden in the same broken-down old cabin from which Daniel Chase had taken the little pistol, she felt relatively safe and secure, though she was certainly cold. For several minutes she'd been weighing her options. She could return to the lodge house and hope she could sneak in without being noticed . . . something sly Daniel could have achieved, but not something she felt confident she could pull off. She could head back into the valley and try to find Sam Underhill, who she knew would protect and help her. But the weather was very bad, the valley piled deep in snow, and she was sure that Sam Underhill was probably deliberately making himself hard to find.

So she kept coming around to her original plan. She'd follow the map that Colfax had crudely drawn, and which she had memorized, find the gold, and bring it back. Then the bad men would have no reason to stay in Texas Gulch, and no one else would have to die.

Arianna didn't look forward to plunging out into the snow, but it made sense to do it now, before the accumulation grew much deeper. And with the snow cutting visibility, she could travel to the pass without fear of being seen from the lodge house.

Closing her eyes and saying a fast, sincere prayer, she slipped out of the cabin and headed for the pass.

Cold, tense, and uncertain, Bushrod and Sam Underhill crouched on the ridgetop, watching the silent tableau of Texas Gulch through the snowfall.

''What should we do, Pap?'' Sam said at last. ''Go down

there? Offer ourselves in place of the people they hold?''

''Don't think that would work,'' Bush said. ''These people are held hostage mostly for what they know, and have seen. Mahaffery would have nothing to gain by letting them go whether he has us or not.''

''Then what can we do?''

Bushrod said nothing.

''Pap?''

''Sam . . . listen to me. I need to tell you about something now. Something that happened back in Texas. Sam, Durham's sons are dead.''

Sam turned to look at his father, puzzled. Bushrod would not look back at him, keeping his eyes fixed on Texas Gulch. ''Dead, Pap?''

''Yes.''

''Danny and Zeke?''

A silent nod.

''Dear Lord, Pap . . . how?''

''It's my fault, son. My fault.''

Now it was coming, Sam realized. The truth at last about what was haunting his father, about what had driven him all the way here from Texas to the Sierras in the wintertime.

''Tell me what happened.''

Bushrod sighed slowly and seemed to descend more deeply into sorrow before Sam's eyes. ''It was . . . Danny. You know how the boy is . . . how he was. Always gentle, never much for hunting, roaming, fishing . . . all the things I had you fellows doing since you were small.''

Sam nodded. Indeed the elder son of Durham and Chasida Underhill had been far from a typical young male Underhill: artistic, kind, prone to be solemn, deeply sympathetic to others and to animals, not prone to horseplay and rowdiness. Sam had watched the boy weep once over a string of fish his father had caught and brought home for supper. Weeping over fish, because he felt sorry for them! Sam had found it appalling, and worried about the lad. Danny's little brother, Zeke, on the other hand, was more the typical Underhill, always eager for some jaunt and adventure with his father or uncles or grandfather.

Bushrod went on. "I'd taken the boys hunting. Danny hadn't wanted to come...but I made him. Told him it would be good for him to come along, that he needed to become a better hunter. Make more of a man out of him. All that kind of thing. God. God forgive me. I wish I hadn't done that."

"How'd it happen, Pap?"

"Very simple, as such things often are. I didn't see the accident itself, so I've had to piece the facts of it together. As best we ever figured, it appears that Danny must have laid his rifle up against a tree, with the lock cocked back. Very, very foolish mistake if he did it, going against everything he'd been taught. But guns and so on were always alien things to Danny, you know. The lessons never took. Anyway, he must have bumped his own rifle, knocked it over. However it happened, it fired...little Zeke never even felt the ball hit him, I'm sure. It entered the back of his head and passed out through his forehead."

"Dear Lord." Sam lowered his head and blinked away tears.

"I was away from camp for a few minutes, down near the river with the horses. I heard the shot...then I heard Danny wailing. The most awful kind of sound...I ran. But by the time I'd gotten there, Danny had reloaded his rifle. No awkwardness about it this time. A perfect, fast job of it ...and before I could reach him to stop him, he'd put the muzzle under his chin, tears streaming down his face...he triggered it with his toe. Punishing himself for having killed his own brother...punishing himself, maybe, for being different, and gentler, and disappointing to his old fool of a grandfather..." Bushrod stopped talking, lowered his head, and sobbed like a child.

Sam had nothing to say. He crouched there, numb and astonished and horrified.

"Pap...it wasn't your fault."

"Yes it was. Yes it was. Those boys were in my care. Those boys were mine to protect . . . and I protected neither of them. Poor Danny. Poor Zeke. Oh, God, if only I could go back. If only I'd not gone down to the river . . . if only I'd thought to make sure Danny hadn't left his rifle cocked like he was so prone to do . . . if only I hadn't forced him to come along to begin with.''

"Pap, none of this was planned. It was an accident.''

"That's what Durham told me. And Chasida. As terrible as it was for them, they never blamed me.'' Bush paused, catching his breath. "And that almost makes it worse. I wish they would blame me. I wish they'd curse me and strike me and tell me what a sad and sorry old fool and failure I am, for letting such a thing happen to my own grandsons.'' Bush cried more, not speaking for a full minute. Then he regained his composure a little, wiping at his face with the heel of his right hand. "Sam, I wish I'd spent more time with Danny, just talking to him. Not about the things I thought he should be interested in, but about what *he* wanted to talk about. I wish I'd just let Danny be Danny. I wish I'd embraced him more, and harped on him less. I wish . . .''

"Hush, Pap. There's no going back, and nothing gained by horsewhipping yourself.''

"Maybe I've already lived too long, Sam. Maybe this hearty and hale old body of mine has done too good a job and kept me around longer than should be.''

"You've told me yourself many a time, Pap: there's no wisdom in questioning the ways and will of God. The things that happen that are beyond us are not for us to understand. We just have to accept what comes. You recall telling me that?''

"Yes.'' Bush actually grinned, feebly. "I'm surprised to hear that it stayed with you, though.''

"It did. But I don't think it's stayed with you. You've forgotten your own lesson.''

"I have, I guess.'' Bush swallowed, hard. "But don't think I haven't tried to persuade myself many a time that

I'm not at fault. I don't like bearing this weight of guilt. But I find I can't shrug it off. It just lingers, like a heavy stone on my shoulders.''

"Why'd you come here, Pap?"

"Part of it was like I said. I'd pined to see you. But the deepest reason, I suppose, is that I was running away. I had to get away from Texas, and all the others . . . had to see if I could find a way to shed this guilt. But it's stayed with me. All the way here, all through the time I spent roaming and asking questions and tracking you down, that burden has stayed on my shoulders, and it stays there still.''

There were things Sam could have said, predictable and wise and well-intentioned, even true, but he knew they would do no good. His father felt just as Sam himself would have felt had their circumstances been reversed. No amount of words would drive away the demon that tormented Bushrod Underhill right now. Sam could only reach over and pat his father's shoulder, silently, hurting for him, praying for him.

Bush dabbed away the last of his tears, took a long, slow breath, and gazed out across the white expanse at Texas Gulch.

"Sam, what did you say the name of that orphan boy was, the one our dead friend back there said was killed in the cave?"

"Daniel. Daniel Chase."

"Daniel. Just like Danny's name."

"That's right."

There was a long silence, then Sam spoke again. "Pap, let's don't let anyone else die. Let's end this thing . . . somehow."

"Yes," Bush said. "Let's do."

At that moment, a voice echoed from Texas Gulch out across the valley. "Underhill! Sam Underhill! I know you're there, for I've caught sight of you twice! Draw near, Mr. Underhill . . . my name's Mahaffery, and there's something going to happen that you'll want to see!"

CHAPTER THIRTY

The Underhills looked at one another. This was an unexpected development.

"Should I reply to him?" Sam asked.

"Don't know," Bushrod said. "Obviously he knows we're here, and who you are. I suppose there's no way any of them can know about me . . . about who I am, anyhow."

"Come on, Pap. Let's get closer."

The two Underhills rose and scrambled down the ridge, sure they were being watched. Maybe watched over the sights of rifles . . . though at this range that wasn't much of a worry. They reached a ridge closer to the mining camp and dropped again to a crouch. Bushrod handed his spyglass to Sam, who opened it and put it against his eye.

"Well! Howdy, there!" Mahaffery's voice called. Sam looked for the man but couldn't see him . . . though there was one open window at the back of the lodge house, and a figure barely hidden in its interior shadow. Probably Mahaffery. "Good to know you a little better . . . that's the clearest view of you I've had!"

Sam called back. "What do you want?"

"Ah! Now I hear your voice. Good! No point in us playing foolish games with one another. What do I want? What I want, Sam—May I call you Sam?—is to show you and your old friend there what comes of interfering with our plans and killing our men. I hope you can see clearly what we're doing. Let me direct your attention to the clear area up past the north end of this building.''

Sam was already looking there. In that clearing stood Bert Mongold, holding up the slumping form of the late Herbert Colfax.

Sam could already guess what was coming.

''That's Mr. Bert Mongold you see there, with your own friend Colfax in his arms. Mr. Colfax has been knocked cold—we're merciful men, to a point. But only to a point. Please observe.''

Mongold let Colfax's body fall, drew a pistol, and fired a ball through Colfax's head.

Sam winced, but when he glanced over at his father, he rolled his eyes.

''That, Mr. Underhill, was to help even the score a little for what you and your old man friend there have done. And let me tell you that more of your friends will be shot, just as Colfax was, unless both of you turn yourselves over to me, right now.''

Sam cupped his hands around his mouth. ''Sorry, Mahaffery! Your partner Winters sang like a songbird before he died. We know Colfax was already dead!''

Bush made a face of pain. ''I sure wish you hadn't done that, Sam.''

Sam reddened as he realized his mistake. ''Oh, no,'' he said softly. ''I hope he doesn't . . .'' Sam trailed off.

What he hoped Mahaffery wouldn't do was in fact just what Mahaffery did.

''Ah, too wise for us to fool, are you?'' Mahaffery yelled. ''You want a fish still wiggling, we can provide that.''

With a growing feeling of dread, Sam and Bush watched in silence as Mongold disappeared back into the lodge house. A few moments passed, and he came out again, his rifle pressed into the small of the back of Leora Winkle.

''Oh, no . . .'' Sam murmured, and his stomach did a turn that made him fearful he'd heave on the spot.

"See her?" Mahaffery yelled from his place of hiding. "Think *this* one's already dead? Don't believe so! But she will be, in one minute, unless you show yourselves and commence to approach us . . . weapons above your heads."

Bush was evaluating the distance. "Sam, if we overload my rifle, and if I can aim high and calculate the drop of the ball just right, there's a chance I might be able to hit that brute. I recall a time when Boone told me about the big siege of Boonesboro, when there was an Indian fellow out waggling his rump at the fort, and one of the men there put an extra charge in his rifle, and aimed high, and—"

"No, Pap," Sam said. "No. We can't risk it. You might miss, or you might hit her instead of him. We've got to go in."

Bush paused. "I reckon we do."

"Time's wasting!" Mahaffery yelled. "Are you coming, or do we stain the snow with this woman's brains?"

Sam stood, rifle high. "Don't shoot her!" he yelled. "We're coming."

"Where's the other one?" Mahaffery yelled back.

Bush stood in silent answer.

"Well! Cooperation . . . that's what I like to see!" Mahaffery said. "Advance, gentlemen—and no tricks. The moment I see anything at all I don't like, that's the moment this woman dies."

Out beyond the pass, half frozen but still determined, Arianna Winkle heard the distant, thin sound of the shot that took off the top of Colfax's head, but she didn't know what to make of it. She prayed no one else had died. And she worried about her mother . . . unaccountably, she felt just then that something was wrong. The impulse to go back and investigate was strong.

But Arianna resisted it. It seemed to her that the quickest way to end this crisis was to find the gold and get it into Mahaffery's hands. Then it all would be over, and she and her mother could go about the business of living their lives.

The snow had lightened a little, and Arianna took advantage of the improved visibility to look around and coordinate the landscape she saw with her memory of Colfax's map. Once she'd comprehended what the man was trying to do, and had connected a few of his crude marks with certain landmarks in this area just beyond the pass, it had seemed fairly simple to get her bearings. With everything covered in heavy snow, however, it was harder to be sure. She felt a compulsion to hurry, but made herself work slowly, and think carefully.

After a few moments she nodded and made for the place the map—if she read it rightly—had indicated the gold would be found. There'd been an X mark on that area of Colfax's map, anyway, and in every story Arianna had read, an X on a map always marked a treasure or something else important.

She advanced, noticing with some alarm how numb her feet were. She wriggled her toes, or tried to, and was distressed to find she couldn't be sure whether she'd succeeded. For more reasons than one she needed to find that gold and get back to where it was warm and safe . . . well, warm, anyway.

She reached the base of a knoll. One not too steep, and easy to climb most times. But she'd never tackled it in the snow before. Still, she was sure she could make it up, and that even old Mr. Colfax could have made it up this slope that night he hid the gold. There hadn't been as much snow at that point. Besides, he'd have been very determined.

She began to climb, examining the ground in front of her before planting any steps. Her progress was slow, and she slipped when she was halfway up and tumbled back down again.

On the second try she was even more careful, with much respect for the course. She succeeded this time, making the top of the knoll, where she discovered a small, flat plateau, covered with snow, as she'd expected, but with an additional aspect that she hadn't.

The snow was heavily disturbed. Someone had dug here very recently. Arianna examined the plowed-up snow with a frown, then noticed the tracks.

Small tracks. A man's tracks, filled in somewhat by the falling snow? Maybe . . . but she didn't think so. Her impression was that these tracks had never been made by a man's foot.

She walked through the disturbed area of the snow, then began to follow the smallish tracks across the remainder of the knoll and down the other side. The slope there was more shallow, and probably, she realized, the route that Colfax had taken up, rather than the steeper one she had climbed. She watched the tracks, following closely, hurrying faster the farther she went.

Her heart was beating very fast, and she wasn't noticing the cold so much.

The slope grew even more shallow, the ground finally leveling entirely. The tracks became fresher, and Arianna moved even faster, the hope that was rising in her heightening.

The snow began to fall hard again, the terrain growing rougher. Arianna slowed, clambering over a few boulders, finding the tracks harder to follow now. The worsening weather made her feel compelled to rush, fearing the trail would be obliterated. Though she wore three layers of heavy trousers under her dress—a necessity in these wintry mountains—her legs were growing extremely cold, and the snow was drifting higher the farther she went. She climbed another stone, entered a small pass between two large, jagged stones . . .

He was in front of her all at once, pistol leveled in her face. She gasped and stepped back. The pistol lowered slowly, and he looked at her in utter surprise.

"Arianna . . . I didn't know it was—"

Before he could finish his sentence, Daniel Chase received the kiss he'd long dreamed of.

"You're alive!" she said. "They said you were dead, Daniel! They said you were killed!"

He shook his head solemnly, looking at her. "No. They didn't even get close to killing me. But I killed one of them. He came in the cave after me, and I shot him. He floated out again on the stream. The other one talked to me, and said he was going to leave me alone. He said he'd leave food . . . and he did."

Arianna was hardly paying attention. She was overwhelmed with joy. In this time of loss and dying, it was heartening indeed to see one who was thought dead actually alive, and seemingly well.

"Where have you lived, Daniel?"

"I have a place. Warm and dry and safe. And Arianna . . . I have the gold. I've been moving it."

"It was on the flat place, back there . . . on top of the hill?"

"Yes. How did you know?"

"Mr. Colfax put it there. He made a map, but nobody understood it but me. Oh, Daniel, I'm so glad you're alive! We can end it all now, Daniel. We can take the gold back and give it to the wicked men, and they'll leave!"

Daniel firmly shook his head. "No, Arianna. That's the last thing that we should do. If they get their gold, they'll kill everyone. I've been thinking about it. We could get them in trouble, all of us, just because of the things we've seen them do. The only reason they've left anyone alive at all so far is that they need someone to do their searching, and to use them as hostages and such if it comes down to it."

Arianna frowned, mulling Daniel's point and finding in it a grim kind of sense. "But what should we do, then?"

"Take the gold with us, like I've been doing. Hide it where they'll never find it. And then . . . I don't know. I don't know. We'll do . . . something."

"Daniel, my mother is still back there with them. She'll worry about me."

"You can't go back there, Arianna. You're lucky to have gotten away, and your mother wouldn't want you to go back. I can keep you safe. I can take you where they'll never find you."

Arianna was torn. She stood there, every kind of emotion coursing through her mind. "My mother, Daniel . . ."

"We'll think of something, Arianna. We'll find a way to help her."

Arianna hesitated.

"I need you to help me look for the rest of the gold, anyway. I think I may have even dropped some of it."

She considered only a few seconds more, then nodded. "All right," she said. "I'll help you."

CHAPTER
THIRTY-ONE

Copp Nolen followed the tracks he'd just found. He was bent almost double, squinting to see in the driving snowfall. Two sets of prints, both left by small-footed persons. One, he was sure, must be Arianna's. But who would have left the others?

One set of tracks was fresher than the other, and whoever left the more recent set certainly appeared to be following the first.

The wind howled and stung coldly against Nolen's face. His coat seemed very inadequate at the moment, and despite the outlaws, the danger, the misery of confinement, at the moment he longed for the warm lodge house. He decided he'd best find Arianna as quickly as possible.

Advancing several more yards, Nolen stopped suddenly and wheeled, facing the wilderness to the west. Squinting, he looked and listened, seeking whatever it was that had whispered at the edges of his awareness just now. Something out there . . . someone.

He saw them then. Two men, heavily bundled. Nearly shapeless figures trudging toward him through the snow. They were armed.

Nolen panicked. Had Mahaffery sent men after him? One of those advancing men was big—Mongold, maybe.

He knew they'd kill him if they caught him. Nolen turned and began to run, or to try to run.

He progressed a dozen yards far too slowly to suit him, and glanced behind him in a panic.

They were coming after him.

Mahaffery strode back and forth, looking with great interest at his two newest prisoners, who stood side by side in the very middle of the lodge house. The outlaw chief wore a half grin, and looked the pair up and down, circling them completely, then stopping to stare Sam Underhill in the face.

"Well, Mr. Underhill, pleased to meet you in person at last. You've been a thorn in my side, sir."

Sam stared at him, silent, then turned his eyes and stared past him, refusing even to acknowledge the outlaw. Mahaffery gave a small, disdainful chuckle, and took a step over to face Bushrod.

"And you, sir . . . judging from the name I heard called by these people when you entered just now, I dare to say that I'm actually facing the famous Bushrod Underhill. Is it true?"

"Back up, mister, if you would. Your breath has a stench worthy of a privy hole."

The hostages laughed, softly, and Mahaffery's left cheek twitched. "Well, Mr. Underhill, I'm sorry about that. I'm afraid you'll just have to endure it."

"Adversity breeds strength," Bushrod said. His eyes remained locked with Mahaffery's.

"You really are Bushrod Underhill?"

"The same."

"I've been told you were still in Texas. How'd you come to be in this valley?"

"Ever heard of something called traveling?"

"But how'd you get in? We had that pass guarded at the start, then all at once, there you were, already in the valley."

"I rode the lightning in from the Brazos country. It's how I travel when I'm in no hurry."

"Believe your own legends, do you, Bushrod?"

"Believe them? Son, I live them."

Mahaffery didn't seem to know what to make of this man. "How old are you, anyhow?"

"Old as the mountains, son. Old as the sky."

"I doubt that. But you're up there in years. Got to be. Yet you're spry and strong."

"My good health comes from the thinking of only pure thoughts and the frequent killing of outlaw rubbish."

Mahaffery laughed. "Your killing days are through, old man."

"You never know."

Mahaffery stuck his face close to Bushrod's. "Oh, I know. I know. You're in *my* hands now, Underhill, and all that sharp-tongue talk of yours will do you no good."

"Your breath, son. Your breath."

Mahaffery pulled back his fist and struck Bushrod hard on the side of the face. But the old man pulled back and turned his head just in time to make the blow glance, and it did much less damage than it would have otherwise. Though Bushrod was rocked on his feet, he didn't fall.

Still, Mahaffery seemed pleased by what he'd done. "You see that, Bert? I just hit Bushrod Underhill himself!" He laughed.

Lennis Yeager stepped forward. "Hell with this!" he said. "What's the point of all this, Jordan? So now we've got two more hostages. Now we've got our phantoms out of the valley. So what? We're still here, still don't have our gold, and the snow's still falling! We're still deep in trouble, still poor as before we started, and you're crowing about having hit Bushrod Underhill! What the hell does it matter?"

Mahaffery, for once, had no answer. He glared at Yeager, lips moving vaguely but no words coming out.

Mongold cleared his throat. "I think he's right, Jordan. We're not going to find that gold. I say let's line these people up and shoot them dead, then get out of these mountains the first time the weather breaks.''

The Colfax women sobbed aloud. The other hostages glanced in terror at one another. The Underhills stood as before, no change in their expressions.

''Think about it, Jordan,'' Mongold went on. ''If that old man made it up these mountains, we can surely make it down again.''

''Shut up!'' Mahaffery said. ''We'll do what has to be done when the right time comes. For now, I've got some more questions for this pair.''

''Hell, they won't answer you,'' Yeager muttered.

Mahaffery ignored him. ''Tell me, Underhills, is that fellow—What's his name? Linfoot, I think—is he still alive?''

''Alive and kicking, and raising an army of savages out there to come in here and scalp you alive,'' Bushrod replied.

Mahaffery drew back to strike the frontiersman again. Sam said sharply, ''Don't do that! I'll answer your questions even if my father won't.''

''Well! Smart man. What about Linfoot, then?''

''Hiram Linfoot is dead. He was killed by one of your men who shot him dead with a rifle. I killed the rifleman with a prospector's pick through the skull. Your other man, fat boy over yonder, didn't linger around long after he found the body. Got a little nervous, I guess.''

''But Linfoot *is* dead.''

''Yes. I hid his corpse with my own hands.''

Mahaffery seemed pleased to hear that. One less potential witness against him to worry about. It wasn't hard for Sam to read the direction of Mahaffery's thoughts. He was seeing before him an opportunity to end every threat against him and his men with a few quick blasts of powder and shot.

''Jordan.'' The speaker was Broadgrass, who had been standing silent for so long that the sound of his voice was mildly startling. ''Where's the little girl? And the man named Nolen?''

Mahaffery looked around, frowning. "What the hell . . . ?"

Mongold and Yeager, equally surprised, swore in unison. Mahaffery wheeled to face Broadgrass. "How long have you been noticing them gone?"

"Just now noticed it." The bland way he said it made the truth of the statement seem doubtful.

"We've got to find them," Mahaffery said. "Bert, you and Lennis, get out there and—"

"No!" Yeager shouted. "Hell, no! I'm sick of this, Jordan! You strut around here like some little piece of royalty, sending us out to do this and that, to get shot and froze and every other kind of thing . . . I'll not do it anymore! This has to stop!"

Mahaffery yanked out his pistol and shoved it into Yeager's face. "Lennis, you're mighty nigh to making yourself useless."

Mongold stepped up. "Don't shoot him, Jordan. Please don't. I'll go look for them. At the very least I can see if there's tracks up toward the pass."

"The way this snow is falling, tracks may already be gone," Broadgrass said.

Mahaffery ignored Broadgrass, and looked at Mongold like a man admiring a faithful dog. "Good man, Bert. I need more like you."

"Don't go, Bert," Yeager said. "This man has gotten too many of us killed. It's time we start directing ourselves instead of letting him shove us around."

"Lennis," Mongold replied, "the reason we can't do that is the very thing you said: There's too few of us left. We can't go dividing up amongst ourselves now."

Yeager glowered and said no more. Broadgrass seemed privately amused, a man to the side of it all, watching but not acting as if he were really a part of it all. It was almost always that way with Conner Broadgrass.

*   *   *

Mahaffery wouldn't allow the Underhills to sit. They were forced to stand as they were, side by side, trophies on display in the center of the room, while Mahaffery paced about, clearly missing his liquor, and cursed and muttered under his breath. Broadgrass was smoking and looking bored, and Lennis Yeager looked like he could either explode or wilt away at any moment.

The sound of relatively distant rifle fire made everyone in the place snap to attention. Mahaffery swore softly and cocked his head, listening. The gunfire came from the vicinity of the pass.

He stomped over and shoved his face almost against Bushrod's. "Who'd you bring with you, old man? Who's up there?"

"I didn't bring a living soul with me. And your breath, son . . . smells to me like you ought to check for a rotten tooth or two."

Mahaffery hit Bushrod again, but once more the old man was able to deflect the worst of it with a deft turn of the head.

"I'm going to kill you, old man. Kill you with my own hands, and enjoy it immensely," Mahaffery said. "Maybe they'll put me in one of those almanacs. 'The Man Who Killed Bushrod Underhill.' I wouldn't mind that at all."

"Somebody's drawing near," Yeager said abruptly.

Broadgrass was looking out a window. "It's Mongold. Running back down."

"Anybody on his tail?"

"No. He's alone. Looks scared to death."

When the hefty outlaw burst into the room he was gasping like his heart and lungs were racing to see which would explode first. He turned a pallid face to Mahaffery. "Men . . . up there . . . tried to . . . take me . . ."

"Men? How many?"

"Two, maybe . . . three . . . got to catch . . . my breath . . ."

"Tried to take you—you mean they tried to kill you?"

"I believe they . . . wanted me hostage . . . but I fired at them . . . got away."

Mahaffery aimed a finger at Bushrod. "You're a lying old devil, and you'll die for it. I don't expect you're going to be sensible and tell me who you've brought with you."

"I believe maybe it was Jesus and the Twelve Disciples."

While Bushrod was busy being difficult, Sam was wondering quite seriously who *was* up at the pass. Maybe whoever it was hadn't followed Bushrod here, but had trailed the outlaws themselves. He had visions of bands of armed officers of the law closing in on that snowy pass, ready to move in and rescue the entrapped citizens of Texas Gulch.

Mahaffery had had enough of Bushrod's sarcastic tongue. He pulled his pistol out. For a terrible moment Sam was sure his father was about to be shot. But Mahaffery pulled back the pistol to club him instead. The first swing hit Bush in the temple and knocked him down on one knee, half stunned. The pistol rose again, the second blow aimed at Bushrod's forehead.

"No!" Sam bellowed, and threw himself between Mahaffery and his father. He groped for Mahaffery's arm, but the outlaw was fast, and diverted the direction of his swing. The pistol struck Sam on the jaw. He grunted in pain. Mahaffery struck him on the head with the follow-up blow, and Sam collapsed. As Bushrod, disoriented, reached out and tried to save the son who moments before had been trying to save him, the third blow hit Sam squarely on the top of the head, breaking the scalp to the bone. Sam pitched to one side, bleeding and unconscious.

Bushrod came to his feet, roaring in fury, and reached for Mahaffery's neck. Mahaffery dodged to the side. Bush would have caught him easily on a better day, but the blow to the temple still had him reeling. He staggered to the side, and Mahaffery managed to hit him a second time, on the back of the head. Bushrod fell to his hands and knees, his head hurt and spinning.

Conner Broadgrass strode up quickly, reached across

Bushrod, and grabbed the arm in which Mahaffery held the pistol.

"Jordan, I'm sorry, but you've just grown too darned aggravating." And with a skillful twist of the hand, he made Mahaffery howl in pain and let go of the pistol. Broadgrass caught it with his free left hand, let go of Mahaffery, and flipped the pistol through the air, catching it again with his right hand. He cocked it, stuck the pistol against the confused Mahaffery's chest, and shot him at point-blank range.

Mahaffery jerked and grunted, though the sound of the roar masked the sound he made. He staggered back, looking in shock at Broadgrass, then down at the bleeding hole in his chest.

"You've shot me!" he said, sounding meek and a lot like his late brother, Searl, in the latter's more childish moments.

"Yes, and I'm going to do it again," Broadgrass said. He dropped the expended pistol, drew his own from his belt, aimed at Mahaffery again, and put a second hole in the already dying outlaw's chest.

Mahaffery sighed slowly and sank to the floor, dying on nearly the same spot where Colfax had breathed his last.

Broadgrass calmly began reloading his pistol. "Sorry I had to do that, folks," he said to the group. "But I swear, I was beginning to grow mighty tired of that man."

CHAPTER
THIRTY-TWO

Mongold and Yeager walked slowly, like dead men who'd been not quite fully reanimated, and gaped at the body of their former leader. Yeager lifted his face slowly and stared at Broadgrass, who calmly finished loading his pistol, stuck it back in his belt, then began reloading Mahaffery's.

Old Man Skinner began singing about Judgment Day again.

"You killed him!" Yeager said. "You killed Jordan!"

"Yep. And ain't it just so quiet and peaceful now?"

"Why the hell did you do it?"

"He deserved it. That man was going to do a Dehaven on us, Lennis. From the moment he left with that Dillow fellow, alone, I knew he wasn't to be trusted. He planned to take that gold for himself, and leave us up here. He'd have gotten back down that mountain again even if he'd had to roll in a snowball."

It took Yeager a moment to digest all that. As for Mongold, he was still staring at the corpse, rather stupidly. "But why'd you choose right now to kill him?"

"Because I'd put up with him as long as I could. And because we couldn't afford to have him get the rest of us killed like he's gotten all our companions killed. And he'd have done it, no doubt. There's somebody out there now, somebody we don't know. Somebody hostile, who's already tried to capture Bert and to kill him when they couldn't catch him. Facing that, men, it's time for a change of leadership and a change of tactics.''

Mongold shook his head. ''I can't believe he's dead. But he is. Look at him. Dead as a stone. Never got his gold back, neither.''

''No, he didn't, and neither will we,'' Broadgrass said. ''That gold is gone, gentlemen. We'd best forget about it and concentrate on getting out of this valley alive.''

Bushrod, meanwhile, was leaning over Sam, who remained unconscious. Examining the broken flesh on Sam's head, Bushrod winced, tore a strip from Sam's shirt, and began pressing on the wound, not too hard, but enough to begin to staunch the flow of blood.

The rest of the people of Texas Gulch were utterly silent, too taken aback and scared to speak. The only exception was Old Man Skinner, still in the midst of his brittle-sounding song.

Yeager gave Broadgrass a cold stare. ''So you were concerned that Mahaffery was willing to cheat us. What about you? You ran out of here, going to the battle, you said, running to help our men fighting out in the valley . . . but once you're out of sight, you turn and go after Mahaffery and Dillow, all by yourself. If you'd found Mahaffery with the gold, would you have brought it back here? Or would it have been *you* trying to make it out of the mountains with all the gold for yourself?''

''I don't believe you trust me, Lennis.''

''I don't.''

''Then you're a wise man, for the wise man doesn't trust anyone without proof. But this time I'm afraid you'll just have to. I would have brought back that gold, Lennis. I swear it. But don't ask me to prove it, for there's no way I can.''

''I think you're looking out for yourself and yourself alone.''

''Then I advise you to cooperate with me, and stay close.

For if I can save myself, maybe I can save you, too."

That seemed to make sense to Yeager, because his antagonistic tone faded a little. "Very well. I don't see much choice, now that you've made the choice for us. But what about these people?"

"Ah, yes. These people. What to do with these people?"

Art Bolton stood. "You've treated us like slaves, like animals. You've talked about us as things and not people. But by heaven, if you seek to murder us, you'll find me, at least, fighting you to the end."

"And me," Joe Skinner said.

"And me." This came, surprisingly to all, from Letitia Colfax.

"Shut up, all of you," Broadgrass said. "I have no desire nor plan to kill any of you."

The looks of surprise that came onto every face were instantly followed by irrepressible expressions of relief.

"What are we going to do, then?" Mongold asked.

"We need these people alive. Whoever is out there will be more restrained with innocent folks to be considered."

"So we're still just pawns to you," Bolton said.

"My friend, in this life every one of us are pawns, trying not to get knocked off the board. But suffice it to say I'm not Jordan Mahaffery. I'm Conner Broadgrass, and though I'll kill when I must, I do try to avoid it."

Bushrod left Sam's side, came to his feet, and faced Broadgrass. "Sir, even though you shot to death the man who would have likely beat myself and my son to death, if he could have, I do want to tell you that I regard you and your ilk there as nothing more than worthless, murdering, thieving, godless, damnable, becursed pieces of dung not fit to breathe the air of this world. I have no regard for you at all. But I have a bargain to offer you."

"Coming from the famous Bushrod Underhill, a bargain is no doubt worth hearing," Broadgrass said, apparently not at all offended by Bushrod's words. "Speak on."

"Whoever is out there is not going to let you leave this

valley by the pass. That's evidenced by the fact that they've already shot at fat boy over there. But there's another way out of this valley, the way by which I came in. I can lead you out again, safely. But I'll not do so unless you pledge to me to leave these people here behind, unharmed.''

"I may need some of these people for hostages, Mr. Underhill, in case we're pursued.''

"You'll have me. I'll be your hostage.''

"You will be, that's true. But you'll also be our guide, and I'll want to make sure you have the right kind of incentive not to lead us astray. But your bargain interests me, and I'm inclined to take it, or a high percentage of it. Tell you what, sir: I'll take you for my hostage, and Mr. Mongold and Mr. Yeager will take one hostage each, of their own choice. The rest of these people may remain here, in this building, tightly tied up. They'll not be tied long; whoever's out there will free them.''

"I'll not have you take hostages other than me. No bargain,'' Bushrod replied.

"Mr. Underhill, you have no choice,'' Broadgrass said firmly.

Bushrod stared at him. "I suppose I don't,'' he admitted.

"So when do we leave?'' Yeager asked.

"Shortly before first light,'' Bushrod replied.

"But what if whoever's up there comes down tonight?''

"Then I suppose you'll have a battle on your hands.''

"Then I say we leave now,'' Mongold said. "Don't give them a chance at us at all. Let them find us long gone when they come down here.''

"Going to be getting dark . . . and cold,'' Bushrod said.

"How long to get us out of this valley?'' Broadgrass asked. "Could you have us out before dark?''

Bush thought it over a few moments, calculating. "I could. It would cut it close.''

"I agree with Bert,'' Broadgrass said. "We don't wait. We don't know how many are up there in that pass, or what

they have in mind. I have no desire to find this place surrounded come morning.''

''Then we'll leave now,'' Bush said.

''You took quite a blow to the head. Can you do it?''

''I've had worse. I can do whatever needs doing.''

Broadgrass turned to Mongold. ''Bert, find some rope.
We've got a whole gang of folks here who need tying up.''

''You really have to do that?'' Bushrod asked.

''Indeed we do,'' Broadgrass replied.

They'd made Bushrod tie up his own son. He hated them
while he did it, but he did it all the same. Few times in his
life had Bushrod Underhill found situations where he felt
almost no sense of control, so this one sat quite uncomfortably with him.

Sam had looked awfully pitiful to Bush while they left
the lodge house. He lay on the floor, semiconscious, his
head raw and bloody. Sam's face had already been bruised
from his ordeal in that pit the first night of this terrible
adventure. All in all, Sam looked almost like a fit candidate
for a coffin.

Broadgrass had had them sneak out of the lodge house,
using the same window that Daniel Chase had crawled
through a time or two. By careful maneuvering and use of
landscape cover, they'd managed to keep the lodge house
between them and the pass, hiding their escape from whoever was up there. Once far enough into the valley, they no
longer had to worry about being seen. Broadgrass relaxed
and turned the guidance over to Bushrod.

Bushrod wasn't inclined to betray Broadgrass, not with
Marica Bolton and Leora Winkle also along as hostages,
being prodded and threatened by Yeager.

After a time of mostly silent, concentrated travel, Broadgrass asked Bushrod, ''How long will it take us to climb
out of this second pass?''

''It's high and difficult. I can't assure you we'll make it
out before dark, especially with the clouds as heavy as they

are. It'll get dark quicker with the clouds. We'd best press on.''

"We will," Broadgrass said. "But I'm afraid there has to be one delay."

"Why?"

"I'm surprised your sharp eye hasn't noticed that Mr. Mongold left us momentarily a little while back. We need to wait here to give him time to catch back up with us."

Indeed Mongold was gone. Bushrod was ashamed of himself for not having noticed. But a departure of one of the outlaws wasn't something he'd anticipated. "Where did he go?" Bushrod asked.

Broadgrass smiled. "A little something was forgotten at the lodge house. He had to run back to take care of it."

A wave of dread rolled through Bushrod. He looked back the way they'd come.

The first trails of dark smoke were beginning to stream into the gray and white sky.

Bushrod stared. He couldn't even find words, and was too numb with shock for tears.

Broadgrass looked at him with an expression of sympathy that wasn't entirely fake. "I am sorry it had to come to that," he said. "But given all the crimes those people have witnessed, we had no choice but to minimize our risks. They had to be disposed of."

Bushrod watched the rising smoke, fury growing inside him.

"Don't worry . . . there was no suffering. Bert had clear directions. Slip back in, make a few deft blows to their heads, enough to knock them out or kill them, then set the fire and flee. If any of them happen to still be alive, Mr. Underhill, they're not feeling a thing. Meanwhile, the fire is a distraction to keep the attention of whoever has come after us."

"I'll see you pay for this, Broadgrass," Bushrod said, voice choking. *Sam, have I let you die, too? Just like*

Danny? Just like Zeke? "I'll see you pay ten-score for the wickedness you've done."

"Now, don't get dramatic on me, sir. You've lived a long time. You know that a man's success or failure doesn't hang on his morality, but on his cleverness. That was Mahaffery's failing. Clever in planning robberies, clever in general as a leader and strategist . . . just not quite clever enough. If I play my hand properly, there's no reason I should have to pay for anything."

"I'll kill you."

"Now, Mr. Underhill, no threats! Would you want to have to watch me put a pistol ball through the pretty head of one of these women? You know I'd do it."

The smoke was rising higher and faster, and now Mongold appeared, loping back toward them at as fast a jog as his weight and the snow accumulation would allow.

Marica and Leora, just now coming to understand what had occurred back at the lodge house, bowed their heads and cried. Bushrod had to struggle not to do the same.

Mongold was red-faced and out of breath. Bushrod eyed him hatefully, hoping the big man's heart would burst here and now. But after some panting, Mongold was able to converse. He actually seemed reinvigorated.

"Didn't take you long, Bert," Broadgrass said. "Did it all go as we'd planned?"

"Indeed it did."

"Are you sure? I'd expected you to be gone longer."

"I'm quick with killing work."

"You clubbed them before you lit the fire, like I told you to do?"

"Every one of them. Blow to the back of the head with the flat of a hatchet." He looked at Bushrod. "Except for Sam Underhill. Him I used my knife on. I'm afraid he died a little slower and harder than the others."

Bushrod lunged at Mongold, knocked him down, and had his hands around the fat neck in an instant. Broadgrass grabbed Marica, pulled his knife, and put it to her throat. "Underhill! Let him go, or she dies!"

Bushrod, with a great groan of suffering that went deep as his soul, let go of Mongold and rolled off. He came to his feet, breathing hard, and stared through wet eyes at the rising billows of smoke back at Texas Gulch.

Mongold got up, rubbing his neck. "You'll die for that, Underhill. I'll make you squeal like your boy did."

"Enough, Bert," Broadgrass said. "We've wasted more time than we could really afford. Underhill, move us on. I'm ready to get out of this valley."

CHAPTER
THIRTY-THREE

Sam Underhill, coughing and choking and very much alive, gritted his teeth, steeled himself against the pain to come, and with a great effort wrenched his right hand free of the ropes that tied it. He'd tensed his wrists while Bushrod tied him up—as loosely as he could get away with—and that had given Sam a slight amount of slack, though not enough to save a good part of his hide when he actually had to pull his hand free.

The bloodied, abraded right hand cleared the rope, and he pushed up, pulling his left hand around and making quick work of the knot. The ropes around his ankles were harder to deal with, and he struggled to keep himself focused on the task amid the rising screams of panic around him.

The fire had come as a surprise, though Sam would later realize he should have expected something like this. The only thing he couldn't figure was why they hadn't killed everyone in the lodge house before they set the blaze, just to make sure nobody got out alive. Maybe whoever had been assigned to the task had simply turned coward and taken the shorter, safer route, figuring that smoke and fire would do the dirty task for him without requiring him to linger under possible endangerment from whoever was up beyond the pass.

While the lodge house filled with smoke and panic, Sam

finished untying his feet, and rose. He went first to Art Bolton and freed him, then the pair of them hurried to untie the terrified, screaming Colfax women, both of whom bolted straight for the door, only to find it blocked closed from outside. New howls of terror escaped them.

Fire licked through the floor on the far end of the lodge house. Sam and Art hurried to free others, who in turn helped their neighbors, and soon all were free. Sam turned to the nearest window, which had also been closed and blocked from the outside, but whoever had done it had worked hurriedly, and it was easy to ram the shutter open. Fresh air spilled in while smoke spilled out, but the inrush of oxygen made the fire rise faster, too.

"Out! Get us *out*!" America Colfax screamed, pounding the door with her fists.

"Out the window, then!" Sam said.

But just as he spoke, something scraped and bumped loudly on the outside of the door. America Colfax screeched harshly and jumped back. "They've come back again! Oh, Lord, they've come back again to kill us all!"

Sam had his doubts that the outlaws would return, but just in case, he picked up a big stick of firewood and held it ready to use as a club.

The door swung open, letting in light and cold and snow and fresh air. Sam gazed at the figures in the doorway, dropped the firewood, and said, "I'll be! Who'd have figured it would be you?"

The newcomers were instantly knocked to the ground outside. America Colfax had bolted out of the lodge house like a panicked cow tearing out of a burning barn, and she was not a small woman.

As the snowfall intensified, the going got harder. The clouds were thick as old syrup, spitting their frozen contents toward the earth but seemingly growing no lighter for shedding the burden. The threat of coming darkness pushed them harder, and Broadgrass, for the first time since he'd come here, was beginning to show signs of strain.

"We need to move faster," he said. "How much farther, old man?"

"Not far. But tell me why I should even cooperate with a man who had my own son murdered, and a houseful of other good people besides?"

"Because if you don't, there'll be three other people murdered: these two women and yourself."

"And if I do lead you out? What happens to us then?"

"Then you live. You have my word."

"I had your word that you'd spare the lives of those back in the big cabin."

"So what do you propose? Die for a certainty here, along with these lovely ladies, or risk trusting me and maybe living once we're past this valley?"

Bushrod stared at him for several moments. "Come on," he said. "I'll show you the way out."

"Are we almost there?"

Bushrod's eye scanned the high bluffs and ridges around them, then stopped for a moment. He was sure he saw someone up on a ledge, in the snow, huddled back against the bluff . . . but a closer look convinced him otherwise. This was just a bit of colored stone, blown free of snow by the hard wind . . .

. . . And he remembered. Sam's story, told in detail. A hunt for the two missing children, a ledge with a colored stone that fooled his eye and led him into a time-wasting climb, and then a fall from that bluff into a pit where there was a cavern entrance, and the corpse of a dead Forty-niner . . .

All these things passed through Bush's mind in no more than three seconds, and by the time a fourth had passed, he knew what he would do. Glancing quickly down, he scanned the base of the bluff, and saw the mouth of the pit that had been Sam's temporary prison.

Another glance up, a taking of measure and bearings . . . yes. Yes, it should work.

"Up there," he said. "There's a cavern up there, impossible to see from below but big enough to walk through. It leads through the ridge and out into a hidden pass on the far side, and that pass leads all the way through the wall of the basin out into the mountains."

"We'll have to climb all the way up there?" Broadgrass said.

" 'Fraid so."

Broadgrass swore loudly.

"You'll have to leave your rifles here below," Bushrod said. "You'll never make that climb with them in hand. Nothing but pistols for you from here on."

Broadgrass clearly hadn't thought of that. He frowned, pursed his lips, then said, "Pistols will have to be enough."

"Conner," Mongold said in a rather small-sounding voice, "I can't make that kind of climb. I'm too big. Too fat."

Broadgrass turned on him. "Is that right, Bert? You sure you can't make it?"

Mongold looked up at the ledge with sorrowful eyes, and nodded. "I'm sure."

"I suppose that makes you useless baggage, then," Broadgrass said. He pulled out his pistol and shot Mongold in the head. The outlaw died without ever having had time to realize what was happening.

The echo of the shot was swallowed by silence that lingered a few moments.

"If I was a murderous, worthless scoundrel like you, I wouldn't have been averse to doing that myself," Bush said quietly, eyeing the corpulant corpse. "That man murdered my son."

"In other circumstances, I might have allowed you the privilege," Broadgrass replied.

Bushrod snapped his head up and showed Broadgrass two piercing eyes. "I hold you as responsible as he was. He may have lit the flame, but you gave the direction."

Broadgrass gave Bush no more than a brief, flickering smile. He went to Mongold and removed the fat man's pistol, which he raised and pointed at Yeager.

"What about you, Lennis?" Broadgrass asked. "Are you a climber?"

Yeager nodded firmly. "A good climber, Conner. Believe me, I'll not slow us down."

Broadgrass seemed satisfied with that answer. He wheeled to face Bushrod.

"Underhill, hear me: if at any point along the way I begin to suspect you've lied to me, or that you're leading me toward anything but a way out of this valley, then you'll be a dead man. No matter what happens to me or to anyone else, you'll be a dead man."

There was a pain in Bushrod Underhill's soul that would have allowed him to reply with full honesty that he didn't think it made much difference to him whether he lived or died. There were two dead grandsons back in Texas whose memories tormented him. And now his own son, hardly found before he was lost, lay inside a burning cabin back in the mining camp. What did it matter whether Bushrod Underhill went on?

Bush said none of this. He merely nodded.

"Let's continue," Broadgrass said.

The lodge house was fully engulfed now, but devoid of human inhabitants. Bert Mongold, anything but a perfectionist, having only half done his assigned task, thus had failed to really do it at all. Every surviving inhabitant of Texas Gulch had gotten out of the lodge house well before the worst of the flames took it over.

The heat was actually pleasant, and given that everyone there had come to perceive the big cabin as no more than a prison, no one mourned the loss of the building.

Sam Underhill, with a blood-crusted, broken scalp and a very bad headache, paused beside Durham and Cordell Underhill, his brothers, watching the flames licking at the logs. Their reunion had been joyous, but there was no time for standing about a moment longer. These brothers had tracked their despondent father all the way from Underhill, Texas, to Texas Gulch, California, and were not about to lose his trail now.

"It'll be dangerous," Sam was saying. "There's three armed men, all desperate, and they have two women hostages along with Pap. They'd kill any one of them at the slightest provocation, if they felt it would help them. The leader for now is a man named Broadgrass, and he's cold and pure mean."

"They can't be out of the valley yet," Cordell said. "The snow's too heavy. Durham and I thought we'd not make it up these mountains, and it's worsened since then."

"No, I doubt they're out of the valley. I also doubt whether Pap will ever take them out. He's bound to have seen the fire at the lodge house. He probably believes right now that I'm dead. Given his state of mind—and Lord, Durham, you don't know how sorry to my soul I am over what happened with your sons—he might decide to bring it all to an end, even if it brings him to an end right along with it."

"He's that bad off?" Durham asked.

"Yes. I've never seen him like he is now."

Durham, with rising urgency, said, "Come on, Cordell. Let's find their trail."

"I'll come, too," said Joe Skinner.

"Have you weapons?" Cordell asked him.

"No," Skinner replied. "They gathered all our weapons when they took us hostage. What ones they didn't take with them, they took the caps from, and emptied the powder in the snow."

"That's no good. I don't know there's much to be gained by your following, if you're unarmed."

"I for one, *will* come along, weapons or not," Art Bolton said. "They have my daughter."

"Then indeed you must come," Durham said. "Sam, are you clear-headed enough after that blow to keep up with us?"

"I am. If I prove not to be, I'll drop behind and let you go on."

"Fine. Let's go get them. Night will fall before we know it."

CHAPTER
THIRTY-FOUR

They crept along the rocky and uneven ledge, which varied in width from two feet to five or more. Bushrod was in the lead, followed by the women, then Yeager, with Broadgrass at the rear. Interesting positioning, Bush thought. Broadgrass had insisted on being last, and Bushrod suspected it was so he could keep Yeager in view at all times. Broadgrass had shot Yeager's partner, after all, and had reason to be wary of Yeager.

"Not too far ahead!" Broadgrass yelled at Bushrod as they edged around a hump on the bluff that made it quite difficult to hang on. "I want you where I can see you!"

"What's the matter, Broadgrass?" Bushrod returned. "You afraid I'll skip right through the mountain and get away from you?"

"Just shut up and lead us on . . . and when you get to that cave mouth, stop before you go in. Let us all catch up together."

Bush's eyes scanned the terrain at the base of the slope. The depths of snow piled there made it hard to make out details, but with that distinctive colored stone ahead as his landmark, Bush was able to know he was near what he was looking for . . . and yes, there it was below. A black, up-turned opening at the base of the cliff, encircled by snow like the open mouth of a hoary-bearded old man. Bush studied its location, the bluff above it, locating the spot on the ledge—the place was mere feet ahead at this point—just above the opening.

He had plans for that spot, but it all depended on positioning himself and Broadgrass right above it, something that wouldn't happen the way they were all aligned right now.

He had to think of something, quickly. In moments he'd be past the right point on the ledge. What he had in mind might work elsewhere on the ledge, without benefit of that pit down there, but on the other hand it might not. The snow was drifted so deeply at the base of the bluff that it would cushion a falling man, perhaps enough to protect a man from death or even serious injury.

When Broadgrass went over, Bush wanted him to hit hard. Fatally hard. And in case he didn't hit fatally hard, to be in a place from which he could not easily exit. And if the same happened to Bush himself, well, so be it. Death would be an escape from grief and ghosts and the pain he'd tried to run from, but which seemed always to catch him anyway.

But with three people between himself and Broadgrass on this narrow ledge, how could he hope to get Broadgrass where he needed him?

At that moment, fate lent a hand, though not in a way that Bushrod would have desired. Beneath the feet of Marica Bolton, a stone moved. Her legs went out from beneath her; her feet went over the rim of the ledge and she fell, clawing at the frozen, rocky ground.

"Marica!" Leora Winkle cried out. "Hold on . . . I'll reach you!"

Marica *was* holding on, her face twisted in fright, her nails digging into the dirty, trampled snow, finding a claw-grip in the gritty, graveled surface of the ledge. The ledge was narrow where she'd fallen, and the entire lower half of her body extended into empty space.

Bushrod turned and began working his way back toward

her, planning to reach down and give her his hand. But Leora was quicker, putting her own hand out before Bush could get there.

Marica reached gratefully for Leora's hand; holding herself for those few moments with only her left hand gripping the ledge . . .

Her grip gave way. What had felt like the rough surface of the ledge itself had been only loose stones frozen in place. Her weight and grip were greater in strength than the feeble cement of ice that held the stones in place, and with a scream Marica was pulled back from the ledge by the weight of her hips and legs, and she fell.

"Marica!" Leora yelled, her cry mixing with that of the plunging woman.

Bushrod winced and felt his heart skip a beat. No. No. He craned his neck, looking over the edge.

Marica was down there, in a drift of snow, lying still. From what he'd heard and seen, he didn't think she'd struck the ledge itself on the way down, but he couldn't be sure.

Leora was in a panic. "Oh, dear Lord! Oh, Marica . . . is she alive?"

"Careful, there," Bushrod warned her. "Don't go falling after her."

"Can you see her?"

"I can," Bushrod said. "She hit in the snow, a heavy drift. She's not moving, but she can't have struck as hard as she would have if there was naught to cushion her."

"What if she's dead?"

"She may be. And if she is, as far as I'm concerned, we can credit our gun-toting friends with another murder."

Yeager turned slowly, hugging the wall, and asked Broadgrass, "What do you want to do? Leave her?"

"Can you tell if she's dead?"

Yeager looked over, cautiously. "She ain't moving."

Broadgrass swore, frowning and thinking. "Can you get in position to put a bullet through her, to make sure she's gone?"

Leora turned so fast she almost fell off herself. "You'd shoot an injured woman in cold blood?"

"I'd shoot my own sister in cold blood if it was necessary."

Yeager said, "Conner, I don't think I want to shoot her."

"You're developing a conscience suddenly, Lennis?"

"I'm tired of all this. I just want out of this valley. I want to go as far away from here as I can."

"These people have seen too much, Lennis. You want to leave them to trouble us with the law later on?"

"We'll never see these people again if we run far enough," Yeager said. "I've been thinking . . . we could leave California. Then none of it would matter. We'd never be caught away from California."

"I have no ambition to leave California," Broadgrass replied. "I've been here too long." He looked down over the ledge. "But I suppose we needn't shoot her. If she's not dead now, she will be soon. Too bad, really. I had plans for that young beauty."

Leora exploded. "You're a beast! You're not even a man! Is that all a human being is to you? Something to use, or to abandon?"

"Ma'am, I grew up in a home where I knew only being used and being abandoned. It's the way of life that I learned, and the way I accept."

"Let me go down to her. I want to make sure she's alive." Tears came. "And I want to find my daughter again."

"Sorry, ma'am. But I need you. You provide protection . . . and perhaps some needed warmth on cold nights."

Leora looked down at Marica, whose body was already being covered by snow. "She moved! I saw her move! She's alive . . . please, let me go to her and help her. We're never going to be a threat to you! We'll never see each other again . . . and besides, I've already decided: if God allows me to live through this, and if He allows me to find my daughter again, I'm taking her back to Texas. There's been nothing here for me but sorrow.''

"Listen to her, Broadgrass," Bushrod said. "Do something decent. For the sake of that poor woman down there, and for the sake of Leora's little girl, let her go. You still have me for a hostage.''

"She could cause me trouble later on.''

Lennis Yeager said, "Well, Conner, you got to consider that the little girl has gotten away, and also that Nolen fellow. So even if we killed both these women, there's still those around who could identify us. So what difference does it make if we spare them? Let her go down and help that woman if she can. They're both likely to die up here before the springtime, anyway, once we're gone.''

"I don't know what's gotten into you, Lennis. This softening is a dangerous change.''

Yeager glared. "So what will you do? Shoot me, like you did poor old Mongold?''

"Would you force me to?''

Yeager pulled out his pistol and aimed it at Broadgrass. "I say this woman goes down to help the other below, if she can. We go on and leave them behind. I say there's been enough bad done in this valley, and that we do no more.''

"Why don't you preach us a sermon, Reverend Yeager?''

Yeager ignored Broadgrass. "Come on," he said to Leora. "You can work your way past me and go back down.''

"Thank you, sir," she said. "God bless you for this.''

"And, Conner, you let her go past you, too. And if you shove her off, I'll shoot you dead.''

Broadgrass was looking at Yeager not with anger, but amusement. "What is this, Lennis? A mutiny?''

"No. Just something that ought to be done. All I want is to get out of this valley alive, forget that gold, and go on.''

Leora was moving back toward Yeager, who kept his eye on Broadgrass and his pistol leveled. When she reached Yeager, he pulled in close to the wall, allowing her to move around him. It seemed a likely time for Broadgrass to act if he planned to do so, yet he did nothing but stand there with a bemused half-smile on his face, as if he were a patient schoolmaster secretly laughing at the silly rebellion of some petty schoolboy.

She got past Yeager safely, and now crept toward Broadgrass, who smiled at her. This was a highly dangerous moment, because her positioning blocked Yeager's potential line of fire at Broadgrass. Just now she was at Broadgrass's mercy; he could shoot her dead with ease.

But for some reason, he did not. She came closer, closer, and finally reached him.

"You'll let me around you?" she asked.

"Of course I will."

Leora drew in a deep breath, went to him, stepped toward the edge of the ledge just enough to clear him, and passed by him as quickly as she safely could, her face inches from his. He smiled and winked, made a kissing sound, then a little false lunge as if to push her off.

He didn't push her, though, and she went on, back down the way they'd come up.

Bush, relieved, prayed for her and for Marica Bolton below. Then he turned his concentration on the situation as it was.

Nobody between him and Broadgrass now except for Yeager.

"Gentlemen, it appears it's just us," Broadgrass said. "Lennis, please put that pistol away. I'm not going to try to hurt you, and God knows there's no longer any gang to lead. Just you, me, and our hostage."

Bushrod was watching Marica below. He could no longer see Leora. He hoped she would get to the base of the bluff and down to where Marica lay in time to help the injured young woman.

"Guess we should move on," Yeager said.

Bush looked down at the gaping hole below and slightly ahead, then calculated once more the place on the ledge where he would need to make his move if it was to work. Somehow he had to bring Broadgrass within his reach at that exact point. But there was still the problem of Yeager, inconveniently positioned between him and Broadgrass.

What the devil. Perhaps he'd be forced to take both of them down with him. Both deserved it. Yeager's turn toward mercy where Leora Winkle and Marica Bolton were concerned wasn't nearly enough to atone for his part in the sins already committed by him and his ilk at Texas Gulch.

An idea came.

"I wouldn't go on with him behind you," Bushrod said to Yeager.

"Why?"

"If I was you, I'd want him in front for the same reason he wants you in front. So he can keep an eye on you."

Yeager made strange expressions as the snow and cold wind battered his face. "Underhill's right," he said to Broadgrass. "I don't trust you back there. We've gone this far with me before you. Now let's got the rest of the way with me behind."

Broadgrass didn't look quite as poised as usual. "If you think I'm going to pass you on this ledge, you're a fool."

"He aims to shoot you like he shot Mongold," Bushrod said.

Yeager brandished his pistol at Broadgrass. "Move on up here. Get in front of me."

"Lennis, I'm not going to shoot you. You have my word."

"And you have mine that I won't shove you down off this ledge when you go past."

Broadgrass flared his nostrils and narrowed one eye, revealing an anger that he was trying to keep hidden. "I'll not pass you."

"I'll kill you! Underhill can lead me out of this valley without you!"

Bushrod looked below. Marica moved again, but the cold snow would quickly rob her of warmth and life. Still no sign of Leora. He supposed she was still making her way down the bluff.

"You'd best shoot him, Yeager," Bushrod said. "You've crossed the line now. He shot Mongold just because he couldn't climb a bluff."

Yeager was trembling, partly from the cold, partly from anger . . . and fear. Broadgrass had always been an intimidating man, like Mahaffery, but in a different fashion. As much as he wanted to kill him right now, Broadgrass was somehow keeping him from it with no more than the coldness of his gaze.

Bush had seen this kind of failure in men before, and knew it would be the end of Yeager. Sure enough, Broadgrass drew back suddenly, letting the curve of the bluff come between him and Yeager. Yeager, panicking, fired. The shot ricocheted off the stone into the emptiness. Yeager dropped his pistol, one of two he'd carried away from Texas Gulch, and scrambled for the second one.

Bushrod dropped to minimize the size of the target he made in case the inevitable answering shot from Broadgrass also missed and hurtled his way.

Broadgrass did not miss. He appeared again, pistol drawn, and shot Yeager through the stomach. Yeager had freed his second pistol and cocked back the lock hammer, but hadn't aimed the weapon yet by the time that Broadgrass's pistol ball tore through him. Reflexively he squeezed the trigger and fired upward.

The ball tore through a great, overhanging mass of heavy snow that had collected on the sloping stone face above the ledge.

The equivalent of a few barrow-loads of snow poured down around Bushrod. He glanced up just as Yeager was pitching over the ledge to fall, dead, mere yards from where Marica lay.

Bushrod might have found a chance to attack an unarmed Broadgrass right then, had not Broadgrass, like Yeager, had the foresight to arm himself with a backup pistol. He put away the emptied one quickly and drew the loaded one in its place, grinning at Bushrod through the smoke of his pistol shot, the echo of which was only now coming back, snow-muffled, from across the wide valley.

"Just me and you now, old man," he said.

A little more snow dumped down on Bushrod, and he heard a strange, ominous noise . . . a kind of heavy, deep, groaning that was quite different from anything he'd heard before.

He comprehended quickly what it was, and the opportunity it gave him.

Bush drew in a deep, groaning breath, clapped a hand dramatically over his chest, and sank back onto the ledge, gasping wildly.

"What's the matter with you, old fellow?"

Bush, still clinging to his chest, began dragging himself farther along the ledge, seemingly trying to come to his feet, then falling down again.

"What the hell are you doing?" Broadgrass yelled, coming after him. "Are you sick?"

"Sick . . ." Bushrod said. "Hurting . . . my chest . . ."

More snow slid off the slope above. Bush hurried. There it was, below . . . the open hole. Days ago a prison for Sam Underhill . . . now to be a burial place for Bushrod Underhill and Conner Broadgrass.

Bush looked toward where Marica lay. To his delight he saw Marica actually rising, and Leora reaching her. The snow into which Marica had fallen had cushioned her sufficiently, it seemed, to let her escape crippling injury. He breathed a prayer of thanks as he watched the two women join and begin a clumsy scramble back down through the drifting snow toward the safer levels away from the bluff.

Good. Maybe they'd get far enough away before the snow avalanched down.

Broadgrass reached Bushrod. "Old man, what's happening here?"

Bushrod looked up at him. "We're going to die, me and you, together."

"Die? Maybe you, old man. Not me."

A loud, low-level rumbling from high above made Bush look skyward and smile.

"It's the end, Mr. Broadgrass. Judgment Day. May Jesus pardon our sins and have mercy on our souls at this, the moment of our death."

Broadgrass seemed to comprehend, but it was far too late. He looked up as the great wall of white came down upon them. At the same moment, Bushrod, still half-lying on the very brink of the ledge, grabbed Broadgrass around the knees and heaved both of them over the side just as the snow hit them.

They rode the crest of the avalanche downward, the open mouth of the pit growing bigger and closer. Then everything was whiteness and darkness all together, and the snow descended and filled the pit and the two men who had plunged into it were seen no more.

Leora Winkle and Marica Bolton reached the edge of the great snowdrift into which Marica had fallen. It had almost proven too great a barrier to allow Leora to reach her, but effort and stubbornness had availed and the pair had gotten just far enough away from the bluff to miss being swept under the snow mass as it fell. Lennis Yeager—still alive after his gunshot and plunge, groping and bleeding and hurting, hadn't been so lucky. The snow had buried him deep.

Battered, frightened, and weeping, the women moved through the snow, looking back to see the ledge along which they'd moved before now devoid of humans.

"Poor Mr. Bushrod!" Leora said. "Poor man!"

"Take me back, Leora," Marica said. "Maybe some of them are still alive."

"Poor Mr. Bushrod," Leora said again. "What a good, good man. God rest him."

"Yes," Marica said. "And God help us."

CHAPTER
THIRTY-FIVE

Bushrod opened his eyes, but it made no difference. All was as utterly black as before. He was lying on his belly, face turned to the side, grit and gravel and very cold rock beneath him.

He lay there for at least a minute before he managed to believe that he was really still alive. How could it be? He'd fallen far, with a world of heavy snow piling down after him.

But here he was. And the most amazing thing was that he could breathe.

Whether he could move, though, was another question, and the truth was he was afraid to try. He'd seen a man once who had been paralyzed from the middle of his back to his feet, and had prayed that such a fate would never be his. And what scared him right now was that he didn't think he felt his lower body at all. Just a general, numb pressure, incredibly heavy.

His arms. That's what he'd start with. He shrugged his right shoulder, successfully, then tried his right hand. That worked, too, and to his joy, he felt his fingers scratching against his thigh while he did so. So there was feeling in his lower body after all . . . the numbness, he surmised, came from incredible cold in which his legs were encased.

His left arm worked, too; he found it was stretched out

beside him, but pulled in closer to his body when he asked it to. He felt his own face, detecting no major cuts, no pits or holes in his skull.

His ability to breathe remained the greatest mystery. The amount of snow that had fallen in atop him and Broadgrass by all rights should have crushed them flat. Yet he wasn't crushed, and even had open space around him. He tried to make sense of it.

As he lay there, thinking, details of what Sam had told him of his own entrapment in this pit began to come to mind. Sam had mentioned a cavern entrance in the pit, with a shielding overcrop of stone above it. As best Bushrod could guess, he must have fallen in such a way that he was rolled by the incoming snow beneath that outcrop of stone. It was a theory that fit the facts. The stone above would keep snow off him, and allow him an air space. It would explain why the upper portion of his body was not buried in snow while his hips and legs were.

It was all surmise, of course, for he was blind in this utter darkness and could verify nothing by sight.

But there might be one way to tell. He recalled how Sam had told him of moving that corpse he'd found. He'd dragged it away from its original place and laid it out in the entrance of the cave at the base of the pit.

If Bush was where he thought he was, he ought to be able to locate that corpse by feel, even if he couldn't see it.

He extended his right arm slowly, feeling around him. All he found was snow and cold rock and gravel. Extending his arm up relative to his head, he groped in the area ahead of him . . . and his hand touched something that felt like old fabric. A bit more exploration, and he closed his hand around something brittle and sticklike, and encased in loose cloth.

A bone. A human bone, probably part of a leg, still clothed. Bush felt like crying in relief. Merely to have some sense of where he was, and why he was alive, was remarkably moving.

Die he yet might in this place, but at least he would know where he was, and that a son he had loved from birth had been in this same place, too. To know this mattered very deeply to Bushrod Underhill.

He closed his hand around the bone and held on. To touch something that he could identify, even something as lifeless and morbid as the bony leg of a leathery corpse, was a connection to the world he'd left behind when he plunged into this dark hole. In its own odd way, it was a comfort.

For a long time Bushrod remained in this posture, unmoving, his eyes open and gazing into a darkness blacker than ink. Against that black screen his mind began to play images of importance to him. His wife, as she had been when she was young. His first children, small and pink and crying, then older, growing strong and making him proud. Old friends, long gone, such as Cephas Frank, and Becker Israel, and the old man Daniel Boone.

And again, his wife. Lorry, the strong, the beautiful, the faithful and loving. Lorry, not as the young girl she had been, but the woman she was now, the wonderful and grand person whom Bush loved more than any other, and who loved him in turn more than she loved herself.

Lying there in that darkness, waiting for death, Bushrod found his mind turning again toward life. He thought of Durham's sons, one dead by the most terrible of accidents, the other by his own hand. Sorrowful, horrific, saddening . . . but unchangeable. What had happened had happened. Bush could cry over it, regret it, blame himself for it . . . but that changed nothing. Healed nothing. It only brought more sorrow to others he loved.

Lorry. Dear Lorry. How could he think of dying while she yet lived? How could he turn away from the greatest treasure he had ever possessed, or ever could?

A cave, opening before him. Sometimes caves went nowhere. Sometimes they led to exits. Ways out to the world beyond.

It was a world that Bushrod realized still mattered to him.

"Lorry, I'll try," he said. "I'll do my best to live."

He put his hands before him and tried to scoot himself forward. The effort was excruciating, and he realized how heavy the weight upon his lower body was, and also how cold and numb his lower extremities were. He gave up his first attempt without being sure whether he'd moved at all.

After a few moments' rest, he tried again. Slowly he went forward, feeling his legs moving under the dead weight of the snow. He dragged twice more, and advanced more than a foot.

A little more rest, and he tried again. This time he got his legs fully out from under the snow. He reached up and determined that he did have room to sit upright beneath the protective stone overhang. Making the attempt, he was rewarded with success. It was odd, sitting on legs he couldn't feel, but at least those legs moved and lived, and the longer he sat, the more feeling began to return. He bowed his head and said a prayer of thanks.

Light. He needed light. Reaching into his pocket, he found phosphorus matches. Hard to tell by feel how dry they were, so he tried one. Nothing. The second match, however, struck fire.

So black was it, and so accustomed had his eyes grown to seeing nothing, that the mere flare of the match made him wince and blink. The brief light bathed the interior of his little chamber with illumination. He saw the snowy wall that blocked him in, the stone above him, the dead man laid flat on the gravelly floor, the dark hole of the cavern opening.

Then the match blew out.

Blew out. Bush realized that the flame had been pulling toward the cavern opening. Drawn by a breeze, obviously. And a breeze had to mean that the cavern was connected to some kind of opening.

By feel he counted the matches remaining on the block. Most of a block. Good. He lit a second one and scooted himself a little farther into the passage, nearer the corpse. He looked into the opening, extending the match in. Hard to tell how deeply it penetrated, but the match flame was definitely drawn toward the opening.

He might try crawling back there in the darkness, feeling his way along and, if lucky, finding a guiding breeze to lead him toward the outside, but he'd much rather have a source of light. His matches wouldn't last long, however, if he used them in continuing succession. He needed a torch of some kind.

His own clothing was cold and sodden. But his long-deceased companion was dressed in dried, nearly crisp rags, and thanks to Sam's placement of the body in the protection of the cavern opening, very little of the snow that had fallen into the pit had gotten onto the corpse's rags.

Bush tore strips of cloth from the dead man's garments and tied these loosely around his wrist. Striking one more match, Bushrod examined the now-exposed legs and discovered that the right was devoid of flesh, nothing but brownish bone remaining. Bushrod shook out the match, reached down, and wrenched loose the thighbone of the left leg.

He wrapped a strip of cloth loosely around one end, leaving the ends of the cloth dangling. He struck fire to this and held the bone by its opposite end. The cloth burned readily and illuminated the cavern much more brightly than had the matches alone.

Bushrod crawled back into the passage, fearing that at any point it might narrow so much it wouldn't accommodate him. At places it did grow small, but on the whole it actually seemed to be enlarging the farther it went.

The first cloth strip was about burned out, so Bush paused to supplement it with a new one, wrapping it around. The flame rose again, and pulled hard in a forward direction. Bush grew encouraged. Even without the visual evidence of the flame, Bush could now faintly feel the draft. A cross-draft actually, indicating at least two openings other than the now-snowblocked one through which he'd entered.

Bush was dismayed for a few moments when he saw a

stone mass at the end of the passage, then realized when he got closer that it was merely a bend in the natural tunnel. The stone mass was the wall of the passage, curving around to face him.

Replenishing his torch as he went along, Bush discovered that the passage grew quite large, and the draft stronger. He experienced overwhelming relief and happiness. He would indeed find a way out. Life would go on. There would be grief and loss and pain, but there would be good, too. His wife, his children, grandchildren . . . himself.

The torch gusted and went out. An unusually strong burst of air, quite cold, had found it. Bush knelt and wrapped a new cloth around the end of the bone, but paused before striking another match.

It seemed he could catch a glint of light in the corner of his eye. Extremely dim, and maybe a trick of vision left from the flicker of the torch in his vision . . . but maybe authentic. When he looked directly at its seeming source, he couldn't see it, but when he gazed to the side of it, the light seemed to return, very faint and moving, rippling.

He lit the match and renewed his torch. Lifting it, he prepared to advance, the tunnel now so large as to allow him to stand nearly straight.

He stopped. The torch's light had caught a reflection on the floor. Stooping, Bushrod examined what he'd found, then picked it up.

A tinderbox, made of battered pewter. Bushrod turned it over. On the back were the initials "C.B." scratched into the metal, roughly, maybe by the head of a nail.

C.B. Conner Broadgrass.

Bush's happiness drained away in an instant.

He advanced, very cautious. The draft grew stronger, and the passage bigger. Before long, that vague flicker of light he'd seen revealed itself more strongly, now there beyond any doubt.

Bush's torch went out again, and this time he didn't even bother to relight it. It wasn't necessary. The passage turned again ahead of him, and reflecting back to him from its walls was firelight.

Bush halted and stared at the light flickering on the stone wall.

"Underhill!"

Bush closed his eyes and shook his head. The voice was that of Broadgrass, and came from the lighted area ahead.

"Underhill, is that you? I'm sure it is . . . who else could it be?"

"So you survived the fall, did you?" Bush answered.

"Indeed. But I didn't think *you* did! If I'd had an inkling, I'd have paused long enough to make sure you never wiggled a toe again. But I had some things on my mind at the time . . . like surviving. Getting out of that hole in the ground. You and me both were lucky not to be crushed alive, Underhill! If not for a fortuitous tumble under that rock, we would have been, you know."

"I suppose we should give thanks for our lives."

"Maybe I'll get around to that someday. But come on around. A couple of things here I want you to take a look at."

Bushrod, the expired thighbone torch still in hand, walked slowly toward the bend in the passage. When he rounded the turn, he was looking into the midst of a large natural chamber in which a big fire blazed, filling the space with light, the smoke rising and being pulled into a crack in the roof, obviously some sort of natural chimney.

Bruised, filthy, wet, clothing torn, face cut and bleeding, left arm hanging broken, Conner Broadgrass sat on a boulder in the middle of the chamber. At his feet were Arianna Winkle and a boy Bushrod didn't know, but whom he guessed at once to be Daniel Chase.

Bushrod's eyes locked with Arianna's. "Hello, young miss," he said. "You've grown a lot since I saw you last in Texas."

He could read her questions. His appearance here was surely an astounding mystery to her. But she asked nothing.

"Where'd you get the pistol?" Bushrod asked.

"The boy had it. Tried to use it, but it misfired on him. Loose flint. But I tightened it after I got it away from him. It'll fire next time."

"Your arm's broken."

"Believe me, that's not news to me. But I don't care that much. I'm very excited, really. Take a look."

Bush just then noticed the strongbox. It sat nearby, atop a leather bag with bank markings on it.

"I have to give these children credit," Broadgrass said. "They found the gold when all the rest of us couldn't. And they had the wisdom to hide it rather than turn it over, because Daniel here knew that when Mahaffery got the gold, he'd have everyone killed. Clever boy. He's even trapped rabbits and such for food."

"So what's your plan now?" Bushrod asked.

"I plan to keep my gold! All mine, now. As soon as possible, I'll take it down the mountain and very much enjoy spending it."

"And the rest of us?"

"I haven't quite decided."

"Don't play games, Broadgrass. You know you plan to kill us."

"Well, now that you mention it . . ."

"You coward. Let these children go and face me."

"Face you? What do you mean, face you?"

"I mean just that! Aim that pistol at me and shoot it, if you have the courage! Go ahead! Shoot me dead right here!"

Broadgrass laughed. "You're insane, old man. I told you I retightened the flint. It'll fire this time. I've seen this pistol fire before. It's the one the boy here used to kill Searl Mahaffery. Ross Romine, too. I have much admiration for this young fellow. Tough and clever, like I was."

Bushrod stepped toward Broadgrass, who started a little and began to rise. Broadgrass brandished the pistol at Arianna. "I'll kill her!"

"If you do, you'll be dead. You've got one shot, Broad-grass. If you use it, it had best be used on me. And it had best be effective."

Broadgrass was on his feet now, raising the pistol, his face going white.

"Move to the side, young ones," Bushrod directed, walking toward Broadgrass.

Daniel and Arianna scrambled away. Broadgrass raised the pistol and thumbed back the lock. "Stop where you are!" he demanded.

Bushrod broke the thigh bone he carried, leaving in his grip a long, sharp splinter. He kept advancing.

Broadgrass fired the pistol. The crack of the shot was intolerably loud in the cave. Bushrod grunted and fell back a step. He looked down and saw blood running down his chest.

"Got me," he said, then began advancing again.

Broadgrass put out a hand to stop him, but Bushrod ducked him. Broadgrass cursed and was about to say something, but Bushrod moved too fast for him. He jammed the sharp end of the splintered thighbone into Broadgrass's right eye, and shoved hard, penetrating deep into the brain.

Broadgrass shuddered and died, falling at Bushrod's feet.

Bushrod looked at the children. "Are you all right?"

"Yes," Daniel Chase replied, staring at Broadgrass's body.

"Good," Bushrod said. He closed his eyes and fell atop the man he'd just killed.

CHAPTER
THIRTY-SIX

Sam Underhill looked down at his father's face, tension building within him until he realized he'd been holding his breath. He let it out in a gust.

"Are you sure, Leora? He opened his eyes?"

"Yes," she said. "Just a flicker, but he did. Keep watch on him. I think he'll be waking up soon."

Sam held his breath again.

Bushrod Underhill awakened slowly. Sam grinned and wanted to weep all at the same time. When at last his father's eyes focused on his, Sam said, "Hello, Pap."

Bushrod's dry lips bent into a smile. "Gone to heaven together, me and my son. Good to see you here, Sam." He grew intense suddenly. "What about Zeke and Danny?"

"Pap, I'm afraid this ain't heaven, and you ain't dead. This is Texas Gulch."

Bushrod looked around, blinking fast. Tears appeared in his eyes. "Sam, I thought you'd burned up."

"We got out, Pap. With the help of somebody you'll want to see. Somebody that followed you all the way from Texas because they were worried about you."

"You mean—"

Cordell was there before Bushrod could finish. He bent over and gently embraced the old man, mindful of the wound in his upper left chest. Broadgrass's rifle ball had entered just enough to avoid striking Bush's heart, and had missed major blood vessels as well.

"Hello, Pap. I'm glad you're alive. Durham's here, too."

Bushrod greeted Durham differently than he had his other sons. "Hello, Durham," he said. "Son, I don't know what to say to you."

"Why wouldn't you?"

"You know why."

"It wasn't your fault, Pap. What happened with Zeke and Danny just . . . happened. I've never blamed you."

Bushrod looked away.

"It'll take you some time, maybe, to see things as they are," Durham said. "But take the time, Pap. Because I want you to stop holding yourself responsible for what was never your responsibility to start with."

"That's right, Pap," Cordell said. "No more running across the country in the dead of winter. You've worried Ma sick."

"Sick? Truly sick?"

"No. But she is mighty worried about you."

Bushrod closed his eyes and wept. "I suppose she must be."

"We're going to take you back to her as soon as you're well enough, Pap. And as soon as the weather clears."

"Sam . . ."

"Right here, Pap."

"How bad hurt am I?"

"I'm afraid it's going to take a lot more than that one little pistol ball to end the days of Bushrod Underhill. The ball's been dug out, by the way. That's one advantage of having a man as senseless as you were. You can dig on him without him feeling it."

"Arianna and the orphan boy . . . ?"

"Both alive. Both fine. Scared, cold, and with things to remember that will probably have them going through nightmares until long after they're grown . . . but they're alive. They credit you. If you hadn't killed Conner Broadgrass, they believe he would have killed them. And I think they're surely right."

"So maybe I've atoned some for Danny and Zeke."

"There's nothing to atone for there, but if you want to see it that way, then see it that way. By the way, if Daniel and Arianna owe you for their lives, you may owe them for yours. Arianna stayed with you in that cave, stopping the bleeding, while Daniel left, came all the way around to the pass, and down into Texas Gulch to take help to you."

"So Daniel had found a third way in and out of the valley . . . through the cave."

"That's right. And he had the good sense to hide the gold in that cave, knowing that if the outlaws got it, it would be the end for all of us."

"The fire . . . how'd you get out?"

"Durham and Cordell arrived in time. They'd run across Copp Nolen out in the mountains . . . he'd sneaked away, at Leora's bidding, to try to find Arianna when she'd gone missing, looking for the gold. We'd have gotten out of the lodge house even if they hadn't shown up, though. Fat boy Mongold didn't do his job right. I suppose he was in a hurry to get away from the phantoms up in the pass who'd shot at him."

"Cordell and Durham."

"That's right. They'd talked to Copp Nolen by then, and knew what was happening here. They were determined not to let any of those outlaws have free passage out of this valley."

Bush looked around. "Where am I?"

"In my cabin," Sam said. "Me and Ben Dillow's, God rest him. He gave up his life trying to save us. In the spring, when the snow melts, we'll seek his bones out there and try to give him a decent burial."

"The woman who fell . . ."

"Marica. She's alive. Leora got her away in time to avoid being crushed in the snowfall. She has a broken ankle and a couple of cracked ribs, but other than that, she's fine."

"What now, Sam?"

"What now? You rest, heal. All of us, I guess, have some resting and healing to do. And in the spring, we go back to Texas."

"We?"

"That's right. I'll not stay here any longer, Pap. I've somehow lost all the desire for gold."

"Gold . . . I know where there's plenty to be had."

"It's gone, Pap."

"Gone?"

"That's right. When nobody was paying attention, Daniel Chase threw it deep into a hole in that cave. Or so he says. It fell a long way, and there was a splash when it hit."

"Why did he do that?"

"He said it was blood gold. It had cost too many lives. He declared it wicked and decided to rid the world of it."

"Imagine that. A boy thinking so deep as that."

"He's a clever lad." Sam paused. "Maybe clever enough to think to hide that gold somewhere for himself."

"It's bank gold. It should be returned."

"Well, it's gone gold now. Whether Daniel tossed it down a hole or hid it, it's out of reach for us or the bank that lost it."

Bush closed his eyes. "I think I'll sleep now."

"Pap, is everything well with you?"

Bush smiled without opening his eyes. "I've found a son I thought dead, to be alive. I've found two other sons willing to follow a foolish old man all the way to California from Texas just because they were worried about him. I've been privileged to help bring an end to a hellish ordeal that never should have befallen a group of innocent people. And I've lived through it, when I was ready, truly ready, to die. I figure there must be a reason . . . more yet to come for Bushrod Underhill. So, yes . . . I think everything is well. Or will be. In time."

"Time, right now, is about all we've got," Sam said.

"It's all we need," Bushrod said. "I think I'm going to sleep now."

"You do that, Pap. I'm going to go build up the fire a little more. The snow's coming in again, harder than ever."

CAMERON JUDD
THE NEW VOICE OF THE OLD WEST

*"Judd is a keen observer of the human heart
as well as a fine action writer."*

—*Publishers Weekly*

THE GLORY RIVER
Raised by a French-born Indian trader among the
Cherokees and Creeks, Bushrod Underhill left the dark
mountains of the American Southeast for the promise of
the open frontier. But across the mighty Mississippi, a
storm of violence awaited young Bushrod—and it would
put his survival skills to the ultimate test...
0-312-96499-4___$5.99 U.S.___$7.99 Can.

SNOW SKY
Tudor Cochran has come to Snow Sky to find some answers
about the suspicious young mining town. And what he
finds is a gathering of enemies, strangers and conspirators
who have all come together around one man's violent
past—and deadly future.
0-312-96647-4___$5.99 U.S.___$7.99 Can.

CORRIGAN
He was young and green when he rode out from his family's Wyoming ranch, a boy sent to bring his wayward brother home to a dying father. Now, Tucker Corrigan was entering a range war. A beleaguered family, a powerful landowner, and Tucker's brother, Jack—a man seven years on the
run—were all at the center of a deadly storm.
0-312-96615-6___$4.99 U.S.___$6.50 Can.

ALL THAT GLITTERS . . .

The time had come, but I hesitated. I didn't feel very heroic. I forced an image of Minnie into my mind. Only through Leviticus Lee could I get the gold I needed to buy her back. Then Lee let out a particularly fearsome scream, and I made my move.

But just as I was about to lunge through the opening between the doors, I heard a shout from inside. "Hold it! I've got my gun on you!"

That was Fairweather's voice—what was he doing in there? He was supposed to enter after me, not before.

Curses, yells, confusion—then a shot, fired just inside the door. Fairweather yelled, fired back. The slug came bursting out through the wall not three inches from my head, sending splinters of wood all over me.

"Enoch, where are you?"

Fairweather's cry was desperate. I moved quickly, wheeling and dodging straight through the gap between the doors—and from the corner of my eye caught the sight of two riders coming around the ridge that Fairweather and I had come across, and riding onto the grounds of the sawmill. Who they were, and why they had come, I didn't know. And there was no time to see . . .

CONFEDERATE
GOLD

CAMERON JUDD

St. Martin's Paperbacks

CONFEDERATE GOLD / DEAD MAN'S GOLD

Confederate Gold copyright © 1993 by Cameron Judd.
Dead Man's Gold copyright © 1999 by Cameron Judd.

All rights reserved.

For information address St. Martin's Press, 175 Fifth Avenue, New York, NY 10010.

ISBN: 0-312-94334-2
EAN: 978-0-312-94334-9

Printed in the United States of America

Confederate Gold Bantam Domain edition / December 1993
St. Martin's Paperbacks edition / June 2000

Dead Man's Gold St. Martin's Paperbacks edition / August 1999

St. Martin's Paperbacks are published by St. Martin's Press, 175 Fifth Avenue, New York, NY 10010.

10 9 8 7 6 5 4 3 2 1

*To the Carrigans of Portland
Mark, Kim, Clay, and Jesse*

CONFEDERATE
GOLD

CHAPTER ONE

SHE LOOKED AT ME THROUGH THE SMOKE OF HER CORN-cob pipe and declared she wanted me to take her home, and I never knew until the day of her death years later whether it was because of a real longing for the place of her raising or because she wanted to give me a way to get myself out of trouble.

"Home?" I said. "Fort Scott *is* home. It's where we make our living. It's where we buried Pap."

"My home is Tennessee," my mother replied. "The living we make here ain't much, and I'm pining for the hills. I want to go back to Rogersville and live with your aunt Kate. I want you to take me."

"It's because of the fight, ain't it!" I said. "You're trying to get me away from here to keep me out of jail."

She leaned forward, that blue glint of her eyes as keen as the flash of a new gun barrel. "Enoch Brand, you ain't never talked back to your mother in twenty-five years of life, and I don't expect you to start now. There's a Tennessee-bound wagon train going to be pulling out soon. We'll be a part of it. I want you to take me home, and there's no more to be said about it."

And that's all that was said about it, and how it all began in that autumn forty-six years ago. Cleveland was in the White House, Geronimo was on a reservation in Florida, the Haymarket anarchists of Chicago were in jail, and the Brand family of Fort Scott, Kansas, was bound for Rogersville, Tennessee, the little town from which we had sprung. That was how Prudence Brand had said it would be, and there was no arguing with her.

The truth was, I was grateful. I needed to get away from Fort Scott as quickly as possible, or find myself in jail for beating Hermes Van Horn half to death. That was the deal I had been offered by the court, but until Ma declared her desire to leave, I hadn't been able to accept it, and my time to choose was running out fast.

I hadn't meant to hurt Hermes so bad. But it was his fault as much as mine, for he had flirted with Minnie, my dear wife, one time too many. A man can only abide so much of that, even when, to be honest, the wife is doing as much of the flirting as the other party.

Minnie had a way of drawing men; I should know, for she had drawn me all the way to the church altar. The trouble was, her attractiveness didn't fade after my ring went around her finger. Men flocked to her like roosters to a hen, and she made little effort to spur them off. It was a vexing thing to endure. I guess that's why I was so rough on Hermes Van Horn when finally I had put up with enough of his lechery: I was unloading on him the full weight of vexation that had been building for a long time.

Minnie hadn't always been an unfaithful-hearted wife. At the beginning of our marriage she was as true as a woman could be. And then had come the great tragedy of her life, one that had jolted her to the heart and left her changed. Nobody ever really knew what happened to bring it about, but the short of it was that her mother was killed. Murdered by shotgun—and the one who did it was Minnie's father, who turned the second barrel on himself when his wife was dead. He had always drunk too much, so much it had gone to his liver and maybe his brain as well. That was how I account for what he did, but like I say, nobody ever really knew.

The murder sent Minnie into a month-long silence. It was like her form was present but her soul was way off somewhere else. And after she came out of it, she was different than the Minnie I had known. The flirting started, the too-long glances at other men, the moodiness, the seeming inability for her to decide whether she really loved me or not. I didn't hold her to fault for it; how could I, knowing what she had gone through? How could I ever think of raising my voice, much less my hand, against a woman who had seen her own mother murdered by her father? Minnie's suffering had changed me as much as it had changed her. It had made me love her more deeply than ever, and given me a world of patience with her trying ways. Maybe too much patience; after you hear my story, you can decide that for yourself.

Of course, a man can grow frustrated in being patient, and frustration can boil over into fury, as it had with Hermes Van Horn. All the anger I had been willing to take out on Minnie I took out on him.

And so now I had to leave, and Ma's declaration gave me the perfect opportunity to do it. In a way, the move would be relatively easy. We were a poor family, always had been, so there were few goods that would have to be carried along to Tennessee. Mostly just some of Ma's old furniture and quilts and other such things that are the treasures of aging widows. Beyond that there were the household goods Minnie and I possessed, and few these were, for we had shared the little rented house at Fort Scott with Ma, and there had been scant room for accumulation.

I would leave behind my smithy fixings, my anvil, hammers, bellows, tongs, and so on, and have them sold. I was a blacksmith in those days, like my father before me had been, and I was good at it, even though I seemed perpetually unable to make a decent living at the forge.

The day after Ma declared our destiny, I set about getting ready to leave. Minnie didn't like the idea at all. She was a Kansan and had never been out of her home state, except to cross the line a few miles into Missouri. She cried and fussed half the night after I told her we were leaving, but this did her no good. She cried and fussed all the time anyway, so I had grown deaf to her complaints.

What would happen soon after would make me

realize that perhaps I should have listened to Minnie more than I did. I would find that not even Prudence Brand could lay out a destiny unalterable by circumstance and a wayward woman. Before this adventure was done, I would find myself not rolling back into Tennessee as anticipated, but deep in the hills of Arkansas, searching for my woman, fighting my way through troubles far worse than those I was fleeing, and following the dangerous path of a strange and obsessed man whose life was wrapped up in a lost strongbox of Confederate gold. But I'm getting ahead of my story.

There were two other families bound for Tennessee from Fort Scott at that time. As bad luck would have it, one of them was the Malan clan, fathered by Bert Malan, uncle-by-marriage of Hermes Van Horn. Bert and I had always gotten along tolerably up until my row with Hermes. After that, however, I could all but smell the bad blood running through his veins every time I got near him.

Only his respect for my mother had led Bert Malan to let us become part of the wagon train at all. I decided to stay as clear of him as possible for the sake of group harmony, and devote my attention solely to driving the wagon, helping Ma with the cooking along the way (Minnie being a sorry cook who complained about the job so much that she usually escaped it), and generally looking out for trouble. There didn't seem much possibility of the latter. After all, this was 1886, modern times, and we would be traveling in settled territory all the way.

Our route would be from Fort Scott to Carthage, Missouri, on to Springfield, across the plateau of the Ozarks to Cape Girardeau, across the river and on into Mound City, Kentucky, then to Paducah, Hopkinsville, Guthery, and into Tennessee about Gallatin. From there we would travel across the midst of the state, over the Cumberland Plateau, into East Tennessee and Knoxville, the stopping point for the rest of the travelers. My family would head on northeast from there, to the old homeplace at Rogersville.

There was no sadness on my part when it came time to roll out of Fort Scott on our big covered wagons. Ma might have felt sad to leave behind the place where she had laid to rest her husband; if so, she hid it, as she always hid her feelings. As for Minnie, she was weepy and maudlin, wiping her tears and nose on the cuff of her jacket, an old castoff of mine that fit her like a tent.

The horses, belonging to a blacksmithing family, were already well-shod. Our two wagons weren't as well off and required quite a bit of repair. By the day of our departure, however, they were in as good a shape as old vehicles could be. The axles were greased, loose sideboards tightened, brakes checked and repaired. Loading followed a sensible pattern, with goods such as skillets and pots, along with foodstuffs, packed on top of those things that would not be required for use during the journey. The canvas

that was stretched across the bows was new and un-
punctured.

Hermes Van Horn came to see off his kin, and
maybe to make sure I was really leaving. I walked up
to him, stuck out my hand, and tried not to stare too
much at the bruises I had left blotching his face. His
round head, marked with the dark impressions of my
fist, reminded me of one of those world globes you
often see in schoolhouses.

"Hermes, I'm sorry we are parting on bad terms,"
I said. "I might have liked you if you could have just
left Minnie alone."

He looked at my extended hand like it held something scooped from the floor of a chicken coop. Without a word he turned away from me, snorting
derisively, and stomped off.

Bert Malan came up to me, a gruff look on his
face. "You trying to pick a fight again, Brand? You
stay clear of him, and of me too, if you know what's
good for you. It ain't out of love for you that I've
agreed to let you come along, you know."

"Just trying to make up for past hurts, Bert," I replied, and turned back to my wagon. All I had tried
to do was be a peacemaker, and even though my effort had been spurned, I felt then and forever
thereafter that I had done the right thing to try.

The caravan set off with a creak and a groan. Minnie was overcome with emotion and crawled back
under the bows and canvas to bury herself among the
bundles and strapped-down furniture. There she cried,
peering out through the back opening. I don't know

what she saw in Kansas that was so all-fired hard to give up. Her own parents were dead and her brothers and sisters well-scattered across the country. I had to wonder if it was Hermes Van Horn she was grieving for. Thinking about that made me mad.

Our family brought up the rear of the caravan, with me driving the final wagon. The one ahead, carrying Ma, was driven by a twenty-year-old member of the Malan family, Joseph Benjamin Malan, whose double name had been shortened down and slurred together for so long that he now went by "Joben." He even spelled it that way, perhaps because he thought doing so was cute and clever, or more likely because he was too stupid to know Joben wasn't a real name.

And stupid he was—one of the worst cases I've ever seen then or since. Joben Malan hadn't made it through the first year of school and couldn't count past twenty without getting crossed up. Even his family considered him an idiot. And lest it appear that I am overharsh in my description of Joben because of what happened between him and Minnie soon thereafter, let me balance things by noting that he was as handsome a man as one would ever meet. He was tall, dark-haired, friendly, and muscular, possessing many qualities women find appealing in a man. My own Minnie, it turned out, was one of those women.

Traveling in the wagon with Minnie and me was Minnie's parrot, a gift to her from one of her brothers the previous Christmas. Minnie, not a very imaginative woman, had given it the name Bird. It was quite a creature, capable of repeating almost anything it heard. Ma had even managed to teach it the first two lines of an Isaac Watts hymn. Minnie was only mildly fond of the bird; Ma liked it a little better but found its chatter hard on the nerves.

My big hound, Squatter, ambled along beside the wagon. He had been my companion since I got him as a pup, and he was a beloved beast. He was strong, easygoing, and a good watchdog, and best of all, loyal. And a man with a wife like Minnie needed loyalty, if only from his hound.

The first day's travel, southward and east, went well. The weather was clear and fine, the road smooth. The more miles that piled up between me and Fort Scott, the better I felt. Maybe back in Tennessee, the home of my youth, I could make a better go of it than I had in Kansas.

We camped that night at Carthage, Missouri, right on schedule. It had been a long day's haul, right at fifty miles, and both beasts and humans were weary. The site of our camp was good, rich with wood and water, and Ma built a roaring fire. After a supper consisting of numerous bowls of soup, I finished the final chores of the day's end and settled back with a pipe. Ma had her pipe out too, and was puffing quite contently. Squatter was sleeping beside her, making her warm and comfortable.

Fifteen or so minutes later I noticed that Minnie wasn't about. I asked Ma, who said she had seen Minnie walking across the camp, up toward where Bert Malan and his kin were encamped. I waited around a little longer for Minnie to return, and she didn't. At last I began to worry for her, and decided to go find her, even if it did mean going where I wasn't welcome.

Bert Malan saw me coming and stood. "What do you want, Brand?"

"I'm looking for Minnie. You seen her?"

"What's that supposed to mean? You implying something?"

"It means I haven't see Minnie in a while, and Ma says she had come over this way. That's what it means, and that's all it means." I swear, this man was aggravating enough to make the Pope cuss.

Joben Malan stood. He had a cup of hot coffee in a tin mug, and instead of holding it by the handle, he was cupping it with his fingers, shifting it to the other hand when it burned him, then shifting it back again when the second hand got too hot. So you can see it's not simple meanness on my part when I say he was stupid.

"I seen her," Joben said. "She was heading for the woods yonder."

"When was that?"

"A good hour ago, I'd say." He looked off in the direction Minnie had gone, and on his good-looking face was a deeply wistful, longing expression. That expression should have forewarned me of troubles to come. "I reckon she'd have hollered if something was wrong. And I'd have been proud to help her if she had, Enoch. I ain't got nothing against you, not me."

And right then, as if Joben's words had triggered it, Minnie's screech came ringing out from the woods.

It brought everyone in the camp to their feet, and sent me scampering. Joben followed, along with Bert and two or three others.

Minnie came racing out of the woods and right into my arms. "He's terrible, he's just terrible!" she yelled. Her face was streaked with tears and she was even more distraught than I was used to seeing her.

"Who's terrible?"

No answer was required, because the man in reference came striding out of the woods right then. It was Dewey Manchester, a hired hand of Bert Malan and driver of one of his three wagons. I hardly knew Manchester, but I did know his reputation. He was a troublemaker and had thrice gotten himself in hot water by acting in unseemly ways toward Fort Scott women. A man had knifed Manchester across the face for pawing his wife once upon a time, and the scar was broad and ugly and only partially hidden by his beard.

"What were you doing back there with my wife?" I demanded.

It was dark, but there was enough moonlight to let me see his maddening grin. "I took me a stroll at the same time she did, that's all. I didn't even know she was there until I stumbled upon her."

"He was watching me!" Minnie said. "I turned around and there he was, and he grabbed at me too!" She held up her arm. "See that scratch? It was his fingernail that done it!"

"Manchester, I'll peel your hide like a pelt if what she's saying is true!" It was a poor choice of words, for Minnie pulled away and looked at me angrily.

"*If* it's true? Of course it's true—you think I'd lie?"

"I'm sorry, Minnie, that's not what I meant."

"I never touched her," Manchester said. He had a cool, smug manner that made me want to light into him right there.

Bert Malan stepped between me and Manchester. "Whatever happened, there's nobody hurt and no reason for this to go on any longer," he said. "Enoch Brand, I suggest you get back to your wagon, and keep a closer watch on your wife."

That made me mad and got the best of my hardpressed restraint. "Bert Malan, you're treading a narrow log. You'd best watch your step, or you might take a tumble right off it."

He lifted a finger and pointed it in my face, squinting down its length like it was a pistol barrel. "It's you who'd best watch your step, Brand. I'm the boss of this train, and I'll throw you off it quicker than you can scratch your backside"—he glanced at the several women present—"your nose. Quicker than you can scratch your nose."

Joben Malan edged up to Minnie. "Are you all right, ma'am?"

She looked at him like she had just noticed his looks for the first time. Like a storybook princess would look at the knight who just saved her. Like Squatter would look at a fresh beefsteak.

"Why, thank you, Joben Malan," she said. Her voice was suddenly a soft, cooing thing, almost musical. It was painful to me to hear it. She hadn't used that voice with me for the longest time.

At that moment Squatter came rushing up. He had stayed back at the fireside with Ma, but had been drawn by the excitement. He must have sensed my hostility toward Manchester, for he snarled and would have leaped on him had I not reached down and grabbed him by his rope collar at the last second.

"That's it—this little gathering is finished," Bert Malan said. "Get on back to your place, Brand, and keep that mastiff away from good folk before it hurts somebody."

I might have spoken my mind to Bert Malan right then if not for my sense that this whole thing was about to get beyond control. With a great effort of will I swallowed my angry words and backed off. "Come on, Squatter," I said. "Come on, Minnie."

"I'm glad you're all right, Mrs. Brand," Joben said. He hadn't looked at me once, just stared at her with a dreamy gaze.

"Thank you, Joben," Minnie said. "You're quite a gentleman."

As we walked together back toward our camp, I asked her what had possessed her to take a stroll into the woods at such an odd time.

"Maybe you ain't noticed, but there's no privies in this camp," she replied.

"Oh."

We went a little farther. "You sure were acting awfully sweet toward Joben back there."

"He's a gentleman. A woman acts kind to gentle-men."

"Are you saying I'm not one?"

"What are you fussing on me so hard for?" She began to act upset, her voice rising. "You're always fussing on me, Enoch. I try to be a good wife, and you just fuss!"

"Don't talk so loud—folks are looking."

"I don't care! Let them look! Let them see a husband dragging his wife off from her home against her will, and see what they think of that!"

I said no more, out of fear of public humiliation. We reached our campsite, and I found myself thinking it was going to be one dreadfully long and trying trip before we made it all the way to Rogersville.

CHAPTER TWO

THE FIRST NIGHT OF THE JOURNEY HAD TAKEN A BAD turn, but I was optimistic enough to hope matters would improve afterward. Instead they only worsened the next day.

Bert Malan despised me more than ever and made no efforts to hide his feelings. For the sake of my mother and wife, I tried to ignore him. He made that difficult, talking about me to the rest of the travelers, calling me a troublemaker who had wrongly beaten his nephew, saying I would have been a murderer if someone hadn't restrained me when I was pounding on Hermes Van Horn. That, more than any other of his words, made me furious, because it wasn't true. Certainly I had given Hermes a severe beating, but at no time would I have lost control to the point of killing him. Blacksmithing had given me much physical strength; I knew the danger of unleashing it, and always kept it in sufficient check. So far, at least.

Minnie also continued to make the journey difficult. Obviously she had become smitten with Joben Malan, and all day, as she sat beside me on the wagon seat, she craned her neck this way and that to catch a glimpse of him on the wagon ahead of us. When I would ask her what she was doing, she would reply that she was merely stretching her back, because it was sore from sleeping on the ground.

Joben was equally taken with Minnie, but had the decency to avoid being too open in his attentions. Of all the Malan family, Joben was the only one who didn't seem down on me because of what had happened in Fort Scott. I might have come to appreciate him for that if only he could have kept his eyes off Minnie. Try as he would, he couldn't. I would catch them glancing meaningfully at each other at odd times, and whenever Joben noticed that I noticed, he would look the other way. Minnie didn't even bother to do that, and it caused me plenty of pain.

Even so, it wasn't Joben Malan who caused me the most concern. It was Manchester, the wagoneer. Like Joben, he was taken with Minnie, but in a way that was obviously more base and dangerous. He had no shame about it, and even seemed to enjoy stirring me up by staring openly at Minnie, and never faltering under my angry responsive glare. He came around close every time the wagons stopped for anything, and when he did, Minnie would draw up close beside me, more for protection than from affection, I suppose. Manchester scared her. He was a frightening man, to be sure. There were rumors that he had once murdered a horse trader in Ohio.

Ma saw the trouble coming even before I did. "We should get out of this wagon train," she told me. "We can go on alone. If we don't, you'll find yourself more trouble."

"I'm a grown man, Ma," I responded. "There's safety in a group. Don't worry. I'll watch my temper."

"Squatter! Here, boy! Here, Squatter!" The voice was high and harsh, and it punctuated its words with whistles.

Squatter made a throaty noise and lifted his head. I sat up. "Shut up, Bird," I said to the squawking parrot. "It's the durn middle of the night."

"Squatter! Here, boy!"

The wind had blown the cloth off the parrot's cage. I replaced it and tied the corners to the thin cage bars to ensure it stayed in place. Then I rolled over to see if the bird had awakened Minnie.

But there was no Minnie there. Her place was empty, the blankets tossed aside.

Squatter was up on his haunches. He looked east, stood, and growled into the dark. Ma was snoring in her bedroll near the fire, oblivious to the world.

I rose. Being in a mixed camp, I had worn my trousers to bed. Throwing my shirt and coat on took only a few seconds, and then I invested a few more in strapping my Colt-bearing gun belt around my waist. I had a bad feeling about this, and worried for Minnie.

The camp was a dark place of banked fires and snoring people. Squatter led me east; he had obviously detected something in that direction. Maybe just a stray dog on the perimeter of the camp. Or maybe

Minnie, God forbid, snatched away by Manchester? But no; surely not. Squatter would have sent up a howl if Manchester had come around our wagon. He despised the man as much as I did.

But he didn't despise Joben. Squatter had always liked Joben Malan, and never even sent up a growl when he was near.

I heard them before I saw them. They were on the far side of a little stand of trees and brush. It *was* Joben there with Minnie; I knew it because her voice had that cooing quality, the one she once had reserved for me.

A great fury rose inside me. My insides felt like a pot on hot boil. I wouldn't abide this. I had beaten Joben's cousin back in Fort Scott. Now I would give the same to Joben, and if it sent me to jail, to jail I'd go.

I stopped, took a deep breath, and forced myself to unbuckle my gun belt. If my temper got the best of me, I didn't want a pistol anywhere handy. I hung the belt over the stub of a branch. Clenching and unclenching my fists in anticipation, I began my advance.

And stopped it as quickly. Joben had just said something that threw the whole situation into a new and more grim light.

"You? What are *you* doing here?" I knew from his tone and the direction toward which he spoke that he wasn't addressing me. Right then, Minnie went, "Oh, no, oh, no!" and I knew that whoever they had seen was quite likely to be Manchester.

"Hello, Joben," another male voice said. I was right; it was Manchester. "What are you doing out here, cuddled up with the wife of another man?"

"You get out of here, Dewey Manchester. You was fired today and there's no cause for you to stay around."

Manchester had been fired? I hadn't heard about that. Of course, the Malans wouldn't have been likely to come running to me with the latest news. Who had fired him? It surely had been Bert Malan. No one else would have had the authority.

"I ain't never been fired until this day," Manchester said. "You want to know something, Joben? I don't like being fired. It ain't a good feeling." There was a pause, during which Manchester must have gestured toward Minnie. "Now, that right there, that's what gives a man a good feeling. But it looks like you already know that, huh?"

Joben said, "It was just that sort of trash-talk that got you fired, Dewey. Now get out of here before I have to work you over."

Manchester laughed. "You, work me over? Pshaw!" He spat on the ground. "You couldn't whip my granny, Joben. Hey now, what do you reckon your daddy would have to say about his own boy out pawing around on the wife of another man, the very day he fired his best hand over a lot less than that? What do you reckon?"

"Joben, I'm going back to the wagon," Minnie said.

And all at once it all broke loose. I couldn't see

them from where I was, and so didn't know what set
it off, but suddenly Minnie screamed, Joben yelled,
and there was a loud scuffling. Manchester was cussing fiercely, and fists pounded flesh. I felt sure the
fists were Manchester's, the flesh Joben's.

Until then I had been transfixed in my tracks, overwhelmed by a sick feeling inside that had sapped the
strength from my anger. I broke out of it, grabbed the
gun belt off the branch and vaulted toward the fight-
ers, breaking into the clearing at the same moment I
got the pistol out of the holster. I flung the empty gun
belt aside. Squatter snarled, barked, and flashed past
me. He had been waiting for me to move; now that I
had, he was in the fight even before I could reach it.

I could tell from some muffled, chopped-off words
that burst out of Joben that Manchester had a pistol.
Something moved in the air; a terrible, metal-against-
bone thud informed me that Manchester had just connected his swung pistol with Joben's skull. Joben fell.
Minnie screamed and ran off into the dark. Squatter
threw his big form against Manchester and had the
bad luck to have his own skull struck by Manchester's
big pistol. I couldn't see the weapon clearly, but figured it was surely the big, outdated Army Colt that
he usually bore.

Manchester's pistol roared. In the brief lightning
flash of its explosion, I saw Joben lying off to the
side, Squatter collapsing at Manchester's feet, and
Manchester's twisted face looking down toward the

dog. It was Squatter, not Joben, who he was trying to kill.

"No!" I yelled hoarsely. Then I was against Manchester, knocking him down, landing atop him and forcing a curse and burst of stinking breath from him. His smoking pistol hit me in the side of the head. I rolled off, came to my feet in a spasmodic motion and swung my own Colt blindly.

He grunted and jerked and fell away from me. My head suddenly began to swim, as if the blow he had landed on me had taken a delayed effect. Groaning, I passed out as I heard shouts and yells from the camp.

One of the last thoughts that went through my mind was the desperate hope that Manchester's shot had somehow managed to miss Squatter. I loved that dog dearly. I didn't want him to die, especially at the hands of a man who was hardly more than a dog himself.

Then I had one more thought as the last of consciousness faded: I might not wake up again. While I was out, there would be nothing to keep Dewey Manchester from killing me—and he was just the kind of man to do it.

CHAPTER THREE

MINNIE'S TEARSTAINED FACE WAS BEFORE ME WHEN I
came to. It wore a look of sincere concern that
touched me, even through the clouds around my
brain. To be cared about by Minnie, to have her fret
over me like she had in our first days—that was all I
could ask. I hungered for her affection, would have
paid any price for her to feel about me as I felt about
her.

"Enoch, you're alive! Oh, I'm so glad!" She bent
over and hugged me. My head throbbed as she jarred
me, but I smiled anyway.

Looking at me across her shoulder was another
face, this one showing nothing but anger. It was Bert
Malan's. The fire lit his countenance but couldn't
erase the darkness of his expression as he glowered
at me. Flicking my eyes around, I saw that I had been
moved back to the main camp and placed within the
circle of yellow cast by the fire. Across from me lay
another person. Joben. He apparently was out cold . . .
or dead.

"Move aside, woman," Malan said to Minnie, putting his hand on her shoulder and rather roughly push-

ing her to the left. She rose and backed away, then went over to where Joben lay.

"Easy . . . on my wife," I said in the loudest voice I could achieve, and that was almost a whisper.

"Your wife is in just about as much trouble as you are, Enoch Brand," Bert Malan said. "I knew I shouldn't have let you into this caravan. My best judgment was against it, and if not for your mother, I'd have never done it. Well, this is what comes of not following my own good sense."

"Manchester . . . where did he go?"

"Manchester? He's long gone. I sent him packing today, the sorry lecher. But you've got worries enough of your own without bringing him into this, Brand. If Joben dies, I'll see you hang for murder."

I tried to sit up. Even as foggy as my thinking was, I could see that a great misunderstanding was under way here. "Wait a minute, Bert. It wasn't me who hit your son. It was Manchester."

"Do tell? Did he use your pistol to do it? There's blood crusting the sight. And Joben's head is laid open."

"Manchester hit Joben. I hit Manchester."

"Did you? Then where is he?"

"He ran off, I reckon. I'm just happy he didn't kill me."

"He was never here, and you know it. You'll not lie your way out of this one."

Hot breath hit my face, then a wet canine tongue licked my cheek. "Squatter! You're alive!"

"Get that hound away from here," Bert instructed

a man standing nearby. The man advanced. Squatter snarled and growled deep in his throat. The man glanced at Malan, shook his head and backed off.

"Why did you do it, Enoch? Why did you hurt Joben?"

"I didn't . . . I told you, it was Manchester."

Bert knelt and spoke so others around couldn't hear. "Listen, Brand—I know Joben has been smit with your wife, and I know that he shouldn't have let himself get that way. But the truth is, that woman of yours is mighty . . . common in her ways, to put it the nicest way possible. She led him on. Tell the truth— you came out here to kill him, didn't you?"

Rising anger was giving me my fortitude again. "I came out here because I woke up and found Minnie gone from beside me. I was afraid somebody had come and dragged her off."

"What? With that big hound of yours guarding your spot? You ask me to believe that story?"

"I figured it was Joben—Squatter never barks at Joben. And I was right. But Manchester showed up before I could get to them. He and Joben fought, and I came in when Joben got knocked down. Manchester hit Squatter too, and shot at him. I managed to pistol-whip Manchester; it's his blood that's on my pistol sight, not Joben's."

"Your pistol also has an empty shell in it. It was you who fired that shot, not Manchester. And you were shooting at Joben. Admit it!"

"No. Because it's not true. That empty has been in my pistol for three days."

Joben groaned. Minnie yelled out, "Glory be! He's come back to us!" and hugged Joben just like she had hugged me earlier, only this hug was more enthusiastic.

Joben moaned in a trembling voice, tried to sit up and failed. Minnie said, "Joben, are you all right?"

The big oaf looked up at her with the blankest of faces and spoke words that evidenced the blankest of minds. "Mama, is that you? Mama, I fell out of the tree!"

Lord help us, I thought. He was fool enough before, and now he's worse.

"Joben, it's me, Minnie!"

"Mama, help me to the outhouse. Hurry, or I won't make it!"

"Well, he's too addled to clarify anything you've said," Bert said.

"Then ask Minnie."

"Her words means nothing. She'd naturally cover for her husband."

Someone stepped up beside me. I looked up and saw Ma's prunish face. Her pipe was clamped between her teeth and she wore a harsh expression.

"Mr. Malan, I don't like the way you're talking to my son," she said.

Malan faced her. "I hope you'll understand, Mrs. Brand. Enoch has injured Joben, just like he injured my nephew Hermes in Fort Scott. I have no choice but to be harsh with him."

"Can you prove he did this?" She waved at Joben, who was still addle-brained and urging "Mama" to take him to the outhouse. A pause, and then he said, very despairingly, "Too late! Too late! I tried to tell you, Mama, but you wouldn't listen!"

Bert Malan ignored his son, around whom everyone was suddenly clearing a wide circle. Even Minnie had backed away. "There's evidence on Enoch's pistol that your son hit Joben," Bert said. "Mrs. Brand, I'm afraid I'm going to have to throw your son and his wife out of this wagon train. You, however, are welcome to stay. I'll have some of the boys drive your wagons."

"Don't believe I want to stay in a train led by a man who's been looking for any bad thing he can find on my boy," she said.

"I'm trying to be fair."

"Pshaw! I heard Enoch saying that your wagoner was the one who hit your son. But you don't appear too interested in checking to see if that is true."

"I'll be straightforward with you, Mrs. Brand: I don't want that daughter-in-law of yours around to entice my boy into doing wrong things."

"Hah! So now we're getting more to the truth! You think my boy and his wife to be so much rubbish! You just been looking for a way to get shut of them, ain't you!"

"I'm sorry you don't understand, Mrs. Brand," he said.

"You must admit that your younger kin have caused a lion's share of trouble for me and mine."

I had managed to sit up by now. "Don't argue with

him, Ma. Let him throw me off," I said. "I can follow on later."

"I won't hear of such as that," she said.

"Well, this can be took up come daylight," Bert said. "At the moment, we should all return to our sleeping places and get what rest we can."

Ma was ready to argue with him, but I reached out and touched her hand. "Let it go, Ma. He's been looking for the chance to do this anyway. It's for the best; if I stay on, there'll be nothing but more trouble."

We went back to the wagon, but slept no more that night. I argued with Ma about the idea of me and Minnie leaving, until at last I had persuaded her not to fight the notion. Furthermore, I convinced her to remain with the wagon train, which could provide her more company and safety than I could alone.

I also had an ulterior motive for keeping Ma in the caravan. I wanted the chance to be alone with Minnie, to try once and for all to win her affections again. That would be hard to do with a third person close by.

It angered me that I would not be given the chance to prove that Manchester, not me, was responsible for hurting Joben. But what did it matter, really? Bert Malan was determined to think the worst of me, no matter what the truth was. I was just glad nobody had been killed in the nocturnal fight, and that I wasn't going to have to put up with Malan any longer. Let the wagon train go on ahead; I could follow a day or so behind, and meet up with Ma in Knoxville.

That is, if Minnie would be cooperative. She was

a miserable woman at the moment. She had just realized that she was about to become an outcast, and
grieved over it like she had been sentenced to death.
When she wandered off again, telling me she wanted
to be alone, I didn't follow her, even though I knew
that most likely "alone" meant being with Joben Malan once more.

We were put off with a couple of riding horses and
one packhorse, my Colt pistol and aging but well-kept
Henry rifle, food, blankets, clothing, and sundry other
items that would see us through as we followed the
wagon train. There was Squatter too, and Bird the
parrot. Ma didn't want to have to put up with its chatter across three states, so I had agreed to keep him
with us.

It really wasn't so much a case of Minnie and I
leaving the wagon train as the train leaving us. We
simply remained in camp while the wagon rolled out.
It was sad to see Ma looking back around the canvas,
watching us recede from her sight.

"It's just as well, I reckon," I told Minnie. "My
head aches something fierce from where Manchester
clouted me. I could use a day or so of rest. Besides,
Minnie, it's a chance for us to be together."

She smiled at me, but it was a sad sort of smile.
Lord knows that woman knew how to make me feel
melancholy to the bottom of my soul.

It was odd, but I slept most of the next day. I say
it was odd because I've always been a light sleeper,
getting by on five or so hours of sleep a night. I sup-

pose it had to do with the blow to the head that I had suffered.

Minnie moped around most of the day, and often I caught her wistfully looking off in the direction the caravan had taken. Most likely she was thinking of Joben.

On the second day I felt much more fit, and we traveled, following the tracks of the wagons. That night we camped on the edge of Springfield, apparently again on the same place the wagon train had put up a night earlier. I judged this based on the dead fires, tracks, tramped earth and such.

"I want to go into town, Enoch," Minnie said.

"Well, I don't blame you for that. We'll go. I might even scrape up enough money for us to have an honest-to-goodness restaurant meal. What do you think of that?"

"I'd like that," she said, and gave me a smile, a real one, not one of her fakes. I was encouraged.

That night in Springfield, dining with Minnie in a restaurant on meager money I had no business spending, was one of the best evenings of my life. I hardly cared right then about the trouble back in Fort Scott, or the subsequent trouble over Manchester and Joben Malan. Perhaps it had all been fate, tossing us around in order to put us into a situation that would draw us closer. Minnie was as pretty a picture as I've ever seen, sitting across that table from me, drinking coffee and eating apple pie that swam in fresh cream. She insisted that we take a bottle of wine with us when we returned to camp, and once there, she poured glass after glass of it down me. Celebrating our marriage, she said.

Holding her as we fell asleep that night—passed out was more like it, in my case—I was glad she was my wife. The best part was that it seemed she was glad of it too.

She was gone the next morning. I followed her horse's tracks almost all the way back to Springfield, right up to an abandoned old livery at the edge of town. There her tracks were joined by the tracks of another horse. I recognized it as Joben Malan's, based on a funny little curl at the end of the one of the horseshoes. I should recognize it; I had made the shoe myself, back in my Fort Scott smithy.

He had come sometime late in the night, while I was passed out from the wine. Had Minnie and Joben planned this mutual escape during that time she was "alone" the night before we left the train? I found my answer quickly—a wadded note at the edge of the clearing. It bore Joben's writing, and instructed Minnie to get me drunk the night we camped near Springfield, and sneak off to meet him at this old stable.

So it had been a sham. All the happiness and closeness of the previous night, that wonderful sense of togetherness in the Springfield restaurant . . . a sham.

Their tracks led south, cutting across the Ozark Plateau and toward Arkansas. Where was Joben taking her? Wherever, it was certainly away from the wagon train. Apparently he had run out on his overbearing father, who was still trying to run his life even though he was a full-grown man . . . at least in body. In brain he was still nothing but a big boy, and probably always would be.

I had mounted and was about to ride away when I heard a an odd but familiar voice. "Farleytown! Farleytown!"

"Bird?"

Indeed it was. The parrot was still in its cage, which was sitting inside the livery door. What would have possessed Minnie to bring the parrot all the way here? The best I could figure was that she had decided on a whim to take the bird wherever it was she and Joben were going, then had changed her mind once she got here and simply dumped the parrot.

"Bird, it's a good thing I found you, eh?"

"Cracker! Cracker! Cracker for the good bird! Farleytown!"

"Farleytown, eh? That's a new one. Who taught you that? Did Minnie teach you that one?"

He fluttered and shifted on his perch as I lifted the cage. "Farleytown! Farleytown!"

"Reckon she must have taught you that one, huh? I never heard of no Farleytown." I was talking at a rapid rate, trying to keep myself from being overwhelmed with sorrow. There's no more depressing thing that to wake up with a head pounding from too much wine, to find the woman you thought you had regained has been playing you for a fool, just to get away from you.

"Farleytown! Farleytown!"

I had been trudging back to my horse, but I

stopped. "Wait a minute—Bird, you might have learned you a word Minnie didn't intend for you to learn! Now, wouldn't that just beat it!"

I rode into Springfield and asked the first man I met if there was a Farleytown anywhere in the region. Yes indeed, he said, though it wasn't real close. Down across the Arkansas line, south and a little westward, maybe seventy, eighty miles from where we were. I thanked him and rode back to camp. I had left Squatter guarding it, and he was glad to see me returning.

"Squatter, the inside of my head feels as ugly as your face. But I reckon I can't let that stop us, can I? We got a ride to make, and it ain't Tennessee we're bound for. We'll go back into Springfield first of all, and I'll send a letter on to Aunt Kate in Tennessee, telling her we might be a little late arriving. Minnie's run off with Joben Malan, and I believe they've gone to Arkansas. We're going to find them, and I'm going to bring Minnie back.

"Guess I'm a fool to love that gal. Lord knows she's brought us enough grief, eh?" I scratched his ears, the way he always liked it. "Better a fool than a quitter, I always say. So fools we'll just have to be. That's right, ain't it, Squatter? That's right."

I wrote the letter to Aunt Kate, asking her to send one of my cousins to meet Ma in Knoxville about the time I anticipated the wagons would get there. Then, with Squatter trotting alongside and the packhorse trailing behind, Bird's cage bobbing on its back, I rode into Springfield and posted the letter. From there we turned southwest and began to ride.

And that is how it was that in the fall of 1886 I aimed for Tennessee and wound up hitting Arkansas, the place where I would meet Leviticus Lee and first hear of the lost Confederate gold.

CHAPTER FOUR

THE DAY BECAME GRAYER, THE SKY HEAVIER AND LOWER-
set, the farther I advanced into the jumbled Ozark
hills and mountains. Even the beauty of the autumn
russets, scarlets, and yellows couldn't brighten the
bloomy atmosphere. Squatter seemed as ill at ease as
his master, sniffing about and growling into the woodlands as we rode.

About dusk I decided we were lost, and felt foolish
for it. I had thought I could find the way to this Farleytown community—for community, rather than real
town, was surely all it was. Now I wasn't all that
confident. Checking the sunset, I realized I had veered
off too directly westward and had managed to leave
the main route.

The forest here was exceedingly full of undergrowth that often reached nearly to the tops of the
rather scrubby trees. But as darkness descended and
I made camp for the night, those scrubby trees seemed
to grow into looming, staring things, and the undergrowth became alive, the breeze running through it
like breath. I hadn't felt such a creeping up and down
my backbone since I was a kid listening to my uncles

tell ghost tales on the porch on summer nights.

Surely Minnie and Joben hadn't come this way. It aggravated me that not only had my misdirection left me out here in this spookish wilderness, but also had slowed me in catching up with them.

"Farleytown! Farleytown!" the parrot screeched out.

"Farleytown, eh?" I grumbled. "I hope that's where we'll find them—else I'll just see how good a parrot will roast on a spit."

Squatter came up, tongue lolling out and dripping, and looked to me for attention. I scratched behind his left ear. "Squatter, I'm glad you're here," I said. "I hate to admit to fearfulness, but I don't like this place. Not a bit."

I had bacon and flour, so I fried some of the former and made biscuits and a big shapeless loaf for Squatter from the latter. The parrot got crumbs, and Squatter ate his loaf smeared with bacon drippings. My beverage was boiled coffee, which I sipped on for an hour or so after the meal. I felt better then, not as wary as before. Soon my head was lolling and my brain growing fuzzy with the coming of sleep.

I jerked upright when Squatter came to his feet, bristling and growling. The parrot let out another "Farleytown!" The fire had died substantially, though enough flames licked up to cast a fair light a few feet around.

Grabbing up my rifle, I looked into the encircling forest. "Who's there? Who's there?"

The parrot echoed, "Who's there?"

"Shut up," I mumbled. Squatter, meanwhile, was continuing his tense growling and edging forward inches at a time.

I kicked a few more sticks onto the fire and let them catch and brighten the scene. Something moved in the brush, and now Squatter sent up a loud, howling bark and looked at me. One command and he would launch into the woods to take on whatever, or whoever, was out there.

"Call off that hound," a rumbling voice said abruptly. It startled me to realize how close the unseen speaker was.

"Show yourself, or I'll turn him onto you," I replied.

The brush moved; Squatter growled like an empty belly as into the firelight stepped one of the strangest men I had ever seen. Back in boyhood I had once read of legends from across the ocean about spirits that inhabit the forest and are somehow an incarnation of trees and brush, leaves and wood. Those old stories were the first things through my mind as I examined the peculiar being before me.

His trousers were rags of wool held up by a rope. A hatchet was stuck into his belt on the left side, and a knife and rusty pistol on the right. His shirt was homemade and shapeless, looking like a particularly crude hunting shirt of the sort worn a century ago. My impression, however, was that this garb had not been made in imitation of any particular design. It was as if the man had simply thrown together a rough garment with a minimum of effort. His hat was of felt, very old and battered, and the front of the brim curled up toward the crown. The dirt-crusted face was bearded, and seemed pallid, though the rich firelight made that hard to be sure of.

And here was the feature that intrigued and then frightened me: The man wore brand new boots, store bought boots, and obviously too big for him. How would such a poor old forest elf as this come by such a fine pair of boots? He wouldn't have the money to buy them, and even if he had, he surely would have bought boots to fit. It was obvious to me that these boots had come from someone else—probably a lost traveler, just like me. And I was willing to bet whoever gave up those boots hadn't done so willingly.

"Who are you, and why are you coming to a man's camp by night?" I asked with deliberate gruffness. I figured it best to grab the advantage here from the outset.

"I smelt your bacon, seen your light," the man said. "My name's Copper. Eb Copper."

"Well, if I'm trespassing on your land or something, I'm sorry. I didn't plan on it. I lost my way." I winced at my own ill-advised words. I had just informed this stranger that I was lost.

"Farleytown!" the bird said.

Abruptly, a second figure appeared, materializing out of the forest. He was younger than the first man, but no more kempt and clean, and no more less ragged. His mouth lolled open as he stared at me, then he turned his gaze toward the parrot. The young fellow had no visible teeth. His hat was new; probably it had belonged to the same unfortunate whose boots now graced the older man's feet.

"Look-air, Papaw! Look-air 'at tawkin' bird!"

"This here's Iradell, my boy," Cooper said. "He likes your bird yonder."

"What do you want from me?"

"Cup of coffee. Biscuit, if you got it. We're lost too."

I didn't buy that. These men were too much part and parcel of this forest for me to believe this was an alien place to them.

" 'At-air bird tawks! Tawks like a man!"

Lord knows I didn't want these men sharing my camp. Squatter's feelings apparently were similar; he was still in a stance for attack. But what could I do? If they intended ill for me, it was better to keep them within view than to send them out of sight.

"Help yourself to the coffee. I'm afraid the biscuits are gone—but I'll make more."

"You're right kind, and we thank you, Mister . . ."

"Cleveland. Hal Cleveland." I felt so mistrustful I didn't see cause to even give my own name, though it would have meant no more to them than the false one I presented.

"Cleveland . . . like the president."

"That's right. Uncle Grover and me, we're close. I suppose he'd send out the army to find me if ever I went missing."

Squatter dropped to his haunches and rested his big head on his paws, keeping an eye on Eb Copper. The younger woodsman, meanwhile, was at the parrot's cage, poking a finger through and guffawing every time the bird said a word.

I made biscuits with one eye on my work and the other on my unwanted guests. The passing of time did nothing to make me feel better about them.

"Where you heading?" Eb Copper asked.

"Just travelling farther south," I replied, not wanting to share any more information about myself than was essential. I was wondering how I was going to manage to sleep with these two in my camp. Hang it, I *wouldn't* sleep. How could I, feeling sure they would bash my head in or shoot me as soon as I did?

"How 'at bird learn to tawk?"

"My wife taught it. It's her bird."

Ed Copper glanced around. "Wife? Where she be?"

"On her way here with her brother. He's a federal marshal," I said. "Though he nearly lost his job here a while back for shooting a man without cause. He didn't like the looks of the fellow, so he just pulled out a shotgun and blasted him right in the loins. It was ugly."

Copper's eyes narrowed. He gnawed his biscuit like a rat. He didn't seem much worried by the stories I was telling. The thing that had him concerned was closer at hand, tangible, and drooling.

"That dog there, how mean is he?"

"Not much mean, unless a man moves too quick around him. Then he'll go for the neck, and I swear you can't stop him once he does. He chewed the head off a fellow one time. The poor old fool had made a move as if to hurt me, and Squatter just went out-of-his-mind-loco." I was doing my best lying in hopes of convincing the two Coppers that it wasn't worth staying around to pluck the feathers from this particular guinea.

Copper stood, stretched, and yawned, Squatter's eye on him the entire time. "Mr. Cleveland, I'm weary. Do you care if we share your camp tonight?"

Glumly I replied, "Make yourself comfortable." There was nothing else I could say.

"Thank you, sir. I'll be proud to brag that I shared a camp with the president's nephew."

"Wanna buy that bird," Iradell Copper said.

"Can't sell it. It's my wife's."

"Want that bird."

"Sorry."

The senior Copper was in the process of removing the hatchet from his belt. He reached for the pistol then, and I watched him intently. If anything was to happen, this seemed a likely moment.

"That's a fine dog you got, Mr. Cleveland. Yes indeedy. I reckon it would protect its master until its last breath, just as you've said."

"Reckon it would."

"That's why I have no choice but to do this, Mr. Cleveland." He pulled the pistol and shot Squatter, right there before my eyes.

"No!" I yelled. "*No!*"

Already Copper had picked up his hatchet and was advancing toward me, his expression very business-like, for this indeed was nothing to him but business.

It was if I were frozen in place, unable to move. His shooting of Squatter had stunned me into paralysis.

I broke out of it too late to dodge the blow. The hatchet went back, came forward, and pain, far more explosive and racking than that inflicted earlier by Manchester the wagoner, cracked like lightning in my head as the flat side of the hatchet struck me. I fell to my knees, then forward onto my face, landing partly atop Squatter.

He whimpered and moved beneath me. "Squatter . . ." I reached up to touch his twitching snout. Then Eb Copper appeared above me, squatting down to examine me.

"I reckon I didn't hit you hard enough," he said.

He hefted up the hatchet again. I closed my eyes and awaited the death blow.

CHAPTER FIVE

I NEVER KNEW WHY EB COPPER DIDN'T KILL ME. MAYBE I passed out at just the right moment and he thought I was already dead. Maybe some grain of mercy remained in his hardened old soul. All I know is that when I had opened my eyes and looked around, I was still in this world.

They had taken everything: guns, food, supplies, even the parrot. All that was left was me, dizzy, hurting, injured, staggering through the darkness on foot, carrying the bloody form of Squatter in my arms. It was cold and hellish. A drizzle fell, the same one that had chilled me back to consciousness. I didn't know where I was going; all I knew was I had to go. Had to keep moving.

Squatter was heavy, straining my muscles and making my twice-injured head ache all the more. Sometimes I would stop and put him down, crouching beside him and stroking him until my breath returned. Then I would pick him up again and proceed through the dark Ozark forest.

I caught myself thinking that it would have been better had they gone ahead and killed me. There re-

mained enough of my old, rational self to repudiate
that despairing notion. "It's good we are alive, Squatter," I said aloud. "As long as we're alive, we can
keep going."

Squatter's blood encrusted my hands. Eb Copper's
bullet had struck the dog in the hindquarters, shattering one of the back legs and leaving an ugly hole. At
the beginning Squatter had howled and thrashed when
I tried to pick him up. Gradually shock had numbed
him, and now he whimpered like a pup as I struggled
along. I was sure he would die. The thought made me
cold inside.

At last I could go no farther. A hill rose beside me,
with a round depression notched into its side. There
dog and man collapsed and lay in a common heap,
falling into a sleep that was more a stupor than a state
of rest.

Morning light awakened me. I was stiff, cold, and
aching. Moving, I heard a guttural canine groan.
Squatter was still beside me, and still living. When I
spoke to him, he wagged his tail weakly.

It crossed my mind that the merciful thing to do
would be to strike him from behind with a big stone
and end his suffering quickly. The thought never became action. This was Squatter, my most faithful
companion. I couldn't bring myself to deliberately
end his life.

Rising, I picked him up and began walking. Weakness overcame me; I discovered that the dime-novel
depictions of people quickly shaking off head injuries
like the kind I had suffered weren't very true to life.

Never had I felt so dizzy and sick. Returning to the place we had spent the night, I lay down with the hound and raked leaves over us. We slept again.

The day dragged past, and we remained where we were. A rain came, but we weren't much dampened, being sheltered by the hill, which was between us and the wind. A rivulet of water ran down a rocky portion of the hillside. Catching some of it in my hands, I drank, and gave some to Squatter as well.

Squatter's wound looked uglier and appeared to be beginning to fester. If that happened, I would have no choice but to find some way to mercifully end his life. I wouldn't let him die the terrible death of infection. If only I had a gun.

Night fell, and I was hungry. Squatter lived even yet . . . and maybe was a bit stronger. I hardly dared believe it, for fear of being disappointed.

I slept hard until morning, and when the light came, I was hungrier than ever, but feeling more stable, more my old self. When I stood, I wasn't as dizzy as I had been. And Squatter still hadn't died.

"Come on, boy," I said. "Today we're finding food. And if we can, help for you. We'll clean that wound, get you well again."

I started to examine the wound, then averted my eyes. The smell of it had struck my nose, and I knew what I would find if I looked. So I didn't look. I just picked up my old friend and started walking though the leafy Ozark hills.

*   *   *

The house seemed to be abandoned. I studied it closely from the cover of the trees for a long time before I dared step into the scrub-filled clearing in which it stood. Built unevenly of logs and roofed in the old style with boards instead of shingles, this must have been the refuge of some Ozark hermit.

Or perhaps of two—a father and son I was not eager to meet again, at least not under these circumstances. At some later time, when I was strong and evenly matched, I might welcome the chance to give my version of the time of day to Eb Copper and son.

The longer I examined the cabin, however, the less I suspected it was occupied by Copper or anyone else. The front door, though intact, stood open, and trash aplenty had been blown in through it. There was a big cobweb across one of the windows, which was broken out.

Rising, I carried Squatter to the door and looked in. Furniture of the roughest sort was inside, draped in cobwebs and covered with leaves and assorted grit that had blown in through the door and broken window. There was a stove in one corner, beside a closed cupboard. A ladder extended up to a loft above the single lower-level room.

"Hello?" I called out, weakly. No answer came.

Confident now that the place was indeed unoccupied, I carried my dog inside and lay him down on a pile of rags that apparently had been another dog's bed at some past time. Squatter was very weak now, and I was sure his last would come soon.

"If we're lucky, there'll be food somewhere here,"

I said. "But we can't bet on it, Squatter. Nobody would go off and just leave food."

I went to the cupboard and opened it, figuring I would find it empty. Instead, I looked in upon several cans of various foods, from peaches to beans. "What the devil's this?" I muttered. Why would anyone have simply abandoned their cabin without taking their food along?

Unless . . .

I glanced up at the loft, moved over to the ladder, put my hand and foot on it . . . then removed them.

"We'll eat first, Squatter," I said. "I'll look up yonder afterward."

There were knives, forks, and spoons in a pile beside the cans. With a knife, I pried open a can of pork meat and dumped it in front of Squatter. He lifted his head just enough to lick at the meat and drag it into his mouth with his tongue. There was very little strength left in the faithful old fellow, and sad it was to see.

I ate beans, peaches, and corn, and never had a meal gone down so well. The food tasted old, but I barely noticed. My stomach, too long empty, grumbled and growled as it adjusted to an overdue filling. I could feel my strength returning even before I downed the last bite.

Squatter was asleep by then, so I covered him with a tattered old blanket I had found. Slipping up into the loft, I set my nerve for what I expected to discover, and was surprised when it wasn't there. Descending, I glanced out a back window. A privy stood at a cockeyed angle across the backyard. There was no back door, so I had to circle around from the front to reach it.

Sure enough, he was in there, what remained of him after several months of death. He was collapsed on the floor of the privy, just a jumble of dried flesh and bone and hide and decaying clothing. I closed the door, swallowed, and hoped I wouldn't lose the meal I had just devoured.

That explained well enough why everything here seemed intact. The corpse had appeared to be that of an old man; I suppose he had been a hermit, just as I had initially thought. Likely I was the first living soul to set foot on this place in all the months since he had died.

I explored his cabin and found little worth the having, with one exception. A long twelve-gauge shotgun was leaned behind the cupboard, almost out of sight, along with a box and a half of shells. On the butt of the shotgun were the roughly carved initials H. J. I cleaned the weapon as best I could and loaded it. Hefting it, I smiled. Being armed again made me feel not so helpless. Let the Coppers come around now, and see how I greeted them!

"Thanks, H. J.," I said aloud. "I'll treat this weapon with care."

And then I thought of Squatter, and the satisfaction of again having a weapon vanished. Now I did have means to end his suffering . . . but did I want to?

I walked over to him, shotgun in hand. Trembling,

I raised it, leveled the double barrels at his head . . .
and he awakened and looked up at me.

The shotgun lowered; I couldn't do it.

"Squatter, poor old boy," I said, kneeling and putting my hand on his head. "Poor old loyal boy . . .
God forgive me, but I just can't bring myself to end
your life. I just can't do it."

Darkness found me sitting beside Squatter, knowing
what my duty was but finding me still unable, or unwilling, to do it. At length my chin dropped and I
dozed.

A noise, a movement outside the cabin . . .

I lifted my head too quickly, making the bruised
places on my skull burst with pain. For several moments I had no idea where I was. There was something cold in my hand. I looked and saw the shotgun,
and then I remembered.

Looking down to see how Squatter was, I was
amazed to find his resting place vacant.

"Squatter?"

His familiar growl rumbled. In the darkness I could
scarcely make him out, standing beside the door.

More movement outside, and not the movement of
wind in the branches. The unmistakable movement of
a man, or men.

If the Coppers were there, by heaven, I would
make them wish they hadn't come around. I stood,
fought dizziness a few moments, and advanced.

My caution was tempered with happiness at seeing

Squatter on his feet again. Maybe he had turned a corner and would be well.

He growled again, and sent out a little bark. He took a step forward, and the back of him collapsed, the wounded leg unable to sustain his weight. I knew then it was sheer force of will that had made him able to rouse from his rag bed. He had detected the creeping man outside and had risen to protect his master.

"Here, boy, nice dog . . ."

The voice came from outside. The man, whoever he was, had heard Squatter's growl. I was pleasantly surprised to realize the voice was different than that of either of the Coppers. Of course, that didn't mean this fellow was necessarily any less dangerous.

There was hardly any light, just a vague, imprecise moonlight that spilled in through the window. Footsteps outside . . . I was about to call out for the prowling man to identify and show himself, when suddenly there was a minuscule change in the shadows, and there he was, looking in the window.

I never knew where Squatter found the strength to make his leap, given that one of his hind legs was useless and he was weakened through and through. With a howl he shot from floor to window; the man outside yelled in fright. Man and beast vanished from my view.

"Squatter!" I shouted. "Squatter!"

Outside there was snarling and barking, cussing and yelling. I yanked open the door and went out. Lifting the shotgun, I fired the contents of one barrel into the sky. The flash and roar of the twelve-gauge was impressively authoritative. The man, whoever he was, cussed again and loped into the woods. Squatter went after him, but he faltered and collapsed.

I ran to him. He rolled onto his side, looking up at me, whimpering. His exertion had taken the last of his strength.

"Good boy, good dog—looking out for me to the end, huh? Good dog."

There wasn't enough light to let me see his eyes clearly, but I could feel the plea in them. I knew what I had to do. Bending down, I nuzzled my face against his ear.

"Good-bye, Squatter. Good-bye. I love you, boy."

The rest I did quickly, so as not to lose the necessary will. Standing, I aimed, closed my eyes, squeezed the trigger.

The roar was the most jolting thing I had ever heard. It rang in my ears, then faded into a silence that seemed to ring even louder. An empty, hollow ringing that wouldn't end.

I knelt beside him and reached down to stroke his fur. But I wouldn't look at him, not just yet. I wanted to touch him while he was yet warm, and think of him for a few more minutes as being as he had always been.

Inside I had the most aching feeling. But I knew I had done the right thing. He would suffer no more.

CHAPTER SIX

I CONTINUED THROUGH THE FOREST A DAY LATER, FEELING more alone than I had ever been. I had remained at the little cabin long enough to get more of my strength back, and to lay Squatter to rest. Once his grave was filled, I decided to dig a second and bury the bones of the old hermit whose remote home had given me refuge. It seemed the decent thing to do; no man should have to go back to the dust from which he came while lying on the floor of a privy.

As I traveled, I kept my eyes open for the sign of any human presence. I was thinking not only of the Coppers, but also of the lone man who had appeared at the cabin window. There had been no sign of him since Squatter ran him off, but one never knew, and the man might be angry over the way he had been treated. If so, he might not treat me very kindly should he come across me alone in the woods. I was glad I had the shotgun.

The remnants of a footpath led from the cabin and through the forest. Figuring this must have been the old hermit's pathway to civilization, I stuck with it. The terrain here was remarkably uneven and convoluted, and at times I felt as if I was crossing my own path. It reminded me of my father's old joke about walking a mountain trail in Kentucky that was so twisted that he met himself coming around a bend.

It wasn't in my destiny to meet myself in such a manner today, but I was to run across a familiar old companion, and some acquaintances I would have preferred not to meet. It all happened very unexpectedly.

Walking through a rugged, area of limestone bluffs and springs that gushed up from the ground, I stopped abruptly when I heard a voice, shrilly cussing. The voice I knew very well; the words it was speaking, however, were quite out of character, for we had always been careful never to let the parrot pick up foul language.

I melted back into the trees and began looking around for the bird. Something fluttered in a treetop nearby, and I spotted it there. It was Minnie's parrot, all right, and he was cussing like a sailor. Obviously Iradell Copper had been busy teaching his kind of vocabulary to his ill-gotten pet. I wondered how the parrot had manage to get away from him.

"Bird! Hey, bird! Whur-ye be, bird?"

The proximity of the speaker startled me. I ducked deeper into my cover and began looking about for Iradell. At the same time, I drew the shotgun closer. If need be, I'd use it.

Iradell Copper came striding up the path, and I swear I smelled him before I saw him. He had an angry look on his face, and the empty cage in his hand.

"Come 'ere, bird, come 'ere afore I skin ya."

If Iradell was here, his father probably was as well. Yet as I looked around, I detected no sign of him. Iradell hadn't seen me. Two options faced me: I could remain where I was and probably escape detection, or I could rise, level the shotgun on the mountaineer, and declare my intention to regain the goods he and his father had stolen from me.

The latter was tempting, especially when I considered that the Coppers were responsible for Squatter's wounding. Even so, it made more practical sense to lie still and let the situation pass. After all, if Eb Copper was nearby, it would be two men against one, and even though I had a shotgun, those odds weren't good.

Something moved farther down the path. It was a horse—*my* horse, stolen from me. Seeing that roused a seething anger inside. Then I noticed that Iradell was wearing my gun belt, and practically gave way to fury. I'd be hanged before I'd let Iradell Copper go away from here on my horse, wearing my gun. For that matter, it was my parrot he was trying to recapture too, at least far more mine than his.

Noting that Eb Copper was still nowhere in sight, I gave into my impulse and stood, leveling the shotgun right at Iradell's midsection. He was so startled that he cussed, stepped back and tripped on a root. That left him on his rump, looking up at me with his mouth gaped open. Come to think of it, I hadn't seen him when his mouth *wasn't* gaped open.

"Hello, Iradell Copper," I said. "You remember me?"

"Don't shoot me, don'cha shoot me!"

"I won't—if you'll be so kind as to give me back what you took from me."

"Ain't never took nothin' from ya!"

"You really are stupid, ain't you? That gun you're wearing, that horse back yonder, even that parrot up in the tree—it's all mine, and you stole it from me, you and your mangy father."

"Ain't never seen ya! Ain't never stole nothin' from ya!"

I began to see how deficient this fellow really was. He truly thought there was something to be gained by denying a guilt as obvious as his. I would realize later that he had been trained to do that by his father, and lacked the sense to see when such a course was futile.

"Get up," I ordered.

He came to his feet. Nervous now, he was drooling at the lip, and didn't even bother to wipe it away.

"Take off that gun belt, very slow."

He did, and let it drop.

"Now back up, into the woods, and wrap your arms around that pine there."

He didn't budge.

"I said for you to back up and . . ."

Iradell was looking past me, and grinning now. I shifted to the side to keep him in view while also looking behind me.

"A man don't like seeing another man holding a

shotgun on his own boy." Eb Copper said the words
coldly. His expression was serious. Almost as serious
as the rifle leveled on me. My rifle, the one he had
stolen.

"You'd best drop that rifle, Copper," I said. "Else
you'll see your boy cut in half when I empty these
barrels."

"You wouldn't do that."

"I would indeed."

"No you wouldn't. Because you know that as soon
as you pull that trigger, you'll be a dead man."

I swung the gun around and trained it on him. We
stood facing off, shotgun against rifle.

"Maybe you're right," I said. "So now maybe I'll
just cut you in half instead of your boy. That way,
when I pull the trigger, it's you who'll be the dead
man."

"I'll shootcha! I'll shootcha!"

Blast it all, I had just made a big blunder. Even as
I had turned the gun on the senior Copper, the junior
had reached down and pulled the Colt from my stolen
gun belt. Now I was caught. I could kill one Copper,
certainly, but would only be cut down myself by the
survivor.

"Good bird! Cracker for the good bird!" the parrot
squawked above my head.

The old man had the boy tie me to a tree, my back
against the trunk and my hands roped together on the
far side. It was a big tree, and Iradell did his best to
make my hands meet, so that when he finished I felt

as if I were stretched on one of those medieval racks. The father and son stepped back and looked at me like sculptors admiring a completed masterpiece.

"We going to leave 'im, Papaw?"

"No sirree, son. We're going to shoot him."

"You won't get away with this, Copper," I said. "This is murder, out and out murder. They'll put you on the gallows for it."

"No, they won't. They'd have to catch me, you see, and that's something ain't nobody been able to do. And what do I care if I got to murder a man? You ain't the first, friend. Me and Iradell, we make our way in this world by doing what we have to. Sometimes we have to take a life or two. That's just they way things go."

"Let me shoot 'im, Papaw! Let me!"

"No, Iradell. Not yet. I want the first shot."

First shot . . . that phrase implied that the first shot wouldn't be the last. Eb Copper intended to have his cruel fun before he completed this job. I pulled at my ropes, wishing I could get at him.

"Use 'at-air shotgun, Papaw! Shoot his leg bones!"

"That's a good idea, Iradell. I got to hand it to you for good ideas."

The old mountaineer laid down the rifle and picked up the shotgun. He opened it, checked the shells, and slammed it shut again. Meanwhile, I was praying what I was sure would be my final prayer, and wishing I had prayed a few more prayers back in the days when death wasn't staring me in the face.

"Well, friend, it's just too bad for you that you

couldn't just leave things be. You had to come pick-ing on my Iradell. I don't stand for such as that. Got no choice but to kill you."

"When they hang you, my ghost will be there to watch," I said. I was talking with bravado, but my mind was full of pictures—Minnie, my mother, my late father, and scenes of the life we had lived.

"Well, let's get it done," he said. He lifted the shot-gun and squinted down the double barrel.

"Farleytown!" the parrot said.

I fought back the urge to close my eyes. In no way was I going to give Copper the satisfaction of seeing me cringe. It was all I could do to keep my eyes on him.

The roar came more quickly than I had expected, and made me yell. For a couple of seconds the world became unreal. Time had frozen. Then I began to re-alize things, one by one.

First off, the shotgun that had fired hadn't been the one in Eb Copper's hands. Second, Eb Copper no longer retained the shotgun. For that matter, he no longer retained the top of his head; someone had fired a blast of buckshot into his skull from a thicket of old briars about fifteen feet to the side. It made a messy and unpleasant sight. Third, Iradell Copper was scrambling for the shotgun his father had dropped when he fell dead. He got it, swung it around, and fired wildly into the thicket. I heard a grunt of pain, followed by another shotgun blast that sent fragments of briar bushes spitting out from the thicket. Iradell was struck in the chest, and died on the way to the ground.

I'm not to proud to confess that I fainted dead away right then from the shock of what I had just seen. If you think it was unmanly of me to do that, I ask you to think about what it would be like to be tied up and awaiting a torturous dispatching, only to have such a horror suddenly occur right in front of you. Then ask yourself if you think you would have done any better.

Awakening, I sat up. No longer was I tied to the tree; I was on the ground, well away from it. Glancing over, I saw the gory bodies of the two Coppers, and gave strong consideration to passing out again.

"Just don't look at them," a man's voice said. I turned and saw him, sitting on his haunches, his sawed-off shotgun laid across his lap and his hands tucked up under his overleaning upper body, out of sight. He was thin, white-bearded man dressed in canvas pants, a thick cotton shirt, black wool coat, and slouch hat. He grinned, showing straight but yellow teeth. "That's the trouble with shotguns. They do so durn much damage. 'Specially these cut-down varieties."

I groaned and laid back down. "I thank you, sir, for saving my life."

"Glad to oblige. I take no pleasure in killing any living soul, but there's times it must be done. Them two, I reckon they earned it."

"My name's Enoch Brand. I'm from Fort Scott, Kansas."

"Well, sir, my name's Lee. Leviticus Lee. And I come from anyplace worth coming from, and several that ain't."

Rolling to the side, I pulled myself back upright, and then settled into a seated position amid the fallen autumn leaves. Looking at Lee, a strange feeling began to form itself somewhere in the pit of my stomach and churn upward through me. It was a kind of combination of joy, terror, relief, sorrow, and most every other feeling you could think of, and when it rose as high as my throat, it came out in uncontrollable laughter, the kind that isn't far from weeping. You've probably seen that happen before at particularly tragic funerals, or maybe even experienced it yourself.

Leviticus Lee seemed to enjoy my display. He grinned, then the laughter spread to him, and we sat guffawing together, while the two deceased Coppers lay in their death blood not twenty feet away. Looking back at it with the hindsight of so many years, it all seems pretty morbid.

"How'd you come across them two?" Lee asked.

I told him how they had come into my camp, eaten my food, knocked me cold, and shot my dog.

"So that dog was wounded when he come at me, huh? My, that must have been quite the critter!"

I was surprised. "That was you at the window? You that Squatter went after?"

"Indeed it was. Lord knows it surprised me too. All I was doing was looking for a roof for the night.

Last time I was through here, there was a feller living there. Known as sort of a hermit, but he'd put folks up who needed it."

"When were you through last?"

"It's been many a year, young man. Many a long year, and a long mile."

I told him I found the hermit's body in the privy, and buried it beside Squatter. Lee seemed to think that a generous thing to do.

"Mr. Brand, you're a fine young man. That I can see. I'm glad I run across you."

"Even though my dog took after you?"

"A good hound looks out for its keeper."

I stood and stretched my legs. It was awfully good to be alive when I fully expected to be dead by now. I expressed the sentiment to Lee.

"I'm glad you're feeling good . . . maybe you can help me out here a minute."

"Just name it."

So far he had sat with his hands tucked up and the shotgun under his torso as he leaned forward over his haunches. Now he lifted his left hand and held it up.

It was about enough to make me faint again. Almost half of Lee's hand was gone, just ripped away. I recalled the grunt of pain that had come from the thicket as Iradell Copper fired that last panicked shot into the brush. The pellets must have caught Lee right in the hand.

I went to him and helped him get seated against a tree, and went to work at once to clean and bandage the ugly wound as best the resources of the moment and place would allow. I was thinking, as I worked, of how this had been the bloodiest, most violent, most frightening day I had experienced in my life.

There was no way for me to know then that before my time with Leviticus Lee was past, there would be much more of the same to come my way, more trouble and adventure than I had ever figured to run across.

CHAPTER SEVEN

WE RECOVERED BOTH MY STOLEN HORSES, MY GUNS, and—with effort—I even managed to catch the parrot and get it back into its cage. Leviticus Lee was riding an old mule; somehow that didn't surprise me. It seemed to fit.

My new companion was an odd fellow, but I liked him. How could I not like a man who had saved me from death at the hands of two mountain murderers? That event had forged an instant bond between me and Lee. And when I found he was bound for the Farleytown area, like I was, I determined to accompany him and find some way to repay the great favor he had done me.

Lee had little to say about himself, leaving me to figure out what I could about him on my own. He did explain his odd name when he mentioned having a late brother named Genesis and a sister named Exodus, who now resided with a husband in New York City. He hadn't seen her in twenty years.

I put Lee's age at about sixty, but I wasn't at all sure about it. He might have been younger by as much as a decade. I say this because everything about the man gave evidence of a difficult life, the kind that can put age on a man before his time. It was in his bearing, his way of talking, his attitude. Lee was a jovial man, yet hardened. Friendly, yet isolated.

He didn't ask me my business, but I told him anyway. In fact, I was just about bubbling over with the need to talk, simply to relieve the tension that had built up in me over my past days of suffering and trial. He found my dedication to finding my wayward wife interesting and maybe unreasonable, given what she had done. Yet he made no effort to change my thinking about her, as some might have. Lee was the type of man who left others to their own way of thinking, asking only that they give him the same freedom.

He knew the terrain, though not with the familiarity of one who had been upon it recently. He informed me that I had never been as lost as I had thought; Farleytown was within a day's ride. He figured he could get us there easily enough, unless the area had changed so much since the early sixties that he didn't recognize the old landmarks.

The early sixties . . . that let me know that Lee hadn't been here since the war. Maybe he had been a soldier. I tucked that piece of supposition away, not thinking it particularly significant at the time.

I let Lee lead the way, and thought all was well, until I noted that our trail had led around to a place we had passed an hour before. We had traveled in a circle.

As I pointed this out to Lee, I suddenly noticed that sweat was pouring off his brow, even though the day was very cool. He held his injured hand tightly against himself; the bandage had soaked through with blood.

"Mr. Lee, I believe that hand is making you sick," I said. "Maybe we ought to put up for a while and let you rest."

"Maybe you're right, Mr. Brand."

Lee wouldn't let me examine his wound, saying it hurt too much to fiddle with it. After we had rested a couple of hours, I suggested that perhaps we should go on. Lee fidgeted and asked if I would mind reaching Farleytown tomorrow rather than today; he was feeling rather peaked and thought it might be well for him to travel no farther today.

I agreed, but with such obvious reluctance that he tried to send me on ahead alone. "There's no cause for you to be held back by a pokey old badger like me. You go on alone—just stick with that trail."

"That's the trail that brought us circling back to here," I replied. "I'd just get myself lost, going alone. Besides, if you're puny, you might need some tending. I don't mind staying."

Truthfully, I did mind a little. I had already had enough of camping in the Ozark woodlands. Besides, too much delay might result in Minnie and Joben going on out of Farleytown—if ever they had gone there at all—and me losing their track completely.

Yet there was nothing else to do but remain. Owing Leviticus Lee my life as I did, I could hardly run out on him while he was feeling sick.

Night came, and still he kept his injured hand to

himself, swearing it needed no attention. Clearly it did. He passed the night in great pain, and by morning I was certain that the shattered hand was putrefying. Already some miscoloration was visible between his cuff and the base of the crude bandage.

"Mr. Lee, we've got to get you into Farleytown and to a doctor. I'm fearing you might be bound to lose that hand."

"I've lost many a hand in my day. But just in poker. Not like this." He laughed, but it really wasn't funny either to me or him.

"Come on, Mr. Lee," I said. "Let's get riding."

I had already readied the horses. Lee rose to head for his—and staggered. Sitting back down hard, right on the ground, he leaned to the side and became sick.

I knew then the hand really was turning bad, and with frightening speed. When he was through with his heaving, I helped him up and managed to get him into the saddle. It was anybody's guess right then whether he would be able to stay in it all the way to Farleytown—and anybody's guess whether we would even be able to find the place.

Fortune smiled, and by following a new fork in the trail, I led us to a wagon road. Heading southwest, it widened, until at last farms and houses came into view.

Farleytown itself was still a mile ahead when Leviticus Lee fell from his saddle. I stopped, ran to him, and knew as soon as I examined the hand that Lee was a sick man indeed.

What to do? He was half senseless, obviously in no shape to ride. To make a litter would take too much time. Looking around, I spotted a two-story house, just visible on the other side of a narrow strip of woodland. If it had been summer, with foliage full, the house would have been invisible.

"Mr. Lee, I'm going to try to get you to yonder house, and see if we can't get a wagon or something to carry you to the doctor. You understand me?"

From its perch on the back of one of the horses, the caged parrot repeated, "Mr. Lee! Mr. Lee!"

"Can you hear 'em coming?" Lee asked fearfully. He stiffened, looked around as if frightened. "The Yanks! I can hear 'em! Listen!"

He was out of his head already. I hadn't known it was so bad. If only he hadn't hid the mounting infection from me, perhaps we could have found some way to deal with the problem before now.

"There's no Yanks here, Mr. Lee. They've been gone more than twenty years now. Come on—let me get you up."

With great struggle I got him to his feet. The prospect of trying to get him onto a horse, even in the belly-down dangling position, was unthinkable. Despite his rather spare build, Leviticus Lee carried a good amount of weight. Or maybe I was just weaker than usual because of all that had happened the last few days.

The curving drive leading through the trees toward the house was really nothing more than a couple of wagon-wheel ruts cut through the woods floor. We had circled halfway around to the house when I heard the rumble of a vehicle approaching behind us. Lee's right arm was draped over my shoulder and I was carrying most of his weight, so it took me a couple of seconds to get us turned around to face the new arrival.

The approaching vehicle was a very creaky buckboard. The driver, an ample fellow dressed in a nice but wrinkled suit of clothes, and wearing a thin mustache on a wide face, pulled the buckboard to a stop, slid on some spectacles that had been in his coat pocket, and eyed us up and down.

"Are you the men who left those horses and such on the road back there?"

"Yes, sir. My name is Enoch Brand. This man with me is Leviticus Lee, and he's hurt. Is that your house ahead?"

"Indeed."

"Well, sir, then you're the man we're seeking. Mr. Lee has been injured in the hand, and the wound is going bad on us. I had wanted to get him to Farleytown, but he has become too sick to ride. If you have a wagon we could cart him on . . ."

"I can do you better than that, Mister . . . Brand, did you say? Take him on to the house, and I'll send my boy to fetch Dr. Ruscher from town."

"I thank you, sir. You're a truly charitable soul."

His name, he said, was Fairweather, Robert Elroy Fairweather, and he was a merchant in Farleytown. He ran a big general store—a store at a crossroads that I would ultimately find pretty much *was* Farleytown—and he provided space upstairs for a retired old physician out of Memphis who had settled in Farleytown to enjoy some ease in his old age. Despite his officially retired status, Dr. J. B. Ruscher was kind enough to keep hours a day or two a week and dispense medical care to the Farleytown people. Quite kind of him, didn't I think?

I agreed that surely it was kind, and in the current situation, might be of life-or-death importance. I didn't worry about saying such a thing with Lee right there to hear it, for clearly he was in a world of his own right now, raving and talking about Yanks and gunshots . . .

And gold coins. Something imprecise and vague and garbled, but those two words made their way out of the welter of nonsense and into my ear. And I could tell that Fairweather heard them too, could tell it from the way his face looked pinched and sharp for just a second . . . could tell it from the way he and I both fell silent for another second thereafter.

The Fairweather family, a sizable bunch, met us on the porch of the house, and Fairweather barked instructions to what looked to be his oldest son. The boy nodded, ran back to the buckboard, turned it, and drove it toward town. And when we had gotten Lee inside and onto a bed in the nearest bedroom, Fairweather sent two more boys out to bring in the horses Lee and I had been forced to abandon on the road.

I sank into a chair, took a deep breath, and closed my eyes in battle against a mounting headache that had started at the base of my skull and was advancing forward. Meanwhile, the Fairweather children—how many were there, anyway? A dozen?—stirred and talked excitedly among themselves, as youngsters will do, and made sounds of disgust when Fairweather pulled away Lee's clotted bandage to reveal the mangled thing that had been a hand.

Fairweather looked at me sternly. "Mr. Brand, it looks to me as if this wound was the result of a shotgun blast."

"It was," I said.

"How did it happen?"

I thought about the terrible incident in the forest, and of Eb and Iradell Copper falling dead from the blasts of Leviticus Lee's sawed-off. How should I answer Fairweather? I wanted to tell the truth—but might the truth result in charges coming against Lee, the very man who had saved my life? I knew nothing of the law; such a thing seemed very possible to me.

And so I lied. "It was my fault," I said. "I dropped a shotgun and it went off. Thank God it hit his hand and not his head."

"Yes. Yes." Fairweather looked at the hand again. "I do hope Dr. Ruscher will hurry."

I stood there, feeling bad for having lied, and wondering if ill would come of it. My mother had always told me that falsehoods carry the price of trouble. I hoped she was wrong.

Leviticus Lee jerked and yelled and said something else about gold—and once again Fairweather and I both pretended we hadn't heard it, while both knew that we had, and that the words had sparked the start of something fierce and greedy in us.

It's a cursed substance, gold. It has brought more tragedy to mankind than anything except maybe the thirst for power. The lust for gold is a destroying lust. I know that now, as an elderly man writing a narrative of an old but clear memory. I learned that bit of wisdom, you see, back in Arkansas in 1886. Learned it so bitterly that I never have been able to forget it.

But at the time I stood in Fairweather's house, beside Leviticus Lee's bed, waiting for the arrival of Dr. J. B. Ruscher, the learning and the bitterness still lay ahead, for me, Leviticus Lee, and the Fairweather family alike.

CHAPTER EIGHT

THE FAIRWEATHER BOY WHO WENT TO TOWN FOR THE doctor must have made a big show of his mission, for when he returned with the aging sawbones, he was followed by a half-dozen local stragglers who wanted to know who the excitement was all about.

"There's a man here, a stranger, named Leviticus Lee, and he's been injured," Robert Fairweather announced to them from his porch. "With him is this gentleman, Mr. Enoch Brand. Now, if you folks will be going, perhaps we can return some semblance of order to this place."

"Leviticus Lee? What loco kind of name is that?" one of them asked.

"An odd one, that's all," Fairweather replied. "Now, be off with you."

Dr. Ruscher, though very old, seemed to know his business. He examined Lee's hand, inquired how it had been hurt (prompting me to repeat my lie—with a little less feeling of guilt this time, the conscience being the most malleable and easily worn-down of man's capacities), and announced that in all likelihood the hand would have to be amputated.

"But there may yet be hope," he said. "I want to stay here through the night, Robert, and see if there is any sign of improvement. If not, I'll have to take it off in the morning."

We moved Lee to an upstairs bedroom, banishing two of the Fairweather sons to sleep in the barn loft. Dr. Ruscher, as good as his word, settled into a chair to pass the night beside Leviticus Lee. I already appreciated the old physician's dedication. How many retired doctors would have gone to this much trouble for a stranger?

I put the parrot's cage into Lee's sickroom to keep Dr. Ruscher company. "It talks, and I'm afraid it's taken up cussing," I said. "It wasn't me or Mr. Lee who taught it that. Just some troublemakers we ran across."

"I'm sure it won't say anything I haven't heard aplenty before now," the doctor said.

When I left the room, he was trying to prompt the bird to talk. Leviticus Lee, meanwhile, was tossing and jabbering out of his head, as before, and I caught myself listening for another mention of gold coins.

Now that things had settled down somewhat, I was able to properly thank the Fairweather family for their hospitality. I counted a total of seven children, five of them boys, and all resembling their father more than their mother.

Speaking of the mother, it was clear from her looks that she didn't much like having two strangers present in her house, and I couldn't much blame her. Lee had already bled on the rug and two beds. But I didn't think that was the real source of her sour attitude.

Blanche Fairweather had already picked up on the fact that Lee had been injured by a shotgun blast. It was my clear impression that she wasn't confident that my tale about an accident was true. Maybe it was some sort of intuition she possessed; whatever, the looks she gave me were the sort you would give a stranger you suspected of having stolen your best china. I tried to be friendly and look harmless, but this didn't make any difference in her ways around me.

"Mr. Brand, how long do you think you'll be staying with us?" she asked me as she busied about to make supper.

"Blanche!" her husband cut in. "What a rude question! Mr. Brand and Mr. Lee are welcome here as long as need be." He looked at me and smiled, one of those too-big smiles like the deacons give visitors at the front door of the church on Sunday mornings. "Besides, my dear, I think these men will prove to be good friends to this family."

Now, what did he mean by that? I figured he had in mind those gold coins Leviticus Lee had raved about, and hoped to get his hands on a few. What he couldn't know, of course, was that I was in no position to help him on that score. I had no idea what or where those coins were supposed to be. They might have been the figment of a raving man's fevered imagination, as far as I knew.

I secretly resented the interest that I sensed Fairweather held in the gold. Lee and *my* partner, not his. If anyone shared in any gold, it should be me.

Without my realizing it, Leviticus Lee had made a jump in my mind from traveling companion to partner. Was it only because of my gratitude to him for saving my life . . . or was I also succumbing to the lure of the mysterious treasure he raved about?

Lee was worse, not better, in the morning, and Dr. Ruscher announced that an amputation was required. "I want you to help me, Mr. Brand."

"Me? Listen, doctor, I'm not too good with blood and such. I might just be in your way . . . especially if I passed out on you."

"I need your help. Blood is blood, and we've all got it, so you can just get over sweating about it. If you're weak of stomach, by gum, you need to be broken of that foolish weakness anyway. I got no patience for the weak of stomach. By gum, where would the world be if we men of medicine turned weak of stomach? Answer me that one!"

Blanche Fairweather scowled at me from the hallway as I entered the room with Dr. Ruscher to begin the operation. Even after I closed the door, I fancied I could feel her angry gaze boring through it.

The doctor had already wrapped Lee's wrist in a cloth soaked in some sort of acidic liquid, maybe carbolic acid, to kill the germs on his skin. With a strong-smelling liquid soaked into a cloth, he put Lee to sleep, and informed me that part of my task would be to make sure he remained knocked out throughout the surgery. He then began cleaning Lee's putrefied wound with a solution that he said was forty grains of chloride of zinc to the ounce of water. "It cleans away the source of the putridity," he explained.

I was already beginning to turn green, and when he got down to the actual business I had to squeeze my eyes shut out of fear I would faint dead away. The doctor didn't let me get away with that for long, however, because I was of no use to him blind.

"Open your eyes and help me keep this arm elevated," he ordered. "You need to man the tourniquet. Come on, man, get hold of yourself! I've got no time for squeamishness. I have to wonder how far medicine would advance if not for folks going all white and pukish every time they see a little blood."

"Sorry," I muttered, and determined to hold my own no matter what.

It was one of the hardest things I have ever done, or ever will do. Dr. Ruscher was a good physician, but even the best amputation job results in more squirting blood and gruesome noises of flesh-and-bone-slicing than anyone would ever want to see or hear. Three or four times I was sure I would faint right there, but with great effort I managed to hold up. When it was all over and Leviticus Lee's stump was neatly bandaged, I sent up a fervent prayer of thanks for an ordeal ended.

"I'm no judge of doctoring, but it appears to me you did that well," I said rather shakily.

"I've removed many a limb, son, back during the war. It's a bad thing to have to do to any man, but better to lose limb than life."

"What will you do with the hand?"

"I'm giving it to you."

"What?" I blanched and waved him off. "No thank you. I got no use for it."

"I'm not joshing with you. Mr. Lee was lucid enough during one stretch last night for me to explain that I was going to have to remove his hand. He agreed, and told me to give it to you for a burial. He said it had been a fine appendage to him, and he wanted it treated properly, not just burned up as rubbish."

"You're really not joshing with me, Doc?"

"I'm not."

"Lord have mercy."

About dusk I set out to fulfill Leviticus Lee's unusual request. The hand, wrapped up in several layers of butcher paper, was in a wooden box I had begged off Fairweather. The box was bigger than necessary, and I had stuffed sawdust and shavings around the enwrapped hand, and tacked down the box top.

I told no one what I was doing, and rode alone. Out the road a ways, I turned right and entered the woods, riding until the undergrowth was too thick for the horse. I left the horse there and walked on across a rise, carrying the box, shovel, and my rifle, which I had brought along in case I ran across any troublesome woodland critters.

One thing about digging a grave for a hand instead of an entire body: It doesn't take long. And that was good, for it was growing dark on me and I didn't want to have to make my way back to the road without light.

I cast the shovel aside, put the box in the hole, and prepared to fill in the hole again. Then I stopped. It didn't seem right to bury part of a man without at least some words being said. But what did you say when you were funeralizing a hand?

"Lord," I said, with hands folded before me and head lowered, "I've come here this evening to lay to rest the left hand of Leviticus Lee. I'm sure it's been a good hand to him. Thank you for giving him use of it for the years he had it, and I hope you'll let him keep its partner for the rest of his days. And that the stump won't hurt him too much while it heals. Amen."

Then I filled the hole, tamped down the dirt, and rolled a couple of nearby rocks in place above the mound. It was getting very dark now; it appeared I'd be going home without the light after all. I hoped I'd have no trouble finding where I had left the horse.

A stirring in the brush behind me . . .

I wheeled. "Who's there?"

No one answered. Might it have been an animal? Just in case, I picked up my rifle, took a step toward the place the noise had come from . . .

Someone moved—not something, but someone, for I could tell it was human—and made a wild scrambling. I raised the rifle.

"I hear you in there! State your business, and show yourself! Why have you been watching me?"

More scrambling; I wondered if whoever it was

had caught his foot on a root or in a tangle.

"All right, I'm coming to face you, and you'd best—"

I cut off with a yell when a gunshot sounded in the thicket and a slug sped past my head. Shards of blasted leaves rocked slowly to earth at the thicket's edge. Now it was my turn to scramble. Ducking to the side, I rolled behind a stump, lifted the rifle and reflexively returned fire. A man's voice sent up a yell and cuss, and then I heard him tear free out of the thicket and run off through the dark woods.

Slowly I stood. When I was satisfied that he was gone, I advanced. There was no light now, and no way to examine the thicket for evidence of who it might have been.

I was mystified, and scared. Whoever it was, he had shot at me in a way that indicated he meant business. But why? I knew no one here, and had made no enemies in Arkansas but the Coppers, and they were dead.

The horse was still there, and I led it out to the road and mounted. By now I was worried. What if the man I had shot died and they blamed me? How could I prove he had fired the first shot? What if they looked back at my trouble in Kansas, tied it together with this, and decided I was such a troublemaker that I needed to be put away for many years? As I've penned here previously, I knew nothing of the law and what could and couldn't be done. Anything, no matter how dreadful, seemed possible to me.

That night I said nothing of what had happened,

not even to Lee. Of course, he was sleeping under the influence of laudanum and was therefore no partner for conversation anyway. The doctor had gone home, promising to return the next day.

"Where have you been?" Blanche Fairweather demanded when I showed up. The bluntness of the question took me back a little, but I supposed she was so used to keeping tabs on her own boys that she had gotten into the habit of forthrightness.

"I had an errand," I said.

"Supper was an hour ago. I fixed a good meal, and you didn't even have the common decency to come to the table."

"I'm sorry. I didn't mean to anger you, Mrs. Fairweather."

"I had to feed that friend of yours upstairs with my own hands, and I didn't much like that either. I was expecting you to do that. It seems the least you could do to repay our kindness to you. I don't have time to be nursemaid to a stranger with a household this size to tend to."

Robert Fairweather walked into the room, and looked aghast when he caught on to the way she was harping at me. This lady made my Minnie, no poor hand at the harping business herself, seem downright kind by contrast. "Dear wife, don't be so harsh with our guest!" Fairweather looked at me, smiling that oversized smile. "Mr. Brand, was that my shovel I saw you carrying back into the barn?"

"Yes, sir. I hope you didn't mind me borrowing it."

"Not at all. You had something to dig up, perhaps?"

"No. To bury."

"Ahhh!" The sparkle in his eye let me know just what he was thinking, and I despised him for it, despite his friendliness. I could read him so easily; he figured me and Leviticus Lee as potential sources of gain, and that was the reason for this exaggerated joviality and kindness of his. Maybe the initial kindness had been true charity, but now . . .

"It was Mr. Lee's hand," I said.

His face fell. "Oh. I see."

I turned to Mrs. Fairweather. "Ma'am, I can tell I anger you, and I'm sorry about it. It wasn't my plan to impose upon you, and I pledge to you we'll be out of your hair as soon as possible. I came to Arkansas to find a straying wife, and there's no need for me to stay here to look for her. If you want, I'll move on out, and come back and get Mr. Lee as soon as he's fit to travel."

She looked hopeful, then peered at her husband, who stepped up and said, "Nonsense, nonsense, Mr. Brand. I insist you remain with us as long as you are in the area. And Mr. Lee as well, of course."

I glanced at Mrs. Fairweather to see how she would react. "He's the man of the house," was all she said, turning quickly on her heel and walking back into the kitchen.

"Blanche has a harsh side to her—don't mind it," Fairweather said. "I'll have a word about it with her later."

"No, sir, please don't not on my account." I could just imagine how she would despise me after being chewed over by her husband about her treatment of me.

"No, no, I don't mind it a bit," he said. "Come in, Mr. Brand, have a cigar with me, if you would. Let me get to know you better."

"Well, thank you, sir, but I'd best be seeing how Mr. Lee is doing upstairs."

"He's fine, fine—just checked on him myself. He's sleeping, so we won't bother him."

I was still shaky from the mysterious shooting encounter in the forest, and hoped my hands weren't trembling too much when I lit the cigar. Meanwhile, Blanche Fairweather walked in, bearing a tray with my supper on it. She set it down before me, on the foot table in front of the sofa.

"I don't let the boys eat in here, but you can, Mr. Brand. You get special treatment here, you see." Her sarcasm had quite an edge.

When she was gone, I wished I could get up and run out. The Fairweather house was becoming an unpleasant place to be. I just wanted to find Minnie, take her back from Joben Malan (if I could figure out how to do it), and get on toward Tennessee.

Of course, if I did that, then I wouldn't know what Leviticus Lee had been talking about when he mentioned the gold coins. And the truth was, I was just as hungry as Robert Fairweather was to know about that.

He leaned back and blew smoke upward. "Buried

a hand! What a task! Heh, heh, heh!" His laugh seemed as false as his comradery. "So that was all it was, huh? Just Mr. Lee's hand?"

"What else would it have been?"

"Eh? Oh, I don't know. Just talking, that's all. Moving my jaws to hear the hinges squeak, you know. Heh, heh!"

It was a long evening before I broke free of him and got to my pallet bed. Even after I did, I couldn't sleep, because I was thinking about the shooting incident in the forest, because Blanche Fairweather's supper was sitting like lead in the base of my stomach, and Leviticus Lee was tossing about on his bed and moaning, and every now and then, I was sure, I could pick up another mention of gold.

I returned the next day to the place I had buried Lee's hand and examined the thicket. There were tracks, and a few dribbles of blood. That confirmed it: My shot had struck whomever it was that had shot at me.

My heart was in my mouth, I scoured the area for a body. I didn't find one. Maybe the wound had been superficial, and whoever it was had just gone home to heal. I hoped so. The urge to get away from this region became all the stronger.

As I was preparing to go, I happened to glance back up to the place where I had buried the hand. What I saw stopped me cold.

The stones I had laid atop the dirt mound were rolled aside, and, to my shock, the box was dug up and the top pried off. I advanced up and looked, amazed and mystified. There was the hand, un-wrapped to the point that it could be identified.

On the ground around was blood. What could it mean?

What else could it mean but one thing? The man I had shot in the thicket must have come back here, even while dripping blood from his wound, and dug up this box to see what was in it. But why? It made no sense.

I thrust the hand back into the box, fist-hammered the top back onto the box, and reburied it by hand. Then I got out of those woods like the devil was nipping my neck.

CHAPTER NINE

THE NEXT MORNING I AWAKENED WITH A CONVICTION that I had best put aside everything except my original purpose in coming to Arkansas. Only the lure of Minnie had brought me here, but so far I hadn't even looked for her, so distracted had I been with murderous mountaineers, Leviticus Lee, and the Fairweathers.

I ate breakfast as quickly as I could, chilled by the unpleasant glare of Blanche Fairweather and equally chilled by the smile of her husband. The children apparently found me fascinating. I was peppered with questions from the little ones all through the meal, questions about me, questions about Leviticus Lee. The former I wasn't willing to answer, and most of the latter I couldn't. Lee was as much a mystery to me as to anyone.

I excused myself and said I was going into Farleytown this morning to see if my wife might be there. I had deliberately waited until after Robert Fairweather had finished his breakfast and left in the buckboard before I made the announcement, because I simply didn't want to have to ride into town with him. After I had fetched my jacket and put on my gun belt, I headed toward the door. Blanche Fairweather followed me and called me to a halt outside.

"Mr. Brand, you may be aware that I don't much like having you here," she said.

"Ma'am, you've made that clear enough in every way you could. But don't worry—I'll be gone soon. It was never my intention to impose on your family."

"I know that. I don't fault you for bringing your injured friend here."

"Then what is it you so dislike about me?"

She looked at me from head to toe, like she was trying to figure out where to begin her criticism. "I don't trust you, Mr. Brand. I've always been told I was an overly suspicious soul, and quite possibly that is true. You're a stranger; I don't know who you are or what you've done. For all I know, you and this Leviticus Lee may be on the run from the law. Maybe he got that wounded hand in a holdup, or a gunfight. I don't know—but here you are, among my children, managing to make them think you're the most interesting man they've ever seen . . . a man who comes out of nowhere." She glanced down at my gun belt. "A man who wears a gun."

"A lot of men wear guns when they travel, Mrs. Fairweather."

She ignored that. "Tell me, Mr. Brand: Why have you really come to Farleytown?"

"To find my wife. I've told you that already."

"It's no wife you're seeking. It's gold."

I cocked my head. "Why do you say that?"

"Because of my husband. He's heard something that your partner said, something about gold coins. He believes that you and your partner know the way to the Confederate gold."

"What Confederate gold?"

"Don't play ignorant with me, Mr. Brand. You know exactly what gold I'm talking abut. It's the same gold that my husband made a fool of himself trying to find ten years ago. He became so obsessed with it that he almost destroyed our life together . . . but in the end he had put all that aside, and became the good man he was born to be. Now you've come, he's changing again. Becoming obsessed with an old myth that I wish to God would just die."

She crossed her arms against the chill of the wind. "Mr. Brand, I would like you to leave this house as soon as you can, and take your friend with you. I'll not be uncharitable and toss him out while he's yet weak from his amputation—but as soon as he's healed, I want you gone."

"I've never had any other intention than that, Mrs. Fairweather." It was odd, but though everything she had said would have seemed prone to make my angry, I didn't feel mad at her. Her rudeness was not without reason; she saw me and Leviticus Lee as threats to the security of her home and the welfare of her husband. I couldn't fault her. "Believe me, you don't want me away from this place any more than I want to be myself." I was thinking of the shooting in the forest, and the oddity of the dug-up hand. The whole thing had spooked me so badly that I didn't feel safe here.

"I'm glad to hear that, sir." She gave me that up-and-down evaluative stare again. "I've seen your kind, Mr. Brand. Trouble follows men like you. I fear it's already followed you into my household."

With that she turned and went back into the house. Her last comments left me a little stunned. Was there really something about me that attracted trouble? Lord knows I couldn't deny that I found more than my share of it, no matter where I went. It was troubling to think that it might not be mere coincidence, that I was some sort of living and breathing magnet for difficulties.

I shook my head. Superstition, that's all that kind of thinking was, and I wasn't a superstitious man. Pulling my coat closer around my collar, I trudged off down the Fairweather's curving drive and toward the road to Farleytown.

Before the day was over, I would be wondering if there wasn't something to be said for superstition after all. By the time I would return to the Fairweather house that day, I would find that, true to Mrs. Fairweather's evaluation, trouble had again followed me.

Here's what happened. I walked into Farleytown and took a look around, thinking that this was surely the ugliest little hamlet I had ever had the misfortune to lay eyes on. Built on a muddy flat where two roads crossed, it was nothing more than a gaggle of buildings that looked like they had been tossed into place out of a giant dice cup. The majority faced each other in two rows. Not even, uniform rows, but haphazard, ragged ones. If you were to hire an artist to paint a portrait of Farleytown in those days, it would have been best to get him thoroughly drunk before handing him his brush and paint board. Only a drunk could properly capture the impression made by this little Arkansas community.

It was easy to pick out Fairweather's big store. It was the first building on the left when you came in from the direction I was walking. It stood two and a half stories tall, had a long and sagging front porch, and was an interesting place to look at, if not an attractive one. It badly needed a new coat of paint, which is only to say that it fit in perfectly with the rest of the town.

Other than the Fairweather store and a smattering of houses up in the hills in the background, there was nothing but a barber parlor, a smithy (much worse-kept than the one I had operated back in Fort Scott), a shop for wagon and buggy repair, a little log church building up on a knoll behind the smithy, and several saloons. Five, maybe six of them, all lined up. It was a sorry little hamlet—just the kind of place a brilliant intellect like Joben Malan would come with a stolen woman.

That set me to thinking: Why, in all seriousness, would Joben have picked this place to come to? Maybe he had kin here; there must have been something to attract him. I went to one of the saloons, which were already open on the pretext of serving meals—mostly of the liquid variety, I noticed—to ask if there were any Malans around Farleytown.

Entering one of the saloons at random, I found a fat barkeep and a single customer. "Come in and set," the barkeep said. He was chewing a cigar and needed a shave. "What'll you have?"

"Cup of coffee. And a biscuit with jam."

"Make it a biscuit with butter, and you can have it. No jam on the premises."

"Fine."

I talked to the barkeep to gain his confidence, and was surprised to find he already had an idea of who I was. Apparently the arrival of myself and Lee at the Fairweather house had generated lots of interest around Farleytown. It wasn't really surprising, when I thought about it further. Probably very little happened around here; it wasn't unlikely that two newcomers arriving under unusual circumstances was the biggest event to hit Farleytown in a year.

"Tell me, sir, do you know anybody of the surname 'Malan' living around here?"

The barkeep screwed up his face, thinking. At the same moment, a pistol blasted just behind the saloon, so loud it made me jump. The barkeep didn't even blink.

"Malan, Malan . . . nope. No Marlans I know of."

Another pistol blast.

"Well, have you by any chance seen a couple, a man and woman, both fine-looking, hereabouts lately?"

"Can't say as I have."

The pistol fired again, and this time a hoot and holler, raised collectively by several male voices, followed.

"What's going on back there anyway?" I asked.

"Paul Merrick's back, that's all."

"Paul Merrick? Who's that?"

"Local fellow, son of Bass Merrick. Richest durn man in the county, Bass Merrick is. He's foreign too. Australian."

"No joshing? I never saw a live Australian before. Nor a dead one, for that matter. What's the shooting about?"

"Paul Merrick likes to bury hens up to the neck and practice his pistol shooting on the heads. That's his way of letting off steam. He's been off in Texas somewhere the last couple of weeks, probably just drinking and running around with women; that's the sort of things he likes to do. He just got back in town this morning."

I finished my coffee and left money on the bar. Heading out, I circled around the block to see the shooting party in the back; there was no shorter route, the saloons all being built in a row with shared side walls, no alleys between.

It was my fault that I didn't notice that my point of emergence was just the place this Paul Merrick had buried his chickens. Just as I circled around the last building, another shot blasted, and a chicken buried right at my feet was called to whatever afterlife awaits feathered creatures. A splatter of chicken blood stained my pants leg. I yelped and danced to the side, probably rather comically, then let out another yell when I saw the blood on my leg. In the confusion of the moment, I thought it was me who had been shot.

The gaggle of men gathered around Paul Merrick— a rather short but well-featured young man of about my own age—reacted with a couple of seconds of stunned silence, followed by an explosion of laughter.

"Well, gent, have I given you a fright?" Paul Merrick called in an accent unlike any I had ever heard. It reminded me of a Britisher's talk, but with a difference—the typical Australian accent, later experience would teach me.

I was just then making sense of what had happened. My temper flared. "You'd best watch where you're shooting, fool! If you'd have hit me, I'd have made you eat that pistol."

Merrick put on an exaggerated expression of fear.

"Whooo! Listen to him, gents! It appears I've roused up a mad hedgehog!"

"Hey, I know who that is," one of Merrick's companions said. But Merrick wasn't listening; he had already lifted his pistol. I don't think he would have done it had he seen that I also had a pistol; my coat hung over the gun belt, however, and he must have assumed I was unarmed.

"Let's see that dance again," he said, and fired.

The bullet struck squarely between my feet and made me prance again. Merrick laughed heartily, and repeated the procedure. Growing furious, but unwilling to draw my pistol at the moment for fear he would shoot me in response, I took two steps toward him;

he again raised his pistol, aimed, and squeezed the trigger.

Click.

Good—his pistol was empty. He had failed to count his prior shots. He gaped at the pistol as I strode up, drew back my fist, and pounded him in the mouth. He fell back with a grunt, tried to sit up, groaned, and fell back again. His mouth was bleeding.

Only then did I realize what I had done. My attack on him had been purely reactive, spurred by his treatment of me. I looked around at the startled men around me.

"We don't want no trouble," one of them said, waving his hands rapidly with palms facing me.

"Neither did I," I replied. "You saw what he was doing with that pistol, and that I did nothing to prompt it."

"We saw it, sure did. Hey, you're that fellow what come in with the old man who lost his hand over at the Fairweather house, ain't you?"

"Never mind who I am. Tell me how this fellow's going to react when he gets his sense back."

Paul Merrick moaned and put his hand to his mouth. He took it away again and studied the blood. "I'm bejiggered if you didn't break my lip!" he said. "I ought to kill you for that!"

He dug into his pocket and pulled out cartridges. Opening the cylinder of his pistol, he spilled the empties onto the ground and started to reload.

I threw back my coattail, pulled out my own pistol

and leveled it at him. "I'd stop right there, if I was you."

He seemed surprised when he realized I was armed, but kept right on loading.

"I said to stop that! Don't make me shoot!"

He didn't stop, and I was left with a choice: Shoot him or knock him cold. The latter seemed the best option. I brought up my Colt and clunked it down on his skull even as he slammed the sixth cartridge into place.

Paul Merrick fell to the side, flopped out on the ground like a scarecrow with its supports kicked out.

I holstered my Colt. "Where does he live?"

The others had scattered back for some distance when Merrick began loading his pistol. Now they closed in again. "He lives just over that hill yonder. Big old house. But I wouldn't go there, if you're thinking that way. His father, he might just shoot you down for this."

"Don't talk foolish," another said. "Bass Merrick would probably pay this feller for keeping his boy from committing a murder."

I bent over and picked up Merrick, hefting him across my shoulder like a feed sack. The effort made my head hurt; it was still tender from the blows it had received in recent days.

"Whatever Bass Merrick thinks about it, I'm taking this one home," I said. "I want to make sure my side of this gets told right."

They watched me haul him off, and I think it impressed them. If so, good. Maybe none of them would try his own hand at getting the best of me, if I came across strong and fearless.

In truth, I was low about what had happened. Once again I had come looking for Minnie and found only troubles. Blanche Fairweather's assessment of me seemed all too accurate. As I strode down the road, looking for the Merrick house and generating laughter from those who saw me, I wondered if life was ever going to get back to normal again.

There it was, a large house, built at the far base of the hill that I had just passed around. It was only one story tall, but sprawling, and with a low-peaked roof. I would see pictures later of similar houses in Australia. Bass Merrick had built his house to remind himself of his homeland.

By now I was puffing from the exertion of carrying my human load, a load which was beginning to come to and groan a little.

Ahead, the big front door of the house opened and a broadly built man emerged. His face was a thicker version of Paul Merrick's; his accent, too, was like Paul Merrick's, but thicker.

"Well, which is it: drunk or shot?"

Odd, how he asked that. It was a question idly presented, as if the answer hardly mattered.

"Neither one. Just pistol-whipped."

"By whom?"

"By me, and with good reason."

The big man looked at me, and a smile spread like melting butter across his face. He threw back his head and laughed.

"My friend, come in and dump that load you carry. My name is Bass Merrick, and I'd like to make your acquaintance."

"You're not going to shoot me for this?"

"Shoot you? Why the bloody devil should I shoot you? I know my son well enough to know that any problem he has, he has brought upon himself."

"He was shooting between my feet to make me dance."

"No! I thought he was shooting chicken heads."

"That too."

I carried Paul Merrick into the house and dumped him on a sofa. He groaned, rolled off onto the floor and sat up.

"Father!" he said when he looked up, bleary-eyed. "How did I get—"

"Shut up, stand up, and fetch me and my friend a beer," Bass Merrick said. "It'll be the first useful thing you've done this day, without a doubt."

CHAPTER TEN

AT THE FAIRWEATHERS' SUPPER TABLE THAT NIGHT I SUG-
gested that perhaps I should find a room in town and
quit imposing on the family. Blanche Fairweather
gave me the most pleasant look I had received from
her since my arrival, but Robert Fairweather waved
his hands and shook his head and said that he
wouldn't even consider it. "You and Mr. Lee are our
guests for as long as you remain," he said. His wife
let out a telling sigh, rose, and went to the kitchen to
replenish the bowl of boiled potatoes.

"I'm sorry you didn't find your wife today," Robert
Fairweather said. "Are you sure she came to Farleytown?"

"Not really. It's just a name that the bird was saying; I figured it had picked it up, hearing her talk
about it."

"It's a bad thing, husbands looking for straying
wives, and all of it laid out in front of decent children
to make them ask questions they shouldn't," Blanche
said icily. She had returned with the refilled bowl in
time to hear my comment.

"Hush, dear," Fairweather said. "Such things happen even to good folk." Then to me: "I heard in the store today that Wilt McCoy's family has a couple of visitors, a man and a woman. The McCoys live some miles north of Farleytown. It might be worth investigating."

"It might. Thank you, Mr. Fairweather."

"For heaven's sake, call me Robert. Or Bob, if it suits you. 'Mr. Fairweather!' Land's sake!"

"I heard in town that you had a fight with Paul Merrick today," one of the boys said. It made me wince. I had hoped that wouldn't get back to the Fairweathers.

"I heard the same—is it true?" Robert Fairweather asked. From his expression I got the feeling he hadn't wanted this to come up either, probably because he knew it would only make his wife more deadset against me. Now that the subject was out, of course, there was no reason to be reticent.

"I'm afraid it is true. But he was the one who caused it."

Blanche Fairweather let out another loud sigh and clicked her fork a little too loudly on her dish—a wordless comment no one missed.

"Oh, I don't doubt it was Paul at fault," Robert Fairweather said. "Paul Merrick is trouble, trouble. That's all he is. Just trouble."

"I heard that you carried him right back to his house after you knocked him out," the oldest boy said. The admiration in his tone was obvious.

"Well, I figured it best to lay what had happened right on the line, without rumors getting started . . . or

Paul Merrick giving only his side of things."

"How did Bass Merrick receive you?"

"Well, I was surprised. He seemed to think it was funny. He made his boy serve me beer."

Blanche piped up sternly: "We don't drink beer in this house, and I don't think it fitting to discuss that foul beverage before the little ones!"

"Land's sake, dear, the little ones see saloons in town every day. There's no reason to pretend such things don't exist," Fairweather said. It was getting to be a pattern: Blanche talking like I was vermin, and Fairweather contradicting her and making it seem I could do no wrong even if I tried. I was more sure than ever that he saw me as a means of potential gain; nothing else could account for him buttering me up all the time, like he did.

"So he treated you well, did he?" Fairweather said to me. "That is odd. But not surprising. There's nothing about Bass Merrick that isn't odd, in my opinion. I don't tend to trust many who come from foreign shores."

"Just who is he anyway?" I asked. "He had little to tell me about himself except that he had just come home from a business trip to Missouri, and that his son had just come home too. Not from business, but from running around in Texas and doing"—I glanced at Blanche's dour face—"doing things he shouldn't."

"Bass Merrick is the richest man within three hundred miles or more," Fairweather said. "He made his fortune in the Ballarat gold fields, married himself an Arkansas girl, and moved here. His wife died shortly after they settled, and he and his son have been on their own ever since. Bass Merrick doesn't so much work as look out for his investments—cattle in Texas, some mining interests here and there, and meat packing up in Missouri. As for his son, he doesn't work at all. He doesn't make money, or invest it. He just spends it. Gambling, women, liquor, you name it."

"Hardly fit talk for the table," Blanche muttered. Fairweather ignored her.

"Merrick must be a smart man, to have made it that rich while he was still young," I said.

"Oh, he's smart, no doubt. A clever fellow. Not everyone likes him, but I've never had any problems. He provides me lots of business, I don't mind saying."

One of the sons spoke. "And Bass Merrick has looked for the Confederate gold too, just like Father has."

Robert Fairweather looked at his son as if the boy had committed some impropriety on the level of pointing out that a guest had a glass eye or six fingers on one hand. His sharp glance shifted my way and softened into a look of embarrassment.

"That might not be the best subject for the moment, eh, Mr. Brand?"

"No, no, it's fine with me. In fact, it gives me a chance to ask what this Confederate gold is supposed to be."

Fairweather's eyes broadened in surprise. "You don't know?"

"No, I don't."

Instantly his eyes narrowed again, and now his expression was one that said, *Of course you know*.

"I'll tell you what the Confederate gold is," Blanche said. "It's an idle tale told by fools and believed by the same."

Fairweather responded angrily, "Blanche, it's your own husband you insult when you say that. You know I've looked for the gold my very self. And so has Bass Merrick, and you certainly can't call him a fool."

"No, because he's had the sense to declare that he no longer believes in that old tale. He's learned to tell when something's real and when it's make-believe."

"I haven't looked for that gold for years now, Blanche," Fairweather said. He paused. "That's not to say it isn't real. It may be that no one has known the right place to look." His glance came my way. "At least, nobody who's come along before now."

I ignored the obvious implication. "Tell me this story," I said. "I ain't lying when I say I don't know it."

Fairweather's smile wasn't his usual gushing beam, but a sort of smirk that indicated he was willing to go along with the game he obviously believed I was playing. "All right, I'll tell you.

"Back in 'sixty-two, in the midst of the war, there was some Confederate payroll money, in gold coins, buried somewhere in the hills around Farleytown. There were some soldiers, six, seven of them, charged with delivering the gold to the payroll officer in a big Rebel camp a few miles south of town. Along the way they ran into a Union patrol, and shots were fired. Some of the gold couriers were killed, but three survived. They ran from the Federals, way back into the hills, and stashed the gold into a crevice somewhere at the base of one of the cliffs hereabouts. And there it lays to this day. Nobody ever came back to claim it."

"How much gold was there?"

"I've got no idea. Must have been plenty, though. It was to be pay for a lot of men."

"Is there any proof this is true?"

"None at all," Blanche said before her husband could answer.

Fairweather frowned at her. "There have been many intelligent people who have believed the story of the Confederate gold. Take Bass Merrick, for instance."

"Or Parker Cuthbert," Blanche said. The children laughed; Fairweather turned red.

"He's an exception," he said. "Blanche, are you trying to make me look a fool before our guest?"

"It's not me who believes in old tales of lost gold," she said. "Now, pardon me, dear, I'm going to start washing up these dishes. Girls, I need your help."

Fairweather, now in a bad mood, shooed the boys away from the table as well. "Now, maybe we can talk without being interrupted," he said.

"Who's this Cuthbert?"

"Oh, just a local idiot and drunk, that's all. He came to Farleytown about five years ago, acting mysterious and like he was something special. He headed out into the hills, and three days later he was back, wailing that 'his' gold was gone. It wound up that

Cuthbert claimed to be one of the soldiers who buried the payroll, you see, and he declared it had been moved from its proper place."

"So what happened to him?"

"He went off his rocker, as they say. Took to drinking and brawling and trying to hurt people, until folks finally left him alone. He lives in a little cabin outside of town now, a place he rents from Bass Merrick, by coincidence. He works odd jobs, takes whatever folks will hand him out, and still pokes around the hills, looking for his gold. He's insane. No question about it."

"But I gather you believe in this gold too."

He looked at me, grinning slyly. "One can't know what a man believes by looking at him . . . can he?"

I was about to say to him that he had it all wrong, that I really didn't know anything about any gold, and hadn't come to Farleytown to find any lost treasure but Minnie Brand. But I didn't get it said, for just as I opened my mouth I remembered Leviticus Lee's raving about gold coins, and wondered if maybe, just maybe, he might really know something about this old legend. Something true. Something that could lead to the gold.

In the interim during which this came to my mind, Fairweather leaned back and said, "You know, I saw Parker Cuthbert today, coming out of one of the saloons. They give him food on 'credit,' which in his case means they give him food, no payment expected. And you know what? He was limping, really bad, and had a bandage around his leg. I turned to a fellow

there with me—buying some flour, he was—and I
said, 'What happened to Parker Cuthbert's leg?' And
you know what he said? He said that the old fool had
gotten himself shot somehow. Stealing chickens, no
doubt. Old Doc Ruscher had to dig a bullet out of his
leg. On 'credit,' of course."

Fairweather laughed, but I didn't. I suppose I must
have had an odd expression, for he looked at me and
asked if I was all right.

"Fine, fine." I rubber my belly as if it were bothering me. "Just a little sour stomach hit me a-sudden,
that's all."

"Blanche's food will do that to you," he said.

"I'll go up and lie down a minute until I feel better," I said.

I was glad to be up and away from that table, so
he couldn't see that I was trembling. The tale about
Parker Cuthbert and the wounded leg had told me
something important: I knew now who it was who
had shot at me while I was burying Leviticus Lee's
hand, and who I had put a slug into in return.

Furthermore, I was beginning to suspect I knew
why.

CHAPTER ELEVEN

WHEN I ENTERED THE UPSTAIRS ROOM TO SLEEP, THE FIRST
thing I noticed was that the parrot's cage was open
and Bird was gone.

Lee was sitting up in bed, looking pale and wan
as with his single hand he thumbed through a picture
book obviously borrowed from one of the younger
Fairweather children.

"How you faring, my friend?" I asked him.

"Tolerable." His voice sounded weak. "Trying to
get used to the notion of going the rest of my days
with only one paw. How's a man supposed to wash
one hand? How's he supposed to carve up his steak,
or dig with a shovel, or do most anything else, for
that matter?"

"I don't know; I got no experience with anybody
one-handed, up until now." I shuffled my feet. "I feel
responsible. It was for my sake you got into that row
with those mountain men and got your hand shot."

"I helped you because I wanted to, so don't worry
about it. I ain't. I can think of worse things to lose
than a hand."

Grinning, I said, "You're a remarkable man, Leviticus Lee."

"Not 'specially so. Not that I can see."

"Well, I sure owe you one. By the way, you been keeping straight our story about how you came to be hurt?"

"Yes, yes—I ain't stupid, you know. It was an accident, all your fault, so on and so on." He grinned weakly. "You know, that Fairweather woman, she questioned me right close about it. I don't think she likes me. Or you either."

"I know it. She thinks we're bad men, I reckon." I waved toward the empty cage. "What happened to Bird?"

Lee looked sheepish. "I turned him loose out the window, Mr. Brand, and I'm ashamed to admit it, for I know it was your wife's critter, not mine." Despite what we had gone through together, I was still Mr. Brand to him, and would remain so perpetually. "That chattering was getting on my nerves, and I just sort of up and did it without really thinking it through. It was durn hard, doing it one-handed. Don't worry— I'll pay you for the bird, soon as I can."

"When will that be? When you find the lost gold?"

My words brought a pall into the room. Lee looked at me in utter silence for almost ten seconds.

"What are you talking about?" he asked at last, even though it was far too late now to play ignorant. His silence had already spoken his full understanding of what I had said.

"About the legend. The old story. The Confederate

payroll gold they say is buried in a crevice somewhere around here."

Again he looked at me for a long time, his facial
muscles in motion beneath his skin, reflecting the
working of his mind. At length the subtle twitching
stopped and he looked at me in a different way, and
I could tell he had made up his mind to be open with
me.

"How'd you figure it out?" he asked.

"I didn't, really, at least not on my own. And the
thing is, there's others who have figured it out too."

"Others?"

"Yes . . . Mr. Fairweather here, for one. I think
that's why he's being so charitable to us. He figures
we've come for the lost gold, and I suppose he ex-
pects he'd be rewarded out of it. Mrs. Fairweather
confirmed that to me, in fact. That's why she despises
us so. Robert Fairweather, you see, used to look for
that gold regular. Apparently it about ruined his marriage until he gave it up at last. And now, since we've
been here, he's started thinking about that gold
again."

Lee swore to himself, then said, "Well, I had
thought I might have raved about that gold some. I'll
tell you the truth about that missing parrot, Mr. Brand.
It was talking about gold coins, repeating things it
must have heard me say. I turned it loose because I
was afraid folks would hear him and start figuring
things out. I see now I was too late."

"There's somebody besides the Fairweathers and
me who've figured it out, I'm sorry to say. That's the

main reason I'm talking to you about this; it's not just me poking into your business. You see, Mr. Lee: I buried your hand like you had asked."

"I'm obliged. A man hates to have his parts just tossed out."

"While I was burying it, somebody took a shot at me. I think it's likely a local man named Parker Cuthbert who did it, a fellow they say is a drunk and an idiot who's been looking for the lost gold for several years now. He was seen in town with a wound in his leg afterward. That's why I think it's him."

"But why would he shoot at you?"

"By the time I buried that hand, word about us had gotten out, names and all. One of Fairweather's boys had talked us up big in town when his pap sent him to fetch the doctor. I figure this Cuthbert heard that Leviticus Lee was in town, and knew somehow that you would know where the gold is hidden. Maybe he even thought you had already recovered it. So when he saw me leaving the house with a shovel, he figured it was the gold I was burying, or digging up, one or the other. Robert Fairweather, by the way, had the same notion, and seemed mighty disappointed when he found out it was just your left paw I was putting away."

Then I told Lee the story of all that had happened, how the shot had been fired, and how I had returned a shot of my own. I told him about the blood on the ground, of how the buried hand had been dug up.

"That's some tale!" he said.

"Mr. Lee, I ask you to tell me straight out: Do you

really know where the Confederate gold is hidden?"

This time, the pause was longer before he answered. "Yep. I sure do."

"Let me throw another guess at you, and you tell me if I'm right: Were you one of the soldiers who buried the gold in the first place?"

"I was."

"Then tell me this: Is it possible that this Cuthbert knows you were one of those soldiers?"

Lee shook his head. "No, and that's what throws me. I never heard of no Cuthbert before. The only men ever alive who knew where the gold was buried was the three of us who hid it. And the other two are dead."

"How'd that happen?"

"The war killed one of them, two days after we hid the gold. His name was Hargrove, Van Hargrove, a boy from Alabama, if I recall aright. The other was Pete Revett, out of Georgia. He lived out the war, but he was killed right after the peace was made. Murdered, before he ever got home. Some kind of brawl in a barroom, I think."

"The war's been over a lot of years now, Mr. Lee. Why did you wait so long to come after the gold?"

"Because up until now, I ain't been free to come after it." He looked somber, and licked his lips. "I was in prison in Missouri up until a few weeks ago. I had me a fight, you see, over a woman. It was right after I got out of the service. The other fellow died. The details ain't important. Suffice it to say that I escaped the noose, but not the bars. I was locked away for more than twenty long years. But the whole time I was in, I knew I'd come get my gold, just as soon as they set me free. That's all that kept me going. All I had to live for."

"*Your* gold?"

"It ain't nobody else's, is it? That gold was the property of the Confederate government. You may not have noticed, but the Confederate government ain't around no more."

I sat down, taking it all in and letting it settle in my mind. It was a remarkable tale, but I couldn't figure out where, or how, Cuthbert worked into it.

"You sure you didn't know any Parker Cuthbert?"

"Never heard the name before in my life."

"Well, he must have heard yours. Somehow he knows you can lead him to the gold. He must want it awful bad, to have shot at me."

Lee settled back. He looked very tired and pale. He moved the stump of his hand and made a face of pain. "It hurts," he said. "I can feel them shot-off fingers hurting, even though there ain't a hand there no more."

"I've heard of that happening," I replied. "You want some more of that laudanum?"

"No, no. It turns me into a slug who can't do nothing but lie and stare at the ceiling. And I got to get out of this bed, quick. My gold's out there, waiting for me." He looked at me closely. "Mr. Brand, I like you. You've stuck by me, and I intend to reward you for it. Just as soon as I get that gold."

The words sent excitement all through me. I didn't

like to admit it to myself, but I was just as gold-hungry as Robert Fairweather, whose ill-concealed and self-serving lust for gain was so repellent.

Yet my self-respect demanded that I not accept Lee's offer—at least, not too readily. "You saved my life, Mr. Lee. You don't owe me a thing—it's me who owes you."

"If I want to share my gold, I can share it," he said. "I want you to benefit from my good fortune. You don't think I'd shut you out, do you? When I get my gold, you'll find fortune smiling. I'll make you well-off enough that your Minnie will come running back to your arms."

I grinned and nodded—and wondered if he really meant what he said. Maybe he was telling me this because he secretly mistrusted me, figuring that if he didn't make me some sort of bribing promise, I might force him to find the gold and then take it for myself. That poisoning thought led to another, and I began to mistrust Lee: What if he sneaked out when I wasn't about and got his gold on his own, and I never got a bit of it?

Not that I had any kind of claim on that gold anyway. If I had been thinking clearly, I would have recognized that. But that's the problem with gold: It keeps you from thinking clearly.

As I said before, gold is a curse. As it brings fortune, it brings misfortune in greater share; as it brings satisfaction and security, it also brings envy and lies and mistrust. Before much more time had passed, I would see all this. At that moment, however, I saw none of it. The promise of a share of the Confederate gold had a gleam so bright it blinded me to all else.

That night the Fairweathers' dogs sent up a racket in the yard. I awakened, oddly tense. Leviticus Lee was deeply asleep; at my insistence he had taken another dose of the liquefied opiate Dr. Ruscher had given him, and wouldn't waken for a long time.

I'm ashamed to confess, even this many years after the fact, as to the real reason I had insisted he take the laudanum. It wasn't out of a charitable desire to ease the pain of his amputation. It was because I knew that as long as he was in a doped stupor, he couldn't rise in the night and get the gold without me.

I rose and went to the window. The night sky was clear, giving me a decent view across the yard. I saw one of the hounds run across, baying. Then something else moved, over near the trees. I caught only the briefest glimpse before it was gone.

It might have been a dog, a cat, a raccoon, or any other type of critter, based on what little I had seen— just motion in the darkness. But I knew what kind of critter it really was: a man, watching the house.

Parker Cuthbert, surely, keeping watch to make sure that Leviticus Lee and his partner didn't sneak out under cover of darkness and take away the gold he lusted for.

It made me furious. I hated Cuthbert right then, a man I had never really seen, and wouldn't know if I met him on the boardwalk. He was a threat, a danger. For a few dark moments I actually wished the shot I had put into him as he hid in that thicket had entered his head instead of his leg.

Never had I entertained a more evil way of thinking—and the worst of it was that I was so taken with gold lust right then that I didn't even notice it was evil.

When I descended for breakfast the next morning, Leviticus Lee was still soundly sleeping. At the table, Robert Fairweather asked me if I was planning to go today to see if the two guests of the McCoy man he had mentioned the day before were Minnie and Joben.

Why is he so interested? I wondered. Was he eager to get me away from the house so he could go up and pump the location of that gold out of Leviticus Lee?

In less than a second I had that thought, and in less than two I designed my strategy. "I believe I will," I replied. "Can you provide me some directions?"

He smiled, reached into the pocket of his shirt and handed me a folded paper. It bore a hand-sketched map.

"I made it last night, before I went to sleep. I figured you'd need it today."

You really do want me out of the house, don't you? Trying to weasel your way into my part of the gold, you two-faced thief! Well, I'll put a stop to your scheme!

Bitter though my thoughts were, my face showed nothing but good humor and pleasantness. "You're mighty kind, Mr. Fairweather . . . Robert, I mean."

"I'd be halfway inclined to go with you, if I wasn't so busy today," he said.

"The store's got you tied down, huh?"

"In a way. I'm doing some work on the store's books today. I always do most of that at home. Lord knows a man can't concentrate on it down at the store, with folks in and out."

"I see." Now I was sure I had detected his ploy. I figured I knew the *real* reason he wanted to stay at home!

Finishing breakfast under the sullen glare of Blanche Fairweather, I rose, excused myself, and headed upstairs. Leviticus Lee was just beginning to waken. Meanwhile, I felt sure, Robert Fairweather was downstairs, eagerly awaiting my departure so that he could come up here and try to prospect my one-handed partner for the whereabouts of the Confederate gold.

"Yes sir, Mr. Robert Fairweather, you do enjoy conversation," I muttered aloud. "Blab, blab, blab, all with that fool smile you think hides so much. Well, my good host, you'll have a bit of trouble having a conversation with Leviticus Lee while I'm away. It's hard to talk to a man who's sound asleep."

I went to Lee's bedside and opened up the bottle of laudanum. Pulling open his mouth, I poured a new dose into him, then pushed up his chin to close his mouth again and make him swallow it. He gurgled and moaned, then settled back into sleep.

"Mr. Fairweather, you just come on in and talk all you want to my good friend here. Just come on in!" I chuckled to myself as I whispered the words.

It was probably the nastiest, sorriest thing I had done in my days, and it only goes to show how bad a turn the prospect of wealth can give to a man's sense of right and wrong.

Heading out to the barn, I fetched and saddled my horse, then began the ride toward the McCoy place. Even though finding Minnie was my goal, my mind was too full of Confederate gold, and of dark satisfaction at the clever trick I had played on Robert Fairweather, to leave much room for thoughts about her.

CHAPTER TWELVE

FAIRWEATHER'S MAP WAS EASY TO FOLLOW, AND I CAME to within view of the McCoy house very quickly. There I stopped, growing nervous. If Minnie was truly here, how would she react to seeing me? And what about Joben? Would he try to fight to keep her?

My thoughts were interrupted by a loud, feminine wail. On the tail end of that came an angry voice, a man's voice. Both the wail and the voice were familiar—and it sounded to me as if Minnie was in distress, and that Joben was causing it.

My protective husbandly instincts took over at once. Spurring my horse, I galloped up to the front of the house, dismounted even while I reined in, and stomped to the door.

It opened before my hand could reach the latch, and Joben Malan came stomping out, his face red and furious. Minnie was wailing in the background.

When Joben saw me, he staggered back like he had seen a walking corpse, and tripped on the threshold. It landed him on his rump, and from that posture he stared up at me with his mouth open.

"Enoch?" he said. A smile started to creep across

his face, then he chuckled. "Enoch, have you come to take her back?"

Minnie, invisible to me somewhere inside the house, stopped her squalling. "Who are you talking to, Joben?"

Joben stood, his face so joyous you would have thought I had just reprieved him from the execution dock. I lifted my hand to shake a fist in his face, but he grabbed the hand when it was only halfway up and started shaking it vigorously.

"Bless you, Enoch Brand, you're a true friend. I never been so glad to see a man, and that's no lie. Hallelujah! Glory be!"

I was so confused now that all my anger was gone. It was me left standing with mouth open and an idiotic expression, worthy of Joben himself, on my face.

"Lord save us, that woman can harp on a man worse than anything! She's like a gnat in your ear that you can't get a pinch on, you know what I mean? God bless you for coming to take her back, Enoch. God bless you!"

"Joben, were you hitting her?"

"Hitting her? Oh no, Enoch, no sir. I just lost my patience and hollered at her. That was enough to get her started crying and fussing. That's all it takes with her."

I couldn't dispute him. My own experience with Minnie had been the same. The woman did go to pieces at the slightest provocation.

"Enoch, how did you know where to find us?"

Joben asked. "I was ready to haul off toward Tennessee just to take her back to you."

"Joben, I asked you who that was you're talking to!" Minnie yelled again.

"It was the parrot," I told him. "It kept saying 'Farleytown.' As best I could figure, it must have picked it up hearing you and Minnie talking about it."

"You're a smart man, Enoch. I never would have figured that out."

"Enoch? Did you say that was Enoch out there?" Minnie said.

"It's me, Minnie!" I yelled in over Joben's shoulder.

"Enoch! Oh, Enoch, thank the Lord you're here! It's a miracle, that's what it is!"

"I see she's not been happy with you any more than you were with her," I commented to Joben. "Now let me ask *you* a question: Why did you bring her to Farleytown, of all places?"

"Relations. Some of my mother's people are here— this is their house, though they ain't present at the moment. They went into town yesterday and ain't come back. It was Minnie's fussing what drove them off, I think. Drove them right out of their own home! Lord, she's a nagging thing! Pretty, but hellacious, downright hellacious."

"Well, I figured it must be relatives, though I looked for them under the Malan name. I never thought about your mother's side of the family."

As I was saying this, Minnie was pushing past Joben and rushing to me. She came into my arms and put a big, wet kiss onto my lips. "Enoch, take me away. Take me back to Fort Scott."

"I can't do that, Minnie."

"Can't do . . . what? You've stopped loving me, Enoch? Is that it? Oh Lord, take my soul, just take it on to glory now!" She began bawling again, all the louder.

"I expect even the Lord would want you to calm down some before you were fit to take to glory or anywhere else," I said. "Further, he might have a few things to say to you about the way you've done your husband. You got no idea all I've been through trying to find you, Minnie. No idea at all. But hush and listen to me. I forgive you for running out on me. I forgive you for taking up with old poop-for-brains here. He's a good-looking man, after all. What I meant a minute ago was that I can't take you back to Fort Scott. It's Tennessee we'll go to."

"Tennessee . . ." She choked down a sob and tried to pull herself together. I handed her a handkerchief and she swabbed the various exudings that emotion had produced all down her face. "Tennessee. You're going to make a hayseed out of me, ain't you! Well, it's my lot. My punishment. I was wrong to run out on you, Enoch. I'll not do it again."

Oh, if only I could have believed that. But I didn't want to wrangle with her over that kind of thing right now. "You were wrong, but like I say, I forgive you. Now, let's get your things together. I'm taking you back to Farleytown to meet some folks who've been kind to me."

"You're a good man, Enoch Brand. A good man," Joben Malan said. "May heaven's blessing be upon you."

I told him to shut up, and he did.

We took a slow pace heading back toward Farley-town. It was good to be with Minnie again, and she seemed truly glad to have me back, despite her consternation over the renewed prospect of having to become a Tennessean. Not far from the place we had left Joben, we tethered the horse and walked together in the woods. Her touch was soft and gentle; I knew now why I loved her so, and why I was willing to forgive her again and again. We found a hidden, mossy place and sank down into it. It was a long time before we got up again.

When we were at last back on the road, most of the day had passed. I had totally forgotten my fears that Robert Fairweather was trying to get me away from the house so he could find out the location of the gold from Leviticus Lee. For one thing, Fairweather had proven truthful in what he had told me about the McCoys' visitors; it apparently hadn't been a mere ruse to get me out of the way, as I had thought. For another, I had Minnie again, and that seemed so marvelous that the gold hardly seemed to matter anymore. I had gone from being a fool for gold and back to being a fool for love.

Minnie didn't talk about her days with Joben Malan until we were on the road again. "He was a hard man to live with, Enoch," Minnie said as she clung to me. We were riding double in my saddle. Her meager bag of the personal possessions she had taken with her when she ran off with Joben swung from the saddle horn. "He had no patience with me, none at all. He wouldn't give me nothing I wanted, wouldn't treat me kind and gentle like you always have."

"Maybe you'll see me in a better light from now on," I said. "I'm a bird in the hand to you, Minnie. But you've never been satisfied with that. You're always casting your eyes into the bushes."

"Not no more, Enoch. I'll never even look at another bird in the bush, no matter how pretty he is."

Life hands everyone a few particularly ironic moments, and this was one of mine. Just as Minnie spoke, who should appear on the road in front of me except Paul Merrick himself. He had a rifle slung casually across the crook of his arm, and wore a big grin. He stood with feet firmly planted and spread, and it was clear his intent was to block our path and stop us. He looked very strong and striking and dangerous, and—wouldn't you know it—with Minnie just having pledged to keep her eyes off bush birds, it was the roadside bushes that Paul Merrick had emerged from.

I felt her pull back behind me, and heard her say "Oh!"

"Hello, Mr. Brand," Paul Merrick said in his Australian tones. This elicited a second "Oh!" from Minnie. "Fancy that we should meet like this, out on the road with nobody around." He glanced right and left. "Well, almost nobody."

From the bushes emerged two more men, both of them young. They carried shotguns and looked nervous, one far more so than the other. Obviously they were cronies or hirelings of Paul Merrick.

"What do you want, Merrick?" I asked. "If you're angry because of me trouncing you, you know you brought it on yourself."

"That? Oh, that's forgotten and done, Mr. Brand. It was your victory, and I congratulate you for it. It's no bleeding revenge I'm after, my friend. It's gold."

Minnie said "Oh!" a third time, then gouged me. "What gold?" she whispered sharply into my left ear. "You've got gold?"

"I don't know what you're talking about," I said to Paul Merrick.

"Don't feed me nonsense, my good friend! You're wasting my time and yours. We both know what I'm talking about. You see, after my little round with you, I asked around a bit. I heard that you came into town with an old codger name of Leviticus Lee. Well, that name might not ring many bells in many minds, but we Merricks, we know some things the average man don't. My father, you see, researched the story of the Confederate gold very thoroughly. Leviticus Lee was one of the three who were assigned to carry that payroll. Therefore, he was one of the three who hid it—and the only survivor of the bunch, incidentally. He's the only man I know of who could put his hands on that gold."

"I heard there's a man named Cuthbert about who claims to be one if the three," I said. I wasn't pleased by how much Merrick knew, and hoped that mention of Cuthbert might somehow confuse the situation in my favor. At the very least, it might reveal something more about Cuthbert, a man in whom I had great interest. After all, he had shot at me, and I was still sure that had been him poking around the Fairweather house in the night.

"Cuthbert? Bah! A fraud and a murderer. That's all he is."

"A murderer?"

"That's right. It was Cuthbert who killed Peter Revett, second of the three who hid the gold. He tried to torture Revett into revealing the location of the gold to him, then killed him after he got the information. But Revett got the last laugh. He lied to him about the whereabouts. It was enough to drive poor old Cuthbert out of his mind. He's a dangerous man, Mr. Brand. He knows nothing of where that gold lies." He shifted the rifle so that now it dangled in his hand. "But Leviticus Lee knows. And by now, maybe you know as well."

"Why should I know such a thing?"

"He's your partner, isn't he? Partners share secrets with one another."

"Who's Leviticus Lee?" Minnie whispered. "And what gold is he talking about?"

"Hush!" I whispered back. Then I spoke to Paul Merrick again. "I don't know where any gold is. If I did, you think I wouldn't have gotten it by now?"

"I hear your partner had an accident and lost a

hand. I hear he's been laid up at the Fairweather house. I figure that's delayed you."

"He's laid up, all right. But I still don't know where the gold is buried."

"Ah, but you can find out, can't you! And that's just what you're going to do for me, Mr. Brand. You're going to find me that gold."

"If you want gold, ask your daddy. I hear he mined aplenty of it in Australia."

"My father and I aren't on the best of terms, Mr. Brand. I have a few . . . habits that tend to become expensive. Right now I've got gambling debts, unknown to my father. I intend to keep them unknown. When you find me that gold, I'll have enough to pay off all my debts, live the way I want to live, and stay in my father's good graces—and his will—for as long as it takes."

"You must be a desperate man, to threaten a lone man and his wife," I said.

"Your wife, is it? Well!" Paul Merrick smiled and tipped his hat. "Good day to you, ma'am. Charmed, absolutely charmed."

"Please sir, please, don't hurt my husband!" she pled in fine dramatic style.

"Hurt him? I don't have any desire to do that, ma'am. Why would I hurt a man whose help I need?"

Now, there was a thought! Why indeed? Immediately I climbed down from the saddle.

"Whoa, there, Mr. Brand! I suggest you stop where you are." Paul Merrick aimed his rifle at my midsection.

"Can't stop yet—I ain't finished," I said, walking straight at him.

"You back off!" he yelled. "Back, you jackass!"

"Should we shoot him?" one of Merrick's cronies asked rather desperately.

"No, no, we need him to—" He broke off, realizing what I already had: He could not afford to harm the very man he was counting on to lead him to the Confederate gold.

I reached Merrick and grabbed his rifle. With minimal effort I wrenched it from his hand.

"Paul, we got to shoot him, we got to!" one of the shotgun bearers said.

"I ain't shooting nobody—ain't enough pay in the world to make me do that!" the other said. He laid down his shotgun and walked away into the woods.

I leveled Merrick's own rifle on him. "Tell the other one to drop his shotgun."

Paul Merrick's face was as red as an overheated furnace. "Drop the . . . no, wait. Aim your shotgun at Mr. Brand's wife."

The man did as he said. I jabbed the rifle muzzle right into Paul Merrick's belly. "Tell him to drop it."

"No. If you're going to shoot me, shoot. Of course, as soon as you do, your wife will die."

"I don't think you've got the guts to do it."

"It's not a question of my courage, Mr. Brand. It's a question of my companion's meanness. He has plenty of it, I assure you. He'll kill her in the flick of an eye."

"Merrick, when this is over . . ." I lowered the rifle

and handed it to him. "All right. You win. I'll do what you want. Just let her go."

"I don't think so."

"What did you say?"

"I'm keeping the lovely Mrs. Brand as a guest of sorts. It's an idea that's just come to me. An inspiration of the moment, you could say. I don't know where your wife has come from or how she came to be here, but her arrival is convenient for my purpose. It appears to me that you care deeply for her. So, if you want to continue to have a wife to care deeply about, it is strongly advised that you cooperate."

"I've already told you I'll cooperate. You don't need to threaten my wife to get my help."

"Let's just consider her collateral, or more accurately, insurance. As long as you cooperate, she'll be safe. If you cross me, she'll be dead. That's no bluff, Mr. Brand. You may count on that."

Minnie was white as paper and looked ready to faint off the horse. "Enoch, don't let them take me!"

"You can't do this, Merrick."

"I don't see a thing in the world to stop me. Certainly you won't. Now, get on with you. Go back to Leviticus Lee, and do whatever you have to do to recover that gold. I want it within three days, and you remember, if there is a sign of law, a sign that you've double-crossed me, the lady will be dead."

"I'll remember."

"Good." He began talking rapidly then, his accent and speed making it hard for me to keep up. What he said, boiled down, was that Minnie would be kept in a place I couldn't find. He then gave me directions to an old shack he said stood in a wild region in the mountains north of town, and told me to meet him there by noon three days hence, with the gold. As soon as it was in his hands, he would free Minnie. And most of all, he told me, I should make sure that Bass Merrick learned of none of this. If he did, Minnie would be killed.

Minnie was crying as they carried her off, but it wasn't her usual dramatic, loud cry. It was a soft, sad, fearful weeping. There was no falsehood or pretense about her now. She was truly scared.

And so was I. So scared I could have been sick. The whole situation staggered my belief. With no more to go on than a stray word from a talking parrot, I had followed my footloose wife through the Ozarks, faced more perils within a handful of days than I had ever dreamed I would in my whole life, and then, almost miraculously, found her again. And now she was taken, and in danger, and I wasn't sure I would ever see her again.

They had left my weapons leaned against a tree a good ways off. I waited until they were out of sight, then collected them. Sad and edgy, I headed back toward Farleytown and the Fairweather house.

I wondered what kind of response I would get from Leviticus Lee when he found that I needed to trade his coveted gold for the safety of my wife. The man had languished in a prison for two decades, living for the day he would recover his lost treasure—and here I was, about to take it from him.

And take it I would, by whatever means were necessary. Minnie's life was at stake, and the gold meant nothing to me now beyond being the necessary means of getting her safely back.

My gold fever was cured. The only treasure I wanted now was the one that I had first come to Arkansas to find, and that was my Minnie.

I rode toward the Fairweather house, my heart as heavy as the red sun that drooped on the western horizon.

CHAPTER THIRTEEN

FEARFUL AND WEARY, I TURNED MY MOUNT OFF THE ROAD to circle back toward the Fairweather house. As soon as the house was in view, I knew something was wrong.

Robert Fairweather was in the yard, pacing back and forth, talking loudly to his family. It was clear that some sort of argument was under way. The children and Blanche Fairweather were assembled on the porch and silhouetted against the backlight of the windows. Fairweather was waving his left hand like a tent-meeting preacher going strong. His right hand hung stiffly at his side, clutching a rifle.

"Look!" Blanche Fairweather declared as I came into view. She raised a finger and pointed it accusingly. "There's the very man who's brought this trouble upon our household!"

"Blanche, God help me, I demand that you close your mouth!" Fairweather bellowed. I noticed at the same moment that he had a bandage around his right upper arm.

"What's happened here?" I asked.

"Leviticus Lee is gone," Fairweather said.

"Gone? You mean he's run off?"

"No—he's been carried away. Abducted."

"What?"

Blanche Fairweather, clearly in no humor to be an obedient wife this night, stepped down from the porch and up to the side of my horse. "It's you who brought that man here, and you who bear the responsibility for the danger that came upon us tonight."

"Blanche, I told you to—"

"Shut up, Robert!" she shouted. "For once, let me have my say!"

I had dismounted by now. She glared at me bitterly. "A man came to our house tonight. He was armed, and forced us to lie on the floor. He took Leviticus Lee away at gunpoint. When Robert tried to stop him, the man shot him in the arm. Shot my husband! And right in front of the children!" Tears rose, but not tears of fear or weakness. These were generated by pure fury.

"Cuthbert?" I asked.

"No. A stranger," Robert Fairweather answered. "And he just grazed my arm muscle here, that's all. The bullet went into the wall."

"Who could he have been?"

"I'd seen him before," Robert Fairweather said. "In town, just in the last month or so, loitering around in front of the saloons. But I don't know him."

"It's you who caused this to happen," Blanche charged again. "I told you that trouble follows you. I've always been able to spot your kind. My own father was one."

"Enoch, do *you* have any idea who it might have been?" Robert Fairweather asked.

"No," I said. "I never knew Leviticus Lee until just before we showed up here. I don't know much about him, or what enemies he might have. Which way did they go?"

"Back to the road, and after that I don't know," Fairweather said. "I was too distracted by this little wound of mine to take notice. But now I'm ready to go after them. That's what I was about to do when you rode up—against my wife's wishes, I should add."

"It's foolishness, Bob," Blanche said. "You're a storekeeper, not a tracker. You should stay here and protect your kin, not go trailing off in the night. Let the constable take care of this."

"She's right about the tracking. We'll never be able to follow them in the dark," I said. A suspicion was starting to roll through my mind. "But there might be a place I can look. It's just a wild guess, but . . ."

Without another word I hefted up into the saddle again and rode toward the road, Robert Fairweather yelling for me to stop long enough to tell him what I was doing. I ignored him; there was no reason at the moment to involve him further in this.

A deep fury drove me now, and a deeper fear. Minnie was a prisoner of a dangerous young man, and the only other person who could lead me to the gold that would buy her freedom was a captive as well.

But a captive of whom? I didn't know . . . but I had a possibility in mind.

I urged my horse to a trot and headed through the darkness on the now-familiar road to Farleytown, trying to ignore my near-exhaustion.

Bass Merrick's house was dark, except for a couple of rooms at the rear. I dismounted and tethered my weary horse in a hidden place, and approached cautiously, on the lookout for dogs or any other thing that might give me away.

Edging around the house, I approached one of the lighted rear windows, hoping to get a look inside. There was no way I could be sure that Leviticus Lee was here, or that Bass Merrick was responsible for his capture.

But it made sense to me that Merrick might be the one. Paul Merrick's words to me earlier indicated that when I was first at the Merrick house, he hadn't yet learned about Leviticus Lee being in town. Given that, it seemed unlikely that Bass Merrick had known about it either. By now, however, surely he did know, just as his son did. And just as surely, he had also recognized Leviticus Lee's name and realized his connection with the Confederate gold.

I might have suspected Paul Merrick as being responsible for Lee's abduction, except for one thing: Today's encounter on the road, Paul Merrick's demands on me, and the capture of Minnie would have been unnecessary if Paul Merrick had planned to take Leviticus Lee himself prisoner. Further, I had gone straight from the encounter with Paul Merrick to the Fairweather house, and there simply wouldn't have been time for the younger Merrick to plan and pull off Lee's abduction in that brief interim. Besides, Paul Merrick didn't strike me as brash enough to set up as brazen and invasive a capture as that which had taken Leviticus Lee. He seemed more the type to bully people in isolation, and with armed companions, as he had done today to Minnie and me.

Since the Fairweathers had specified that Parker Cuthbert wasn't Lee's captor, that left only Bass Merrick as a likely suspect. My working theory was that Bass Merrick had, like his son, come to realize that Leviticus Lee could lead him to the gold he coveted. But unlike his son, he had decided to go straight to the source itself, rather than taking the indirect route of trying to get the gold through me. It was virtually certain that Bass Merrick knew nothing of what his son had done today; Paul Merrick seemed very intent on making sure his father did not find out what he was up to.

The window was covered with thick drapes, making it impossible to see inside. I could hear muffled and unintelligible male voices, but try as I would, I could not detect if one of them was Lee.

Moving to another window, I had an equal lack of success. Now I was bewildered. I could hardly knock on Bass Merrick's door and say, excuse me, but did you kidnap my partner, and would you mind giving him back? Nor could I burst in like some dime-novel hero and free the captive . . . if he was even here.

As I dawdled and wondered what to do, a door opened around the corner. A rear door was there—

and someone was coming out of it. There were no bushes immediately at hand to hide me, and no place to go but back toward the front of the house, or to the woods at the side.

I opted for the latter, and made a dash that I hoped would be quick and quiet. On the third step, however, my foot trod a stick, which snapped loudly. I lunged forward all the faster, and my other foot caught the remnant of the same branch and sent me flat onto my face.

"Hey, hey you there—hold it!"

There was no point in trying to run now. As I stood, the man who had emerged from the house was upon me, and others were coming out to join him. I brushed myself off as I was surrounded. The fellows reeked of cigar smoke and whiskey.

"Who are you, and what are you doing here?" one asked.

"Where's Mr. Merrick?" I asked.

In one of those cases of appropriate timing, Bass Merrick came out that same rear door. "What's all this, now?" he boomed.

"Got us a fellow who was poking around under the window," my captor said. "Don't know who he is."

"It's me, Mr. Merrick—Enoch Brand."

"Mr. Brand? Well—isn't this interesting! Come down here and join me and my friends. We're in the midst of a ripping good poker game." His tone was friendly on the surface, but sounded threatening and suspicious just beneath.

"I'm afraid I don't have the time or money for a

poker game," I said. "Maybe the best thing would be for me to just go."

"No. Come in. I insist."

I didn't want to go in. If in fact Leviticus Lee was a prisoner here, the odds were I would be taken prisoner as well. And then what would happen to Minnie?

"I'd really best be going," I muttered.

"Stay," he said. His hand slid into a pocket and came out holding a derringer. "I'm afraid I have to know why you've come poking around my house in the dark of night."

He had me taken into a back room, then sent the others out and closed the door behind them. Sitting down in front of me, he crossed his legs and toyed with the little pistol. He didn't aim it at me, but neither did he put it away.

"Mr. Brand, I'm not pleased when folks come poking around my place like you were. It makes me want to ask a lot of questions."

"Let me ask you one first, Mr. Merrick. Where is Leviticus Lee?"

He reacted immediately to the mention of the name. His eyes flashed and a little smile danced across his face for a second or two. "Leviticus Lee! A well-known name to me. Had I known at the time you were last here that you are a companion to the good Mr. Lee, I would have found you even more interesting than I did. But why should I know where Mr. Lee is? It's my understanding that he's a guest at the Fairweather house, just like you."

"He was. He's gone now. Abducted."

"Abducted?" He had no smile now. "In what way?"

"Someone came into the house with a gun, forced the family to hold still, and took him off. Robert Fairweather tried to stop them, and took a wound in the arm for his effort."

Merrick seemed intrigued, and mulled over what I had told him. He brightened in quick comprehension. "Aha! So you thought that perhaps I was responsible, and came here to see—is that it?"

"I couldn't help but suspect you. I'm told you have looked for the Confederate gold for a long time. A man with your knowledge of the lore of the gold would know that Leviticus Lee is the key to finding it."

"*Was* the key, you should say. I'm convinced that the gold existed, but that now it's gone."

"Gone?"

"Yes. I've explored these hills, traced down every shred of evidence, poked through every cave. I don't think the gold is here anymore."

I didn't want to hear that. Without the gold I couldn't get back Minnie. "You think it was taken by someone?"

"Maybe. Or maybe the crevice it was hidden in shifted or opened wider, or was flooded out. The gold could have dropped into the very bowels of the earth. If it's here, it's buried so deep now that it can't be found."

"You sound awfully certain. What grounds do you have for being so sure?"

"I'm not sure, really—it's just speculation. Suffice it to say that I don't feel that looking for the Confederate gold is worthy of any more of my time than I've already given it in years past. I gave up that search some time ago. I don't believe that even Leviticus Lee could put his hand on that gold now. And so, you can see, there's no reason I would have bothered to abduct him. What good could he have done me? Besides, I'm no kidnapper. It's not my style."

I didn't know whether to believe him. But certainly I wasn't going to argue with him, with all the proverbial cards in his hand. "But if not you, then who?"

He smiled an almost mysterious smile. "I might suspect my son, but my son is far away from here. He wasn't much happy about the way I 'shamed' him in front of you—that was his word, 'shamed.' He was all huffed up, let me tell you. So he took off back to Texas and his saloon girls and drinking partners."

That's what you believe, I thought. I could tell him a few things about what his son had really been doing—but I wouldn't, not until I knew he was trustworthy.

"If I were you, I'd investigate a man named Parker Cuthbert. He's something of a town fool, but he also happens to be the person here most obsessed with the Confederate gold. He might know enough to be aware of Leviticus Lee's connection with that gold. And he would be just the kind to pull something like this."

"I've heard of Cuthbert. But the Fairweathers say

it wasn't him who came into their house."

"Well, then maybe it was someone he had hired, or promised a cut of the gold."

I hadn't thought of that possibility. It made sense. "I hear that Cuthbert lives in a house you own. Where can I find him?"

"He did live in it. I threw him out three days ago; I doubt the word has spread yet. He hadn't paid rent for five or six months, and local folk said he'd been acting threatening and dangerous lately. I had my fill of him, and gave him the boot."

"So where's he staying?"

"Who knows? For all I know, he's lodging in a cave. I've given a lot of help to that bloody fool, and I don't care about him anymore."

"Will you let me leave?" I asked.

He smiled slowly. "I will. And I hope you find your partner safe and sound. Let me know what happens. I'm as concerned as you are."

I nodded and headed for the door. The others outside gave me uncertain, dark glances, then looked at Merrick as he followed me out. "It's all right," he said. "Give him back his pistol. He can go."

As I rode away from Bass Merrick's house, I did so with several new convictions. One, I didn't trust the senior Merrick any more than the younger one, even though he had let me go. Something in his manner, something in the way he had held that derringer throughout our conversation, something about the overconfident way he assured me there was no gold to be found . . . it just didn't ring convincing.

He had said he was as concerned as I was about Leviticus Lee, yet he offered me no assistance in finding him. And he had taken great pains to make it clear that he no longer had any sort of affiliation with the mysterious Parker Cuthbert.

But I wasn't buying. There was something odd here, something rather sinister. I was glad I had said nothing about what Paul Merrick had done. Let Bass Merrick believe he was really in Texas, at least for now. To have said otherwise would have endangered Minnie.

It was very late now, and I was so weary I could hardly stay in the saddle. I could do nothing more tonight to find Leviticus Lee. In the morning I would have to seek help from Robert Fairweather.

I longed to return to the Fairweather house and get some sleep, but the prospect of facing off with Blanche Fairweather was too much to take. The way I felt, the way I feared for Minnie's safety, I might just lose control of myself and raise a hand against Blanche Fairweather if I had to choke down any more of her bile.

Outside Farleytown I found a barn that stood out of sight of its affiliated farmhouse. I stabled my horse and fed it on some hay. Then I wrapped my coat around myself, lay down on a pile of hay, and immediately fell into an exhausted sleep.

The sound of riders on the nearby road awakened me. Creeping to the wall, I looked out through a knothole. Three horsemen came past. A chill ran through me. Were these incidental travelers—or had Bass Merrick had me followed?

If the latter, at least I had escaped them, for they had gone right past the barn. Lying down again, I resumed my sleep.

CHAPTER FOURTEEN

WHEN I RODE INTO HIS YARD THE NEXT MORNING, ROBERT Fairweather seemed hardly less agitated than he had been the prior evening. He came running out of his house to meet me. His wife came to the door but did not come out; she looked harshly at me from its shadows.

"Did you find him?" Fairweather asked urgently. "Where did you go? Where is he? Where is he?"

"I don't have him," I replied. "But I think I know who might. The man who captured him could have been working on behalf of Parker Cuthbert."

"Yes, I suppose he could have," Fairweather said after he thought about it a couple of seconds. "I never considered that Cuthbert might have someone else do the dirty part of the work for him. But where did you go last night?"

"On a chase after a wild goose. It's not important. Listen, Fairweather, I came back here for only one reason. I want you to tell me where Parker Cuthbert might go if he wanted to be out of view. He's no longer in his house. Bass Merrick threw him out because he quit paying his rent."

"I didn't know that . . . let's see, let me think . . ." He rubbed his chin. After a few moments his face brightened. "The old sawmill!" he declared. "That's a likely spot. I know Cuthbert has been known to go there to drink with some of his friends, if you could call them that."

"Tell me how to get there."

"Wait, my friend, wait. I've been thinking, and Blanche and I have been talking. I think we should notify the constable, just as she suggested. This is becoming far too criminal to be handled by regular folk like you and me."

"No," I replied. "No law." I was thinking of Minnie and what might happen to her if word somehow reached Paul Merrick that I had gone to the law. He would be bound to think I had gone to report his kidnapping of Minnie. Paul Merrick surely had eyes all around; if I did anything too peculiar, he would doubtlessly learn of it. Even going to Bass Merrick's house had been risky, but in this case necessary.

Blanche came into the yard now. "See, husband? He fears the law. Why? What does he have to hide?"

I wanted to scream at her, to tell her to shut up and mind her own affairs before she got an innocent person or two killed. But I kept myself calm, took a deep breath, and said, "Please—let me explain. I'm going to tell you something in confidence, and if you betray me, my wife might pay for it with her life."

"Your wife?"

"That's right. Your hunch was right, Robert. My wife was at the McCoy house, just as you had thought—the McCoys turned out to be relatives of Joben Malan's mother. I went and fetched her away from there."

"Then where is she now?"

"She's been taken captured too, just like Leviticus Lee. But the difference is I know who has her. It's Paul Merrick. He stopped us on the road and took her hostage. The price of me getting her back is finding the Confederate gold for him. If I go to the law, he'll kill her. I'm sure he would." I looked up at Blanche Fairweather. "That's the reason I don't want to bring the constable into this, ma'am. I hope you can understand that."

"God spare us!" Robert Fairweather said. "What a terrible thing!" He stopped, thinking. "Wait a minute—might it not be Paul Merrick who took Leviticus Lee as well?"

"I don't think so," and I explained my reasons for that opinion. "But whoever has Leviticus Lee," I added, "I've got to find him. Without him I can't find the gold and get my wife back. It's not a matter of greed or gain anymore. It's a matter of Minnie's survival."

"I see." Fairweather rubbed his chin again. "My friend, I'm going to help you. I'll get my rifle and head out to the sawmill with you, and if Leviticus Lee is a prisoner there, then by Jove, we'll set him free! I'm not afraid of Parker Cuthbert."

"We still don't know for sure it's Cuthbert," I reminded him. "Nor do we know that Lee is at the old mill."

"No," Fairweather said. "But I can't think of any better options to pursue at the moment. Can you?"

"No." I stuck out my hand, and actually got a lump in my throat. My earlier greed-inspired distrust of the man was gone. He now knew that even if the gold was found, it would have to be paid out in ransom, yet he was still willing to give me aid. I knew then how wrong I had been about the man, and how blind my own greed for the gold had made me. "I accept your help. Right now I'm desperate enough to take help from anyone willing to give it."

Blanche grasped her husband's shoulder and wheeled him around to face her. "You can't get involved in this—it might be dangerous!"

"Blanche, think of Enoch's wife! Good heavens, woman, if it was you in danger, I'd certainly want someone to help me get you back!"

"How do we know he even has a wife? Why have you been so quick to trust him? It's the gold—that's it. You have gold flashing in your eyes again, and it's making you blind. You still think you can get your hands on it. Your duty is to your own family, to your *own* wife, not to this man's—if she even exists!"

"She exists," I said. "And I intend to see that she continues to exist." Looking to Robert Fairweather, I said, "But your wife is right about your duties. I need your help, but I won't fault you if you back out. Just tell where the mill is, and I'll do this alone."

"Nonsense. I'm going with you."

Blanche Fairweather spat toward me. "I hate you!" she said. "Why did you have to come to our house at all? If my husband goes with you, I'll, I'll . . ."

"You'll go inside, say prayers for my safety, and wait for my return," Robert Fairweather said. "My mind is made up, Blanche. I'll hear no more from you about it."

She looked at me with a venomous gaze. "There may be more than praying that I can do," she said, and stomped back into the house.

"What does she mean by that?" I asked.

"Never mind her—she speaks her mind too freely," Robert Fairweather said. "I'll go get my guns and horse, and we'll be off."

"Robert, I want you know how much I appreciate this, and that—"

"Hush, son," he said. "Time's wasting."

He went about readying for our venture. When he came back out, he handed me my Henry rifle and a couple of leftover breakfast biscuits with tenderloins stuck in them. I had been so wrought up that I hadn't even noticed how hungry I was.

Armed and mounted, and with me gnawing the biscuits, we set out, Fairweather leading the way toward the old sawmill, and—I hoped—to my captured friend Leviticus Lee.

We wound through scraggly, dark forests, under tall limestone cliffs, along streams, up narrow, abandoned roads, and finally reached a rutted, overgrown route that followed the crest of a ridge. I heard a river splashing along somewhere beyond the trees.

"This is the old sawmill road," Fairweather said. "Not many use it now."

I had dismounted and was investigating the ground. "Somebody used it recently," I said. "Take a look."

There were tracks, relatively fresh, of three horses. I followed them on foot a little ways, and then discovered something else. A strip of white cotton cloth, darkened at one side with blood.

"Look at this, Robert," I said. "Looks to me like a piece of bandage."

"Yes . . . just like the one Leviticus Lee had on that stump of his."

"How far to the sawmill?"

"About a mile."

"No one works there now?"

"It's been abandoned for a couple of years. All that's left is the building."

"If Cuthbert or anyone *is* there, will they be able to see us before we come close?"

"Not unless we round the last ridge and enter on the main road. When we get near the point, I suggest we tie our horses and go over the ridge on foot, and approach the mill from the side. That way we can get a good look at what might be going on before they have much chance to see us."

"They have three horses," I said. "Assuming they brought one to carry Leviticus Lee, that means there's only two men involved. Probably Cuthbert and whoever it was who actually came into your house."

We went on. The autumn Ozark countryside was

fantastically beautiful, but I hardly noticed it. I wondered what we were riding into.

A new thought came to me. What if someone was being held at the sawmill—but what if it wasn't Leviticus Lee? This might be the hidden place Minnie was being kept.

What then? Would it be wise to attempt a rescue, or would that simply endanger her? Thinking about it made me nervous. I decided to withhold all such judgment making until we knew what the situation truly was.

That mile of travel was the longest I have ever known. By the time we reached the ridge that Fairweather had mentioned, the relatively few minutes that had passed seemed like hours. We hid the horses, drew out rifles, and looked at each other.

It struck me then what a ludicrous little army we made—a Kansas blacksmith and a small-town Arkansas merchant, going in to rescue a one-handed former convict from a violent, gold-obsessed town drunk. It really did seem rather funny, in a way.

I felt no inclination to laugh.

"Lead the way," I said to Fairweather.

"All right. Up this way here, quiet and easy, would be the best. I suggest we—"

He cut off suddenly, having heard the same thing I had. A yell of pain—a man's yell. The cry was muffled by distance and distorted by suffering, but it sounded for all the world like Leviticus Lee's voice to me.

Funny, how hearing that cry caused us to forget

our planned caution. We scrambled up that ridge like berry-picking boys racing each other toward a particularly productive blackberry vine.

Another yell echoed up, this one virtually a scream. No question about it now—that was Leviticus Lee's voice. Obviously he was in great torment.

"Merciful heaven—I think they're torturing him!" Fairweather whispered.

The sawmill, visible when we topped the ridge and hid in the brush to peer over, was a rambling, rough old structure with a roof half caved in and big pieces of the walls missing. It appeared that parts of the building had been cannibalized over its two years of abandonment and used in other structures. We could see no sign of human life, but the evidence of our ears was entirely sufficient.

"There's their horses," I said, pointing toward the rear of the sawmill, where three hobbled horses picked at dried winter grasses.

"I recognize that old sorrel," Fairweather said. "That's Parker Cuthbert's horse."

Another scream came to our ears. It made me wince.

"I wonder what they're doing to him?" Fairweather said.

"Working on that stump of his, I'll bet." The thought of that kind of cruelty made me angry. Good. I would need anger, and every other motivator I could think of, to do what needed doing.

"We got to go down there," I said. "It appears to me the direct approach will be best."

"What do you mean? Just walk in on them?"

"Why not?"

He shrugged. "I can't think of any better plan. If we can surprise them, maybe we can have them disarmed before they can react."

"We'd best split up—you go in the back, and I'll go in the front. Hitting them from two sides would be to our advantage. We'll get down there together, then when you're stationed at the back, I'll bust right in through the front there. Likely that'll fluster them. When their attention is on me, that's when you need to come in. Keep a sharp ear, all right?"

He nodded resolutely. "I'll do it. By Jove, we'll get that poor man out of there."

Leviticus Lee was screaming again, begging them to stop whatever it was they were doing. I heard another voice, yelling just as loudly as Lee's. "You want us to stop? We'll stop when you tell us where that gold is!"

"That's Cuthbert's voice!" Fairweather said.

Lee, his voice tight with pain but defiant in tone nonetheless, shouted back at his tormentor, inviting him to make a permanent trip to the nether regions.

Fairweather I looked at each other, both of us knowing that if Cuthbert was desperate enough torture a man, he wouldn't be likely to give up without resistance.

"It's not too late for you to walk away from this," I said.

He paused, swallowed, blinked. Then he shook his

head. "No. Especially not now that I've heard those screams."

"All right. Be careful."

"I will."

"Well, now's the time," I said. "Let's go."

"Let's go," Fairweather repeated.

And we went.

CHAPTER FIFTEEN

I DIDN'T DARE ALLOW MYSELF TIME TO THINK, FOR IF I did, it would lead to hesitation, and hesitation could bring death to me, Fairweather, or Leviticus Lee.

Using brush and trees for cover, I circled down toward the front corner of the big, unpainted building. It was a dark and rather grim-looking structure, two stories tall, with a heavy iron-ribboned jack ladder leading down from the upper saw floor into the river, which ran directly behind the building. The jack ladder, up which logs had once been hauled for sawing, was one of the few items remaining from the mill's active days. The saws and steam engine apparatus to drive them had been removed.

The place was remarkably clean, the slabs and other saw leavings having inevitably been taken for firewood by local folk. What trash there was now was mostly empty bottles tossed down by the drunks who apparently used this as a hideaway. As I carefully made my way among the bottles, making sure not to cause any clinks or breakage to give me away, I wondered how many of these emptied containers had been drained by Parker Cuthbert.

I glanced down the side of the mill and saw Fair-weather moving into position. He darted to the jack ladder, crouched beneath it, and gave me a brief wave to acknowledge his success in traveling unseen.

Waving back, I took a deep breath and began creeping toward the big front door, a double-gated affair that was almost completely closed. Leviticus Lee was screaming again; the sound came from just inside the front doors. When I came bursting through, I would be directly upon them.

I had a certain curiosity to see Parker Cuthbert, a mysterious and faceless figure so far. I imagined him as a husky, brutish creature, topped by thick, wild hair as dark as his squinted eyes. His nose surely was bulbous and etched with veins, courtesy of his drinking habit.

Well, the time had come . . . but I hesitated. Now that the moment was at hand, I didn't feel very heroic. I forced an image of Minnie into my mind. Only through Leviticus Lee could I get the gold I needed to buy her back. Then Lee let out a particularly fearsome scream, and I made my move.

But just as I was about to lunge through the opening between the doors, I heard a shout from inside. "Hold it! I've got my gun on you!"

That was Robert Fairweather's voice—what was he doing in there? He was supposed to enter after me, not before. Had he misheard something and taken it for my signal?

Curses, yells, confusion—then a shot, fired just inside the door. Fairweather yelled, fired back. The slug came bursting out through the wall not three inches from my head, sending splinters of wood all over me.

"Enoch, where are you?"

Fairweather's cry was desperate. I moved quickly, wheeling and dodging straight through the gap between the doors—and from the corner of my eye caught sight, just as I disappeared, of two riders coming around the ridge that Fairweather and I had come across, and riding onto the grounds of the sawmill. Who they were or why they had come, I didn't know, and there was no time to see.

The scene that met me inside was as confused as I had anticipated, yet the details of it revealed themselves starkly. There was Leviticus Lee, tied down on a large log, with his handless arm stretched out and tied along the length of a board, which served as a splint to keep him from bending his elbow. His bandage had been pulled off, and it appeared that his torture had consisted of pressure being applied by a second board at the point of his wound.

Two men were in motion as I came in, one surely being Cuthbert and the other his assistant. One, a man with a completely bald head and large ears, was diving behind a pile of rotting lumber, taking cover. The other, a tall, thin man with shuck-colored hair, was already positioned behind one of the big poles that supported the rather barnlike building. He fired off a shot from his Remington pistol toward the far end of the mill, then turned when I came in, cussed, and ripped off a second shot toward me. Fortunately, he missed, but he did manage to drive me back outside again.

A lot of good my appearance had done! More shots rang inside the sawmill. Somewhere in there, Fairweather was trying to hold his own, and still wondering why I wasn't there to help.

I had to go back in, and was about to do so when more rifle fire erupted, this time from behind me. A bullet thunked into the wall above me and passed inside the sawmill. Remembering the two riders I had seen, I wheeled and ducked at the same time, coming down on the backs of my heels with my shoulders against the plank wall.

"No, Billy, no!" a youthful voice cried. "That's Mr. Brand!"

I saw the one who had shot at me—a lanky fellow in an oversized coat and straw hat. He was standing in an odd-looking, bow-legged half squat beside his horse, holding a smoking Henry rifle almost like mine. I caught the glitter of a tin badge on his black coat.

"She went and got the constable anyway!" I said out loud to myself. I recognized the youth with the lawman to be Fairweather's oldest son; he must have served as his mother's messenger boy.

So confused was the situation now that I didn't even have time to consider the implications of this new development. I reentered the sawmill to again attempt the relief of Robert Fairweather and the rescue of Leviticus Lee.

This time the tall man with the Remington was not

at his previous post. In fact, I could see him nowhere. Once inside, I headed straight for Lee, who was yelling and writhing for freedom. Pulling a pocketknife from my coat, I said, "Hold still—let me cut you loose!"

Then the bald man popped up behind his woodpile, pistol in hand, and fired almost point-blank at me. The shot passed so close to my head that it clipped off some hair. I yelled and fired my Henry, and the bullet buried itself in the wood.

Immediately I vaulted over the woodpile, for I knew I had to rid myself of the bald man's threat before I could hope to free Lee. From across the sawmill Fairweather's yell, another cry for help, came ringing; I was encouraged to know he was still alive.

I landed on top of the bald man and drove my knee into his belly. He let out an "Oooof!" and tried to point his pistol into my face, but I deflected it, then hit him in the head with the stock of my Henry. It knocked him silly, but not out cold.

Just then I was aware of a shadow looming up behind me. It was the tall man with the Remington. He aimed and would have fired, but suddenly he spasmed and fell, simultaneous with the sound of a shot from the far end of the mill.

"I got him!" Robert Fairweather shouted.

Then began a quick succession of events that I would go through in my mind a million times thereafter, looking for whatever would have stopped it from happening, and never being able to find it. It was the confusion that caused it; that's the best all these years of assessment have been able to come up with. Confusion, and the speed of human reaction, and the inability of the mind to keep control of behavior once it begins running full-steam.

Here's the progression: I struck the bald man a second, lighter blow, designed to render him unconscious, but not kill him. Then Leviticus Lee sent up a holler, a warning, telling me to look out behind. I stood, wheeling around, as a figure came through the door. As I leveled my Henry, I saw two things—first, that the man at the door was the constable, and second, that Robert Fairweather had come out of his place of hiding at the far end of the stable and showed himself abruptly.

I remember seeing the constable raising his rifle, hearing myself yell out the word "No!" as loudly as I could, and then seeing and hearing the explosion of the constable's shot. At the other end of the building, Robert Fairweather took the slug right through the chest and jerked back and down like a dog hitting the end of its leash on a dead run. I yelled another no, then saw the constable's face go white. He dropped his rifle, recognizing who he had just shot. God help us, I thought, he's hardly more than a boy himself. A boy with a tin badge and a trigger finger that reacted before his mind could stop it.

The young constable collapsed to his knees, burying his face in his hands and crying in horror, "Oh, God forgive me, God forgive me, I've kilt Bob Fairweather!" At the same time, the Fairweather boy was running toward the collapsed heap that was his father, and then he was kneeling beside him, feeling his bloody chest, and at last crying himself as he slumped over and put his arms around the body as if he could squeeze the life back into it.

I knew then that Robert Fairweather was dead, and the thought made me sick clear through to the center of my very being. I stood there, watching the constable cry, until at last an urging voice managed to cut through the fog inside my ears and I realized that Leviticus Lee was begging me to free him.

Moving like a human machine, I stepped across the woodpile and also across the body of the tall man with the Remington. He was dead too. I opened my jackknife and sawed through Leviticus Lee's bonds while the sounds of grief rose on both sides of us.

There's no need to break down bit by bit all that had happened to lead up to the tragedy, or every detail of what happened immediately afterward. I'll turn things backward and give the broad strokes of the latter first.

After the constable got hold of himself again, he went from sad to angry, and turned a lot of venom on me and Leviticus Lee, on the grounds, as best I could tell from his nonsensical raving, that our presence in this county was the reason all this had happened, and therefore we were to be held to blame.

So he put us under arrest and hauled us off. Lee was taken somewhere "safe," they told me, but wouldn't tell me where. As for me, I was taken to Farleytown and stuck into the constable's "jail," a shack with double-thick walls, bars on the single window, and a rusty old cell door that fit in behind the regular one. The constable had built the thing himself out of what had been a woodshed near his own house. It provided the only secure place in the county to hold prisoners, except, of course, for the real jail at the county seat.

I was in despair, as you could suppose, not only about the death of Robert Fairweather, but also over being locked up when it was so pressing to get the gold and buy back Minnie. I almost told the constable about Minnie's capture, but held back because I saw he was so distraught about what had happened at the sawmill that he would either not believe me or would do something crazy in response and get Minnie killed.

Besides, I was fairly sure I could get out of this so-called jail, if it came to that.

Now, back to the sawmill tragedy and what led to it. Some of what I relate here I learned immediately after the incidents; other information came later, and some is based on my best supposition.

The bald man I had struck behind the woodpile in the sawmill was Parker Cuthbert. He didn't look a thing like I had pictured him. As suspected, he had hired the other man, the lanky one with the pistol, to capture Lee from the Fairweather house. The lanky man, who I later learned went by the name Jimbo Rollins, was a small-time criminal from Texas who had come to Arkansas fleeing a robbery charge, and had taken up with Cuthbert as a drinking partner. Robert Fairweather's shot had struck him in the upper chest and killed him instantly.

My blows to Cuthbert had knocked him out, but did no further damage. He too was arrested because of the horrible thing he had done to Leviticus Lee, and was taken to Dr. Ruscher's house under hired guard—a couple of locals who agreed to watch him while he was laid up. Cuthbert came to with both his guards sound asleep, and simply walked out the door. After that he couldn't be found.

As I had surmised, Blanche Fairweather was responsible for the constable coming into the picture. She had sent her son to get him just as soon as Fairweather and I had ridden out; the boy and constable had then come together to the sawmill.

No one ever knew what had caused Robert Fairweather to enter the sawmill before he should have. I suppose he mistook one of Leviticus Lee's yells as my signal. Whatever the case, it was that mistake, more than any other factor, that led to the tragedy.

The death of Robert Fairweather grieved me deeply. I felt responsible, even though it wasn't directly my fault. I knew in my heart that the person most at fault wasn't me, or even the constable who had fired the shot. It was my own Minnie, whose unfaithfulness was what had led me to Arkansas in the first place.

I paced inside the little woodshed jail, feeling like a kettle on full boil with nobody to take it off the stove. The constable was nowhere around, as best I could tell. Hours passed, and the light faded. There wasn't so much as a candle inside my prison, nor even a bed.

At length I lay down on the dirt floor and dozed off. It was very dark when the outside door opened. There, on the other side of the inner barred door, stood the constable, holding a lighted lantern.

And beside him was Blanche Fairweather.

CHAPTER SIXTEEN

HER FACE LOOKED LIKE THAT OF A DEAD WOMAN. No tears, no expression, nothing but an ashen, barren expression. She stared at me in silence. The only sound was a quiet, choked weeping from the constable.

"Mrs. Fairweather," I said falteringly. "I'm sorry about what happened to your husband."

"Sorry," she repeated. "Sorry, you say." She closed her eyes. "I knew when I first saw you that tragedy would come upon my family. I don't know how I knew it, but I did."

"Mrs. Fairweather, it wasn't me who killed your husband," I said. The constable gave a louder sob, then lowered his head. He had made the cycle from grief to fury and back around to even deeper grief. His hands shook, making the lantern light tremble. I felt a great sympathy for him. He was just a young man, and he had made a mistake that he would never be able to put behind him. "It was an accidental death," I quickly went on. "Just an accident, caused by the confusion. There's really no one to blame."

The constable sat the lantern on the ground and began to cry in earnest, leaning against the frame of the door. For half a minute it was like that, the constable weeping, and Mrs. Fairweather and I standing, looking at each other without words.

At last the constable turned and lurched off into the darkness, thoroughly overcome. Mrs. Fairweather hadn't yet shed a tear.

"It was him who shot Mr. Fairweather," I said. "He didn't really mean to do it. He didn't know what was going on—he just reacted, that's all."

"You've destroyed my family," she said.

"It wasn't me, Mrs. Fairweather. It wasn't me."

"I don't care who pulled the trigger. If you hadn't come into my household, none of this would have happened."

"I know that, ma'am. I've been sitting here alone, going over and over that same thought in my mind. But none of this was intended. None of it."

"But the result is the same."

"Yes . . . yes."

"He's dead, Mr. Brand—my husband is dead. I'm left a widow, and my children have no father."

"I want to make it up to you, somehow. Want to do something . . ."

"Do something?" Now, the first tears welled in her eyes. "Do something? What will you do? Raise my Bob up from the dead? Return him to me like he was before?"

How could I answer that? I stood silent.

"You can do nothing, Mr. Brand. Nothing but pay the price for what you did." And she reached into the pocket of her jacket and produced a small pistol.

Trembling, she lifted it and aimed it into my face.

"Mrs. Fairweather, what will you gain by pulling that trigger?"

"Satisfaction. Vengeance. Justice."

"No. Your children have already lost a father. You'll deprive them of a mother as well. It will be murder if you kill me. And it won't be justice. *I didn't kill your husband!*"

"You're responsible all the same! I hate you!"

"Then hate me. But I didn't kill him. You have to understand that."

"Oh, you think I should use this pistol on that poor constable? You think I should blame him because he was the one who pulled the trigger? Because I don't— you've said with your own lips that it wasn't really his fault. It was an accident, one that would have never happened if you hadn't come to us uninvited."

"I came uninvited because my companion needed help. But you may recall that we weren't uninvited for long. Mr. Fairweather made it clear he wanted us to stay."

"Yes—because of the gold lust you revived in him. You cause it. You and your foul old partner. That's why I despise you. That's why I want the pleasure of seeing you die just like Bob died."

I saw then the depth of her hatred for me, a hatred I never would fully comprehend. She was able to see the truth of the constable's innocence with surprising ease, but where I was concerned, her mind was closed and locked. All her thoughts about me were irrational and bitter.

"I don't think you should use that pistol on me or anyone else, ma'am," I said. "And I think you're right not to blame the constable. But you're wrong to blame me or Leviticus Lee. Your husband came with me to that sawmill because he was a merciful-hearted man. There was far more to the man than gold lust; I know that now. He didn't want my wife to be murdered over a pile of lost gold, or Leviticus Lee to suffer at the hands of an evil man like Cuthbert. Your husband wouldn't want you to do what you're wanting to do, Mrs. Fairweather. And if you do it, you'll profane his memory and destroy what remains of your life. And a lot remains—all those beautiful children who need you. Think about it, and put away the pistol."

She began to cry very hard. The pistol lowered. "I hate you, hate you," she said. "I'll always hate you!"

The constable reappeared. His face was streaked and red, but he was not crying now. He had seen what was going on, and knew his duty. "Mrs. Fairweather, let me have the pistol," he said. "Please, give it to me."

She let the gun fall. He knelt and picked it up. Blanche Fairweather sobbed, turned away and ran off. I heard her climbing aboard the wagon upon which she had come, heard her drive off in the direction of her house.

"She told me she had to see you," the constable told me. "That's why I brought her. I didn't know she had a gun. If I had, I never would have—"

"I know. It's all right."

"I'll never be able to forget what it was like to see him fall, to know that I killed him." He looked off in the direction Blanche Fairweather had gone. "She's wrong to blame you. It's me who's responsible for Bob's death."

"It wasn't your fault. You were trying to do the right thing. There's no one blaming you."

"I feel responsible."

"No more than I do. We all had a hand in this. But none of us planned it. None of us wanted it to happen."

He looked at me wearily. Then, as if on impulse, he dug out a key, opened the inner barred door, swung it open with a creak, stepped back and waved his hand. "Get out," he said.

"What?"

"Get out. Your guns and things are yonder in my house, inside the back door. Take them and go. Your horse and saddle are yonder at my stock shed."

He was setting me free! I couldn't believe it.

"Thank you," I said. "I appreciate—"

"Shut up! Just shut up and go. Get out of this county and don't come back."

"I will get out." To myself I mentally added: *But not until I've gotten Minnie back again.*

He was still standing in the little shed door when I rode away. I breathed a prayer for him, than one for Minnie, and then another for myself.

I had told Blanche Fairweather that I would do something to make up for the death of her husband.

And I had meant it. What that would be, I had no idea. Yet I had to try.

But only after Minnie was safe. How could I get her back? At this point I hadn't yet learned where they had put Leviticus Lee, and there was no time to waste on a cold search for him. Nor did I have any notion of where Paul Merrick had stashed Minnie, nor if she was even still alive. If Paul Merrick had learned of the incident at the old sawmill, he might have panicked and already gotten rid of her.

I knew of only one place that might hold the answers I needed. I would have to go to Bass Merrick and reveal to him what his son had done. Maybe he would know where Paul Merrick might have taken Minnie. Maybe he would know where they had put Leviticus Lee. Maybe he would know something, anything at all, to help me—if only he would. I remembered the riders who passed me in the night, the ones who very well might have been sent by Bass Merrick to follow me. I had no grounds to trust the man at all.

Nor had I any other options. If Bass Merrick wouldn't help me, then there was no one else who could.

I was on the darkest stretch of the dark road when Parker Cuthbert appeared before me. He had a bandage on his bald head and a pistol in his shaking hand. He ordered me to stop, dismount, and throw down my pistols. I didn't know where he had come from; at that point I had no knowledge of his placement in and escape from the home of Dr. Ruscher.

"I knew I'd find you," he said. I could smell the liquor on his breath from where I stood. "You know where it is? Do you?"

"If you're talking about that gold, no, I don't know."

"You're a liar. You're a partner of Leviticus Lee. You know! You got to know!"

"No. Put the gun away, Cuthbert. You've dug a deep enough hole for yourself as it is."

"I'll not see my gold taken off by a stranger. It's my gold—I've searched for it for many a year. I've even kilt for it."

"Pete Revett?"

"Yeah, Pete Revett. Pete Revett the liar. He and me, we were friends once. He told me about hiding the gold. But he wouldn't tell me where it was. Said it was to be his, and his alone. He wasn't no friend at all. So I made him talk, made him tell me where he hid it, and then I kilt him. But he lied to me. It wasn't where he said it was. He had lied." He waved the pistol threateningly. "You won't lie. You'll take me to that gold. I would have had it by now if you hadn't come messing in my affairs. Leviticus Lee would have sung it out in good time if you hadn't interfered. Now you can make up for the trouble you've caused. You can take me to that gold as good as he could have."

"I don't know where it is. I'm not lying."

He clicked the hammer of the pistol. "You know— and if you don't talk, I'll kill you."

"Then what? With me dead, there's nobody to lead you."

"So you admit it! You *do* know!"

What could I do? The man was drunk, crazed, obsessed. I had no doubt he really would kill me if I overly frustrated him. So I nodded. "All right. You win. I'll take you to the gold."

He laughed like a child about to be handed a pound box of chocolate. "Smart man, smart man you are," he said. "Step aside. I'm going to ride that horse of yours, and you're going to walk in front of me, straight to that gold. One false move, and I'll kill you."

"I can't take you to it now—it's too dark. We'd never be able to find it in the dark."

"We can sure give it a try, now, can't we! Step aside!"

I had not the slightest notion where to go, so I walked along the main road. "I don't like this," Cuthbert said after a few minutes. "Somebody'll see us here. Where you heading?"

"The gold is near the old sawmill," I said, pulling the locale out of the blue. It was one of the few places I knew how to get to. "Tell me something, Cuthbert—was that you who shot at me when I was burying Leviticus Lee's hand?"

"I wouldn't have done it if you hadn't come after me. I was watching the house. I figured you had the gold and were going to hide it for a time."

"You want that gold mighty bad, don't you?"

"More than anything, friend, more than anything.

Listen to me: If we're heading toward the sawmill, there's a back road we can take. It's a little longer, but there's less chance we'll be seen."

Longer sounded fine to me; it would give me more time to come up with some scheme to get myself out of this. I dug around for ways to stall. "Wait a minute—we'll have to have a shovel. And a light."

"Light? What, is the gold down in a cave or something?"

"That's right."

He stopped. "There ain't no caves within a mile of that sawmill. What are you trying to pull?"

He had caught me in my own lie, but I faltered only a half second. "No caves you know of, you mean. The entrance is covered. That's why we need the shovel."

"Well, then we'll steal one along the way. There's a house or two we'll be passing." Suddenly he turned. "Wait—did you hear something?"

Indeed I had—it sounded like riders on the road behind us. But I said, "I didn't hear anything."

"There's somebody back yonder! Get off the road! Get!"

It was one of those sudden inspirations. I lunged forward, dropped to my knees and slid right under the horse. Then I let out a big yell, lunged up, and butted hard against the horse's belly with my shoulders.

As I had hoped, the horse spooked and reared. I rolled out from beneath to avoid being hammered by the hoofs. Parker Cuthbert, completely unready for my unexpected maneuver, and none too steady anyway because of his drunken state, hooted in surprise and was bucked clean off the horse. He landed on his back on the road just as the riders we had heard, three of them, came around the bend and into view.

It was too dark to make out who they were right away. All I could see was that the lead rider had a long shotgun. He stopped his horse, looked over the dark scene as best he could, then aimed the shotgun down at Cuthbert.

"Parker! So I've come looking for a treasure guide and found only a maggot." It was Bass Merrick's unmistakable Australian voice.

"Mr. Merrick!" I said, stepping forward.

"Well, I'll be!" he said. "Is that you, Brand? It was you I came looking for. I was just on my way to the constable to see about bailing you out—I heard about the incident at the old sawmill, and your arrest. I'm glad to find you. I have need of you."

"Enoch? *Enoch!*"

It was Minnie's voice, coming from behind Merrick. For a moment I was too stunned to react, then I darted toward her. "Minnie! Thank God!"

Merrick lowered his shotgun and shoved the muzzle into my chest. It caught me hard; my feet kicked out from beneath me and I fell onto my rump with an undignified thud.

"Not so fast, Mr. Brand," he said. "Not so fast. There'll be time for reunions later, after our business is done."

"But how did you find her?"

"I know my son's hiding places. It was easy for

me to get her. And that's the point to be stressed: *I* got her, not you. If you want her back, you'll have to earn her."

I was dismayed. "How?"

"Same deal my son offered you, the only difference being that this time you're dealing with me, not my pipsqueak of a boy. He's a loser, that one. Always has been. But I confess that this time he had him a good notion."

"How did you find out what he had done?"

"Paul's no judge of men—it's one of his many flaws. One of his 'friends' who was in on his little plan decided that I might reward him for sharing the scheme with me. Thought I might want to take it over, you see. He was right. Me and my man Jim, here"—he indicated the rider with him—"we just rode out and fetched your woman there right from Paul's grasping fingers. Now she's my prisoner, and you're dealing with me."

"Where's Paul?"

"Ran off pouting, and no doubt halfway to Texas by now. But enough talk. Have we got ourselves a deal, Mr. Brand? Gold for me, wife for you?"

I was so sick of this, so weary and hopeless, that I felt I could have fallen down in the road and died without complaint, just to escape. But all I could do was agree.

Parker Cuthbert rose. "Wait, Merrick. This here's *my* prisoner, not yours. And that gold is rightly mine too! You'll not snatch it from me!"

"Parker, Parker, Parker—if only you had any notion how wearying a man you are!" Merrick replied. "Don't you know that all the time I've given you a house to live in and put up with your presence, it's been on the slim chance that you might find that gold? If you had, you think I would have let you keep it? You're a bloody fool. You always have been."

"I thought you didn't believe that gold exists any longer," I said.

Merrick laughed. "So I said. But one never knows, does one! The more I thought about it, the more wonderfully possible the whole thing began to seem again. There may well be Confederate gold hidden in these mountains after all." His voice lowered and became coldly threatening. "You'd bloody well better hope there is too, Mr. Brand, if you want your dear woman back there to be safely yours again."

I could hear Minnie crying back in the darkness. I wanted so badly to go to her.

"I'll find your gold, Mr. Merrick. I'll find it for you—and when I do, I hope you choke on it."

Merrick laughed loudly. He seemed to think it was a very fine joke indeed.

Right then Parker Cuthbert made his move. He had dropped his pistol when the horse bucked him, but now he dove for it and retrieved it. In one swift roll he raised the pistol in both hands and shot Merrick's partner through the neck. The man pitched backward off his horse and thudded to the dirt. Minnie screamed, and Merrick swore. Cuthbert's second shot was aimed for Merrick, and it hit. Merrick took the slug in the shoulder and almost fell from his own mount. Cuthbert's third shot would have ended the encounter in his favor if he hadn't veered too much to the right and missed Merrick by little more than a hand's breadth.

That gave Merrick time enough to aim and fire. The shotgun's roar was fiercely loud, and the buckshot hit Parker Cuthbert squarely in the midsection. No second blast was required; it was immediately clear that Parker Cuthbert would no longer be a threat to anyone.

I headed straight for Minnie, hoping to somehow get my hands on her and get us away from here. It was a hopeless notion from the outset. Bass Merrick swung up his shotgun and brought it down on my skull. I fell to the ground, gripping the back of my head, then rolled over onto my back with a groan. Minnie was screaming.

"Shut up!" Merrick barked at her. From his voice I could tell he was hurting. He aimed the shotgun at her and looked down at me. "Mr. Brand, I wouldn't advise you to try anything like that again. There's still a loaded barrel in this shotgun, and I'll not hesitate to make your pretty wife look not so pretty anymore. Do you understand me?"

I sat up, my head throbbing. "I understand."

"Good. Now, stand up. We're going back to my house to patch me up, and then you're going to set out on a gold-retrieval venture, Mr. Brand. And you'll succeed, without any tricks, without any law, and without any hitch, or the lovely missus here will be a dead woman."

CHAPTER SEVENTEEN

WE MADE OUR WAY BACK TO BASS MERRICK'S HOUSE. Merrick's swore beneath his breath at the pain of his wound, and from his manner it was clear he was deeply disturbed by the killing of his underling, not to mention his own injury. And that was bad. Disturbed men react more than think, and often in irrational and dangerous ways.

And as Minnie reluctantly bandaged Merrick's wounded shoulder back at his house, the man seemed both irrational and dangerous to me. It scared me, more for Minnie's sake than my own. The way things had gone lately, I didn't expect anything but problems for myself. I was ready to handle whatever was tossed my way. But Minnie—that was different. If something should happen to her, that would be more than I could handle. Seeing the panic rising in Merrick, who until now had seemed the type to always be on top of his situation, was truly frightening.

"You're going to fetch that gold for me and bring it back here," he said, holding my own pistol on me with his good hand even as Minnie worked on his bloody shoulder. "I expect it in hand before sundown, or else I'll do what requires doing." I knew what that meant, and so did Minnie. Yet she didn't bawl out or collapse, as I might have expected. Perhaps the ordeals she had suffered had actually toughened her up a bit.

"Mr. Merrick, I won't lie to you. I don't know where that gold is. I never have known. Only Leviticus Lee knows."

If eyes could shoot lightning, his would have fried me thoroughly at that moment. "Mr. Brand, that had best be a bluff, for if it isn't, then you have no potential but to do me harm. And those who would do me harm are quickly swept away."

This was a dangerous man indeed. Even more dangerous than his son. "All right. I admit it was a bluff. I'll go get the gold."

What else could I have said? Anything else would have cost the life of my wife, and that of myself.

"Get on with you," Merrick said. "And if I catch even a whiff of law or treachery on your part, I'll make you a widower quicker than you can spit."

Alone in the night, I wondered what I could do. Where was Leviticus Lee? Given the torture inflicted on him in the old sawmill, was he even in condition to lead me to the gold, even if I could find him?

For that matter, would he be willing to do it? He had spent two decades of his life behind prison bars, living for the chance to gain the lost gold. He wouldn't be willing to turn it over to a man like Bass

Merrick, simply to save the life of a man he really hardly knew—would he?

I had to hope he would, for without it there was no hope at all. Bass Merrick had taken all my weapons. I wouldn't even be able to force Lee to help me, if such became necessary.

"Slow down and think," I said aloud to myself. "Where would they have taken Lee after the sawmill fight? Where?"

I had been hauled off and locked up, and Lee taken elsewhere. Realization struck, a realization so obvious it made me laugh. Lee was weak and injured after his ordeal at the mill. Where else would they take him but to Dr. Ruscher?

Encouraged, I increased my speed and rode toward Farleytown and the Fairweather store. It didn't strike me until I was in sight of the place that Dr. Ruscher only practiced there; his residence was elsewhere.

The window of his office in the store building was dark. Dismay swept over me. I had to find him, somehow.

My eyes turned to the saloons. Farleytown, though well-populated with drinking places, was no mining or railhead cattle town. The saloons didn't run all night. All that faced me was a row of dark buildings.

Dark . . . but not entirely. In the rear of one of the saloons a light burned. It was the same saloon, I recalled, that I had visited the day Paul Merrick was shooting the heads off buried chickens in the back.

I ran across the street and pounded the door so hard it rattled the adjacent window. Sure enough, there was somebody in the rear, and as he approached, I made him out to be the barkeep I had talked to before.

"What the devil are you doing?" he yelled through the door. "I'm closed!" Over his shoulder I saw another person—a woman, seated at a table. The lamplight revealed a frilly, rather revealing dress. A soiled dove, no doubt, sharing the barkeep's liquor, and probably more.

"I need Dr. Ruscher," I said back through the door. "Where does he live?"

He opened the door and looked at me in a way that indicated he had just recalled my face. "Head up past the store—third house on the hill there, with a building behind it where he lays up sick folks sometimes. You hurt or something?"

"No. But I'm afraid somebody will be. Thanks, friend. No time to explain."

I took off on a lope toward the indicated house. I heard the saloon door close and lock, as the barkeep returned to his woman.

Dr. Ruscher adjusted his spectacles, lifted the lighted lamp he held, and looked at me with the bewilderment common to folks who have been roused from sleep at the oddest of hours. He ran fingers through his white hair and ushered me in.

"Mr. Brand, are you ill? And what are you doing running free—I thought you had been locked up."

"There's no time for me to explain myself right now, Doctor. I'm looking for Leviticus Lee. Is he here?"

"He was. He isn't now."

"Then where is he?"

"I don't know. I had him here. But this afternoon, when I went to check on him, he was gone. The constable had posted some guards over him and Parker Cuthbert, but after Cuthbert got free, the guards just walked away. I suppose they figured Mr. Lee was too weak to run off. They were wrong."

"No, no, no!" I burst out. "He can't be gone! I've got to find him! You have no idea where he went?"

Dr. Ruscher gave me a probing look. "Well, if I had to take a guess, I'd say he went after his gold."

"His gold . . ."

He said, "Come in. Let me show you something."

He led me to his kitchen. On the table were spread papers—mostly maps, showing the local region. I looked uncomprehendingly at them, then understood. "So you've looked for the Confederate gold too?"

"That's why I moved here upon my retirement, Mr. Brand. It was an interesting legend, and it attracted me. Oh, I've never been obsessed with it, like some; in fact, I've kept my interest in the legend entirely private. But it's been a good diversion for an old man. I've tromped around the mountains from time to time, trying to find it, with no more luck than anyone else. I suspect Mr. Lee may prove a more effective searcher."

"I think we will. He was one of the three who first hid it."

"Ah! I had thought that might be the case! Fascinating! That explains his ravings about the gold coins."

"You heard it too, obviously."

"Yes. It didn't take me long to figure out what gold coins he was talking about. You know, I had a feeling about that man, one of those unexplainable intuitions. I knew he had something to do with that gold. Fascinating! Just fascinating!"

"Dr. Ruscher, I've got no time to explain my situation right now. Suffice it to say that I've got to find Leviticus Lee very quickly, and the gold too. Otherwise an innocent woman is going to die."

He frowned. "Die?" He seemed to withdraw. "Mr. Brand, I don't know what you're getting at, but I don't like the sound of it."

"I wish I could explain it more. All I can do is ask you to trust me, even though I know you've got no grounds for doing so. Dr. Ruscher, the woman who may die is my wife. Believe me, this is no fraud, no trick on my part to try to get something I've got no claim on." I waved at his maps. "Do you have any idea of what general area the gold is?"

"Nothing definite, but . . ." He paused, chewing his lip. "All right. Very well. I'll trust you. You have the look of honest desperation about you. Come, sit down. I'll show you what I can. But understand that this is nothing more than my best speculation, based on the study I've done concerning the legend, and my own explorations."

It was a meager lead, but all I had. I sat down, and

he pulled up a chair beside me. Adjusting the lamp, he took up his maps and began to talk.

It was still dark when I left his house, but the first hints of dawn were lighting the eastern sky. I rode my weary horse into the mountains, following the route Dr. Ruscher had laid out. I had no real hope of finding the gold on my own. My hope was that Dr. Ruscher's information would lead me to the general area Leviticus Lee would have gone to recover his gold. With good fortune, I might be able to find him there—unless he had already come and gone.

I went as far in the dark as I could without risking the loss of my trail. This was unfamiliar terrain to me; it would be difficult under the best of circumstances to find my way. Finally I reached a point where I felt it prudent to wait for the full light of day before continuing. That time of waiting, though less than an hour in duration, seemed to last three times that long. I tried to relax, to let my weary body retrieve a little strength.

When the sun was finally up, I continued. Dr. Ruscher had scrawled a crude map for me, indicating various natural points of reference for me to look for. I was well-aware as I went on that I might be wasting my time. Dr. Ruscher had admitted that his study of the probable whereabouts of the gold had led him to conclusions at variance with those of most other treasure hunters. If the doctor's reasoning was faulty, I might be going farther away from Leviticus Lee, rather than nearer him.

Time seemed to have speeded up; as I made my way through valleys and beneath bluffs, up hills and down treacherous slopes, it seemed I was making progress far too slowly. Aching and tired, I forced the horse on, knowing it was as exhausted as I was. At last the land became too rough for riding to remain feasible. I abandoned and tied my horse and proceeded on foot.

Until finally I was there. A narrow valley opened before me, and leading into it the remains of an old and abandoned road. In a thicket I saw the rotting remains of an old wagon. A military vehicle? Not enough remained for me to tell.

I descended into the valley. To my left rose a sheer limestone cliff, marked with cracks and crevices that might lead into caverns. At the base of the cliff I stopped, looking around.

I cupped my hands to my mouth. "Leviticus Lee!" I yelled as loudly as I could. "Leviticus Lee! Are you here?"

My call echoed away through the wild Ozark land. I raised the yell again. Still only silence in response.

Then, so close to me that I started in surprise, a voice replied, "Mr. Brand, is that you?"

"Leviticus!"

He was not thirty feet from me, lying in a bare spot behind a clump of scrubby brush. I could just make him out.

I circled the brush so quickly I almost fell atop him. He was on his back, looking as weak as death.

In his hand he gripped a very rusty old Chicopee saber, like the Union cavalrymen had carried back in the war. And beneath his other arm was an equally rusted old box.

A strongbox. Marked with the letters C.S.A.

"Mr. Lee—you found it! You found the gold!"

"That I did, Mr. Brand. But I'm afraid I've nigh killed myself doing it."

And indeed he did look bad. Very bad. His face was pale, and I had seen healthier countenances than his in many a coffin.

I knelt beside him. "Are you hurt?"

"I was hurt before I started. Wasn't in any shape to do this. But I couldn't wait. I sneaked out of that doctor's place and came on out for the gold. Didn't know if I could find it, but I did. I looked for the big crevice, and dug. Sure enough, there was the saber. We had marked the spot with it." He weakly lifted the old blade. "An old Union saber—Pete Revett had come by it some way or another, and carried it. We buried it beneath an overhanging rock to mark the place. Once I found the saber, finding the gold was easy. Or as easy as any job can be for a man freshly deprived of one of his paws."

I examined the stump. It was blackened and ugly, and stank. Parker Cuthbert's abuse of the wound during Lee's ordeal at the sawmill had obviously badly damaged the arm. "Mr. Lee, this is bad. Real bad. We got to get you back to Dr. Ruscher, or I'm afraid this will poison you to death."

"It might. Wouldn't that be something! To find the gold, and then die."

"I've got a horse not far away. We'll get you on it and take you back. And then—" I cut off, dreading what I had to say. "And then I have to take that gold from you, Mr. Lee. Not for myself. For Minnie's life."

"Take my gold? You think you can . . . what do you mean . . . ." He stammered into silence, and looked at me like I was Judas himself.

"Please, hear me out. Then you'll understand."

He lifted the saber and thrust it at me, driving me back. Weakly he stood. "You want my gold, and you'll have to fight me for it. Fight me clean to the death!"

"Listen to me. Just listen. That's all I ask right now. Just hear me out."

He was trembling very badly. The saber drooped to the ground, and he collapsed onto his rump. "All right, start talking. I don't appear in much shape to fight anyhow."

I told him the story, as best I could, from start to finish. He took it in without comment. Then he stood again, leaning on the saber like a cane. He looked down at the strongbox, sighed, and said: "Take it, then. Give it to Merrick, and buy back your woman."

"You mean that?"

"I mean it."

I could do nothing but stare at him. And I'm not ashamed to say that the tears rose in my eyes and spilled out.

"God bless you, Leviticus Lee," I said. "You're a saint. A saint, as sure as the world."

He shook his head. "No," he said. "Not a saint. Just a fool, that's all. Just an old fool with a heart that's even softer than his head."

CHAPTER EIGHTEEN

"WE'LL GO BACK TOGETHER," I TOLD HIM. "YOU NEED TO be looked at by Dr. Ruscher."

"No," he said. "I won't go back there. Too dangerous for me. When I sneaked off, I was still officially under the custody of the constable, and I can't afford an escape accusation. No sir. I'll stay here."

"You're in rough shape, Mr. Lee."

"I'll make it. Get on with you—get that gold to Bass Merrick and get your woman back before my old heart hardens up and makes me change my mind."

Any other time I would have argued with him harder, because he clearly did need medical attention. But my mind was full of Minnie right now; all I could afford to care about what getting her back. So I took the strongbox, thanked Leviticus Lee again, and returned to my horse.

With some cord from my saddlebags I strapped the strongbox onto the saddle behind me. Riding back through the rugged countryside toward the Merrick house, I thought how fine a man Leviticus

Lee was, how remarkable it was that he was so willing to give up the gold that he had centered his life around, all to help me regain my captured wife. It was a sacrifice greater than many would have been willing to make. That a rough old former convict like Leviticus Lee would make it was astounding, even unbelievable.

I reined to a stop. *Unbelievable*, I thought again.

Dismounting, I loosened the ties around the strongbox and hefted it off and onto the ground. The lock was already broken away; Lee probably had done that. Kneeling, I took hold of the lid, closed my eyes, then opened the strongbox. Then I sat there, fearing to open my eyes again, for I knew what I would see was a box filled with stones or dirt.

I willed my eyes open, and what I saw took my breath. Gold coins, gleaming in the sun, and piled to the top of the strongbox. For a full minute I could do nothing but stare.

"Leviticus Lee, you really did it after all!" I said aloud. "You really are a saint—you really are!"

There was something different about the Merrick house, some vague change in the atmosphere that gave warning to my instincts as soon as I arrived. How I wished I had a weapon! I would have even welcomed the feel in my hand of that rusty old saber of Leviticus Lee's.

Dismounting in the yard, I took the strongbox and walked with it in hand up to the front door. As I was about to call for entrance, I noticed the door was slightly ajar.

My instincts were still sounding an alarm. So rather than call, I carefully pushed open the door and peered inside.

"Mr. Merrick? Mr. Merrick—I'm here. Where are you?"

No voice answered, but I heard a slight scuffling movement in the room beyond. I entered warily.

"Mr. Merrick, is that you?"

Then I rounded the sofa and saw him.

Bass Merrick lay on his back on the floor, staring up at the ceiling above him. But he saw nothing. He was dead, his chest bloody and punctured by at least three shots.

I dropped the strongbox in surprise and gaped at the ugly corpse for a few moments. Then panic began to rise. "Minnie? *Minnie*! Where are you?"

"She's right here, Mr. Brand."

I pivoted. Paul Merrick stood in the doorway to the next room. His left arm was around Minnie, and his right hand held a pistol that was aimed at her head.

"Minnie—are you all right? Has he hurt you?"

"She's as fine as fine can be," Paul Merrick replied. "And if that strongbox contains what I hope it does, she'll continue to be fine. If it doesn't, she'll be joining my dear father in the great world beyond, and you will too."

"Did you do this?" I asked, pointing at Bass Merrick's corpse.

"He deserved it," Paul Merrick said. "He humiliated me one time too many. This was my scheme, my plan, and he took it away from me. Took over my plan, and took your wife for his own hostage. I started off toward Texas, figuring that this time I'd never come back. But I had to come back and settle my grievances once and for all. I couldn't stand the thought of letting him get that gold. That gold will be mine alone. *Mine*."

"Well, I've got it," I said, nudging the strongbox with my toe. "It's all there, and it's yours. Just give me my wife."

"All in good time," he said. "Open that box. I want to see it."

I knelt and opened the lid. Paul Merrick's eyes widened at the sight of the coins, and he smiled broadly, hungrily, and swore in awe at the sight. And indeed it was a sight worth seeing, a sight to rouse a fierce, ravenous greed in any man. But at that moment I was immune to the lure. All I wanted was my woman.

"You've got your gold. Now give me my wife," I said, standing.

He shoved her toward me without even glancing away from the box. I took her in my arms, hugged her to myself, whispered her name in her ear. I had never felt a feeling of relief and utter devotion to match the one running through me right then.

Paul Merrick knelt beside the box, chuckling to himself, his eyes as bright as flame. He looked at the coins a moment, then dug his fingers into them . . .

And the flame of his eye died. He drew in a sharp breath, pulled out a handful of the box's contents, stared at it, then with a curse threw it all down. What he had held was a few gold coins, and much more loose gravel.

Leviticus Lee had betrayed me. He had emptied the strongbox, filled with gravel, and covered the gravel with a thin layer of gold coins. The vast majority of the gold wasn't here at all.

So that was why he hadn't come back with me! Even now, he was surely making his escape as fast as he could, taking the bulk of the Confederate gold with him.

It was the most disillusioning experience in my life. Leviticus Lee was no saint. He was a traitor, a scoundrel, a man willing to see me and my wife killed, just as long as he could get his gold.

Paul Merrick rose, leveling his pistol. "You thought you could betray me, did you? Where's the rest of it, Mr. Brand? Where's my gold?"

"I don't have it, I swear. Leviticus Lee has it, up in the mountains where he found it. I didn't know about this, Merrick. I swear to you I didn't know. He betrayed me too."

"You're a bloody liar, Brand! I ought to kill you and your trollop right now!"

My mind worked quickly, searching for a way out. "No," I said. "You kill us, and you'll never find the rest of the gold. Let Minnie go. I'll take you to where I found Lee. He's in bad condition—he can't have gotten far. We'll get the rest of the gold. But please, just let Minnie go."

He considered my words, then nodded tersely. "All right. We'll do it—but your wife comes along with us, and if anything goes wrong, anything at all, she'll be the first to die. You keep that in mind, Mr. Brand."

He herded us before him like sheep before a mounted shepherd. He had traded his pistol for his father's shotgun, so that he could easily hit us should we try to flee.

Minnie was pale but calm; I was proud of her. She wasn't the emotional and rather weak girl she had been before. She was stronger, more in control of herself. I wouldn't have willingly put her through the ordeals she had suffered for anything in the world, but I was glad to see the maturing effect they had wrought on her.

Life with Minnie might be better and happier now—if we survived this day to have a life together at all.

It seemed to take an eternity to make it back to the place I had left Leviticus Lee, and all the time I was conscious of the escape opportunity Lee was enjoying, and wondering how far he had gone. He might not have been as weak as he seemed to be; it might have all been pretense and fraud.

I was dismayed, but not surprised, to find no trace of Lee when we reached the clearing. Stopping, I looked around helplessly. I was exhausted, out of tricks, out of defenses. Leviticus Lee had left Minnie and me in a hopeless state, and I had no question about Paul Merrick would murder us as mercilessly as he had murdered his own father.

"He's gone?" Merrick asked.

I nodded.

Merrick shook his head. "I don't believe you."

"Look around. You can see for yourself that he isn't here."

"He never was here—that's my guess. It's you who found the gold, and you who are holding it out on me. You can put your hand on it if you want. You're just hoping I'll give up and turn tail." He lifted the shotgun. "Well, you're wrong."

Sometimes, when all hope is gone, defiance rises in its place. That happened to me. I stepped forward two paces. "If you're going to kill me, then do it. But let Minnie go."

"You really love that woman, don't you, Brand?"

"Yes. Let her go. She's had no hand in any of this."

He smiled, shook his head. "No. No. I can't let either one of you go, can I? After all, you both know I killed my father."

He was right. I felt a chill. Why hadn't I realized already that, gold or no gold, Paul Merrick couldn't let us live? We could implicate him for murder.

"What's your plan, Merrick? To blame your father's death on me?"

"Precisely, Mr. Brand. You came to rob my father, to extort from him, to bribe him—any old tale will do—and you grew violent and killed him. I pursued you into the hills and brought you down. A good and dramatic ending to the story of Bass Merrick's life, don't you think?"

"Don't kill us," I said. "I do know where the gold is. Let us live, and you can have it—and our silence." Such a pledge, I knew, could never save us, but maybe it would buy us time.

"Now you're cooperating! Good man! All right, take me to it."

I glanced around, as if looking for a sign or landmark, but in fact looking for anything at all that might help me gain the upper hand. By chance I spotted a flat stone slab that sat at a slight angle against the cliff base. Behind it was the dark opening of a cavern. Looking at the dirt around the opening, I saw Leviticus Lee's footmarks. This must have been the very place the gold had been hidden!

"It's in here," I said, and headed over to the cavern.

Paul Merrick brought Minnie with him. I squeezed between the slab and the cliff, and into the hole. Minnie came next. Merrick remained outside, peering in through the gap.

"You have a candle, or lamp?"

"No," I said. "I had a candle when I first came in for the gold, but it's burned away now. I got no matches, so unless you have some, we'll have to feel our way along to the gold."

He was hesitant. "This is a trick."

"No trick."

He shook his head. "Send the woman out again. You go and get the gold alone. If you don't come out with it, she dies."

I could have almost broken down and cried. In the darkness there would have been hope of me over-coming Merrick and getting the shotgun away from him. Now the situation was as hopeless as before—even more so, because Minnie's life now depended on me coming out of the cave with a cache of gold coins, when in fact no such cache existed.

"All right," I said. "All right."

With no other options before me, I edged back into the dark cavern, my back against the wall, my palms flat against the damp, dank stone. When I was several yards in, I felt in my pocket and found my box of matches. I had lied to Merrick about not having any.

I struck a match and held it up, then examined the floor. Sure enough, there were tracks here, both com-ing and going, matching Leviticus Lee's boots, and a drip or two of candle wax along the way. Addition-ally, there was a long, continuous furrow that might have been made by the corner of a strongbox if it was being dragged out—and a one-handed man would have had little option but to drag it.

Encouraged, I went forward, lighting my way with

matches. At length I reached a sort of room with a natural stone shelf on one side, and by match light found the stub of a candle. Leviticus Lee must have left it. With my next-to-the-last match I lit the candle and looked around.

It was easy to tell where the strongbox had sat. There were plenty of tracks on the cave floor, and depressions left where Leviticus Lee had knelt. I could picture the scene: Lee kneeling in the golden light of his candle before this stone altar upon which sat the thing that mattered more to him than anything in the world—even more than the lives of innocent people.

I vowed to myself that if Minnie was killed or hurt, and I survived, I would track down Leviticus Lee and make him pay for what he had done.

Well, I had found the room, but what good did it do me? There was no gold here to be taken out to Paul Merrick. I searched for a scheme and came up cold.

And then the candle flame blew out as a cold wind brushed my face. In the darkness I dug for my last match—then realized the darkness wasn't complete, and further, that the wind had not blown in from the entrance that had led me here, but from the opposite direction.

There it was—a shaft of sunlight, filtering in around the next corner. This hidden cave had not one opening, but two.

My mind worked frantically, and I smiled. Not much of a chance, I thought. But at least a chance.

I headed for the newly discovered opening, praying it would be large enough to accommodate me, and far enough away from the place Paul Merrick was to keep him from seeing me.

CHAPTER NINETEEN

ONLY WITH EXCRUCIATING EFFORT DID I SQUEEZE MY WAY
through the narrow secondary passage to the outside.
I found myself on the far side of the hill from the
cliff that overlooked the clearing where Merrick
waited for me. Covered with slime and grease from
the cavern, I began making my way over the hill and
toward the bluff.

I paused long enough to find a large stone, about
the size of a man's head. Picking it up, I hefted it the
rest of the distance.

When the edge of the bluff came into view, I put
down the stone, dropped to my belly, and snaked over
to look down. There, maybe twenty-five feet below,
was Paul Merrick, standing at the end of the slab that
mostly covered the cavern opening. He was alternat-
ing between looking into the opening and glancing
back to make sure Minnie wasn't making a break for
freedom. She was in the center of the clearing, sitting
on the ground, a very sad and hopeless look on her
face.

I crabbed back from the edge of the cliff and got
my rock. This time I proceeded on foot, right to the

edge. Looking over, I gauged the angle of drop, the speed of the fall, and so on. I intended for this stone to strike Paul Merrick right on the crown of his head, and with any luck, to crack his skull thoroughly.

If Minnie hadn't spotted me and let out a gasp just as I dropped the stone, I think it would have worked. As it was, Merrick reacted to her noise by shifting his head a little, and the stone didn't make a direct hit. Nevertheless, it bashed the back of his skull soundly, drove his face into the rock and made him drop the shotgun. He collapsed, blood streaming down over the back of his neck and his collar.

Summoning my courage, I sat on the edge of the cliff, swung my feet over and pushed off. It was a long, long drop, seeming more like a hundred feet than the twenty or twenty-five it really was. I hit much harder than I had anticipated, my legs folding up beneath me like those hinged sectional yardsticks that store clerks carry in their pockets. The impact drove the breath from me, so that when I stood up and turned to face Merrick, I was completely unable to draw in air.

Fortunately, Merrick was in as bad or worse a shape than I was. The impact of the stone had stunned him, and he thrashed about like a drunken sailor freshly fallen overboard. I lurched toward him, hands extended to grab his throat. He tripped backward, landed on his rump, and his left hand found the shotgun he had dropped.

He raised it and fired; pellets fanned above my head. I was not even in shape to flinch or duck. I

continued my advance, grabbing the end of the shotgun and yanking it out of his hand. It flipped through
the air and landed in the clearing, near the place Minnie had been.

I say "had been" because she wasn't there anymore. She had taken off on a run as soon as I dropped
over the cliff. Good for her. I hoped she would get
far away, and survive no matter what became of me.

Paul Merrick and I struggled for the longest time
at the base of the cliff. It was a primal struggle, a
time of grit and sweat and blood and determination,
and how long it lasted I can't say, but Minnie later
swore it must have been an hour or more. We moved
all across that clearing, each of us keeping half an eye
on that shotgun, for one barrel remained loaded. At
three points I almost got my hands on it, only to be
dragged away each time by Paul Merrick.

I had just gotten in a fierce blow to his chin when
he drove up his knee and caught me in the gut. I fell
back to the edge of the rocky clearing, and when I
tried to get up, I couldn't. And in the meantime, Merrick had staggered over and managed to get the shotgun.

That motivated me enough to make my next attempt at rising more successful. I tried to run, but
didn't make it far before I fell again, onto my face
this time. Merrick laughed as best his heaving lungs
would allow, and came after me. When I rolled over,
he was above me, his back toward a surrounding jumble of boulders, his trembling legs spread and slightly
bent, and the shotgun wavering in his hands but man-

aging to keep a sufficiently lethal aim right at my face.

"Mr. Brand, it's time for your last good-bye," Paul Merrick said.

I closed my eyes and prepared for the blast, but instead all I heard was a strange, choked cry. When I looked up, Paul Merrick was still standing there, staring down at his chest, from which a long, pointed, rust-colored object was protruding. For a couple of seconds I was confused, then I recognized it as the point and eight additional inches of the saber that Leviticus Lee had dug up. Paul Merrick made a few more choking sounds, then wheeled so that his back was toward me. The saber was still in him; now it was the handle and base of the long blade that was visible to me.

Paul Merrick had been run through, and the man who had done it was Leviticus Lee. He had emerged from the rocks behind Merrick as he was about to kill me. Had Lee had a hook in place of his missing hand, it would have been like a scene from some boys' novel of pirate adventure on the high seas.

Merrick screamed in fury, then lowered the shotgun and fired. Leviticus Lee took the blast in the midsection; the impact kicked him back against the rocks.

Merrick dropped the shotgun, gripped the blade that pierced him, and staggered off to the midst of the clearing. There he dropped to his knees. Twisting his head, he looked at me with a wild glare, like a man fresh-roused from sleep, moved his lips as if to say something that just wouldn't come out, and then fell straight forward, digging his right ear, and the tip of the saber, into the dirt below him.

"Why'd you come back, Mr. Lee? Why?"

He was barely conscious, and the blood rising into his mouth made it hard for him to talk. "Had to . . . felt guilty, you know . . . about what I had done . . ."

"You were coming back to help me?"

"Yes . . . tried to leave . . . with the gold . . . conscience wouldn't let me. Durn conscience . . . plagues a man, you know."

He closed his eyes and swallowed some blood. I told him not to talk anymore, but he did anyway. "I was too weak . . . to carry the gold all the way . . . to Merrick's. Buried it . . . back yonder . . . map to get you there—it's in my pocket."

From his bloodied coat pocket I withdrew an old envelope. On the back of it was a map scrawled and marked with an X, showing the path from the main road to the new resting place of the old Confederate treasure.

"Mr. Lee, I'm going to get Dr. Ruscher," I said. "You rest, and I'll be back with him quick as I can."

"Too late, too late, Mr. Brand." He was making the most terrible noises in his shattered chest. "Lay me . . . in the cave."

Tears rose and came down my face. I wiped them away and nodded. "All right, Mr. Lee."

"Thank you . . . Mr. Brand. The gold . . . it's yours. You get it . . . spend it for me—hear?"

"Don't die, Mr. Lee. Please don't die."

"Don't think . . . it's up to me now," he said.

I cradled his head in my arms until the last rattling breath passed from him. Then, with tears in my eyes, I dragged his battered old form into the cavern that had hidden his treasure for so many years, and laid him to rest on the rock shelf.

When I came again into the light, I was wishing I had known him in other circumstances, and better. He had swept into my life and out again, and my life wouldn't be the same again because of him, yet he remained to me mostly a stranger, and now always would.

I found Minnie hiding in the woods about a quarter mile from the clearing. I told her what had happened, and in silence we walked together back toward Farleytown. I could have taken Paul Merrick's horse, which was tied in the woods, but it didn't seen prudent to risk being seen on the horse of a man who would at some point be found in a remote clearing, with an old saber jammed all the way through him.

I took the envelope Leviticus Lee had given me and examined the crude map etched onto it. Minnie saw it and asked what it was, and I told her. Her eyes got big and she looked at me with wild joy.

"Then we can go get it! Enoch, we're rich!"

"No," I said. "That gold has cost too many lives. I don't want a single coin of it; if we had it, I swear I believe it would ruin us. There's another that gold rightly should go to, and I aim to see that it does."

She couldn't believe it. She fussed and cried and yelled like the Minnie I had always known, and when we reached the road she turned and stomped off, declaring she was leaving me and I shouldn't come after her, because she never wanted to see me again.

Yes, indeed, Minnie was still the woman I had known. If she had matured in her ordeals, it hadn't stuck.

I circled around Farleytown to avoid being seen. On a tree trunk hung a fading old campaign sign from a past county election; I yanked this down and folded it. Then I continued on until I got near the Fairweather place, at which point I went out onto the main road to the place where their drive circled back toward the house.

There I knelt and dug from my pocket the stub of a pencil. On the back of the campaign flyer I scrawled these words:

Mrs. Fairweather—

I know there's nothing to take the place of your husband, but I told you I would do what I could, and so I have. The map stuck here was made by Leviticus Lee, and if you follow it you will find wealth aplenty to see you and your young ones through the rest of your days. I am sorry about all that has happened, but want you to know again that I did not kill your husband.

Yours truly,
Enoch Brand

P.S.—When you find the gold, I hope you will share some of it with Dr. Ruscher. He is deserving of it.

I folded the paper, wrote "Blanche Fairweather" on the top fold, and put away the pencil. By now a couple of the Fairweather dogs had come from the house and were sniffing around me. I grabbed one of them and tied the note to the hemp collar around its neck, using a strip tore from my coat lining. Then I set out down the road, and watched long enough to make sure the dog headed back to the house.

I really hoped that Blanche Fairweather would go claim the Confederate gold. Perhaps, by letting the gold go to a good use like the care of a fatherless family, some atonement would be made for all the sorrow the cursed treasure had brought to so many.

Just then I heard a noise above me in the trees, then a voice: "Gold coins! Pretty gold coins!"

I looked up at the familiar creature in the branches. "That's right, Bird," I said. "Pretty gold coins."

Then I set off, heading down the road to overtake my still-straying wife before she got all the way to the next county.